I0762283

The 3rd Faerie Tale Romance

THE FROST GATE

a Retelling of Snow White

by

HANNA SANDVIG

Illustrations by Hanna Sandvig
Formatting by Enchanted Ink Publishing

Hardcover ISBN: 978-1-7780229-7-5

First Published: June 2022

I dedicate this story to my dear chickens.
Wait, I mean children! My dear children.

Author's Note

To help you with all the Irish and Norse names and words, I've included a faerie glossary, a pronunciation guide, and an illustrated guide to the magic runes used in The Frost Gate at the back of the book, as well as on my website: HannaSandvig.com

I did my best to make them all spoiler-free but it's hard to avoid any hints, so I put it at the back for you to decide when you want to read it.

TÍR NA NÓG
N
W
E
S
the DWARVEN KINGDOM
the UNSEELIE COURT
KILINAIRE CASTLE
INNER SEA
the ELDER FAE
the ISLE OF MIST
PORT DELFARE
SOUTHERN GRASSLANDS
the SEELIE COURT

THE TOPAZ GATE

NIDAVELLIR

THE FROST GATE

THE PISKIE TREE

THE SECRET COTTAGE

HWATH FOREST

ASRAI VILLAGES

AN OLD FOREST GATE

THE UNSEELIE KINGDOM

N
W
E
S
LIADAN'S ISLAND
THE RUINED GATE
THE ICE GATE
BRONACH'S CABIN
THE LICHEN GATE
SKYRETAINE
THE BHANMHOR SLIABHRAON RANGE
A CROSSROAD GATE
KILNAIRE
THE ROSE GATE
CLÍODHNA'S COTTAGE

PART 1

Chapter 1

Neve

I TRULY BELIEVE THERE ARE TWO THINGS that will always make you feel better. Time and salted caramel apple pie.

That was the advice I gave the crying customer deciding on her order, anyway.

"I'm in a bit of a hurry," sniffled the pretty blonde girl. "So I guess I'll go with the pie. And a medium flat white, please."

"You got it." I rang her up at the till. "Medium flat white," I called to my mom as I passed the teary-eyed girl a slice of pie in a paper box. "You'll meet someone better. I know it."

"Thanks." She dabbed her eyes with a napkin and moved to the other end of the counter to wait for her drink.

I breathed a sigh of relief when I saw that she had been the last person in line. The girl collected her coffee and waved tearfully as she left. And with that, the morning rush at Pie in the Sky, the café I ran with my parents, was finally over. As the only café in Pilot Bay—if you didn't count the coffee bar at the gas station, and I did *not*—we were always pretty busy, but this morning had been a lot.

"She's here, Neve." My mom wiped down the pale blue counter. "Sorry to run out on you, but your dad and I need to hurry to make it to our meeting with the coffee roaster in Nelson. Can you keep an eye on things while you have your tea?"

"Of course, Mom."

"Thanks, sweetie. We'll see you at home." My mom gave me a side hug and kissed my cheek. Gone were the days when she could give me a peck on top of my head.

My dad waved from the kitchen door, and then they disappeared out the back.

After I retied the folded red bandana around my black curls and smoothed down the pink apron covering my red vintage-style polka-dot dress, I plated the last two slices of apple pie and poured Earl Grey tea into two mismatched floral teacups.

The only customer left in the café waited for me at her usual table by the window. She said she liked to sit where she could watch people, which was very on-brand for her. Nobody I knew was nosier than my aunt.

I set the tray down on the table and leaned over to give Aunt Chloe a hug, her soft gray curls brushing my cheek. She was technically my godmother, not my aunt, but as my parents' closest friend, she'd been a constant presence in my life as long as I could remember.

"Good morning, honey." Aunt Chloe's gold-rimmed glasses fogged a little as she took a sip of the tea. "Mmmm . . . perfect. How are you today? Have the chicks hatched yet?"

I pulled out my own chair and sat, smoothing my skirt. "I think today's the day! Five of the eggs had pipped by this morning, and I even saw a little beak poking out of one. If I lean my head right up against the incubator, I can hear them cheeping inside. It's killing me to be away from them all day, but I know I can't just skip work to stare at my eggs."

"How many chicks are you expecting?" Aunt Chloe took a bite of pastry.

"Hopefully seven."

I had ordered ten fertilized, heritage breed eggs. When I had held each egg up to a flashlight two weeks ago, three were empty inside. It was hard to give them up, especially since one had been a breed I was very excited about, but from all the research I had done, seven out of ten was still pretty good.

I couldn't wait to have my own chicks. My parents had always fallen firmly on the *no pets* side of things. Running the café kept us all too busy, but they'd finally caved and had even ordered me a chicken coop last month for my twentieth birthday. After all, chickens weren't actually pets. They were for eggs. And saying our breakfast sandwiches were made with local eggs was sure to be a good draw.

At least, that's what I told my parents. Of course the chickens were going to be pets.

"You'll have to text me when they hatch." Aunt Chloe took another bite of pie. "This is very good, by the way."

"Hmm." I tilted my head.

"Still not right?" My godmother knew I'd been experimenting with apple pies for years. One could call it an obsession, but I just couldn't get the recipe right.

"I mean, it's good." I sighed. "Obviously it's good. I made it."

"I sense a *but*."

I took a bite of my pie. The pastry wasn't the problem. Light and flaky. I'd made it with butter, of course. There's always a debate about butter versus lard among pastry enthusiasts, but as a vegetarian, my choice was clear.

The apples were perfectly cooked with just a little bit of firmness left, the tart flavor pairing beautifully with notes of cinnamon and clove. And, of course, the salted caramel drizzle on top was genius, if I did say so myself. Still . . .

"It's the apples."

"The apples are delicious!"

"I know." I frowned at the glossy filling, made with a new variety I had convinced the local fruit stand owner to track down. "They're just not the right apples."

"I've never known anyone as obsessed with apples as you." Aunt Chloe finished off her pastry and licked her fork clean. "I'm shocked that you don't have any on your arm." She waved a hand at my left arm, covered in tattoos.

While it wasn't technically my first tattoo, I'd started on the sleeve at seventeen—when my parents had finally relented after years of my begging—with a white owl on my shoulder. And though the pink flowers inked around the Celtic knots on my arm were actually apple blossoms, I still had a space saved on my bicep for an apple. But not just any apple.

"I just wish I could figure out what kind of apples my mother baked with."

"Roberta doesn't bake," Aunt Chloe correctly pointed out. My mom was brilliant with bookkeeping and responsible for the gorgeous shabby-chic feel of the café, but my dad ran the kitchen. Or at least, he *had*, until I took over most of the baking in high school.

"I know, but I've always had this perfect memory of my mother's apple pie. But, like you said, Mom doesn't bake, so all I can think is that it must be from . . ." I trailed off.

"Your birth mother." She patted my hand.

"It's strange, right?" I said. "To not remember anything about her? Only apple pie? I was five years old when Mom and Dad adopted me. I don't want to sound like I'm ungrateful," I added. "I have the best parents ever. And there's this nosy old family friend who visits the café every day." I winked at my godmother and she smiled. "But still, who doesn't remember anything at all from before they were five? Not so much as a hazy memory of riding a tricycle before my very clear memory of meeting my parents. All I've got from before is a weird Irish name, and an even weirder tattoo."

I rubbed the rune on the inside of my left wrist—the ink that had been there since before my parents adopted me—still unusually clear and sharp after all this time. Two *X*s, one on top of the other, with a line connecting them and a dot at the top and bottom. Just plain black lines. Not what I would have chosen for *baby's first tattoo.*

"Neve is a beautiful name," protested Aunt Chloe.

"Yes, it was so beautiful when the kids in elementary school called me *Heavy Nevy* because no one can figure out that it's pronounced *Nev,* not *Nevy.*"

Aunt Chloe looked like she wanted to say something but thought better of it and took another sip of tea.

"Audrey can tell me what her high scores were on Mario Kart when she was two and a half. My doctor says my lack of memories is probably trauma, but that doesn't help. I know it's not much, but I'd feel better if I could just figure out which variety of apple I'm looking for." I tapped my red nails on the side of my teacup.

"Well, I'm sure you'll figure it out. And I'll happily keep eating your experiments while you do. Speaking of Audrey . . ." Aunt Chloe set down her teacup. "Have you heard from her recently?"

"She just finished up her exams last week, and then Gavin took her to Rome." I fished out my phone and found the photo Audrey had sent me. I showed my godmother the shot of my blonde best friend and her dark-haired Irish boyfriend in front of the Trevi Fountain. "Look at this dessert they had yesterday." I swiped to the next photo and showed Aunt Chloe the *Crostata Ricotta e Visciole*. "I'll have to see if I can find some visciola jam online. I'd love to try and make it."

"What about traveling yourself? Wouldn't you like to try that fancy Italian cheesecake firsthand in Rome?"

"I don't know. Maybe someday. Now that I'm working here full time . . ." I waved my hand around the snug café. "I don't want to leave Mom and Dad in a lurch."

Truthfully, Audrey had been harassing me to go on a trip with her and Gavin ever since my graduation almost two years ago. She had even offered to fly me out to Italy this week.

The two of them were always traveling and sending me photos from around the world. I wouldn't have guessed that Gavin came from money when I met him during his time as an exchange student at our high school. And I did want to spend time with her. My best friend seemed allergic to coming home, and I missed her. But I'd given Audrey the same excuse I always did about the café. Truth was, I didn't like to leave our little town hidden in the mountains of the Kootenay region of British Columbia.

Every time my family went away—even for a short trip—my parents always seemed so anxious. And when I had spent the weekend with Audrey and Gavin one Christmas—honestly, only in Nelson, not even out of the Kootenays—Mom had actually cried with relief when I got back. Was that overkill? It had felt like overkill. But I hated to worry them.

"Maybe in the fall," said Aunt Chloe.

"Maybe," I answered easily.

My godmother looked at her watch. "I need to open up the library. I'll send Amber over later for our afternoon tea."

"I still can't believe Amber Watson is learning to be a librarian."

Amber had been a year behind me in school, and saying that she had been trouble was putting it mildly. I'd heard she had a tough childhood before coming to Pilot Bay to be raised by her two older sisters, both of whom were now married. But she must have changed, or my godmother would never have taken her on at the library, let alone rented her a room at her house.

"Turns out she's a natural at . . . sorting books." Aunt Chloe sat up straighter in her chair and looked over my shoulder. Something unreadable flashed across her face before smoothing into a mischievous smile. "There's a cute boy checking you out."

Chapter 2

Neve

"A CUTE BOY, EH?" I GAVE HER a sidelong glance, rubbing the rune tattoo on my inner wrist absentmindedly. It felt warm. Had I bumped it against the teapot earlier? "I didn't even hear anyone come in."

"You should see if he needs anything." Aunt Chloe dabbed her lips with a napkin. "Coffee? Tea? A date for Friday night?"

"Do all aunts meddle as much as you?"

"I'm special." She stacked her plate, saucer, and teacup on the tray.

"You are, indeed." I stood and cleaned up my dishes. "Well, I'd better get back to work, then."

After another hug, my godmother left, and I picked up the tray before turning around. I nearly dropped the dishes on the floor. I had never in my life seen anyone less deserving of the title *cute boy*.

No one with shoulders filling out a black t-shirt like that could be called a *boy*. And "cute" was a word for puppies—and maybe round-faced, freckle-nosed schoolboys. Not a man so tall that his knees bumped up against the antique table he sat at. Not a man with cheekbones that could cut glass, black hair shaved up the sides with ropes of waist-length locs, dark umber skin, and dark brown, almost black eyes that were . . . Well, crap.

He was definitely glaring at me.

"Do you even know what *checking out* means, Aunt Chloe?" I muttered under my breath as I walked past him to set the tray on the counter.

Every now and then we got a customer who didn't understand how coffee shops worked, and thought I would bring them a menu or something. Clearly, he thought he had been waiting too long. I really had to stop taking breaks with my café apron on.

Taking a deep breath, I walked over to the sexy customer with the rage simmering in his near-black eyes.

"Were you talking to yourself?" The man furrowed his eyebrows at me. One had a thin scar bisecting it—which did not add to his bad-boy appeal at all.

And he has excellent hearing, I added mentally.

He had a rich Irish accent—not the norm for interior British Columbia. Was he visiting the exchange students from Ireland? He looked too old to be part of the high school's program.

"Can I get you anything to eat or drink?" I waved my hand at the chalkboard menu above the bar. "As you can see, we have . . . Actually, we're out of today's apple pie, but we do still have lemon meringue and huckleberry pie, and breakfast cookies the size of your head." I eyed him. "Well, a normal person's head. Not a giant's head."

Whoops! I pressed my lips shut as his eyes narrowed. My mom was always reminding me that I didn't need to say every thought in my head out loud.

"I don't eat sweet things." He tapped his long fingers irritably on the lace tablecloth, a gold ring sparkling on his right pinky.

"Right. You came to the café for some mid-morning . . . pizza?" I glanced back at the display packed with cookies, cupcakes, and fruit pastries.

The man continued to frown at me. I was missing my chicks hatching for *this?*

"You probably just want a drink, then. We have tea, we have apple cider, my dad makes a pumpkin spice latte that is not a copycat of the Starbucks drink, no matter what you may have heard from Mrs. Fenly . . ." Wow, something about him really brought out my rambling side.

"Are Mr. or Mrs. Klassen here?"

"My parents are out for the day. Can I take a message?"

He looked disgruntled. "No."

I waited for him to get up and leave, but he just sat there looking annoyed.

"Okay. Are you sure you don't want anything? You might think you don't like sweets, but my carrot pineapple muffins are—"

"Nothing insipid," he interrupted.

Insipid? *My* baking? Honestly!

"No sweets." I tapped my foot. "Black coffee, then?" *Like your heart?*

"Fine." The man glanced at the door, apparently done with our conversation. Rude.

"Ooookay, you can . . ." I waved my hand at the pickup station at the end of the counter. He just looked at me. "I'll bring it over, shall I?"

The man gave a curt nod. I unclenched my fists as I walked to the counter, feeling his eyes burning into my back.

"Doesn't like sweets," I muttered, pouring a scoop of coffee beans into the grinder. "Nothing insipid." I added another scoop. "We wouldn't want to accidentally eat anything *delicious*." I looked up for a moment. He tapped his foot impatiently, watching the door again. I added three more scoops.

When I sniffed the finished drink, my nostrils burned a little. "Perfect."

My lone customer was still staring at the door with his arms crossed when I returned.

"Your coffee." I set the drink down, careful not to spill a drop on the tablecloth. It might eat through the lace. I gave him my sweetest smile. "Enjoy!"

I waited until he took his first sip and was gratified by the involuntary cough.

"I made it myself."

The man looked me straight in the eyes and took another long sip, this time only twitching ever so slightly. "Perfect."

"Great!" I said. "You can pay at the front when you're ready to go."

I turned to leave, but the man reached out and grabbed my wrist.

"*Excuse* me." I shook off his firm grip and nervously stepped back.

"*Niamh*."

Something about the way he said my name—his accent changing the short *Nev* to the Irish *Neevf*—felt so familiar. I shook my head.

"How do you know my name?" I took another step back. Had he been listening to my conversation with Aunt Chloe? Creepy.

"Don't go out tonight," he continued, ignoring my question. "And lock your doors."

"Excuse me? Who do you think you are?" Never mind that I had no intention of going out tonight. I had baby chicks to snuggle. But that was none of his business.

"It's not safe."

A chill swept through my body. "Are you threatening me?"

"Just promise me you'll stay at your house."

"I think you should leave. Don't worry about paying."

The strange man pushed his chair back and towered over me. I was five foot ten and all curves. The softness of my genetics—and love of pie—hid the strength I'd developed through years of training that had made me the three-time regional champion in longsword martial arts. All in all, it took quite a lot to make me feel *small.* This man was definitely quite a lot.

He looked at me with those near-black eyes for a long moment before turning to go.

As he left the coffee shop, I could have sworn that, for a moment, I saw him in a black tunic and leather pants, the flash of a large silver axe strapped to his back. But when I blinked, he strode past the window in his black t-shirt and dark jeans.

"I forgot my laptop," Dad called from the back room, startling a yelp out of me. "Neve, are you okay?" He poked his head out. "You look even paler than normal."

I attempted a weak smile. "Rude customer. I'll be fine. I just need a few minutes."

"Of course." Dad looked at me worriedly. "Lock the door for a bit if you need to. Take all the time you need."

I thought back to the stranger's withering stare. "Time might not be enough. I'm going to bake some more apple pie."

Chapter 3

Kylian

FROSTY AIR HIT ME AS I STEPPED through the Ice Gate. I removed the gold ring—enchanted with a glamour to make me appear human—and tucked it into a pocket of my leather pants before taking another step forward, away from the sharp drop behind me.

The Ice Gate, crafted in intricate frozen swirls, arched at the edge of a sheer cliff. The long drop to the forest below could kill a fae ten times over, no matter how many runes he might use.

My least favorite of the queen's faoladh lounged on the steps of carved ice in his high fae form. Even without the fur he grew every night in his wolf form, Dylan was as unaffected by the cold as the rest of the Unseelie fae who lived at Skyretaine. I'd call it a kindness on the queen's part, but she just didn't want her minions freezing in the permanent winter she had created to keep Skyretaine Castle encased in enchanted ice.

"Message for me, pup?" I didn't so much as glance at the blond boy as I descended the steps curving down from the gate's platform, my eyes fixed on the icy spires of the Unseelie castle.

Dylan fell into step behind me. "The queen wants to see you."

"Does she now?"

That couldn't mean anything good. Hopefully, Moriath hadn't figured out how I'd spent my morning. I had kept my distance all this time for Niamh's safety, but now that the princess had reached adulthood, the protective wards had begun to unravel. Even though I knew she wasn't without a protector, I couldn't help checking when I felt the *ingwaz* rune on my wrist awaken.

I shook my head, remembering my encounter with the curvy spitfire, the bitter taste of the drink she had made *especially for me* still lingering in my mouth. She had a spine of solid ice, that girl. Well, good. She would need it for what was coming.

"Aren't you supposed to be in Pilot Bay?" I asked him.

"Queen Moriath called all the faoladh back this morning."

A chill ran down my spine. "All the Pilot Bay wolves?"

"*All* the wolves."

"From all six of the towns we're watching?"

"Yes, yes, and the wolves stationed across the Unseelie Kingdom. All the wolves."

I tapped my fingers against my thigh as I faced the imposing castle doors, eyeing the carved creatures of ice curving around the doorframe. The guardians of Skyretaine, asleep for now.

"Right away, she said." Dylan stopped beside me and I shot the pup a look that had him shrinking back. "Lord Kylian, sir," he added.

I gave him a curt nod, my hand on the door. The giant, sleeping dragon of ice opened one eye to see who was at the door, and then closed it again.

"Make sure the rest of the wolves are ready," I told Dylan before stepping through the door and shutting it behind me.

Moriath's faoladh were her greatest treasure, a collection of beautiful young fae men whom she'd lured in with promises of love and power. Each one had been her whole world for anywhere from a handful of days to a few months, or once—in Dylan's case—for a full year. But, inevitably, she tired of each one and added them to her pack. Fae by day, wolves by night. Fanatically loyal to their queen. And, as Huntsman, I was responsible for the whole bloodthirsty lot of them.

I rolled up my right sleeve as I walked, revealing the tattoos that swirled up my arm. Like the powerful runes covering my left arm, these knotwork tattoos were spellcrafted with ink mixed with enchanted gold, but these also had a drop of a wolf's blood that bound that wolf to me through the matching ink over their hearts. I could track each wolf and compel his obedience. For all Moriath's skill with blood magic, she would never mar her perfect skin with spelled ink. Not when she had her trusted Huntsman to bear the marks for her.

I ran a finger over each symbol. Dylan was right. All the wolves were at the castle for the first time in two hundred years. Well, all of them but one.

The iron heels of my boots echoed on the stone floor as I strode through the empty halls of the castle. Once, there had been plush rugs, velvet curtains, and masterful paintings of previous Unseelie rulers to soften the echoes. Once, the halls had been filled with the bustle of courtiers, pets, servants, and a loving family with two beautiful little girls. Today, not even a frightened scullery maid ran across my path. They must be hiding. All wise creatures stayed out of the way when Moriath was in a mood. My mind sifted through all the things that might be upsetting the Unseelie queen today, and I prayed that I wasn't one of them.

When I finally reached the door to Moriath's solar, I didn't even have to raise my hand to knock.

"Enter," she commanded.

I didn't need to school my features into respectful disinterest before I walked through the door. That had been my only expression for nearly two hundred years.

Golden eyes bored into me. Ránach, Moriath's familiar, watched from her roost in the corner, the dark head of the peregrine falcon tracking my path toward her mistress.

The Unseelie queen had her back to me. Her long white hair was bound in a thick braid that fell to her knees, studded with flashing gemstones. Fur and tiny crystals trimmed her white dress. A crown of sparkling diamonds set in gold filigree rested on a stand beside her. The gems were tall and tapered, like a row of icicles, with two graceful white antlers reaching up above them.

"Huntsman." Moriath turned, and a wave of power rolled off her, forcing me to kneel with my head bowed.

She snapped her fingers, and the power rolled back. I slowly looked up, first to the hand toying with her sapphire necklace and then at the expression in her pale, icy eyes. It was worse than I had feared.

Moriath wasn't angry.

She was happy.

No, not just happy. The Unseelie queen positively glowed with excitement.

She waved me over. "Come here, come here!"

I rose from my knees and stood beside the queen, looking at the gold basin studded with diamonds and filled to the brim with water.

"*Scáthán, scáthán,*" she murmured. *Mirror, mirror.* "Show me the most powerful Unseelie fae."

"My Queen, you've been trying this for—"

She held up her hand, and her power snapped my mouth shut. "Just watch, Kylian."

Fine. I watched in silence. At first, it looked the same as every other time I had seen the queen scry this way. Nothing but empty black water. But then, slowly, the water rippled to show an image of a small human town next to a lake, nestled against forested mountains. Pilot Bay.

"You've been able to narrow it down, then?" I asked when she allowed me to speak again, forcing myself to sound impressed and not worried. I had been right to take the risk and warn the princess after feeling how thin the wards had become today.

"That doddering old fool of a banshee thought she was so smart, warding six different towns so that I couldn't tell where she had hidden the child," Moriath huffed. "So much trouble to keep my sweet little niece alive and that crown out of my grasp. Who would have guessed the child would be so powerful? I should have had you carve out Maeve's heart when we had the chance, like you did with Niamh."

I said nothing, grateful that both princesses were still out of the queen's reach. Anyway, Moriath wasn't interested in my opinion.

"The old crone's wards are finally failing," the queen gleefully said.

"I'll ready the faoladh and take them through the gate," I said with a bow. It was a pity she'd made us dig out the gate in the old mine. We'd get to Pilot Bay faster than I'd prefer, but at least Moriath didn't know where in town to look. I could warn Niamh's foster parents and have them prepare the princess to leave.

"Wait." Moriath shot out a hand, her grip on my arm painful as her long nails dug into my black linen sleeve. "It's changing. There's more."

We both peered down into the mirror as the water rippled and cleared again, this time revealing the Klassens' snug farmhouse surrounded by trees. No time for a warning, then. I'd have to move fast.

The queen turned to me, eyes bright.

"The wards are nearly gone. With your runes, you should be able to get through them now. Bring me Maeve's heart—attached to her body, if you can. I'd like to remove it myself, but do whatever it takes." The queen glanced scornfully at the antlered crown on its stand, a beautifully crafted—but powerless—replica of her obsession. "I'm done waiting," she said. "The *true* Unseelie crown shall be mine tonight."

Chapter 4

Neve

THE MOMENT I GOT OFF WORK, I sprinted home. Not because some grumpy stranger told me to, but to check on my babies. I threw off my boots and navy hoodie and ran up the stairs two at a time. I jumped onto my vintage floral bedspread and peered into the foggy depths of the incubator next to the stack of childhood books on my nightstand.

Come on, come on, come on.

I grinned once I made out five little puff balls cheeping around inside the incubator. Each chick was a different breed of chicken, so the babies were all different shades of white, brown, and yellow. Two eggs remained. The dark brown egg had cracked and was rocking back and forth. The light brown egg had pipped, and I could see the tip of a little beak peeking through the hole.

I nervously watched as the hatched chicks climbed around the egg shards, knocking the remaining eggs around the incubator.

My mom poked her head into my room. "Did they hatch yet?"

"Five have, two to go." I scooted over to make room and patted my bed. "Come see."

She sat beside me, and we watched together as the dark brown egg cracked further, revealing damp black fluff. A moment later, a little black chick tumbled out, showing its pale throat and wingtips.

"Good baby," I whispered to the chick as it lay resting from its hard work.

"Why aren't you taking them out?" Mom asked.

"You're not supposed to take them out until they're all hatched and dry. The last one might not hatch if I let the cold, dry air in, and those two are still a little wet from hatching. See?" I pointed at a yellow chick and the new black one. "If they were with a mama hen, she would still be sitting on them to keep them safe."

"I was tempted to sit on you sometimes when you were little," Mom teased, kissing my curly, dark hair. "Always up a tree or running off with your wooden sword. Mother hens have it easy."

I smiled, leaning against her.

"Will that last egg hatch, do you think?" she asked.

"It will." It had to. "You can do it, little one." I could hardly breathe as I watched the light brown egg.

It rocked once, then stopped.

"Come on." I leaned forward. The other chicks had fallen asleep in little heaps of baby fluff.

The pale egg cracked, and I gripped Mom's hand. One

more crack and a silver head emerged, dark with the dampness of hatching.

"Yes!" I jumped up, throwing my arms in the air and knocking *Tales of the Unseelie Fae* from the top of the stack of books by the incubator.

"Dinner's ready." My dad knocked on the doorframe as he entered the room. "I take it they all hatched?"

"All seven!" I did a little happy dance, my eyes glued to the chicks who were all awake again to welcome their newest companion.

Dad crouched down to inspect the incubator.

"How can you tell which ones are hens and which are roosters?" asked my mom.

"I can't." I sat back down on the bed beside her, still bouncing with excitement. "Probably not for a couple more months."

"And then you want the hens for their eggs. But are the roosters . . . ?" Dad drew a finger across his neck.

I gasped. "Absolutely not! It's good to keep at least one rooster. They keep the hens safe from predators and reduce infighting."

"And if you have more than one?" asked my dad. "Do we make soup?"

I waved an accusing finger at my dad. "No one is going to be soup!" He never really understood my vegetarian choices.

"I suppose we'll cross that bridge when we come to it." Dad stood and put a hand on Mom's shoulder. "Can you help me set the table?"

"Of course, dear. They're very cute, Neve." Mom kissed the side of my head and followed my father out. "I'm sure there won't be too many roosters to get rid of."

"Don't listen to them. I won't let anything happen to

you," I whispered to the baby chicks. "Nobody's going to be soup."

Later that evening as I helped my mom wash up the dishes, I stripped off my ruffle-topped rubber gloves and looked at the rune tattooed on the underside of my wrist.

"What is it?" Mom set a stack of plates on the counter. "Is there a hole in your glove?"

"No. It's weird. My tattoo feels warm. That's the second time today." I rubbed the tattoo. It looked normal.

My mom's eyes widened. "I'm just gonna go . . . talk to your dad for a moment." She hurried out of the kitchen.

"I don't know why you're telling me that," I called after her, wiping my hands on my apron.

I suddenly felt overcome by a sense of worry and determination. I shook my head and it faded. What was I worried about? I should be over the interaction with that man at the café this morning. I had totally forgotten to tell my parents about him. I'd have to mention it to my mom when she came back in.

The feeling of worry rose up again. Weird. Maybe I needed a cup of tea? I set the kettle to heat on the stove and picked my rubber gloves back up.

As I did, I caught a flash of someone running past the kitchen window. *What?*

The door crashed open, and the man from the café burst into my kitchen, dark locs swirling. I screamed, throwing my ruffled gloves at the intruder.

"That's good," he said, batting the gloves away. "Scream again."

I did, because not only had he just broken down my front door, he was brandishing a large silver axe.

The man now wore tall black boots, and black leather pants with a dagger strapped to his thigh. His black linen tunic had the sleeves rolled up to reveal dark tattooed runes covering his left arm and a design of Celtic knots encircling his right. How had I not noticed those before?

The top of his hair was pulled up in a thick knot of locs, revealing tapered ears like some sort of elf. But even that paled in comparison to the double-headed, rune-inscribed weapon he gripped in both hands.

Anger suddenly burned through me. How *dare* he bring an axe into my kitchen!

"Okay, mister, I don't know who you think you are, but you have ten seconds to get out of here!" I started backing toward the living room. Why didn't I keep a sword in the kitchen?

My parents rushed into the room.

"Stop!" I held out my hands, wanting to keep them away from the crazy axe murderer. But just when I thought that I couldn't possibly be any more shocked, they both ran up to the intruder.

"Lord Kylian." My mom gave what would have looked like a curtsy, had she not been in jeans. "It's time, then?"

"What time?" I pulled my mom back, and she put her arm around me. "Who *is* this guy?"

"The wards protecting this house are failing," the man—elf? Kylian?—said, strapping the axe to the leather harness on his back. "Niamh must leave with me immediately."

"It's *Neve*, and I'm not going anywhere with you." I took another step back, dragging my mom with me.

Kylian looked at my parents. "You should tell her what's going on. You have three minutes."

My mother wrung her hands. "We need more time."

"Fine." Kylian glanced out the window. "Seven minutes. Pack while you talk." He stalked into the living room.

My mom and dad exchanged a look, then mom nodded and dashed for the stairs. My dad rummaged through a drawer, pulling out a paper lunch bag.

"So tell me, Dad." I tried to keep my voice steady but failed.

"Kiddo, you're not originally from here." He threw an orange and a granola bar into the bag.

"I know I'm not from Pilot Bay." My voice ratcheted up a notch. "You've told me all this."

"Well . . . you're not actually from the human realm. Pass me the muffins?"

"The *human realm?*" I grabbed the muffin container from the counter and tossed it to him. "What are you talking about?"

"This is taking too long." The axe murderer paced back across the kitchen. "You're the crown princess of the Unseelie fae. Get your coat."

"The *what?*"

"Four minutes." Kylian looked out the kitchen window again, and I stared at his pointed ears. He must be a fae then.

When I felt my own ears, they were still as rounded—as *human*—as ever. Wouldn't I know if I was some sort of *faerie*?

"Your parents were killed," my mom said, hurrying back in. "Moriath, who now calls herself the queen of the Unseelie fae, murdered them and took their throne. In order to protect you, Kylian stole you away and brought you to the human realm. To a couple who had always wanted children." She paused to tuck a curl behind my ear. "We always knew you would have to leave someday, my dear."

A strange, yipping howl from outside made the hair on the back of my neck stand on end.

Kylian cursed under his breath, then stuck his head out the broken kitchen door and yelled, "She's hiding. Give me a minute."

He turned back to me. "The wolves are here for you now. They're trying to get through the weakened barrier. I can't stall much longer without raising suspicion. Say your goodbyes."

Another howl rose from the cover of the trees. More wolves joined in from all around the farmhouse.

The blood drained from my face. "When you say wolves, do you mean *actual* wolves?"

"I wish they were ordinary wolves. You should put some boots on," suggested Kylian. "Unless you want me to carry you over my shoulder to the fae realm."

I squeezed my eyes shut. "This is a mistake. How can I be a threat to some evil faerie queen? And a princess? I'm *not* a princess. I'm Neve Klassen. Pie baker. Chicken mom." Maybe when I reopened my eyes, this hallucination would disappear.

I startled at a gentle touch of rough fingers on my jaw. I opened my eyes and my breath caught to find Kylian standing so close that his twisted ropes of black hair brushed my arm.

He tilted my chin, forcing me to look up at him. "Unless we draw them away, Moriath's wolves will break through soon. They will kill anyone who gets in their way, but the faoladh don't care about your foster parents. They just want you. So we have to leave now, Princess. Understand?"

I studied him. Intense? Yes. Lacking in civilized communication skills? Definitely. But I didn't think he was lying. He looked down at me with quiet determination, and something in me settled.

I focused on my parents watching us with tears in their eyes and knew that I'd do anything to protect them.

"I can really trust this guy?" I asked my mom.

"Lord Kylian saved your life fifteen years ago and brought you to us." My mom squeezed my hands. "If Moriath has found you, he's the only one who can keep you safe." She hugged me tight. "You have to go."

"Now," added Kylian. "Boots."

The kettle whistled on the stove. I could barely hear it over my spinning thoughts.

I put a hand to my forehead, trying to pull myself together. "I need to get something."

"Your sword?" asked Kylian.

"How do you know about . . . ? Never mind. Mom, fill a hot water bottle." I ran up the stairs.

"Okay," she called back.

I burst into my room and found my backpack in the closet. Then I dug through my pile of books to find the notebook with all my apple-pie-making notes. No way was I leaving that behind.

My mom bustled into the room with the flannel-covered hot water bottle and my boots. "Here you go, sweetie."

"Thank you." I slid the rubber bottle into the bottom of the backpack, then pulled off my apron to make a nest on top of it.

"Your time is up." Kylian appeared in the doorway with his arms crossed, looking incredibly grouchy and impatient—in other words, his usual expression—and decidedly out of place in my extremely girly bedroom.

"Here's your sword, honey." My dad squeezed past the fae and set my sheathed sword on the bed.

I lifted the top of the incubator and carefully picked up the first fluffy baby.

"It'll be okay, sweetheart," I whispered, nestling the yellow chick into my backpack.

"What are you doing?" Kylian loomed over me as I picked up two black chicks, one with a pale face, and snuggled them in next to their siblings. "You're running for your *life*. You can't bring tiny animals along."

"Don't raise your voice in front of the babies." I tucked in the next chick, white with feathered feet. "I just hatched these. Do you know how long it took me to convince my parents? To pick out the perfect heritage breeds?" I nestled another pale yellow chick into my bag, then a brown and yellow baby. The first few had already snuggled down to sleep in their warm nest. "Three weeks I've incubated them at the perfect temperature, and do you know what my father wants to do with them?"

Kylian raised an eyebrow.

"Turn them into soup!" My voice went up an octave. "Soup! Would you turn *this?*" I held up the last tiny silver puffball, its feathered legs still not completely dry. "Into *soup?*" The chick sneezed.

"Of course not."

"Well *good*."

"It's much too small. Doesn't have any meat on its bones."

"*Men*." I tucked the last one in with its siblings and zipped my backpack closed.

"That can't be safe for the chickens." He was trying to reason with me. He should ask my parents how hard it was to change my mind once it was set.

"They send chicks in the mail. They're warm. They'll be fine." I slid a bag of chick feed into the front pocket.

"What if they make a noise and give away your location?" He tapped his fingers on his leg impatiently.

"It's dark in there. They're already asleep." I grabbed a hoodie and wished I had time to change out of my red dress into pants.

"Be reasonable, Princess," he tried again.

I whirled on him. "You barge in here and upend my entire life, tell me I'm a faerie princess, expect me to follow you to who-knows-where, and *I'm* the one who needs to be reasonable?" I shouldered my backpack. "These are my emotional support chickens. They're coming."

"I don't—"

I held up my hand. "You said we were in a hurry. Do you really have time to stand around and argue with me? I go, the chickens go!"

We glared at each other for a moment before he sighed and handed me my scabbard.

"Well, then. Strap on your sword, Princess. You're all going to Faerie."

Chapter 5

Neve

I STOOD AT THE BACK DOOR, LOOKING out its little window into the quickly darkening forest behind the farmhouse.

"She needs a sandwich, Sam, not lemon tarts," my mom muttered from the kitchen.

I didn't know if I'd need a bagged lunch at all for wherever I was going, but that was my parents for you. When in doubt, pack some food.

"I'll go first." Kylian stood behind me in the entryway. "I'll tell the wolves that you escaped south while I searched for you. You count to ten, then run as fast as you can toward the Wolf Gate."

"The what now?"

"It's a gate, a portal that links to other gates in this realm and in Faerie. This one is well hidden as an arch of branches due east." He pointed through the trees. "You should reach it in no more than five minutes if you run."

"Ah, yes. Perfect directions. No way I'll miss that in the dark."

"I will do my best to lure them away from you while maintaining my cover with the Unseelie queen," Kylian continued, ignoring my snark, "then circle back to meet you at the gate."

"Or wherever I happen to be in the forest." I rolled my eyes, then turned to see my mom slide the lunch bag into the front pocket of my backpack. "Thanks, Mom." I kissed her cheek.

"Read this when you have time, sweetie." My mom tucked in an envelope beside the food, and I nodded.

"If I'm delayed," Kylian continued, "and the wolves catch up to you, step through the gate and think of roses climbing up aspen trees. It should take you to another location in these woods where I can find you. But even if that doesn't work, anywhere it takes you will be better than here. Are you listening, Princess?"

I shook my head. "I thought I saw something glittering. Must have been my imagination."

"The faoladh are trying to get through the wards. Put your hood on so they can't see your hair."

"What's wrong with my hair?" I pulled my hood up.

"Hopefully it's dark enough out there that they won't notice the color. Ten seconds." He yanked the door open and jogged off, yelling something to the wolves in the trees.

We had better survive this. I needed a proper explanation.

I pushed that all aside for now and started to count.

One . . . two . . . three. I tightened my sword belt and adjusted the straps of the backpack containing my precious cargo.

Four . . . five . . . six. I double-knotted the laces of my black combat boots—the only footwear in the house I could actually run in, as my runners were at the gym.

Seven . . . eight . . . nine. "We love you, darling." My parents gave me a quick kiss and hug.

Ten.

"Don't leave the house tonight," I warned them.

When they nodded, I dashed out the door and down the porch steps.

The sun had sunk behind the mountains, and the world was painted in blues and silvers as I raced across my yard. I glanced back one more time to see my parents tearfully waving goodbye, and then I hit the edge of the forest. Shadows surrounded me as the trees blocked out the fading evening light.

My eyes adjusted to the twilight as I ran. All I could hear was my own heavy breathing and the pounding of my footsteps. Maybe, just maybe, Kylian had succeeded in drawing the wolves away from me.

But soon, I heard growls behind me. Glancing over my shoulder, I almost stumbled at the sight of the largest wolves I'd ever seen. I didn't have a lot of experience with wolves, but the ones I'd seen at the Calgary Zoo were not the size of small ponies. These weren't ordinary wolves, though. Kylian had called them *faoladh.* According to my book on the Unseelie fae, these were the Celtic version of werewolves.

Fear gave me speed, but I knew there was no way a chubby baker, no matter how long her legs were, could outrun giant wolves. I had trained for strength, not sprinting speed.

I ducked behind a large tree and the first wolf kept running, momentum carrying him past me. My heart hammered in my chest. In all my years of learning to use my sword, even when sparring hand to hand, I'd never really thought I would have to hurt someone.

But not only could these wolves kill me—or drag me off to their queen—what would they do to the chicks if they caught me? I wiped my sweaty hands on my skirt and took a deep breath.

"It'll be okay, babies," I whispered to my backpack as I drew my sword.

I held my breath, waiting for a wolf to approach.

A twig snapped. There. I swung out from behind the tree and cracked the black wolf on the side of the head with the pommel of my sword.

"It's just like a training dummy," I squeaked as the wolf fell at my feet. Dead? Unconscious? "Training dummy!"

The remaining wolves scrambled back. Obviously, they had not been expecting their prey to have teeth. One of the wolves lifted its muzzle to howl, and more howls answered it from all around me. I widened my stance. The light grew dimmer as more and more glowing eyes surrounded me in the dark forest.

"I've got her, boys. Good work. Stay behind me." Kylian stalked toward me with a murderous expression on his face that had me questioning everything he had told me earlier. As he came closer, the circle of wolves crowded in as well, a step behind.

I adjusted my grip on the hilt of my sword. Even if he was on my side, could we really take on so many wolves? There must be *fifty* surrounding us now.

Suddenly, a bright, golden light blinded me. The wolves whimpered and yelped. When my vision cleared, Kylian had stumbled a few steps back, his arm thrown up to protect his face.

In front of me, holding a staff that blazed with light in one hand and a blue sapphire the size of a chicken egg in the other was . . .

"Aunt Chloe?" My jaw dropped in disbelief.

"Hello, sweetheart," Aunt Chloe said cheerfully, still in her cardigan and slacks from this morning. The sapphire she held emitted a pulse of blue light, and all the wolves took another stumbling step back. A faint golden shimmer enveloped us like a bubble. "I've got this, my dear. The two of you get going."

Did she mean Kylian? He squinted at my godmother's staff but didn't make any move to go. A hand brushed my sleeve, and I spun, sword up.

"Not a wolf! Not a wolf!" The pretty brown-haired girl threw her hands up in the air.

I blinked in surprise. "Amber Watson?"

"Apprentice faerie godmother, at your service," Amber said with a curtsy. "Gem, please," she called to my aunt.

"Catch!" Aunt Chloe tossed Amber the sapphire, and the shimmering golden bubble traveled with it.

Amber caught the gem neatly and waved it at me. "Follow me!" She took off running, then added over her shoulder, "Stay close so the shield protects us both."

I hurriedly sheathed my sword and jogged after her. "Will she be okay?" I asked when I caught up. "Aunt Chloe, I mean." And Kylian? Was he truly on my side? Surely he wouldn't hurt my aunt.

"Oh, sure. It'd take more than a bunch of little wolves to take Clíodhna down. Don't worry about her."

"Clíodhna?"

"She's epic, but she can explain that later. I need to get you to the Wolf Gate." Amber slowed and held up the sapphire, which was shining brightly in the dark forest. "There's the trail."

I squinted through the gloom. "I'll take your word for it."

"Now, I don't mean to pry, but your backpack is cheeping."

"The chicks!" I patted the bottom of my bag. "I hope they're doing okay."

"Chicks, like . . . chickens?" asked Amber.

"Yes," I said, rather defensively.

"All right." Amber shrugged. "That's not even the weirdest thing that's happened this week."

"So, you're not *really* learning to be a librarian?" I ducked under a branch.

"Oh, I am. Well, I'm not, like, in school for it or anything, but if you need to know anything about the Dewey Decimal System, I'm your girl." She stopped and squinted into the dark forest, then continued walking. "Surprised?"

"You've never struck me as much of a reader, that's all. Isn't Isobel the bookish one in your family?"

"Hey, I read a book this month! Well, listened. It was an audiobook. Okay, it was an audio novella. But Miss Chloe says it counts." She walked on for a minute before adding, "But you're right. I'm not working at the library for the love of books. Your aunt's been teaching me magic, which you should be very grateful for right now, as this ward seems to be working for me." She tossed the sapphire and caught it in her other hand. "Okay, that gate should be around here somewhere."

As Amber slowed, I noticed that we actually *were* following a faint trail.

"Here it is." She held the sapphire up, but, as far as I could tell, they were simply two trees, their branches reaching together above the path.

"Right, Kylian. I totally would have found this on my own," I muttered.

"Yeah, it's pretty hard to see if you're not looking for it. Which is, you know, the point." She reached out her free hand. "Are you ready to go?"

I thought of my parents at home in our farmhouse, of the café filled with the smells of sugar and coffee. Of everything I had ever known and loved.

"Do I have a choice?" I asked.

"Well, you *could* wait and travel to Faerie with the wolves instead," said Amber.

"Fine." I sighed, then squared my shoulders. "Let's go."

I took her hand, and together, we stepped away from my whole world.

Chapter 6

Kylian

"So, huntsman." The queen frowned at me, the antlered crown on her head and Ránach perched on the back of her throne. The wolves lounged around the pillars and the raised dais of the vaulted throne room, even though the sun was up. Moriath preferred her pets silent. "That did not go as well as I would have hoped."

I knelt and lowered my head. "I take full responsibility, Your Majesty."

The weight of her fury pushed against me until she abruptly pulled her power back, making me fight to remain steady.

"As you should." Moriath tapped her long fingernails against the stone armrest of her throne. "Still. Clíodhna. To think she's escaped my notice all these years in that human village."

I rose to my feet, relieved that the queen's fury was redirected. "It seems she was masquerading as a librarian." The ancient Banshee queen had been living a quiet life in Pilot Bay while she watched over her goddaughter, Princess Niamh, but that was over now that she'd revealed herself by helping Niamh escape the wolves.

"A *librarian.* She'll pay for this," spat Moriath. She scratched a black wolf behind his ear. "Now. Where should we look for the princess, boys?" She looked around the room. "My Huntsman seems to be all out of luck."

My left eye twitched, but I remained silent. At least the queen still believed it was Niamh's little sister who had eluded her. Disappointing Moriath was nothing compared to her finding out that I'd betrayed her by keeping the crown princess alive. Maybe I'd keep my head a little longer.

It had been too dark for Moriath to see any details by scrying, and none of the wolves had seemed to know any better, even when they'd faced off with the princess. What a force Niamh had been with her sword. Even in that impractical red dress, with a backpack full of chickens, she had been fierce enough to give the faoladh pause.

"Any ideas?" Moriath tilted her head.

The wolf at her feet whimpered.

"Dylan? Up with you, then." Moriath pointed at the wolf, and a ring on her finger flashed.

Dylan stretched up into his fae form and straightened his tunic. "That human girl. She could help."

"Which one?" Moriath asked through clenched teeth. "You'll have to be more specific. That realm is crawling with them."

"Audrey, Your Majesty," Dylan replied. "The one that helped Gavin escape."

"Ah, yes." The queen leaned back on her throne, her eyes narrowed. "Another disappointment. How long have you failed in retrieving that rogue wolf, Huntsman?"

"Too long, Your Majesty." I bowed. There were so few times I'd allowed myself to work against Moriath. Too many *mistakes* and I would have lost the ability to watch over Niamh. But I hadn't been able to make myself drag the only good faoladh and his human partner back to face the queen's wrath once they'd escaped.

"Quite so." She turned back to Dylan. "What of the girl?"

"She was very close to the princess. If we can find Audrey, she might be helpful in finding Niamh." Dylan smirked. "Or, if not, we can use her as bait."

"I do like bait," the queen mused. She suddenly stiffened, her eyes snapping to Dylan's face. "*What* did you just say?"

I froze.

"You mean Princess *Maeve*," I corrected Dylan. My fingers itched to unhook my axe. My legs tensed to run. "Niamh is dead."

"Right, that's what I thought, too." Dylan tilted his head. "Until I saw who we were chasing in the forest. You forget, Huntsman, that my family spent a lot of time here at Skyretaine before our beautiful queen's rule began. Niamh was only a child then, but there's no mistaking which princess is which." He winked at me. "Maeve was a redhead."

I cursed under my breath. Dylan was one of a handful of faoladh who had spent time posing as exchange students at the high school in Pilot Bay while searching for the lost princess. No amount of dim lighting or hoods would have mattered because he already knew what Niamh looked like.

What I *hadn't* realized was that the pup had known the princesses before my time at Skyretaine. Trust Dylan to keep that knowledge to himself until he found the right moment to impress the queen.

"Niamh *lives*," Moriath seethed, eyes darkening, her knuckles white on the arms of her throne.

I began backing away. Slowly, as I would with a feral animal. "*Raidho*," I whispered under my breath. "*Thurisaz*." The runes for speed and protection flared on my arm. "My Queen." I held up my hands.

"What do you have to say for yourself, *Huntsman*?" she spat. "Whose heart did you bring me to gain my trust?"

I could feel her power gathering. My mind raced with stories to tell her, lies to keep me at her side, where I could keep interfering with her search. But I'd seen that look in her eyes countless times, just before she killed someone. There was no time to try to convince her to trust me again.

"Maybe he didn't betray you, My Queen." Dylan looked gleeful. He had always chafed under my authority. He obviously relished bringing me down. "Maybe he's just really, *really* bad at catching one little girl. Well, two girls and one wolf, I suppose. Not very mighty after all, are you, *Huntsman*?"

Moriath surged to her feet, and a blast of power threw me back. The wolves whimpered from the wave of magic as I flew through the air to hit the back wall. I lay there for a moment, winded. If I hadn't activated the protection rune, the force would have broken every bone in my body. I had to get up. I had to run before the runes wore off or she used more power.

I pulled myself to my feet and bolted for the exit. Her blow had been an unintended blessing. I was past all the wolves and into the hall before they realized what was happening. I needed every advantage I could get because I didn't dare exert any of my own influence over the wolves. Not only would Moriath counter it, she might remember what else my Huntsman tattoos allowed me to do.

"Get him!" Moriath yelled, her voice shaking the walls of the castle. "Each of you bring me a piece of that *traitor*!"

The gate. I had to reach the Ice Gate before she thought to seal it against me and strip my powers. I ran through the front door, not even glancing at the gargoyles or the guardian ice dragon. But I could hear them. Hear the ice splintering as they came to life to obey their mistress's wishes.

None of them were fast enough. Not the creatures of ice. Not the howling wolves. Not even the ice queen herself. I had been planning for this moment, training for it for two hundred years.

I reached the gate and hesitated, standing at the cliff's edge. If she had sealed it, I wouldn't portal anywhere. If it was sealed, I would be jumping straight to my death. But death was certain if I didn't try.

I leapt, but my hesitation cost me. A gray wolf launched himself up the stairs and bit into my left shoulder as I jumped through the gate of ice.

We fell, and I briefly had the grim satisfaction that if I was falling to my death, at least I was taking Dylan with me. But then we hit snow. The roll down the icy bank knocked Dylan away from me. My jump had taken us through the Ice Gate to an old forest gate, just as I had hoped.

I glanced around to quickly get my bearings. Behind me, a waterfall tumbled over the bank we had just rolled down. The river rushed beside us, deep and rapid enough not to freeze and dark against the surrounding snow. The shallow pools along the edge were covered in thin ice, and a mound of snow covered each rock.

Dylan scrambled to his feet, drawing his sword. He was fae again, now that he was away from Moriath's influence.

I tried not to wince as I unfastened my axe. Dylan's teeth had certainly done some damage to my shoulder before he'd shifted into his fae form.

"Getting sore, old man?" Dylan taunted, picking his way toward me over snow-covered stones.

I resisted the urge to roll my eyes, settling for twirling the giant silver axe without a hint of struggle.

"You should run home now, pup." I tried to put my Huntsman compulsion into my words but failed. I knew without looking that Moriath had already stripped the power from the tattoos she had given me. Unfortunate, but not unexpected. Thankfully, the queen couldn't do anything about my runes.

"Run? And miss this chance to impress our queen by bringing her your heart?"

He lunged for my chest, and I knocked his sword to the side just in time.

"Or maybe your head this time." Dylan danced back. "I hear hearts can be faked."

"You think she'll make you Huntsman?" I scoffed, easily dodging his next attack.

"Well, I can't do a worse job than you." Dylan circled me, avoiding the edge of the dark water. "I'm tired of spending my nights as a wolf. I'm sure if I take care of you, she'll be very grateful. And how hard can it be to find two little girls? If you actually try, I mean."

I weighed my options, then backed into the shallows of the river where my heavier bulk would give me an advantage, making me stronger against the current.

Should I kill this pup, here and now? It would be awfully satisfying to smack that smirk off his face for good. I stepped back farther, carefully finding my footing on the slippery rocks of the river bed. I could feel the frigid water pushing at the leather of my boots, nearly coming to their tops.

Dylan was a conniving narcissist, and Faerie would be a safer place without him in it, but I still hesitated. *Danu* knew I'd done a lot of things during my time as Huntsman that I wasn't proud of. But the wolves had been entrusted to my care, and I'd never outright killed one of them.

"Going for a swim?" Dylan smirked. "That's one way to run away, but that axe of yours can't be a great flotation device."

"The water's lovely. Come and see." I beckoned, counting on the boy's ego to override his common sense.

Sure enough, he lunged forward, splashing into the water. I blocked his blow with my axe, his sword not even making a dent on the ash haft which was strengthened by the runes etched onto its silver head. I countered with a swing of my axe, and Dylan spun away in what would have been a very clever move if the boy's foot hadn't slid on the unstable river rocks.

Dylan yelped as he stumbled forward, trying to find his footing. He slammed into me and pushed us both deeper into the river. He flailed erratically, too quickly for me to dodge with the rushing water slowing my legs. I felt his blade graze my side.

I shoved the pup away from me, sending him flying toward the riverbank. The momentum made me stumble back farther, and I looked down to see red swirling from my side. Not just a scratch then.

What he hadn't been able to accomplish with skill, the boy had managed with clumsiness.

"*Sowulo,*" I mumbled weakly as I crashed back into the roaring river, but my head spun, and the healing rune didn't flare.

I could hear Dylan in the distance, heckling me as he staggered back up the bank toward the gate. With any luck, he would think me dead in the frozen river. And with the weight of my silver axe tugging me down into the icy, rushing water, I wasn't sure he'd be wrong.

Chapter 7

Neve

AMBER AND I EMERGED UNDER A TALL arch of rough-hewn stone into a cold and misty morning.

"This is Faerie?" I waved at the moss-covered rocks heaped around us. "I have to admit, I was expecting a castle or something." Of course, I couldn't see more than a foot in any direction, so maybe there was a castle in the mist somewhere?

"Welcome to Tír na nÓg! The northern part, to be precise. Home of the Unseelie fae—and your birthplace, I hear. This should be the Ruined Gate on Liadan's Island." Amber glanced around. "Yep, looks right. I've only been here once, but you don't forget all the rocks."

"If you say so."

"Now, I have to head back and see how Miss Chloe is doing, but someone is going to meet you here. Oooh, I want to tell you so bad!" Amber bounced on her toes. "But surprises are fun, too. It'll be better as a surprise."

"What will?" I peered into the mist.

"You'll see! Okay, I'm sure I'll see you soon. Bye!" Amber waved the sapphire at me, then stepped back through the gate, disappearing from sight.

"I can't feel my fingers," complained a female voice from somewhere through the mist.

Shock ran through me. It couldn't be.

"Do stop your whining, child," came a husky woman's voice in reply.

"It's just so *cold*. If you have to drag me out to meet a guest, the least you could have done was give me enough warning to make a cup of coffee."

There was no mistaking that voice. It had to be her.

"I offered you a lovely cup of stinging nettle tea," continued the second voice.

Someone gagged.

"If you add some honey, it's actually pretty good," came a third voice. Male.

"Traitor."

What was my best friend doing in Faerie? I followed the voices through the mist, walking around giant boulders.

"I've been doing some research," said the husky voice, "and that vile beverage you drink is actually very bad for your health."

"Lies."

"Well, human child, you can drink your poison soon enough. Our visitor has arrived. This way, Princess!" the husky voice called.

Finally, the speakers came into view as the mist started to dissipate.

"Audrey?!" I gasped at the blonde, red-hoodie-clad girl.

My best friend spun around and shrieked. She dashed for me and threw her arms around my neck.

"Neve!" Audrey pulled back and adjusted her glasses. "Gavin, it's Neve!"

I stared at the friend I had known since kindergarten—first grade for her—stunned.

"Hi, Neve." Gavin stood up, balancing a teacup in his hands. Audrey's tall, dark-haired boyfriend wore jeans and a black hoodie with the sleeves shoved up to show Celtic tattoos peeking out on his left arm. He looked just like I remembered him. Except . . .

"You have pointy ears," I said, stupidly.

"Yeah." Gavin laughed, tugging on one of the steel plugs that pierced his earlobes.

"That's not the half of it," Audrey confided. "He also turns into a wolf every night. He's all black and furry. It's adorable."

"You, Gavin, Amber, Aunt Chloe . . . Does *everyone* know about Faerie?"

"Not *everyone*," said Audrey.

"Amber's sisters, though," pointed out Gavin. "Isobel's a Seelie princess now, right?"

"Oh, yeah, and Ella's the Seelie queen." Audrey turned to me. "You know, Ella Daniels? She was in your grade in high school."

I blinked at her. "What?"

"Well, that's not important," said Audrey. "That's Seelie Kingdom stuff. You're Unseelie, so we're probably not going to run into them up here."

"I need to sit down."

"Let's get you inside and have some breakfast." The husky voice belonged to a tall woman with long black hair, olive skin, and golden eyes slitted like a cat's. She took a sip from her teacup and smiled at me, showing her sharp canines. "You might want to take a step back, child."

"Always so dramatic, Liadan." Audrey rolled her eyes, but she did drag me back another step from the rocks.

Once we were well away from the giant stone archway rising above the fading mist, the woman, Liadan, snapped her fingers, and the gate collapsed. The stones in the clearing began to rumble and shift around, shedding their moss and rolling together, stone on top of stone, to form a tall tower with three balconies, a shingled roof, and a smoking chimney. The tower's windows glowed with a warm golden light.

"Time for breakfast." Liadan swept past us, her velvet skirts trailing behind as she opened the door.

"Finally." Audrey hooked her arm through mine, pulling me through the doorway and up a curving stone staircase. "Gavin is baking cinnamon rolls. Hopefully, they're ready by now."

"How?" I asked as we emerged into a snug kitchen with glossy wooden cabinets and shelves with bottles of herbs and spices. Velvet-cushioned chairs surrounded a long wooden table, and a wide arched doorway led to a sitting area with two plush armchairs and a sofa. I could hear a fireplace crackling, and sure enough, the smells of cinnamon and brown sugar filled the air.

"Liadan's a cait sìth," explained Audrey.

"Like in my book?" I tried to remember the illustrated page. "A cat shifter, but she can only shift nine times. And the last time, she's stuck in cat form forever?"

"Well, yes." Audrey looked at me in surprise. "That's pretty accurate. But the important part is that she can channel boatloads of magic."

"No weapons in the house!" Liadan set a copper kettle on the stove as Gavin pulled the cinnamon rolls out of the oven.

"You can tuck your hoodie and sword in the closet over here." Audrey opened a tall door beside the stairs.

I pulled off my backpack and handed it to her as I unbuckled my sword belt.

"Wait a minute." Audrey held the pack up to her ear. "Do you know that you have birds in here?" My friend pulled me over to the blue velvet sofa and set my bag on the cushion between us. "Okay." She unzipped the top and peered in. "Why do you have a backpack full of baby chickens?"

"Are they okay?" I reached inside and picked one up, examining the little golden puffball before placing it back in. I ran my hands over them. All seven were moving. I pulled out the little silver one that had still been damp when I put it in. "How are you doing, honey?" I asked. The chick sneezed and snuggled down into my hand.

"These are the chicks I told you I was incubating," I explained to Audrey.

"So you decided to bring them to Faerie with you? In your backpack?"

"I had no choice." I handed her the white chick with fluffy legs.

"I can see that. Who could leave someone this cute behind?" She snuggled the chick up against her chest.

"Do you two ladies want tea or coffee?" called Gavin from the kitchen.

"Very funny," Audrey shot back.

"Coffee, please, Gavin." I needed *something* to convince me I was actually awake.

"She takes cream and sugar," added Audrey before turning back to me. "Please explain why you had no choice but to bring seven baby chicks along." She rubbed the white chick against her cheek. "Other than the obvious reason, I mean."

"I had to bring them along because they're my responsibility. Otherwise, who knows what could have happened to them? Someone might have *eaten* them."

Liadan loomed over us. "They do look very delicious."

Audrey gasped and snuggled the chick closer. "These are pets, not kitty treats!"

"Pity." Liadan swept back into the kitchen.

Gavin brought over two large earthenware mugs of coffee. "I'll go cook some eggs to go with the cinnamon rolls. No offense," he added to the backpack.

Audrey laughed and settled back into her corner of the sofa. "So, are you okay? You look as white as a ghost. Which is only, you know, a shade or two paler than your normal self."

I tilted my head back and closed my eyes. "It's been quite an evening. Morning?" I peeked at her. "What time is it here?"

"Coffee time." Audrey took a sip and sighed happily.

"That's all day for you," I teased my friend.

"Mmm, so true." She took another sip and closed her eyes. "Coffee-with-breakfast time. Maybe eight-ish? So why are you in Faerie now? What happened?"

I filled her in on my day so far. That I was apparently an Unseelie princess, someone named Kylian had come to *probably* rescue me, and my godmother was of the faerie variety.

"This is crazy though, right?" I asked, once I had caught her up. "I would know if I was a faerie. I'd have, like, pointy ears or wings or something?"

"Well . . ." Audrey peered at me through her glasses and then tucked my hair behind my ear. "Now that you mention it."

I gaped at my friend. "I do *not* have pointy ears."

She grimaced and pulled out her phone, taking a photo and handing it to me.

I stared at my image on the phone. At my sharply-tapered ears.

"This has to be a filter or something." I ran my finger over the pointed tip of my ear. "It's not a filter. What . . . *how?*"

Audrey turned my head and examined my ear. "Looks like a temporary transformation spell is wearing off." She squinted. "I'm guessing from what's left that it was cast on you when you were little, and coming to Faerie triggered its end. This is some next-level spellcrafting. I've seen visual glamours, but they need an enchanted object to work. Liadan," she called to the elegant woman through the arched doorway, "did you have anything to do with this?"

"I did not." Liadan didn't look up from her book at the table. "Clíodhna is her godmother, and she is more than capable."

"She means your Aunt Chloe." Audrey let my curls fall back into place. "I like the ears, though. It's a good look on you."

I dropped the phone onto the cushion and rubbed my temples.

"How long have you known all this?" I asked her. "Why didn't you tell me?" I waved my hand around the tower. "*This* is kind of a big secret." I tried to keep the hurt out of my voice, but I couldn't believe she had been lying to me all this time.

"Breakfast," Gavin announced.

We tucked the chicks back in the bag, and Gavin passed us each a plate with a plump cinnamon roll, fluffy scrambled eggs, and a sliced orange.

"Thank you, wolf boy." Audrey tilted her head and Gavin kissed her on the cheek.

"I'll let you guys finish catching up," Gavin said before sitting at the table with Liadan.

"It all began the summer after I graduated high school," started Audrey.

"When you and Gavin traveled to France?" I took a bite of egg.

"Well, actually, before that," she said. "You see, the wolves you saw in the forest are Queen Moriath's minions, and Gavin used to be one, too."

"What? Like the whole time he went to our school?"

"Yep," she said. "Also Dylan. They were looking for the lost Unseelie princess. Moriath is obsessed with some magic crown."

"Wait, your ex-boyfriend is also a faoladh? You have a thing for dating Unseelie minions?" I took a bite of my cinnamon roll. It tasted really good. Gavin obviously knew his way around a kitchen. "I never liked Dylan, you know."

Audrey grimaced. "I know. Apparently, I like my boys dangerous and able to turn into canines." She shrugged. "Everyone's got a type, right? Anyway, Dylan didn't take our breakup very well, and Gavin was trying to escape from Moriath. So we ended up on the run together. He saved me, actually."

"You saved me back," called Gavin.

"Stop eavesdropping!" Audrey turned back to me. "We couldn't come back to Pilot Bay because, of course, the person they were looking for all that time . . ."

"Was me," I finished.

"Correct. And your godmother didn't want a couple of Unseelie fugitives drawing attention to you."

I sighed. "I suppose it makes sense. So all those emails you've sent me from your travels? None of them were true?"

"Oh, they were. Just not the whole truth," said Audrey. "And I really have been going to college. Just not *at* college." She took a bite of her orange. "I'm taking the courses online.

We spend half our time here with Liadan and half our time in the human realm. But we can't stay in one place for too long. Just long enough to access the internet so I can hand in my assignments and to test out some projects that I'm working on. I have to keep rehacking Gavin's tracking spell so the Huntsman doesn't find us, and I need the magic of Faerie to do that."

I blinked, trying to keep up. "You can hack spells?"

"Oooh." She clapped her hands. "I'm so happy I can finally show you what I've been working on!"

Chapter 8

Neve

WHAT AUDREY HAD BEEN WORKING ON TURNED out to be a combination of faerie magic and human technology. She'd always been a tech genius, perhaps even too much for her own good, which was why she had gone into computer science after graduating.

After finding out that she had the Sight, Liadan had offered to teach her magic as well. Or rather, *spellcrafting*, the art of creating and changing spells.

"It's a lot like working with code," explained Audrey. "If code were, you know, kind of alive and sometimes out to get you."

"It might as well be for all I know about it," I reminded my friend. "Most of us didn't grow up building, and then programming, our own computers. But what does that have to do with magic?"

"Okay, let me start from the beginning. Magic is everywhere in Faerie, and anyone can use it to do small magic."

"Even me? What's small magic?" I finished off my orange.

"Anything that uses the magic around you. People can channel different amounts, but anyone can use it to light candles, heal a cut, keep your coffee warm, that sort of thing." Audrey reached over and held my coffee mug for a minute, and it started steaming again. "Small magic. You'll get the hang of it."

"I could heat up cookies without a microwave?" I took a sip of my steaming coffee.

"Yeah, probably." Audrey thought about it for a minute, then shook her head. "Anyway, spellcrafters have the Sight—the ability to see the magic around us—and we can learn to cast more complex spells by infusing objects with magic, which anyone can then use."

"What sort of objects?" I looked around the snug living area.

"Gold is best," Audrey explained. "Silver's better for weapons because it's stronger. Gems are for storing raw energy, but it's hard to get your hands on gems big enough to be worth it."

"What about iron?" I asked. "Is it poisonous for faeries?" I tried to remember what it had said in my book.

"That depends on how it's used. Iron's for blood magic," she said grimly. "We're not into that. Anyway, did you bring your phone?"

"I think so. It should still be in my hoodie pocket from work."

"Sweet!" She ran to the closet and grabbed my phone, then waved me over to sit at the table next to her.

"Are you gonna hook her up to the network?" asked Gavin, stacking our dishes in the sink of soapy water.

"Sure am." Audrey set our phones next to each other on the table. "Oh, you got a new one!" She hummed happily while typing in a password and unlocking my screen. "I hear the camera is amazing on this model."

"How do you know my password?" I asked.

"You're very predictable." Audrey squinted at her phone, and an aura of golden runes intermixed with zeros and ones surrounded it. She made a motion with her fingers and the pattern duplicated into her other hand. She spun the new pattern around, adjusting little bits of what must be the code.

"How're you doing that?" I asked. "The glowy stuff?"

"You can *see* it?" she squealed. "Gavin! She can see it!"

Gavin gave us a soapy thumbs up.

"I knew you were awesome." Audrey went back to playing with the code. "You have the Sight, too."

"I still have no idea what you're doing," I told her.

"I'm making it so that you can . . ." She pressed the golden pattern over my phone, where it sparked and then disappeared, sinking into the screen. "There. Now you can call anyone on the FPN."

I blinked at her.

"The Faerie Phone Network."

"Which is only me and Audrey," added Gavin.

"Well, yes, that's true. I keep trying to convince Liadan to get a phone, but she is not interested in our 'ridiculous human technology.'" She mimicked Liadan's husky voice.

Liadan glanced up from the book she was reading. "If you spent half as much time looking at spellbooks as you do playing with that thing, you'd be a full-fledged spellcrafter already."

"But, Liadan, a new phone would come with a nice box!" called Audrey. "I know how much you cats like *boxes*."

Liadan ignored her, already back to her reading.

"All right, that's step one." Audrey handed me back my phone. "I haven't figured out how to send a signal between realms, so we both have to be in Faerie for it to work."

The screen looked the same, but the spot where I'd usually see the signal strength had been replaced by a little glittering star icon. Suddenly, a notification popped up that I had eleven new emails.

"How am I getting emails?" I glanced up to see Audrey tapping on her phone.

"They're from me." She threw her arms around me. "I wanted to tell you everything so badly. I wrote you emails over the past two years, but I couldn't send them. I saved them all. I just . . . I don't want you to think it was easy for me, keeping this from you." She pulled back and wiped her eyes on her sleeve. "Read them later, okay?"

I nodded, tears in my own eyes.

Audrey took a deep breath. "Okay. Next step is a charger. You only have twenty percent of your battery left. Do you ever plug this thing in?"

"Occasionally." To be fair, it was usually at about ten percent.

"I'll go see if I have all the parts I need to make you one." My friend dashed up the stairs.

I took another sip of coffee. This might be the strangest day I'd ever had, but it was really nice to see Audrey.

Liadan looked up from her book. "It's time."

"What?" Gavin pulled the plug to drain the sink.

"Audrey, it's time!" Liadan called.

"Time for what, you cryptic feline?" Audrey yelled from upstairs.

"Visitors." Liadan snapped her book shut and stood. "Come, come." She waved us along. "I've never disassembled the tower with living creatures inside. I suppose you could stay if you would like to be part of an experiment." She poked her head up the stairs. "Audrey, would you like to be part of an experiment?"

"I'm coming!"

Gavin dried his hands and hung up the tea towel before passing me my hoodie.

"Thank you." I snatched up my backpack as well. I wasn't sure what the whole *experiment on living things* entailed, but it didn't sound like something I should inflict on the babies.

Audrey ran down from upstairs and collided in the kitchen with Gavin. He handed her hoodie over and she paused to kiss him before pulling it on.

"*Later*, children." Liadan swept past us and exited in a rustle of velvet and silk.

I shouldered my bag and followed Audrey and Gavin down the stairs out of the tower.

The mist had dissipated around the tower, but it was still a cold morning. What time of year was it in Faerie?

"Can't you get your visitors to come on nicer days?" Audrey rubbed her arms, and Gavin pulled her back against him, wrapping his arms around her. "And don't you find it incredibly inconvenient to have to disassemble your entire house every time somebody comes to visit?"

Liadan glowered at her and snapped her fingers. The tower began to tumble apart.

"I mean, *you* built this thing," Audrey continued. "What kind of poor planning was that?"

"I planned the creation of the Ruined Gate in detail. It keeps people from poking through my things while I'm out." Liadan examined her fingernails. "Besides, I generally plan not to have visitors at all. You may recall that I didn't actually invite any of you." She waved her arm at the three of us.

"No, you just dragged me here against my will," said Audrey.

"I suppose that's true." Liadan glanced at her. "Only the first time, though. You just keep coming back."

"Who's visiting, anyway?" Audrey asked.

"So impatient, human child."

The rocks all settled into place, some of them creating the Ruined Gate, the rest littering the mossy field. If I hadn't just been in her tower, I would have thought I was looking at ancient ruins.

A minute later, Amber jumped through the gate, followed by Aunt Chloe.

"Miss Chloe!" Audrey rushed over and hugged my godmother.

"Thank you, Liadan," Aunt Chloe called.

The cait sìth nodded. "Clíodhna."

I held back. I wasn't actually sure how I felt about Aunt Chloe lying to me my entire life—the parts that I could remember, at least—or about her telling my best friend to stay away from me, even if she felt it was for my own good. I looked off into the misty forest as Gavin and Amber greeted each other awkwardly, like you do with people from high school you hadn't known well.

"Oh, sweetheart." Aunt Chloe came over to give me a big hug, and despite myself, I sank into her comforting warmth for a long moment. Then I stepped back and let her see the hurt in my eyes. She smoothed back my hair. "It's been a lot, I know."

"You can explain everything to us when we get inside," suggested Audrey. "Maybe with another round of coffee. *Hot* coffee."

"We're expecting one more," said Liadan.

"Ooh!" Amber clapped her hands. "Who?"

Aunt Chloe just tilted her head and nodded.

"The only other person who has access to the Ruined Gate," said Liadan, as if that answered everything.

"How are the chicks?" Amber patted my backpack.

"You brought your chicks?" asked Aunt Chloe, surprised.

"They seem good," I said. "Although, one is sneez—" I cut off as my rune flared with warmth.

A tall shape stepped through the gate.

"That's the *Huntsman.*" Gavin grabbed Audrey's hand and pulled her behind him.

"Calm yourself, pup." Liadan rolled her eyes. "He's on our side."

"He's been chasing us for the past two years of human time," Gavin snarled. "Who knows how long it's been in faerie time."

Human time? Faerie time? I felt overwhelmed again by how much I didn't know. Everything needed to slow down long enough for me to get some explanations. And possibly a nap. Whatever time it was here, it felt like forever since I'd woken up at home.

"I think I would have noticed if Moriath's Huntsman was *on my side.*" Gavin didn't move, but he didn't relax either.

Kylian took a step forward. He was soaking wet, water dripping from his long locs, his black tunic plastered against his powerful frame.

"In all that time, you may have noticed that I never actually caught you." He rested his silver axe on the ground. "Despite the ink Moriath put on you. Didn't you ever find that odd?"

Gavin nudged Audrey another step back. "It's gonna take more than that for me to trust you."

Kylian grunted.

Aunt Chloe put her hand on Gavin's arm. "It truly is fine, Gavin. We'll explain everything once we get inside."

"If Liadan says he's on our side, then he must be." Audrey slid under Gavin's arm and patted his chest. "And I like the part about *inside*."

She continued on, saying something about making a fresh pot of coffee, but my attention was fixed on Kylian. The tall man's left shoulder hung a little funny, and though his face looked as impassive as ever, I couldn't help but notice the way his jaw clenched as he gingerly touched his side. When he pulled his hand away, the palm dripped red.

He looked up again and caught me watching him. "I'm glad you're safe, Princess," he said in a low voice. Then his eyes rolled back, and he collapsed on the ground.

Chapter 9

Neve

Audrey and I convinced Gavin to help us carry Kylian up the stairs. Amber came behind with his axe.

"Lay him on the sofa," Liadan ordered, spreading out a quilt with a wave of her hand.

We set him on the quilt—some of us more gently than others—and Aunt Chloe knelt down and pulled up Kylian's shirt. I gasped. A deep wound bled red against his muscled side.

"Not bad, eh?" Amber elbowed me, wiggling her eyebrows.

"He's *bleeding out*, Amber," I protested.

"He'll be fine. We're in Faerie."

"Amber." Aunt Chloe waved her apprentice over. "Why don't you work on his shoulder while I heal his side."

"Got it!"

I took off my pack and hoodie, pulling the brown chick out for comfort while they examined Kylian. As I paced around the tower, I noticed that the room seemed to have grown. It felt just as snug and comfortable with seven occupants as it had been with four, but not any more cramped.

Audrey patted my shoulder. "He'll be okay."

I didn't know how to explain my anxiety over a man I had only met a few hours ago. He had frightened me, upended my entire life, and not once had he even come close to properly explaining why. Or smiling, for that matter. But when I looked at him lying there, I couldn't shake the feeling that I *should* know him. That we had met somewhere before. It was like something in me tugged toward him. But that was ridiculous. It had been a very long day. I must be imagining things.

"Whatever." I shrugged, dragging my eyes away from the injured fae. "He doesn't even like dessert."

"That's a red flag if I ever heard one," teased Audrey. She petted the chick in my hands with one finger. The chick glowered at her. "Not to knock your cool backpack, but maybe we could upgrade the chicken accommodations?"

With Gavin's help, we located a wooden crate and lined it with an old towel. When it was settled by the fireplace, I carefully tucked the baby chicks into it. Six of them poked around, exploring their new home, but the white chick blinked sleepily before curling up for a nap. I pulled out the container of chick feed, and Audrey found a little dish for water. The chicks could technically go another day before they needed to eat, but I wanted to make sure they had the option to try if they were hungry.

I emptied out my bag and held up the apron I had nestled them into with a grimace. "I guess this is going in the trash."

Liadan walked past with a cup of tea and waved her hand, muttering something about wasteful children. The stains disappeared, and the apron looked cleaner than I had ever seen it. It was even ironed.

"Teach me that one next, Liadan," called Audrey. "I don't think any magic will save that sandwich though." She wrinkled her nose as I pulled out a flat ham sandwich.

"I won't even show you the muffin." I crumpled up the paper bag of broken pumpkin raisin and bran with a sigh. Poor muffin.

"That should do it. Good work, Amber." Aunt Chloe patted her apprentice's shoulder.

Amber smiled up at Aunt Chloe, and I peeked over at their patient. His clothes were dry and the rips gone—Liadan again, no doubt—and while his normally warm complexion still looked a little ashen, he breathed peacefully.

A sense of relief washed over me. I hadn't realized just how worried I had been. I shook my head. Obviously, I didn't want *anyone* to die in Liadan's sitting room. I'd feel the same about any acquaintance, surely.

"So, Liadan, how have you been?" Aunt Chloe settled back into an armchair.

I shook out my apron with a snap, and everyone turned to look at me, even the chicks.

"No *how-have-you-beens*," I firmly said, tying on the apron. "Here's what's going to happen. I'm going to make pie, and *you*," I added, pointing around to each person in the tower, "are going to explain everything. But first." I tucked a chick into each of my big apron pockets. "Liadan, do you have any apples?"

Once I had gathered what I needed, everyone but the still-unconscious Kylian sat at the kitchen table. I could have sworn I had seen only four chairs earlier, but somehow everyone had a seat and enough room at the table.

My hands shook slightly as I pulled the big earthenware bowl in front of me. I rolled my shoulders, needing to ground myself in the recipe I knew best. Like watching a favorite movie or bundling up in an old quilt, baking apple pie was comforting. Something easy and familiar even when my world had been turned upside down.

"Okay, Aunt Chloe, you start explaining. Everyone else, peel an apple."

"She's awfully bossy," Amber murmured.

"That's good. She's going to be queen," my godmother reminded her.

"That!" I pointed a wooden spoon at her. "That's what I mean. Explain."

"Sam and Roberta told you that you're the Unseelie crown princess?" Aunt Chloe picked up an apple and a knife.

"And that some queen is trying to kill me. But why?" I scooped flour into a bowl with a chipped teacup that Gavin swore worked as a one-cup measure. He had become quite the cook while traveling with Audrey.

Aunt Chloe glanced over at Liadan. "Maybe you should start. You knew the girls better back then."

"True." Liadan took a sip of her tea. "Once upon a time, there were three sisters—Oonagh, Moriath, and Bronach."

"Ugh, Bronach is the worst." Audrey made a face. Everyone looked at her. "Sorry, I know Moriath's the evil queen and trying to kill Neve and all, but Bronach *did* trap Liadan in an iron cage that one time."

"Thank you, child. It truly was a trial. She didn't even offer me any peppermint tea. I knew she had some. I could smell it." Liadan paused in memory, then shook her head. "The girls' parents were powerful fae. Their father had an affinity for plants, and their mother was a spellcrafter who worked with ice. Bronach inherited her father's magic, while Oonagh and Moriath inherited their mother's. Moriath had more raw power than her sisters, more than anyone had seen in generations. Her parents made sure she knew it. She was insufferable at court, honestly."

"So was she, like, a princess?" asked Amber. "Was that why she was at court?"

"Wait!" Audrey dropped her apple. "Liadan, are *you* a princess?"

"Human child." Liadan blinked at Amber. "You've spent altogether too much time in the Seelie Kingdom. And, Audrey, you should know better. Apart from our monarchs, the Unseelie don't care about such titles. You have power, or you don't. Not everyone has to rule some tiny court of flowers."

"Peppermint Princess?" mused Audrey. "No, no. Catnip Princess!"

Liadan stared at Audrey, who sighed and went back to peeling apples.

"The Unseelie crown doesn't automatically pass down the royal line," continued the cait sìth. "The crown belongs to the strongest and most powerful of the Unseelie fae. Usually, that's the royal family, as generations of Unseelie rulers have married powerful fae in order to keep the crown in their family. Moriath's parents rightfully assumed that she would be chosen to marry the crown prince, Fionnbharr—your father, Niamh. They groomed Moriath to be the future queen, placing all their hopes and ambitions on her. And when the girls were children, it seemed like all would go as planned."

"Until the Yule Ball," said Aunt Chloe.

Liadan nodded. "We were both there when Moriath's parents presented their daughters at court. They were so proud of Moriath. Her beauty, her power."

"But Fionnbharr only had eyes for Oonagh." Aunt Chloe smiled, remembering.

"My mother," I whispered.

Aunt Chloe nodded. "Yes, dear."

I rolled the names around in my head. Oonagh and Fionnbharr. All my life, I had wondered who my parents were. Imagined some human girl who gave up a baby she had been too young to keep. A father who hadn't known I existed. But we had been a family. What had they looked like? Did I still have relatives somewhere? I tucked my little questions away for later. For now, I needed the big ones answered.

"Fionnbharr pestered his parents until they gave in and allowed the love match." Liadan swirled the tea in the bottom of her cup. "And they lived happily ever after."

I looked at her expectantly.

"For six hundred and forty years," she amended. "Not bad, honestly."

"The trouble started when you were a little girl, only three. Your mother, Queen Oonagh, was killed in a battle with Fiachra, the former Seelie king," Aunt Chloe said, picking up the tale. "I'd always found the circumstances around her death suspicious, and after recently learning that Moriath and Fiachra had been in league with each other for many years, I have no doubt that she arranged for your mother's death. Your father was left with two tiny girls and a kingdom to rule on his own."

"Wait." I paused, a spoon of baking powder forgotten in my hand. "I have a sister? Where is she? Can I meet her?" In all my wonderings about my birth parents, I had never thought about having a sibling.

"Maeve," confirmed my godmother. "She was two years younger than you."

My heart fell. "Was?"

"Time goes more quickly in Faerie." Amber bit into an apple. "Mostly."

"What does that mean?" My head spun with all the things I didn't understand as I dumped the baking powder into the bowl.

"You'll see when you go back to the human realm," Amber said. "A week in Faerie might be an hour there. Or five minutes. Or a day. It's hard to keep track, but on average, time moves maybe . . . ten times as fast? So your sister might be older than you now, if she's been living in Faerie. She's not dead though, right?"

"She's missing," said Gavin. "That's who Moriath was looking for. Kylian was supposed to have killed Neve when she was little."

"He was *what?*" I spun to look at the unconscious Huntsman. "Never mind. Back up." I closed my eyes, took a deep breath, then sprinkled sugar and salt into the bowl. This was testing even the comforting powers of pie baking. "If you jump around, I'll never get this straight."

"King Fionnbharr, your father, remarried quickly." Aunt Chloe peeled an apple in one long spiral. "He wanted to give you girls a mother and to have someone help rule the Unseelie Kingdom. He chose someone he knew well. Someone who had always claimed to love her nieces as if they were her own daughters."

"Moriath." I stirred the dry ingredients together.

"Even though it was so soon after your mother's death, your father seemed to love her," said Aunt Chloe. "And he was happy to have a partner again. In Tír na nÓg, the spouse of the king or queen becomes a co-ruler alongside them. It's believed to bring balance and to ease the burden of ruling."

"If you can call it ruling, in Moriath's case." Liadan drained her teacup.

Aunt Chloe nodded. "Things began to change. Noble families stopped visiting Skyretaine."

"Sky Train?" I added butter to the bowl and began cutting it in with a fork.

"The Unseelie castle where your family lived," she explained. "Then there were stories of people disappearing, creatures stirring in the darkening forests."

"And my father didn't do anything?" I cracked an egg into the teacup, added a splash of vinegar, then filled the cup the rest of the way with cold water.

"He didn't seem to see it," said Aunt Chloe. "Moriath was careful, and he wouldn't hear anything against his new queen."

"She enchanted him," said Liadan.

"She must have," agreed my godmother. "Rumors are one thing, but the Fionnbharr we knew would never have stood by and done nothing when Moriath traded Maeve to the Aziza."

"She *traded* my sister?" I asked. "For what?"

"For me," came a low voice from the sitting room. "Although, she regretted that decision today."

Chapter 10

Neve

Everyone turned to see Kylian leveraging himself up to a sitting position. He lifted his shirt to examine his healed wound, and I looked away *almost* immediately. This wasn't the time to be distracted by abs, and I still needed to sort out this whole "was he Moriath's evil minion?" thing. But I could say, just as an observation, that whatever his duties as Huntsman were, they kept him quite fit.

"Lady Clíodhna," he said. "I assume you used your healing magic to take care of me. My thanks."

"I helped." Amber stuck up her hand, and Kylian nodded at her.

"Come and sit," said Audrey. "Do you want a cup of coffee?"

"That depends." Kylian gave me a pointed look. "Who made it?"

Amber glanced between the two of us, looking rather amused, and I went back to pouring my egg mixture into the bowl.

"It's quite safe. I'm too busy making more vile sweet things," I said.

Kylian sat at the table and accepted a mug from Audrey with a grunt of thanks. He and Gavin shared a look, then they both nodded and looked away. Had they really just sorted out all their issues that quickly? *Men.*

"Perhaps you can tell the rest of the story, Kylian." Aunt Chloe waved her paring knife at him. "You were there for more of it than I was."

Kylian nodded and took a sip of coffee. "Your aunt Moriath wanted to get rid of the two of you."

"Why?" I asked. "We were just little kids."

"Even though you were just children," said Kylian, "there was no telling how powerful you would become as you grew. Moriath wanted the crown. She would not let a couple of children get in her way."

"So she traded my sister for you?" I asked.

"There's an old tradition in Faerie," he said, "where rulers exchange their children to be fostered in each other's kingdoms in order to forge alliances and to act as hostages to prevent war."

"Your kingdom was at war with this one?" I glanced at Kylian to find him frowning at his coffee cup. Maybe he wasn't actually grumpy all the time. Maybe he just had one of those faces. Perhaps I had overreacted at the café? On the other hand, he *had* shaved at least two years off my life when he burst into my kitchen with that axe, so I didn't feel *too* bad about the coffee incident.

"No, it wasn't about international politics for Moriath." He shook his head. "She only cared about the crown. She didn't dare kill Maeve, not while your father still lived, but if your sister joined another kingdom—and was bound into their royal family with a betrothal agreement—then she would no longer be Unseelie and the crown wouldn't pass to her. So, Moriath arranged a trade with my parents, the rulers of the Aziza fae, and sent Maeve as far away as possible. After all, Maeve was the second child. A political marriage wouldn't raise any eyebrows."

I blinked at Kylian. "That's terrible. How old was she? How old were *you*?"

"I was twelve. Don't give me that face, Princess. It was a long time ago, and I had my reasons for going along with it. I was older than my twin sister had been when she was traded away to the Seelie Kingdom."

There was a lot more in there that I was curious about, but I let it go for now.

"So then my father died?"

Kylian nodded. "I had been at Skyretaine a little over a year. King Fionnbharr's health began to decline, and the healers couldn't figure out what was wrong. He just slowly became more and more tired, and Moriath gradually took over ruling the Unseelie Kingdom. But he had always been good to me, treating me like a son for that year, so when I heard that he was dying and saw the servants rushing about, I went to say goodbye. He didn't have the strength to tell me much, but he knew he didn't have much time left. He asked me to take care of you. I think Moriath's enchantment weakened there at the end, at least a little, and he understood enough to be rightfully worried about leaving you in your aunt's care. He told me how to contact Clíodhna, should I need to."

"I'm guessing you needed to." I mixed the dough, kneading it until it came together, then covered it with a tea towel. "How are the apples coming? Oh. Thank you."

Amber, Audrey, and Gavin, listening intently, had peeled and sliced a giant heap of them.

"Your father hadn't even been buried when Moriath tried to kill you," Kylian continued. "She was in a rage. Your father was dead, and as the queen and most powerful Unseelie fae--or so she believed--the crown should have passed to her. It had disappeared instead. She blamed you."

"She blamed the preschooler?" I scooped the apples I needed into a glass bowl.

"Yes," he said. "And rightfully so. Even then, your power was remarkable."

"That's ridiculous." I added sugar and spices to the apples. "I don't have any power. But go on."

"Moriath wanted two things," said Kylian. "She wanted you dead, and she wanted to see if I would support her or not."

"You were only thirteen," I clarified.

"And already growing into a formidable warrior with a talent for rune magic," said Aunt Chloe. "Although not quite as tall as he is now."

Kylian inclined his head. "Moriath doesn't like to waste things if she doesn't have to. I'm sure she was tempted to get rid of me as well, if only because it would have endangered Maeve's life as a hostage. But I'd taken care not to give the queen any reason to distrust me. Moriath decided to solve two problems at once. She told me to take you out into the woods and bring back your heart. You still had too many supporters at the castle for her to do it herself."

"Were you tempted?" I asked, rolling out the pie crust.

"Never."

I glanced up to see his dark eyes intent on me. I quickly looked back at my dough.

"Kylian contacted me," said Aunt Chloe, "and we met in the forest. I knew a couple in the human realm who had spent time in Faerie when they were younger. They had always wanted a child, so we took you to Pilot Bay."

"To the Klassens." I carefully placed the pie crust in the pan. "And Moriath just believed you when you told her that I was dead?"

"I brought the queen a pig's heart and told her it was yours," said Kylian.

I dry heaved.

"She thought you were dead, but when the crown didn't appear, she sent out her spies and learned that Maeve had never reached my home kingdom to be bonded to my brother. My parents had lied and said she arrived safely because admitting that they had lost her would have put my life at risk. Moriath was furious. She's been searching for your sister all this time to finish Maeve off and get the crown."

"So she hasn't found either of us in, what . . . fifteen years?" I was glad that this mysterious sister was so good at hiding, yet I couldn't help but wish that I could meet her. I dusted my hands off on my apron and reached for the bowl of sliced apples.

"It's been well over two hundred," said Liadan.

"I'm over *two hundred?*" I almost dropped the pie filling, bowl and all, onto the crust.

"No, child. You're twenty. Time moves slower in the human realm, remember?"

"Oh, right." I filled the pie crust with the spiced apples. "And you haven't found Maeve either? No one knows where she is?"

"That's a mystery that's been bothering me for years," Aunt Chloe admitted. "I don't know how she's been hidden for so long, even from me." She tapped her fingers on the table, then shook her head and continued. "When we placed you with Sam and Roberta, we built all the layers of protection we could manage around you, Pilot Bay, and five other towns. It wasn't until recently that Moriath gave up searching in Faerie and started carefully scrying for Maeve in the human realm. Four years ago—in human time—she found the areas that were warded against her and sent her wolves to sniff around. But even though Moriath believed Maeve to be in one of the warded towns, she didn't know which one—or even what your sister looked like now that she was grown."

"It drove her insane." Gavin smiled.

"But none of the glamours or wards were meant to last forever," continued Aunt Chloe. "It was all just to keep you safe as you grew up."

"And now I'm grown up?" I asked. Everyone just watched me. "I guess I am." I placed the top crust on the pie and crimped the edges with a fork. "So, what am I supposed to do now? Fend for myself?"

"Of course not," said Liadan. "Now, you're supposed to defeat Moriath and reclaim the Unseelie throne."

The fork clattered to the floor as I gaped at them all. "I'm sorry. What did you just say?"

The cold misty air hit me like a slap when I escaped the tower. I welcomed the chill and the quiet after all those people staring at me with their expectations. People I thought I had known, like Aunt Chloe with all her secrets, and people who acted like they knew me. Like they had a *right* to tell me what my life should look like.

I found a rock to sit on and pulled the envelope out of my hoodie pocket, then hesitated. Once I opened this letter, would I lose my adoptive parents too? Two more people I thought I knew? I blinked back tears, feeling the sting of betrayal.

But in the end, I missed them more than I was mad at them, so I tore open the envelope, desperate for some connection to home.

Two papers were neatly folded inside, a bit crumpled from their time in my backpack.

The first one was in my mom's neat printing.

Hi Sweetie,

Now that you're twenty, I know your time with us is going to end soon. I might not get the chance for a proper explanation, so I'm writing this note in case you have to leave in a hurry.

First of all, I'm sorry that we couldn't tell you this sooner. Your Aunt Chloe decided that it would be safest for you if you believed you were truly a human child. These last few years with Moriath's wolves searching Pilot Bay for you have proved her right. We never wanted to hide your true identity from you. Neve, you are strong and kind, and we are so proud of the woman you've grown to be. Nothing about what I'm going to tell you changes who you really are.

Your father and I didn't meet in culinary school like we told you. We met in Faerie. Yes, just like your book. All those stories are true—selkies, dragons, and all. He had been recruited to work at Skyretaine Castle as a pastry chef because of his talents, and I was just a girl who fell through the wrong gate and wound up as a kitchen maid. We always wanted children, but it wasn't meant to be. This isn't about us though, it's about you.

You always wondered about your birth parents, but how could I tell you that they were the Unseelie king and queen? Or that you had a little sister like you always wanted, but she was in another kingdom, far away? I hope you can meet Maeve someday, and I wish I could tell you more about them all now, but we only ever saw your family from a distance. I do know that your parents loved you and your sister very much.

You were always getting into scrapes, but you seemed so happy. Little Princess Niamh. I hope it isn't too confusing that we adjusted your name. The spelling and pronunciation they use in Tír na nÓg would have drawn Moriath's attention, but we kept it close so that you would still feel like it belonged to you when you grew up. Sorry, I'm getting ahead of myself.

When your mother died and your father married Moriath, it wasn't safe for humans to remain in the Unseelie Kingdom, so Chloe helped us to escape and settle in Pilot Bay. Soon after, she showed up with young Lord Kylian and you. We tried to convince him to stay here with us, but his sense of duty was too strong. He knew you'd be safer if he could tell Moriath that he had killed you. He was so young still. It broke my heart.

You cried when he left, but Chloe blocked your memories. She glamoured your fae ears and set up wards of protection around our home and the town. She's been watching over you ever since, and in his own way, Lord Kylian has as well. We haven't seen him, but the wolves masquerading as Irish exchange students haven't discovered you, even after years of poking about. That can only have been due to his interference.

But Chloe's wards were only meant to allow you the time to grow up. I know that soon the time will come for you to return to Tír na nÓg. Just know that even if it seems like everything you knew wasn't real, the way we love you is the truest thing in our lives. We're so blessed to have you for our daughter and are so, so grateful for the fifteen years we've been your mom and dad.

This isn't goodbye. We'll see you again as soon as it's safe.

Love you forever,
Mom

My tears fell, but they weren't the only ones staining the paper. My mom had always been a crier, just like me.

The second paper was just a short note in my dad's messy cursive, a butter stain in the top corner.

Neve, don't forget to chill the butter properly when you make pie crust, or you know your adopted Mennonite ancestors will be disappointed in you. And don't eat too much cookie dough while you're gone. You know the raw flour and eggs aren't good for you.

Your mom is giving me a look. You know the one. She thinks I should write more, but you already know how proud I am of you. Nothing about you being a princess changes that.

Love you, kiddo,
Dad

I laughed, inhaling a short hiccup through my tears. I reread both letters two more times before carefully folding them back up. I could feel their love in their words, and I knew they were right. Nothing that had happened today changed who I was or who my family was. I'd do whatever I needed to make sure they were safe, and then I'd go back to where I belonged. Back home.

Chapter 11

Kylian

I FOUND NIAMH BEHIND THE TOWER, SITTING on a mossy rock at the edge of the forest, huddled in her hoodie.

Wordlessly, I sat beside her and offered her a plate of apple pie.

"Do you want a bite first?" she asked without looking at me.

The scent of butter, fruit, and sugar wafted up from the plate, but I grunted and shook my head. It had been a long time since I had allowed myself an indulgence like that.

"Of course you don't." She sighed and took the plate from me. Her small, pale fingers brushed against mine, warm in the cold air. "So, you've all planned my life out for me. What do *you* think I'm doing next?" Niamh stabbed her fork aggressively into the pie.

"We keep you hidden from Moriath while we gather allies, then we take back your throne." Simple. Or so I had thought before meeting grown-up Niamh.

"I am *not* a queen." She glared at me. "Not even a princess like you keep calling me. And I didn't ask to be involved in some royal conspiracy." She took a bite of pie and then waved her fork at me. "So, thank you very much for not killing me. Twice. But take your plans elsewhere."

"Princess," I began.

"Not a princess."

"I didn't save your life *twice* for a *thank you*."

"Well, then, why *did* you save my life?" she demanded. "Just because I'm so cute?"

A memory shot through me of the child princess she had been, climbing trees with scraped knees, blue eyes sparkling.

She rolled her eyes when I didn't answer. "Obviously not that."

I shook off the memory. "I saved your life, *Princess*, for the kingdom." How could I make her understand? "You're the only one who can match Moriath for power."

"I don't know what kind of power you *think* I have, other than making killer apple pies. Are you sure you don't want a bite? I think this might be my best one yet." She tilted her head. "It's not quite right. Definitely closer though. Maybe my mother's apples were from . . . Never mind."

"The Unseelie fae are suffering under Moriath's rule. They need you."

"I know that's supposed to mean something to me, but that just sounds like something out of a story. I wasn't raised to rule some fairytale country. My parents are Sam and Roberta Klassen. I grew up in Pilot Bay, and I'm a baker. I'll just stay right here with my chicks and work on my recipe until it's safe to go home." Niamh ate her last bite of pie. "I wonder if Liadan has any other varieties of apples . . ."

"Let me explain." I willed her to look at me, but she just shook her head.

"There's nothing more to explain. You're going to have to find another Unseelie queen, and anytime you want some pie, you can stop by the tower." Niamh jerked her thumb toward Liadan's home. "Which, since you don't eat dessert, will be never. Have a nice life!" She stood up and handed me the plate and fork while she brushed crumbs off her skirt. "Now, if you don't mind, I'm going to go inside and check on my babies."

"Wait." I set down the plate and surged to my feet. I had never been good with words.

It didn't matter that she didn't want anything to do with me, but how could I get her to understand how much the kingdom needed her? I had done my best these long years, but it hadn't done anything more than inconvenience Moriath. And now that I wasn't Huntsman anymore . . . "You have to listen."

She pointedly ignored me, continuing to talk to herself as she walked toward the tower, before letting out a sharp *yip*.

Liadan's tower collapsed in a crash of tumbling stone, revealing our allies on the far side of the clearing.

"The chicks!" Niamh darted over to the group.

Of *course* the animals were the first thing she worried about. I held back, letting her talk to her friends.

"Don't worry." Audrey passed Niamh her backpack and sword belt. "I got them for you. They're all packed up and ready to travel with a fresh hot water bottle. I didn't have all the parts to make you a charger though, so take it easy with that phone."

“But I’m not going anywhere.” The princess set her sword on the ground so she could unzip her backpack and look inside.

“We will entrust Niamh’s safety to you, Kylian.” Liadan’s golden eyes regarded me steadily.

I nodded. Niamh might not want anything to do with me, but between her headstrong nature and Moriath’s obsession with getting the crown, I didn’t trust anyone else to keep the princess alive.

When I looked back at Niamh, she had an odd expression on her face.

“What is it, child?” asked Liadan.

“I still don’t remember any of this.” Niamh wrinkled her nose.

“But?” prompted the cait sìth.

“But when you call me Niamh . . . it feels more like *me* than Neve does. Like it’s actually my name.” She sighed. “It makes it hard to not believe you.”

Liadan nodded. “You were very young when I last saw you, but I assure you, child, you truly are Princess Niamh of the Unseelie fae. I was present at your christening.”

“I’ll take the name, but the princess part is still not happening. Oh Liadan, can’t I stay here?” begged Niamh, not noticing when I picked up her sword for her. “I’m very quiet.”

“You are not,” said Liadan.

“I’ll cook *all* your meals. I’m working on a muffin recipe that I think you would be very into.” She batted her eyelashes at the cait sìth.

“Child, Moriath’s powers are strong,” she said. “Stronger even than mine. Now that she knows you’re alive, she’ll be scrying for you in her mirror. I’ve kept her away for as long as I can, but you need to be somewhere safer. This is not a fortress." The cait sìth turned to me. "I've contacted Ulrik. They've unlocked the Topaz Gate for you."

I inclined my head. "Thank you, Lady Liadan." I exhaled in relief. Nidavellir was the perfect place to take Niamh, and she would be much safer arriving by gate.

"You will be able to learn a great deal about ruling a kingdom in Nidavellir, child," Liadan told Niamh.

"Aunt Chloe?" Niamh abruptly hurried over to her godmother, who was talking to her apprentice in a low voice. "Where are you going? Can I tag along?"

"It bothers me to admit this, but I do seem to have lost Maeve," Clíodhna said with a sigh. "I haven't been able to spend enough time in Faerie to track her down, what with Moriath so upset with me. I have some friends that I want to check in with now that Her Royal Evilness is distracted by her plans for your demise."

"I wish I could help," said the princess. "Is there any way you can unblock my memories? Maybe I could help find her! And then we can ask her if *she* wants to be the Unseelie queen." She shot me a look over her godmother's shoulder, and I just raised an eyebrow.

"I'm afraid you were very young when I put the memory blocks in place. I can't reverse it, but now that you're in Faerie, some bits and pieces might come back to you. Regardless, I'm afraid that bringing you along would draw too much attention now that Moriath knows to scry for you. We can't have her finding Maeve before we do." She hugged Niamh. "I'm sorry, my dear. You'll be safe with Kylian."

Niamh squeezed her godmother in return and stepped back. "Will you check on my mom and dad at home for me? I know you guys said there were wards and whatnot, but I'm worried about them."

"Of course." Clíodhna smiled at Niamh. "I'll stop in for tea before we go."

"Where *are* you guys going?" Niamh asked.

Clíodhna just smiled. She loved her secrets.

"Amber?" asked Niamh.

Amber tossed her golden brown hair. "You know as much as I do. Clíodhna never tells me anything."

"Keeps things interesting," teased Clíodhna.

"Yeah, but it's hard to know which shoes to pack, you know?" Amber turned back to Niamh. "Audrey hooked my phone up to her faerie network, so I'll tell you when I know something. If we're in Faerie, that is. It's not as good as a pocket dragon, but mine abandoned me for Haru, so . . ." She shrugged.

"Dragon? Never mind." Niamh shook her head and turned to Audrey, who was tying the laces on her red shoes. "And where are *you* going? I just found you!" She set down her backpack and tackled her friend in a hug, knocking them both over.

While Audrey dove into an explanation about the project she needed parts for, Gavin walked over to me.

"All that time," Gavin said in a low voice, "you were never really Moriath's right hand?"

I could tell he wanted to believe it. Of all Moriath's wolves, Gavin had always had the softest heart, only joining up to try to help his older brother—now long dead, like so many others.

"I was everything you believed me to be." I picked up Niamh's backpack and set it beside her sword. The peeping inside quieted. "It was what I had to be. To keep her safe."

Gavin nodded thoughtfully, and we both watched the girls while they helped each other up, chattering the whole time.

"Well, I guess I don't have to look over my shoulder for your scary self anymore." Gavin stuck his hands in his pockets.

"Don't let your guard down," I said. "I wasn't trying that hard." I pushed up my right sleeve, not surprised to find that all the Huntsman tattoos the queen had given me were now dormant. It wasn't just Dylan that I would be unable to track or influence. It had been too much to hope that Moriath would forget and leave me that advantage. I'd have to rely on my runes. Even Gavin's mark had faded to a dull black. "Moriath will send someone more motivated after you now." I nodded at Audrey. "I assume she's been scrambling your tracking tattoo."

Gavin nodded. "She tried to remove it, but Moriath's spell is too strong."

"Keep her safe." Niamh had a hard road ahead. She'd need her friend. "And watch your back."

"Same to you." Gavin clapped his hand on my shoulder.

I froze, stunned by the gesture of camaraderie. When was the last time someone had touched me out of friendship?

"Sorry." Gavin pulled his hand back. "I—"

A flash of bright light and dark red smoke suddenly exploded in the center of the pile of stones beside the girls. We all stared in shock as it cleared to reveal a gasping Dylan, looking as white as a ghost, an amulet of iron in his fist.

In a flash, he pulled Niamh to him, his sword to her throat.

I slowly unfastened my axe, focused on nothing but that blade pressed into her skin. Wolf or not, he'd die for touching her.

"Hey, Dylan, how'd you get here without a gate?"

The boy jerked his attention to Audrey. "You!" His grip on his sword wavered. "I'll be back for you next."

"Mmm, you can't teleport with more than one person, eh? Is that the amulet's restriction or . . . ?" Audrey narrowed her eyes thoughtfully. "Nope, it's yours. Too bad you don't have more power. That's a nasty bit of blood magic, but the theory behind it is *interesting*."

"Audrey, please step back," murmured Gavin.

"Oh, I just think it's funny that Moriath didn't give him more resources. I bet she didn't think he'd actually be able to catch us." Audrey winked at Dylan. "After all, we did lock him up in his own cell that one time."

Dylan's pasty face flushed with rage, his attention now fully on Niamh's friend. "When I bring the princess to my queen, she'll make me Huntsman, and there will be nowhere you can hide from me, you stupid little girl!"

Good, keep him distracted. I took a step closer. Niamh's arm suddenly shot up, and she shoved Dylan's sword hand, dropping to the ground in a beautiful roll. I lunged for him, swinging my axe, but I swung through empty air. The boy was already flying backward. He somersaulted through the air and disappeared through the Ruined Gate.

"*Liadan.*" I spun to face the cait sìth, who had the look of a cat playing with a mouse.

"No murders on my tower, if you please." She sniffed. "Do you know how much power is in these stones? I shudder to think what would happen if someone spilled blood in violence on them."

"He'll be trouble." I helped Niamh to her feet, surreptitiously checking her for injuries. She didn't look at me, instead unzipping her backpack to check on her chicks again. *Honestly.*

"You'll just have to kill him elsewhere." Liadan shrugged. "Speaking of elsewhere, it's time for you all to leave. Not only do I need to reset my wards, but it has been over one hundred years since I last had so much company at once." The cait sìth yawned. "I need a nap. Possibly for another hundred years. So off you go. I want to rebuild my bedroom."

After yet more hugs, the others left through the Ruined Gate. It was time for us to go.

"Princess," I started, strapping on my axe.

"Stop calling me *Princess*."

I passed Niamh her sword. She could be as mad as she wanted, so long as she came with me. Maybe Ulf and Ulrik would have better luck convincing her.

Niamh took a deep breath, pulling herself together.

"Fine. Apparently, we can't stay here." She threw up her hands. "Where are you taking me?"

"To see some old friends of your parents," I said.

She gave me a sidelong glance. "Older than you?"

"Much." I held out my hand.

She eyed it like I had a snake on the end of my arm.

I sighed. "We need to be in physical contact, or you won't make it to Nidavellir."

"Nidavellir?" Her eyes sparked with curiosity, and she reluctantly placed her hand in mine.

Her fingers were small and smooth against my calloused palm, but I ignored the sensation, tugging her to the gate. "We're going under the mountain. It's time for you to meet the dwarves."

PART 2

Chapter 12

Niamh

When Kylian said *dwarves* and *under the mountain*, I pictured some sort of dark, damp cave situation. I couldn't have been more shocked to step into a bright, well-lit courtyard. Yes, it was indoors, but it was a garden, not a cave. Intricately tiled marble paths wound between mossy beds containing the most beautiful mushrooms I had ever seen. The fungi grew in every shape and color I could imagine, little toadstools nestling under towering fungi that reached up like trees toward the vaulted ceiling.

Kylian dropped my hand.

I turned back to see what we had just stepped through and gasped at the gorgeous archway studded with a rainbow of giant crystals in gold settings.

"This is amazing." I smacked Kylian's arm. "Isn't this amazing?"

He grunted, looking down at the arm I'd just hit.

I winced. "Sorry."

"I see you're admiring the Topaz Gate."

I spun around to find a girl behind us, about three feet tall but with the features of someone closer to my age. Her dark red hair was coiled into two braided buns, and freckles spotted her friendly face. She wore a sword belt over a simple blue tunic and brown leather leggings under tall fur-trimmed boots.

"You must be Princess Niamh and Lord Kylian. Welcome to Nidavellir!"

"I'm not a prin—wait a minute. Are your lights made from mushrooms?" I stared at the chandelier suspended from the ceiling. A cluster of glowing golden mushrooms grew down from a mossy circle in the marble ceiling, strung with faceted white crystals that scattered sparkling light around the courtyard.

"Sure are! Don't touch them. They're poisonous." The girl's nose wrinkled as she smiled. "I'm Estrid. The kings sent me to fetch you. Come on!" She set off through the courtyard.

I took a step and then squealed when an adorable purple salamander with gold crystals running down its back scampered past my feet.

"Did you see that?" I crouched down, looking to see where the creature had gone.

"You'd better hurry and catch up." Kylian tapped his fingers on his leg. "Unless you know your way around Nidavellir?"

"Oh!" I set off across the courtyard after the dwarven girl. I didn't have to look to know that Kylian walked close behind me. Despite saying that these were friends of my parents, he sure seemed twitchy. Maybe that was just his regular state.

"You have more than one king?" I asked Estrid when I

caught up with her at the entrance to a hallway of pale marble with veins of crystal looping in abstract swirls along the walls.

"Oh, right. You were raised by humans. You probably don't know anything about the Dvergr people. The Tuatha Dé Danann call us dwarves," she added at my quizzical look.

The Tuatha Dé Danann were, according to my book, the tall, human-looking fae. I supposed I was a Tuatha Dé Danann. As for dwarves . . .

"I only know what I learned from *Lord of the Rings*," I said.

Estrid gave me a puzzled look.

"It's a movie trilogy. Well, books, actually. Never mind. I know nothing."

"Usually, we only have one ruler. When the king or queen dies, we choose a new monarch. A master craftsman who has created something truly beneficial for all the Dvergr. Like Queen Solveig, who developed the first steam engine, or King Hreidmar, who nurtured the mushrooms we use for our lights instead of torches and candles."

"Oh, I like that." I glanced at the smaller bioluminescent mushrooms growing like sconces out of the walls every few feet. "It makes so much more sense than just showing up at someone's house and telling them that they're the next ruler of some kingdom they've never heard of."

Kylian snorted.

"Um, that's true." Estrid glanced back at me before turning down another tunnel. Kylian and I ducked through the archway and followed. "When the Dvergr were invaded by the Dökkálfar elves and fled our home in Álfheimr across the oceans to Tír na nÓg—long before I was born—we lost Queen Solveig. She sacrificed herself to buy our people time to escape. It was Ulrik who designed the steam-powered ships and the navigation crystals that brought us safely to these shores."

"So they made him king," I guessed.

"Then when they arrived here, it was Ulrik's brother, Ulf, who created the crystal-powered stone cutters that allowed us to carve all of Nidavellir from the mountain rocks. The vote was tied, so they both decided to rule together."

"And that works?" I asked.

"Oh, they bicker, to be sure, as all brothers do," she said. "But they agree on the important things. Here we are." She stopped at an arched doorway and gestured to the guards at the door. "Weapons, please."

I unbuckled my sword and handed it over. Beside me, Kylian looked physically pained as he relinquished his axe and dagger. Estrid raised an eyebrow at him, and he sighed and passed over four more daggers.

"We'll get these back to you in no time." Estrid nodded to the guard who bowed and left with the armful of weapons.

The tension in Kylian went up two more notches.

I put my hand on his arm. "Why are you so twitchy? I thought this was the safest place to stash me?"

"I'm not twitchy, Princess." He stared down at my hand on his arm, and I realized that he certainly didn't *look* tense. The muscles in his arm weren't even clenched. Still, I somehow felt that he wasn't as relaxed as he appeared.

"Okay, then." I removed my hand from his arm, only to see Estrid peering at his tattoos.

Kylian glanced at her and rolled his sleeves down casually, but not before I caught sight of the rune on the underside of his arm.

"Hey, that looks just like my—"

"They're waiting for us," Kylian reminded me.

I narrowed my eyes at him but entered the throne room with Estrid. Kylian came a step behind.

"Have you ever considered, Ulf," a gruff voice rumbled through the majestic vaulted throne room, "how much more satisfying your wins would be if you didn't cheat?"

We walked down a carpet of emerald green moss bordered by purple crystals and pale blue mushrooms, both of which seemed to be growing right out of the edge of the moss. At the end of the hall, suspended over the two thrones, a graceful tangle of giant mushrooms glowed. The light caused the gold and gems of the empty thrones below to shimmer.

Off to the side, sitting on heaps of cushions with a low wooden table between them, sat two older, long-haired dwarven men crowned with gold circlets.

"I don't cheat," said the small man. His braided red beard matched Estrid's hair, but was streaked with white. "I just forget the rules sometimes."

"Well, it's easy to forget the rules when you're making up new ones all the time." The second dwarf stroked his braided black beard streaked with silver, then moved a polished stone piece on the game board sitting on the table.

Estrid clapped her hands. "Papa! Uncle Ulrik! Your guests are here."

"Yes, yes." The red-bearded dwarf poked his brother. "Ulrik, it's little Niamh!" Ulf stood, arms outstretched. "How are you, my dear?"

I bent down and hugged the old man without thinking, like my arms remembered him, even if my mind didn't.

"You were a much more comfortable height when you were younger," he said.

"Sorry." I hugged the other king and straightened.

Kylian remained where he was, hugging no one.

"Apology accepted." Ulf settled back down onto the cushions. "And Lord Kylian? Not evil after all, just as I suspected."

"*I'm* the one who always told *you* that he was obviously working against Moriath," groused Ulrik.

"Well, *I'm* the one who reminded *you* that he was a very polite young man when we met him. Not at all the sort to hurt a sweet little princess. We're happy to have you back for a visit." Ulf waved at the Huntsman.

Kylian just nodded in greeting, but that sense of unease dissipated. Had he been worried about what the kings would think of him? And how was I able to tell? I was probably just imagining it.

"So chatty." Ulf winked at me conspiratorially, and I couldn't help laughing. "Estrid, my dear, could you run and grab our guests some refreshments?"

"I just sent a girl in with . . ." She trailed off, and we all looked at the four plates stacked on the ground beside the table, empty but for crumbs. "Never mind," she said. "I'll go get refreshments."

"Thank you, my dear." Ulf patted her cheek and she left, muttering something about high blood pressure.

"Sit, sit." Ulrik pulled out a couple of cushions and set them in front of the low table.

I sat, adjusting my red skirt. Kylian leaned up against the wall and crossed his arms. Okay, then. I set my backpack down beside me and unzipped it to check on the chicks.

"I say." Ulrik leaned forward. "Do you have chickens in there?"

"Yes." I ran my hand over the little white chick. It nuzzled up against my fingers, so I lifted it out and let it curl up in my lap. "I know it's strange, but they've only just hatched, so I'm trying to keep them safe."

"Too small for supper then," Ulrik said to his brother.

I shifted the backpack closer.

"So, Niamh," Ulf said to me, "you've decided to come and reclaim the Unseelie throne."

"And about time," Ulrik cut in. "I've never been comfortable with that Moriath on the throne. Remember when Fionnbharr brought her to meet us? Niamh was just a little thing." The king nudged his brother, who nodded in agreement. "It's the last time we saw you and your young man here. But Moriath . . ." He leaned forward. "She doesn't like soup. Very unnatural." He shook his head.

"Do you like soup?" Ulf asked me, seriously.

"Yes?"

"Well, that's a relief," he said, and Ulrik nodded.

"But I'm not planning to reclaim anything." I stroked the little chick falling asleep in the folds of my dress. Must be nice. I held in a yawn. "I only just found out that I'm fae. I don't know anything about the Unseelie Kingdom. I don't think I'd be a very good ruler."

The two kings gave each other a look.

"But I do thank you very much for your hospitality," I quickly added.

Ulrik nodded. "Of course. It's the least we can do to take in King Fionnbharr and Queen Oonagh's child after all they did for us. I just wish we could have prevented this tragedy from ever happening."

"Kylian said you were friends of my parents. How did you know them? What were they like?"

Ulf's eyebrows shot up. "You don't remember anything?"

I shook my head—the same way I'd answered that question countless times to people over the years. But now, I finally knew that there was something magical going on with my missing memories. I'd have to see if I could get more information out of Kylian later.

"The Dvergr people," Ulrik said solemnly, "are in your parents' debt. When we arrived in Tír na nÓg, we came with nothing. Just our lives and the clothes on our backs. Our small supply of gemstones had been used to power the ships on the voyage over, and we had precious little food left. We were prepared to throw ourselves on the mercy of the rulers of this new land and knew that we might have to work as laborers or servants to support and feed our families. But your parents met us on the rocky shores, and the hosts around them were not warriors as we had feared. Certainly, there were some, but instead of swords, we were met with food and blankets." Both kings' eyes were wet with tears. "And that wasn't the half of it," he continued. "They gifted us these mountains to be a new home for the Dvergr people, with the agreement of the great Northern dragons who nest in this range. Luckily for us, dragons are more interested in the outsides of mountains."

"They can even become strong allies and protectors when sent regular gifts of gemstones," Ulf added with a wink.

Ulrik leaned over and patted my hand. "So, as you can see, giving you and your young man here a safe place to stay doesn't even scratch the surface of the debt our people owe to your family."

"He's not . . . Never mind. What if Moriath attacks your kingdom?" I asked.

"Do you think Sofie would eat her, or would Hedda?" Ulrik asked his brother.

"Oh, definitely Sofie," Ulf said. "She likes icy food."

Estrid returned with four plates of food. Kylian immediately picked up a deep-fried chicken leg, ignoring my glare. Apparently, his refusal to eat my baking wasn't about *health* food.

"Eat," Ulrik urged, munching on a rib. "You must be famished after all that *running for your life* earlier. Liadan told us all about it."

I stared at my plate. There were pieces of fried chicken, ribs, sausage, and some kind of stuffed meatballs.

"I'm not really that hungry."

"Come now, try the sausage." Ulf waved a chicken bone at me. "It's excellent."

"Actually . . ." If I was going to be staying here, I'd need to eat eventually. "I don't eat meat."

The kings blinked at me.

"But meat is *delicious*." Ulrik's eyes widened.

I held up the fuzzy white chick. "I just can't eat something that used to be alive. Look at her!"

"Maybe I'll just switch to the ribs." Ulrik set down his chicken leg, uncomfortably looking away from the chick's eyes. "Out of respect."

"What about fish?" Ulf waved Estrid over. "Does the kitchen have any fish?"

"Still a living thing," I sighed. "I don't want to be any trouble, though. What about mushrooms? You must eat mushrooms." I looked around at all the mushrooms in the throne room.

"Aren't mushrooms alive, though?" asked Ulrik, completely serious.

"Well, yes, but that's not . . . Never mind. I'll eat later." I yawned widely.

"Let's find you a place to rest." Estrid patted my shoulder. "I'll have the kitchen make you something with *vegetables*." She gave the kings a pointed look.

Ulf leaned over to his brother. "Don't be too upset. At least she eats soup."

Chapter 13

Niamh

After I said goodbye to the kings, Estrid led Kylian and me through the tunnels to our new home. Unlike the quiet courtyard and passages around the Topaz Gate, dwarves of all ages bustled past us. I tried not to stare at the small citizens of Nidavellir, but they certainly gaped at us. We were hard to miss—Kylian's head nearly scraped the ceiling, and we both had to duck through the arched doorways between tunnels.

The dwarves were a colorful bunch, with tunics and dresses in all shades, and sparkling crystals set in rings, hat bands, and belts. Some adults carried tiny baby dwarves in slings or pulled knee-high children in baskets that floated behind like magical wagons, trailing a golden glow from the gems that must have powered them.

"So you're a princess then, Estrid?" I asked, following her through the busy, mushroom-lit hallways, Kylian again at my back.

"Oh, no. Like I told you earlier, my father being king doesn't make me any closer to ruling myself. My brother, maybe. He's an incredible craftsman. I'm just a warrior. What would I invent to improve the lives of my people?"

"Do you think we can convince the Unseelie fae to be that logical?" I dodged a little black-haired dwarf girl chasing . . . Was that a mole? "Someone with the right skills should be in charge, not someone who only knows how to make pie."

"Is that truly your only skill?" She glanced back at me with a raised eyebrow.

"My parents have been teaching me how to run a bakery, not a kingdom."

"And what does that entail?"

"Oh, you know, keeping track of the money."

"Economics." She nodded.

"Ordering supplies and shipping out orders." I tilted my head. What was that roaring sound?

"Import-export," she said. "Got it. What else?"

I thought. "Managing the staff. All three of them."

"Leadership." She grinned back at me. "You're right. Absolutely no skills for running a country."

"Th-that's not the same," I sputtered, and then froze as the source of the roaring I'd been hearing revealed itself.

We had entered a vast cavern where a massive underground waterfall cascaded down a crystal-studded cliff face and into a deep pool. Tiny glowing fish darted among bioluminescent seaweed in a rainbow of pastel colors, and laughing children splashed while their parents sat and gossiped. These people weren't dwarves. From their shimmering blue-scaled skin, long black hair, and webbed feet, I recognized them from my faerie book. They had to be asrai, the faeries who lived in ponds and creeks. What were they doing under a mountain?

Along the walls of the cavern, stairs carved into the stone led up to balconies and window boxes with little gardens of bioluminescent mushrooms. I caught sight of more dwarves peering out their windows at us.

"This way!" hollered Estrid over the roar of the waterfall. "I gave you an exterior suite," she added once we were farther away from the noise. "I thought you might find it more comfortable."

"How far up is it?" I eyed the stairs nervously. There had to be hundreds of them.

"You're on the thirty-second floor."

"I'll just never come down, I guess." I groaned and adjusted my pack. "I might need a piggyback." I smiled sweetly at Kylian, who raised an eyebrow.

Estrid laughed. "That's one option. But, personally, I'm taking the elevator."

"Oh, thank goodness." I sighed in relief, following the dwarf to what almost looked like a birdcage crafted from gray metal, the top and bottom ringed with blue crystals.

When we were all in, Estrid shut the door and showed us the controls that made the magic crystals light up, powering the elevator. I leaned over the waist-high sides and peered down at the pool below as we rose high into the air on a track cut into the side of the cavern.

"Please don't do that." Kylian snagged the loop of my backpack and hauled me back from the view.

"It has a safety rail," I protested.

"For people half your height," he pointed out.

"Fine, fine," I grumbled as we came to a stop.

Estrid led us along a sidewalk edged with a knee-high stone wall. Little salamanders of all colors, with crystal backs and horns, scurried past.

"Here we are." The dwarf stopped at a door of warm, polished wood. "Put your hand on the doorknob."

I grabbed the crystal knob and felt a warm pulse go through my hand as the crystal lit up. Kylian did the same thing.

"Now this door will only open for you," Estrid said. "Not that we expect any trouble," she quickly added to Kylian. "I just thought you might be more comfortable that way."

He nodded. "Thank you."

"I'll send someone up with mushroom soup for you," she added with a wink to me. "Get settled in."

My stomach rumbled. "Thanks."

"I'm always telling them that it wouldn't hurt to eat a few vegetables now and then." Estrid rolled her eyes, then waved and walked back toward the elevator.

Kylian entered the suite first, then opened the doors to the two spacious bedrooms, checking for assassins? Dragons? Who knew? I wandered in after him and found myself in a cozy sitting area with a lit fireplace. The chairs and sofa had been carved from pink-streaked marble, then covered with gold velvet cushions, looking like they would comfortably fit an eight-year-old child.

Kylian grunted in approval when he spotted our weapons on the low marble table, clean and shining.

"They even sharpened them." He examined a dagger before sliding it into its sheath on his belt.

I walked past him, curious about what lay behind the heavy velvet curtains on the other side of the room.

"Wait." Kylian jerked his head up. "Let me check first."

Ignoring him, I pushed past the curtains to a bright, sunlit balcony. I gasped as the cold air hit me.

"You shouldn't just—" Kylian burst through behind me.

"Shhh." I poked his shoulder. "Look!"

The view beyond the waist-high carved stone wall of the balcony entranced me. We were nestled into the side of a mountain, with towering snow-capped peaks all around. Evergreen trees, dusted with snow like powdered sugar, created a lush forest below before giving way to short, twisted trees, then sheer snowy peaks as the mountains climbed higher.

Balconies like ours dotted the mountains around us, and I could see more signs of dwarven civilization in the mountain across from us, the gap bridged by a graceful stone arch. Towers rose here and there in the distance. Nidavellir was more than just an underground castle. It was a vast kingdom built into a mountain range.

The sky above was a brilliant cobalt blue, but I shivered as a gust of wind blew sparkling snowflakes across the balcony from the surrounding trees.

"We should go inside, Princess," said Kylian.

"Wait." I grabbed his arm.

"You're very . . . handsy," he remarked.

"It's called normal human behavior, Kylian. Well, *fae* behavior. Well, actually, I don't know, but *look*." I pointed up at the enormous silver dragon clutching the side of one of the peaks. The dragon launched itself from the summit, its silver scales glinting under the sun.

"Do you think that's Sofie or Hedda?" I whispered.

"I don't actually know the names of—"

"There's a baby!" I squealed, gripping his arm tighter as a smaller silver dragon—only as long as a school bus—flew after its mother, swooping in circles until they disappeared from sight behind another mountaintop. I shivered again, craning my neck to see if any other epic magical creatures were outside the window.

"We really should go inside, Princess," said Kylian.

"I'm not that cold," I lied.

Another gust of wind blasted sparkling ice crystals around us, pricking my skin.

"Maybe not," he said, "but think of the chicks." He turned me around and gave me a light push toward the curtains.

"Oh, the chicks. Right!" I dashed inside and pulled off my backpack. I dropped my hoodie on the floor before I sat down on the plush rug in front of the fire. Unzipping my backpack, I felt inside carefully. They all seemed okay. The heat of the hot water bottle was starting to fade, but it wasn't cool yet.

"Hello, babies." I pulled each one out. "Don't go outside," I told a yellow one as I set it down, "or you will be dinner for an owl or maybe a very small dragon." I looked back at Kylian. "The chicks are all good."

He scooped my hoodie off the floor and hung it by the door.

"Weren't you cold out there?" I motioned to the tunic sleeves he had rolled back up.

"I'm fine." The tall warrior sat beside me on the ground, watching the chicks.

"I didn't think you'd be worried about the chicks," I said. "I thought you didn't care about them."

"I don't." Kylian frowned at the little black chick as it wandered up to his leg. He plucked it up and set it on his palm. "Explain it to me. What is so important about these birds that you could not leave them behind with your parents? Do you really think they would go against your wishes and eat the creatures?"

I scooped three chicks into my lap and smiled as they climbed around my red, polka-dotted skirt.

"Probably not," I admitted.

"I understand that you don't want them to be eaten," Kylian persisted, peering at the black chick as it sat happily on his palm. "Even though people eat chickens all the time. But I'm sure they could have found them a good home."

"You're right." I watched the chicks on the floor as they explored their surroundings. "I guess I feel responsible for them. I've wanted them for so long. I researched chicken breeds for years and special-ordered these eggs online. You probably don't know what that is . . ."

"I've spent time in the human realm, Princess," Kylian murmured as the little black chick curled up on his hand. "I know about the internet."

"Oh, okay." That did surprise me, but I supposed it made sense if his wolves had been in Pilot Bay for years. "I selected them based on temperament, the color of eggs they'd lay, and, of course, how cute the chickens would grow up to be." I leaned back, propping myself up on my hands. "Then you burst into my life—which I had all planned out, by the way—and informed me that I was never going to have the future I'd planned. You took me away from the only parents I've ever known and the town I've never been away from for more than a weekend. I guess I just wanted one small thing—well, *seven* small things—to remind me of who I am. I don't think that's too much to ask."

Kylian looked down at the little black chick. The chick looked up at him. "I suppose not. Do these creatures have names?"

I straightened. "I'm glad you asked."

I reached into my backpack and pulled out my container of chick feed. The pale orange chick ran over and climbed right into the container as soon as I took the lid off, chirping happily. The other chicks scurried over after it.

"I haven't had time to think of any yet, what with all the running for our lives. Let's see . . ." I picked up the white chick, brushing its soft, furry legs. "This one is a Silkie. It will grow up to be fluffy all over, even its head. I think . . . Meringue. Light and sweet, just like you. Are you a girl? I think you're a girl."

"How can you tell?" asked Kylian.

"It's a vibe. Just go with it." I kissed Meringue on the head and set her down, picking up the pale orange chick, a Buff Orpington. "Now, what do you want to be called? What do you think, mighty Huntsman?"

"Call it Orange."

"What?" I squinted at him.

"Because it's orange." He attempted to set the black chick down, but it hopped back up onto his leg.

"You're terrible at this." I peered at the orange chick. Female? I was getting girl vibes. Probably just wishful thinking. After all, more hens meant more eggs. Still, I couldn't shake the sense that I could tell.

"You asked," Kylian said with a shrug.

"Hmm, how about Clementine?"

Kylian just looked at me.

"It's a fancy orange." I set Clementine down—I could swear the chick was happy with her name—and picked up the pale yellow chick. No, it hadn't been wishful thinking. "This one is definitely a boy."

"If you say so." Kylian nudged the black chick now curled up on his leg, its whole body rising and falling with its sleeping breaths.

"This little guy is a Buff Polish. You're going to look hilarious when you grow up," I informed the little rooster. "Majestic, yes, but also a bit dopey with the long-feathered hairdo. You need a name that's awesome but also ridiculous." I thought for a moment. "Snickerdoodle."

"What's a snickerdoodle?"

"A delicious sugary cookie. You'd hate it." I set the chick down and picked up the orange and brown chick, hopefully a Belgian d'Uccle. She—definitely a she—squawked in protest at leaving her meal. If looks could kill, this little chicken would be an assassin. "Spicy thing, aren't you? Do you like spices, Huntsman? Or are you allergic to flavor in general?"

"Paprika," said Kylian. "That one is kind of a dark orange, like paprika."

"Huh." I set down the grumpy chick. "We can call her Pip for short."

I examined the remaining chicks as they ate. The gray chick—a hen—would grow up to be a Blue Cochin with fluffy feathered legs, and the black and white baby rooster would hopefully be a Silver Laced Wyandotte, with black-edged white feathers.

"Latte," I decided, watching the gray chick sneeze as she munched her food. "She looks like a London Fog. And Waffles for that one."

"Waffles?" asked Kylian.

"I like Waffles." I shrugged as the little rooster tried to break up a scuffle between two other chicks. One day old and already such leadership potential.

"What about this one?" Kylian poked the black chick. The little hen nuzzled his finger.

"That one seems attached to you, Huntsman. Maybe she thinks you're her mother, what with all the black." I waved a hand at his attire. "What do you think?"

Kylian plucked the chick up to eye level. She blinked happily at him. "It's the same color as that coffee you tried to poison me with."

"Hmm, how about Espresso? We can call her Essie for sho—" I broke into a sudden yawn. I had forgotten how tired I was while exploring this magical kingdom.

"Whatever makes you happy, Princess." Kylian handed me the chick and stood, carefully avoiding the chicks underfoot as he retrieved his axe and hung it beside the door.

It made me feel strangely safe. I shook my head. How had I gone from screaming at this man to being happy that he was sleeping in the room next to mine? Maybe I was simply too tired to keep fighting with him. For today, anyway. It was hard to stay mad at someone who named chickens with me, even if he hated pie.

I yawned again, bigger this time.

"All right, Princess." Kylian had retrieved a basket of food from the doorstep while I'd struggled to keep my eyes open. "Food and then sleep."

"Not a princess." I dug into the mushroom soup and biscuits with my eyes half closed.

"Bed," ordered Kylian as soon as I had finished.

"So bossy," I mumbled as I shuffled to the nearest bedroom, then braced myself on the door frame. "Wait. The chicks . . . Oh."

Kylian stood behind me with the seven chicks sleeping in the basket our supper had come in.

"Don't worry, Princess. I'll take care of you."

I smiled sleepily at Kylian as he set the chicks by my banked fireplace and realized, as he softly closed the door behind him, that I believed him.

As I fell asleep in a bedroom realms away from the one I had woken up in, feeling safe and warm, one last thought drifted through my mind. Who would take care of him?

Chapter 14

Niamh

I WOKE UP TO A KNOCK ON the outside door. Where was I? Why was I in a very luxurious—but not terribly big—four-poster bed draped with rose-colored velvet curtains and heaped with silk pillows?

Oh, right. The dwarves.

I sat up in what was probably a king-sized bed if you were four feet tall.

"Who's there?" commanded a gruff voice. Kylian.

I threw back my covers and grimaced at my wrinkled dress from the day before. I must have fallen asleep in my clothes. But would the dwarves even have pajamas in my size? I snagged a quilt from the bed and wrapped it around my shoulders to ward off the morning chill.

"Go back to sleep," I told the chicks as they rustled around in their basket near the bedroom's fireplace. "I'll get your breakfast after I see what the fuss is about."

I opened my bedroom door and then yelped as I tripped over a heap of blankets. Had Kylian slept outside my door?

I untangled my foot from a quilt. "Who are you yelling at out here?"

Kylian stood fully clothed but barefoot, axe at the ready as he cracked the front door open.

"It's just breakfast, my lord," squeaked a small voice from the other side of the door.

I put my hand over Kylian's on the axe. "I'm starving. Surely Moriath can't have figured out where I am yet."

He gave me a sharp look. "As someone who has been working for the woman who's wanted you dead for the past two centuries, I would say you greatly underestimate her."

"But *breakfast*," I pleaded.

Kylian relented and opened the door. I expected a dwarf and was surprised to see a delicate girl about four feet tall with pale blue skin and shining black hair in a braid down her back. From her coloring and the shimmering scales scattered on her cheeks and hands, I recognized her as another asrai. What *were* they doing in Nidavellir?

The girl pushed in a cart with a teapot and covered plates, padding softly in fur-lined boots that disappeared under a simple green dress with an apron over it. She glanced nervously at Kylian, who watched her carefully as she began to set trays on the table.

"Thank you," I said, trying to put her at ease. I helped by transferring the teapot to the table.

"Oh no, Princess Niamh!" she exclaimed. "I can do that."

"It's fine." Correcting her about the princess part would probably just make her more flustered.

"Is that . . ." Her eyes darted nervously to Kylian. "*The Huntsman*?" she whispered.

"Um, yes. It is. But don't worry. He's on our side." I set the teacups on the table.

"That's what they told me, Your Highness." The fae girl gulped. "But it's hard to believe after all the things I've heard—"

Kylian cleared his throat, and she jumped.

I scowled at him. "He's quite safe, I assure you." I smiled at the girl again. "Thank you for the food."

"I'll be back for your dishes," the asrai girl squeaked and then scampered out the door.

"Do you have to glare?" I asked Kylian the moment she left. Pulling the lids off the trays, I found mushroom popovers, fried eggs, smoked fish, and oatmeal with berries.

"It doesn't matter if I glare or not." Kylian sat, glaring even more at the tiny chair. "They'll still be afraid."

"I suppose you have a reputation." I heaped a plate with eggs and popovers.

"More than a reputation, Princess." Kylian's face didn't change, but I could somehow feel the pain behind his words.

"If you ever want to talk about—"

"Is that the chicks?" Kylian speared a slice of fish from the platter.

"The chicks!" I dropped my popover and darted to the other room where the little birds were all climbing over each other in the basket, peeping loudly. "Who wants breakfast?"

After I released the chicks into the sitting room with food and water, and cleaned up after three of them with a cloth I found in the bathroom, I realized that Kylian had completely distracted me from trying to talk about his past.

His victory this time, but I was more determined than ever to figure out what he was hiding.

Estrid showed up with a basket of clothes for me as we finished breakfast.

"I'm sorry," she told Kylian. "It was hard enough finding Princess Niamh clothes, never mind your giant self." She waved up at him.

"I don't need a change of clothes," said Kylian.

"Really?" I said. "We seem to be roommates, and I don't want you to start getting smelly."

He raised an eyebrow. "These clothes are spelled against damage, dirt, and *smells*."

"So you only have one outfit?" I sipped my tea.

"I had another tunic and pants at the castle."

"Exactly the same as this one?"

"Of course." He finished up his fish.

"Have you ever thought about wearing some color?"

"Black is very practical." Kylian plucked at his tunic. "Especially in the dark."

"True," I said. "But I bet seafoam blue would look great against your skin tone."

Estrid choked on a laugh. "I'll just put these in your room."

"Can you watch her?" Kylian asked the dwarf. "I want to have a look at your training area before I assess the princess's education with the sword."

"Of course." Estrid adjusted her hold on the basket on her hip and nearly tripped over Pip. "Is that chick glaring at me?"

"Some chickens—and fae Huntsmen, for that matter—just look naturally grumpy." I finished my tea. "And I don't need a babysitter. I can take care of myself."

"That's what we're going to find out." Kylian strapped on his axe.

Ominous.

"Is fetching clothes a usual part of a warrior's job?" I asked the dwarf, scooping up Essie as the black chick attempted to follow Kylian out the door.

"Nope," Estrid said cheerfully. "I'm just nosy. We don't get royal visitors very often."

She set the clothes on my unmade bed, and I tucked the chicks back into the basket by the still-warm fireplace. They were still too little to spend much time running around away from the heat.

"How did you find human-sized clothes?" I peered into the basket on the bed. "I mean—" What kind of fae was I, again? "—Tuatha Dé Danann sized?"

"I tracked down a trunk that belonged to your mother," said Estrid. "She stored it here for when she visited. I thought they might fit you better than anything from my closet."

I lifted out a dark pink silk bodice and flipped it over. It was missing the ribbons to cinch it up.

Estrid examined the bodice. "I'll try to find some laces for that. The color suits you."

"These were my mother's?" I looked through the clothes, hoping to find something that would spark a memory. All I could tell so far was that my mother had dressed in the same colors I loved: reds, pinks, sapphire blues, and emerald greens.

"That's what the housekeeper tells me. I never met her. I'm only seventy-five."

"Okay." I pulled out a long gown of red velvet and held it up against my chest, trying not to be disappointed that I still couldn't remember my birth mother at all. "How exactly does aging work here?"

"What do you mean? And if Lord Kylian wants you in the training ring this morning, you'll be better off with pants than that."

I laid the dress on the bed and looked through the basket for anything that resembled activewear. "Well, you look the same age as me, and I'm only twenty. And Kylian says he's over two hundred, which seems . . ."

"Like a long time to wear only black?" said Estrid.

"Impossible." I pulled out a pair of brown leather pants. What were the odds they would fit my curvy figure?

"Well, how does aging work in the human realm? I've heard mortals die awfully quickly."

"Well, you're born and you grow up." I tugged on the pants under my dress. "And then you get older, and then you die. Usually before you're one hundred."

"*One hundred?* That's even less than I thought! Barely enough time to get anything done."

"I guess." I did up the buttons on the side of the waist. "Whoa, these fit perfectly! Was my mother the exact same size as me?" I pulled up my wrinkled skirt and admired how the leather hugged my curves without being too tight. The fitted pants were much more flexible than I'd assumed.

"Similar, I'd guess, but pants like that are usually spelled to adjust the fit and add flexibility."

"So this is what I'd want to wear for a really big dinner?"

Estrid laughed. "Also, you know, for fighting."

"Sweet!" I found a navy tank top made out of linen, or something like that, and traded my wrinkled dress for the shirt. "So if two hundred isn't old, do you stay children for decades here?"

"Nice tattoos. And no. In Faerie, you grow steadily until you reach adulthood, the same as in the human realm."

"Thanks." I had been eyeing Estrid's own ink peeking out from her sleeves. "What age is adulthood?" I asked.

"Twentyish?" Estrid shrugged. "And then the magic of Faerie preserves you, slowing your aging. We generally live to be around a thousand."

"A *thousand?*" I yelped. The chicks all popped up from their basket to stare at me. "Sorry, babies." I gripped a sweater to my chest. "I'm going to live for nine hundred and eighty more years?"

"So long as that Huntsman of yours keeps you away from your homicidal aunt, you probably will."

I sat on the bed, stunned. It made sense, based on everything I'd been told, but still. A *thousand?*

"And that's the same for all faeries?" I blinked at Estrid, who waved a pair of socks at me. "What about humans?" I thought of Audrey and her fae boyfriend.

"Yep, even for humans living here. It's thanks to the magic of Faerie. It's not anything to do with us."

"I wonder how old my chickens will live to be." I watched the chicks clambering around in their basket as I pulled the socks on.

"I suppose they'll live longer here." Estrid shrugged. "I don't know a lot about birds."

Someone knocked on the outside door.

"I'll go get that so your Huntsman doesn't have my head." Estrid nudged a chick aside with her foot.

I laughed as I pulled a green sweater over my head. "He's really not that scary."

She gave me a look from the bedroom door. "To you, maybe. I can't say what he'd do to me if something happened to you on my watch."

The knock at the door was, of course, just the asrai girl

who had brought our breakfast, back with her cart to collect the dishes.

"Thank you," I said. "Tell the cook it was delicious. I might need the recipe for those mushroom popovers."

"I'll let her know." The girl smiled, obviously more at ease without the big, scary Huntsman lurking around.

"What's your name?" I started stacking plates.

"Cara, Your Highness."

"Are there a lot of asrai living in the dwarven kingdom?" I asked.

"About a hundred and fifty of us, Highness." She gathered the cutlery from the table.

"That many?" I blinked, surprised. I'd gotten the impression that only the dwarves and the dragons lived here.

"Not so many," said Cara sadly. "We're the only ones who were able to flee when the queen dammed up our creeks and rivers to extract the water magic. She flooded the villages my people built in the shallows of enchanted streams and enslaved anyone who resisted moving. Some of the glaistig came to help us, and he burned their villages down too."

My stomach knotted. "*He?*"

"The Huntsman and his faoladh, Your Highness." Cara looked around nervously.

"Oh." The plate I had been lifting clattered to the table.

"How many fae were killed?" asked Estrid, watching my reaction.

"We lost our homes, but even the littlest asrai can swim like a fish. Many were taken captive, but our people are slippery. More and more escape and join us here with the dwarves, where we're safe."

"And the glaistig?" I remembered the goat-legged fae with their curling horns from my book.

"They were lucky. The Huntsman wanted to scare them first and sent threats before he came with fire. They were all able to flee to Nidavellir, but many lost all their belongings."

"I'm so sorry." I went back to stacking plates with a lump in my throat.

"We've been waiting for you for a long time, Your Highness." Cara gave me a small hopeful smile.

I didn't know what to tell her. Telling the bossy Huntsman that I didn't want to be a queen seemed a lot easier than saying it to this wistful asrai girl.

"I'm glad I got to meet you, Cara." I put the last of the dishes on her cart. "Will I see you with lunch?"

"Oh!" The asrai wiped the table clean. "I'm supposed to deliver a message. Lady Estrid is to take you to the west training arena. I believe you'll have your lunch there."

"And then supper with the kings tonight," said Estrid.

"Sounds like I have a busy day, but I'm sure I'll see you again soon." I smiled at Cara.

Estrid watched me with interest.

"What?" I asked when Cara left. "Are you back to telling me how well-equipped a queen I am? I don't even know what's been happening to my people."

"*Your people* are they, now?" Estrid smirked.

"You know what I mean."

"Oh, I do," she said.

"Kylian told me that he'd been working for Moriath all this time, but I don't think I really realized what that meant." I tugged one of my curls. "It's just hard to believe he'd do those things."

Estrid shook her head. "My dad and Uncle Ulrik always believed that he was good despite the stories coming in from the refugees. I have to agree that for all the horrors Kylian brought down as the arm of the Unseelie queen, there have always been little stories that didn't quite match up. So many near misses and lucky escapes. Especially with children."

"You think he's been working against her all this time?" Why did I so desperately want to believe that?

Estrid nodded. "It's what makes the most sense. Besides, could anyone protecting *you*—the most open and genuinely sweet person I've ever met—be that bad? An evil villain, together with the girl who keeps baby chicks in her backpack?"

"We're not *together,*" I grumbled. "Not only does he not eat sweets, but I'm not staying here to be together with *anyone.* Aunt Chloe is going to find my sister, and I'm going home—once it's safe. Anyway, not *together.*"

She laughed. "That's not what I meant, but if that's where your mind is wandering . . ."

"Isn't it time to go?" I grabbed my boots and sat on a tiny chair to tie them on.

"By all means, *Princess.* Let's go meet up with that scary hot Huntsman that you're *not together* with and see what you can do."

Chapter 15

Kylian

A LAUGH BROKE ME OUT OF MY thoughts, and I looked up from the practice sword I had been examining. Niamh entered the gym with the young dwarven warrior.

The princess laughed more easily than anyone I'd ever met and with none of the edge to her humor that I'd grown used to with Moriath and her faoladh.

"Thank you." I nodded to Estrid. "I can take it from here."

"I'll be back later with your lunch," said the dwarf.

"Oh, is food delivery one of your duties, too?" Niamh laughed again.

"Of course." Estrid winked at her and left.

I had no idea what they were on about.

"So, now what?" Niamh looked like she belonged in Tír na

nÓg with her fae sweater and leather pants, but her hair was tied back with the red bandana she had worn in the café.

I shook away the memory of the ill-fated cup of coffee. "Now we see what you've learned in your lessons."

She drew her sword. "Let's do it."

"Practice weapons." I held out my hand for the sword.

"Are you afraid I'll hurt you?" she asked.

I raised an eyebrow at her. "Terrified." I opened my hand again.

"All right, all right." Niamh sheathed the sword and unbuckled her belt, handing it over to me. "But be nice to her," she said. "My parents got her for me on my sixteenth birthday. She's a replica of this sweet sword from *Tales of the Unseelie Fae*. Check out the knotwork on the pommel."

"It's not a replica." I set her sword on the weapons bench. "This was your mother's sword."

"*What?*"

"Your father gave it to me before he died. He wanted you to have it when you were old enough to wield it. I couldn't leave much with your human parents, certainly nothing enchanted, but it's a good sword, and I wanted you to train with a proper weapon."

Niamh just stared at me with her mouth open.

"You never wondered why the Klassens didn't sign you up for a more typical human sport?"

"I never really thought about it."

I passed her a practice sword that was a similar length and weight to hers. "How many human girls start learning sword-work when they're five?"

"I mean, there was a class of us when the teacher moved to Pilot Bay."

I waited for her to make the connections.

"Although . . . People at the HEMA tournaments *were* always surprised that we had such an excellent teacher—and in a tiny town in the interior of British Columbia. Wait. Master Neil is a human, right?"

"Of course," I said. "Master *Niall* is a human who spent five hundred years training under a fae swordmaster in your father's court."

She looked like she wanted to ask more, so I picked up a sword of my own, and she automatically stepped into a ready stance. Good. She'd done well to develop the strength to hold the hand-and-a-half steadily in a one-handed grip.

I had her run through some basic drills and was happy to see that she had good muscle memory. She had all the basics down to the point of instinct. Unfortunately, that left her mind free for questions.

"I haven't seen you use a sword before," she said. "Why do you use the axe?"

I shrugged, continuing to test her basics. "The axe is more imposing."

"Oh, right," she said. "It's part of your very scary Huntsman vibe."

With anyone else, I would have tried harder to maintain that *very scary Huntsman vibe*, as she put it. But I couldn't help it. Once she knew who I truly was, she would stop teasing me and smiling at me. Stop touching me without even realizing she was doing it.

"Okay, good," I said. "Your form is excellent."

"As it should be." Niamh's cheeks were flushed pink from exertion. "I *do* practice four days a week. I'm ranked top of my age class nationally."

"You fight pampered human children." I couldn't resist a smirk. "Let's see what you can do against an actual opponent."

"Oh, you're on." She held up a hand. "In a second. Hold this." She passed me her sword. "I need to take off a layer."

I was about to say that in a real fight, we don't stop to get comfortable first, but I found myself speechless as she pulled her green sweater off. Her undershirt rode up, revealing a slice of soft white skin before she tugged it back down, shaking out her black curls.

"What?" she asked, noticing my stare.

Was my mouth open? No, thank *Danu.*

"It's a lot of tattoos, I know." Niamh tossed her sweater to the side. "Not very princess-like."

Oh right, the tattoos. Unlike mine, hers were purely decorative. I'd seen the mix of pink blossoms and bands of knotwork that day at the café, but her capped sleeve had hidden the white owl on her shoulder, the wings stretching across her collarbone and shoulder blade. I tore my gaze away from her smooth throat only to be snagged by the rune on the inside of her arm. The match to the one on my own arm.

"Right." Niamh pointed at me. "You distracted me earlier. What is the deal with this one?" She tapped her finger against her *ingwaz* rune. "I've had it for as long as I can remember, which is very weird. Who tattoos a five-year-old? And you have the same one. Care to explain?"

I shook my head. "Not today." I tossed her the practice sword, and she caught it expertly with one hand.

"It gets warm," she said. "Whenever you're around."

"The wards on your magic must be breaking down."

She scowled at me. "That doesn't explain anything."

"All right, Princess," I started.

"I have a name," she pointed out. "As I've told you multiple times."

She didn't realize how many of my barriers she had bashed through already. I needed to keep this last one for as long as

I could manage. I had to remember who she was, and she needed to remember what I was.

She wasn't wrong, though. I needed to explain the runes at some point.

"I'll tell you what." I twirled my practice sword, but she didn't even glance at the flashy distraction. Good. "I'll tell you about the runes if you can best me in a sparring match."

She narrowed her eyes, considering.

There was no way she could match up to my decades of battle experience, but it would do her good to have an incentive to show me her skill without holding back today.

With no warning, she lunged, and I barely got my blade up in time to parry her blow.

She sidestepped quickly, pulling back with a grin. "I accept your terms."

I spun my sword again, getting a feel for the dull blade as we circled each other, before attacking with a series of blows. I held back my strength but none of my speed, though everything felt slow without active runes.

Niamh parried beautifully, moving with a speed to match mine, even if her reach wasn't quite as long. Her blade slid along mine and she spun, almost slashing my shoulder before I disengaged, pulling back and considering. I wanted to see her skill, but I might need to stop holding back if I wanted to avoid discussing the *ingwaz* rune today.

Niamh laughed as she stepped into a thrust.

"Something amusing you, Princess?" I asked, blocking and attacking with three fast strokes.

"It's just fun to fight someone so skilled. I've been getting bored sparring at the club." She dodged, slipping under my strike and almost tapping my chest before I pulled back. A pretty move, but risky. She was used to fighting for points, not blood. It was obvious from her chatter and sparkling eyes. I'd have to watch her in a real battle.

She feinted right, then thrust up stunningly fast. I wrenched my attention away from those eyes and parried with a twist of my sword, trying to use my strength to my advantage as I closed the space between us. My goal was to disarm her, but I must have misjudged my force because, instead of pinning her sword to her body, I knocked her off balance.

Niamh tumbled back, a shocked expression wiping the smile from her face as she fell, rolling her ankle with a whimper. I lunged forward and grabbed her free arm instinctively, only to find myself falling with her. Before I could blink, I was flat on my back, Niamh's knee on my chest, her sword at my throat.

"I don't use that move on the pampered human children." Niamh leaned so close to me that strands of her hair brushed my cheek. "And I didn't think the big and scary Huntsman would fall for such a trick."

I tried to pull myself together, stunned by our closeness more than the fall.

"Very impressive, Princess," I said dryly. "You win. Can we get up now?"

"Oh." She blinked, only now realizing how close we were. "Right." She stood and then leaned back against the wall of the practice room to catch her breath. "The runes!" she hollered as I walked across the room to grab a flask of water. "Explain."

I took a long drink, thinking about what I would say as she slid down to sit on the floor, practice sword on her lap.

When I sat down beside her, she snagged the water from me and took a drink. After swallowing, she handed it back.

"Tell. Me. What. This. Is." She tapped the rune on my arm to punctuate each word.

"Runes are different from regular tattoos." I rolled up my sleeves so she could see the symbols covering my arms. "The runes contain magic. Spelled gold dust is mixed into the ink. If I say the rune's name, it activates the spell."

"So these all do something?" She ran a finger over my arm.

I fought back a shiver. *She's just very touchy*, I reminded myself.

"This one's for speed." I tapped *raidho*, then *daegaz*. "This one's for night vision."

She pointed to *thurisaz*.

"Protection," I said.

"I want some," she breathed.

I considered. It actually wasn't a bad idea. The more advantages she had, the safer I would feel. "Talk to Estrid. She has runes. She'll know who does runecrafting in Nidavellir." After all, she couldn't very well go to the master runecrafter who had done my ink.

"Okay, then what does this one mean?" She pointed to her *ingwaz* rune. "Can I jump really high?"

"Not exactly." I leaned my head back against the wall. "Moriath didn't just arrange for a hostage trade of me for your sister," I started slowly. "Your father would never have agreed to that no matter how weak he was."

"Okay," she said. "Then what did he agree to?"

"In order to cement alliances between our people, you and I were betrothed."

She gaped. "To get married?"

"Yes."

"When I was five?"

"Three," I corrected.

"*What?*"

"Almost four. It didn't matter how old you were or how old I was. It was a political arrangement designed to give Moriath a good reason to be rid of your sister."

"Wow. Just . . ." She shook her head. "But what does that have to do with the tattoo?"

"That's the *ingwaz* rune," I softly said. "We were given them when the betrothal was finalized."

"Do all people here get ink done when they get engaged?"

"It's not common among the Unseelie fae, but it was part of the arrangement. We were too young to be married, but this proved the intent."

She stared at her arm as if it were an alien creature. "You told me all your runes do something. What does this one do?"

"It magically binds a couple together," I said, "and lets them feel when the other is near or in danger."

"How do we get rid of them?" She turned her arm over to hide the rune.

Of course. That was the expected response when you're told you've been betrothed to someone you've never met. And it had always been my intention to sever the bond. In time.

"We'll find someone to remove the rune. Your spell-crafter friend could probably do it," I said. "When you're out of danger."

Niamh critically eyed my rune. "So they haven't been removed yet because you were using it to spy on me?"

"It's not spying, Princess. I can't see you or hear your thoughts. I don't even know exactly where you are. But we left the runes in place so that I would know if you were ever in danger. Your godmother thought it would be best."

"Oh, Aunt Chloe, you have a lot to answer for," muttered Niamh.

"As soon as Moriath is defeated, we will have the runes removed," I said.

"The sooner the better." She pushed herself up to standing. "I have to go. I can't . . . I have to go."

I pushed down my conflicted feelings and stood too.

"Lunchtime!" Estrid called from the doorway, waving a couple of cloth-wrapped bundles. "Did I miss all the fun?"

"No fun here." Niamh stalked past her out of the room. Estrid looked at me with wide eyes, and I jerked my head for her to follow the princess. She tossed me a lunch bundle and dashed after Niamh.

Her response was good. It was what it needed to be. We might have been betrothed as children, but I had no right to think of her in any way except as her protector now.

The man she ended up marrying would be the Unseelie king, and I had given up any thought of that when I became Moriath's Huntsman.

Chapter 16

Niamh

"DID YOU KNOW?" I DEMANDED AS I stormed out of the training room.

"Did I know what?" Estrid ran after me. "And must you walk so fast? You have very long legs."

I stopped and pointed to the rune on my arm.

"You have runes, too?" Estrid caught up and peered at my arm. "I must have missed it in all the other tattoos. Oh, I see. That's your betrothal rune."

"Argh!" I threw my hands up. "I hoped he was making it all up. I guess not."

"Right, because the matching one belongs to . . ." She glanced back down the hallway.

"To *tall, dark, and grumpy* back there. So, you *did* know about this madness?" I started walking again. "Who marries off a three-year-old?"

"Well, technically, you're not . . ." Estrid trailed off when I scowled at her. "I mean, it's not uncommon in kingdoms with ridiculous succession laws like yours." She ran to catch up with me again. "From what I've heard, the Unseelie often marry for power, and your Huntsman is brimming with it. The tales I've heard of him?" She shook her head. "Truly unbelievable."

"It's just all so *ridiculous*. What if I fell in love with somebody else?"

"Um, are you in love with somebody else?" asked Estrid.

"That's not the point!" I kept walking.

I didn't know how to explain why I felt so upset. What did it matter if some father I didn't even remember had married—fine, *betrothed*—me off as a preschooler for power? Or allowed Moriath to do it? Either way, that was all in the past. I had a family who loved me now.

But if every adopted child daydreamed about having parents who were royalty, the real dream was that your biological parents loved you more than anything. Would have raised you if they could. I could forgive my birth father for dying, but could I forgive him for allowing Moriath to use me as some sort of political pawn instead of letting me choose my own life?

Suddenly, I wanted nothing more than to hug my mom and dad. Oh, I hoped they were okay. Everyone kept telling me how much slower time went back home, so it was probably too early to expect a text from Amber. Aunt Chloe was probably still having tea with my parents. Or waiting for Amber to pack her shoes.

"If you were planning to return to your suite, we should have turned back there." Estrid pointed at a hallway behind me.

"I don't want to go back to my room." I shook my hands. "I need . . . I need . . ."

"A run? A nap? A drink?"

"A kitchen," I said firmly.

"Okay, you're hungry. That explains the rage. You should see me when I'm hungry." She held up my lunch. "But I did bring you food, so you don't have to go anywhere."

"I'm not *hungry* hungry. I just need to bake."

By the time we reached the kitchens, my anger had died down to a restless annoyance. Like the rest of Nidavellir, the kitchen was spacious but built for people half my size. Even through my simmering rage, I couldn't help but notice the clever dwarven engineering. Everything from stoves, and what appeared to be fridges, to mixers, all boasted elegant shining metal designs and seemed to run on steam power.

"How does it all work?" I peered at the turning gears as they rotated some unfortunate animal on a spit.

"It's powered by magic-infused crystals and steam from the hot springs in the mountain," said Estrid, "like all the devices and heating in Nidavellir. Now, what's going to make you feel better?"

"Going back home," I said grumpily. "And a tattoo removal." I scowled at my arm.

"I mean, no one abducted you, right? Do you actually want to go home?"

"More than anything." How could I explain that, although I'd technically agreed to everything that had happened since Kylian had burst into my house, I hadn't really had any other choice? I shivered, remembering the glowing eyes of the wolves in the forest around my home. "But I can't. I'll stay, but I need to make a pie."

"Got it," said Estrid. "I mean, not really, but sure."

She led me through the noisy kitchen, crowded with busy cooks, and I couldn't stop staring. Yes, most were dwarves, but I also recognized many other creatures from *Tales of the Unseelie Fae*. There were more asrai, tree-like draoi, short brownies with mottled brown skin, goat-legged glaistigs, and even tiny-winged piskies sprinkling sugar over a row of cookies.

They all stopped and bowed as I went past, and I heard a flurry of whispers behind me. Word had spread that their princess was alive and in Nidavellir. What else were they saying about me? I waved and smiled, feeling a bit awkward.

Estrid pulled me over to a dwarf wearing an apron around his waist and a fabric cap. "Gustav, this is Niamh, the Unseelie princess."

Gustav bowed. "Your Highness."

"And she wants to make a pie."

"Oh, but we can make you any kind you like," protested the chef.

"I know, I know." I still felt twitchy with nervous energy. "I just love to bake. It calms me."

"And she could really use some calming," Estrid told Gustav behind her hand.

"I see." It was clear that Gustav did not see. "Of course, Princess. Our kitchen is yours. What do you need?"

I brought up my recipe in my head. "Butter, flour, salt, sugar, baking powder, cinnamon, white vinegar, an egg." I thought for a minute. "And cloves."

Gustav waved over a gawking glaistig girl with little horns sprouting through her brown curls. "Nora, gather supplies for the princess."

The girl nodded and scampered off.

"Anything else?"

"What kind of apples do you have?"

Gustav clapped his hands. "Everyone, please continue working. The kings will not be impressed if the feast is late tonight." He turned back to me. "I will show you the storeroom, Your Highness." Gustav beckoned, and I followed him through the kitchen. Everyone we passed stared at me until they caught the chef's stern gaze.

"And make some salads!" Estrid added, hurrying after me.

"You don't have to come," I told her as Gustav led us through a well-stocked pantry where Nora was putting together a basket of supplies for me. "You must be busy."

"I am busy." She sighed. "Busy watching you!" The dwarf girl winked. "This is officially my job now when Kylian's not around. Orders from the kings."

"I can take care of myself."

"Says the girl who left her sword in the training gym," commented Estrid.

"Fine, I'm not used to worrying about my safety," I said as we passed through a cool room with rows of shelves holding rounds of aging cheese. "Honestly, though, who's going to attack me in the kitchen? Your dad said that Moriath can't even get into Nidavellir."

"That's true, but she gained the Unseelie throne through tricks and treachery, not force, so it's best not to underestimate her."

"Here we are." Gustav opened the door to a cave so cold that I wished I had not left my new sweater behind along with my sword.

Braids of onions and garlic hung from the earthen ceiling above barrels of potatoes, carrots, and other root vegetables. Shelves against the rough walls held baskets of nuts, dried fruit, pears, and, of course, apples.

"There must be over fifty kinds of apples in here." I stared at the wall of fruit ranging from reds to yellows to greens to pale pink.

"It was a good harvest year," said Gustav proudly. "This is just what we use for the royal kitchen. You should see the common storage caverns."

"How do you grow apples underground?"

"We don't, Your Highness." Gustav laughed. "At the base of the mountain, we have fields and pastures, and there are terraces up the south side with orchards." He waved at the apples. "Take your pick."

"How can I choose?" I picked up a pale pink apple and sniffed it. Mild and sweet with a hint of blossom. I took a bite. "This is the best apple I've ever tasted," I said around a mouthful.

"Rose Lady." Gustav nodded. "Delicious indeed. Not my choice for baking, though."

"Oh, I know. It's too crunchy. I'm just hungry now."

"I have your lunch," Estrid reminded me. "Pick some apples and then eat something. You can't live on questions and annoyance, you know. You also need food."

"Mm-hmm." I examined the apples and picked up a few to smell while Gustav found me a basket. Finally, I narrowed it down to six varieties to try and grabbed a few of each to take back to the kitchen. Gustav took the basket from me despite my protests. I wouldn't have made it quite so heavy if I had known he would insist.

"So you're really into apples?" Estrid had also grabbed an apple to munch on as we headed back to the kitchen.

"I've been trying to recreate a pie from my childhood," I said. "It's the only thing I remember from before . . . you know."

Estrid nodded, mouth full of apple.

"I've never been able to get it right, and I think it's because I was using apples from the human realm. And it turns out I'm not, well, *human*."

Gustav set the basket on a section of the long workbench that had been raised to my height by using clever knobs in the legs. Metal bowls, a pile of knives and wooden spoons, and the ingredients I'd requested waited for me.

"Let me know if you need anything else, Your Highness." Gustav bowed and disappeared into the busy kitchen.

"Thanks, Gustav," I called after him.

"So, do you think these are winners?" Estrid pulled out a yellow apple with a blush of red on one side.

"I don't know," I said. "I have to bake them to know for sure."

"And you're going to bake six pies?"

"No," I corrected her. "*We* are going to bake six pies. Well, tarts, technically."

"Oh no." Estrid held up her hands. "I'm just a—"

"Just a warrior. I know. You said." I handed her an apple and a knife. "Which means you're good with a blade. Get peeling."

"I'll peel if you eat your lunch." Estrid waggled the knife at the napkin-wrapped food on the table.

What was in it? My stomach growled.

"Okay, deal." I snagged the parcel and opened it up to find a mushroom and garlic hand pie, a wedge of cheese, and some purple baby carrots.

Estrid got to work on the lower table beside me, and I lost myself in the rhythm of preparing pie crust, the steps as familiar to me as my sword drills. I felt my pulse calm and my mind clear while I worked, taking bites of my lunch as I went.

The glaistig girl, Nora, brought me a selection of pie plates, and I chose a set of six-inch tart tins, then separated my dough into twelve balls.

"Tell me about rune magic." I rolled out the first tart shell. "It's like magic tattoos?"

"Basically, yes." Estrid pushed up her left sleeve and showed me her tattoos.

"Those look like Kylian's," I commented, staring at the graceful runes swirling up her arm.

Estrid nodded. "These are Futhark runes from our homeland. Rune magic was developed by the elves back in Álfheimr. The fae here in Tír na nÓg tried to translate the runes to Gaeilge Ársa, but they were never able to adapt the rune magic to their language."

"But everybody also speaks English," I pointed out.

"What?" Estrid tilted her head.

"We're speaking English right now." I looked at her, confused.

"Is that a human language? We're speaking Gaeilge Ársa. The dwarves learned it from your people, and most of us younger dwarves speak both now that we have so many Unseelie living here."

"What do you mean, that's what we're speaking?" I set the rolling pin down and stared at her.

"Listen to my words," she said slowly. "What are you talking about?"

I sat down heavily. For the first time, I noticed she was right. We *weren't* speaking English. How long had I been speaking another language without even noticing?

"But how?" I said. "I've never been any good with languages."

Estrid shrugged. "You spoke it until you were five."

"But I don't remember anything!" I threw my hands up.

"Apparently, you do." Estrid picked up a new apple to peel. "Apple pie and Gaeilge Ársa."

"Apparently," I grumbled, more annoyed at my hidden memories than ever, as I rolled out another tart shell.

Chapter 17

Niamh

ESTRID PEELED APPLES AND LET ME PROCESS everything in the way I knew best.

After pressing the dough into the tart pans and slicing the perfectly peeled apples into thin wedges, I started to feel more myself. The combination of precise, focused motions and the comfort of a recipe I knew so well had worked its magic yet again.

"It was just a bit of a shock." I carefully fluted the edges of each tart with my fingertips.

"Which part? Finding out that you're fae? A princess? Being hunted by an evil queen? Or that you're bonded to that one over there?" Estrid jerked her head in the direction of the training area.

"It really has been a long couple of days." I finished the last tart and pulled over a nearby stool to sit with a sigh.

Gustav came by with Nora, and they each loaded three tarts onto a tray.

"Thank you," I said. "They bake at . . ." I trailed off as Gustav stared me down. "I mean, I'm sure you know how to bake pies."

"Your Highness." Gustav gave me an indignant nod before whisking the tray away, his assistant trailing behind.

With the tarts taken care of, I turned back to Estrid. "I'm referring to today's revelation." I flipped my wrist over on the table. "In all the stories I made up about this tattoo as a kid, a magic engagement ring was not one of them. Kylian says we're just keeping them for safety." I glared at the rune. "He's not expecting us to go through with it. But being magically bonded to someone without my consent and not even knowing about it for all this time? It's unsettling." I rubbed my wrist. The familiar tattoo felt alien now.

"May I see?" Estrid held out a hand.

"Why?" I gave her my arm.

"I'm a runecrafter. Maybe I can tell you something about it."

"Not *just* a warrior, then?" I teased.

"It's not a big deal. Runecrafting isn't like *real* crafting." Estrid nodded, her red braids bouncing. "I thought I recognized Master Brynjar's work."

"Who?" I stared at the inked lines with new interest.

"The runecrafter I apprenticed under." Estrid didn't look up from my rune. "There's something about this *ingwaz*. The ink looks the same but the underlying spell has . . ."

"What?"

Estrid shook her head. "I'm not sure. It's safe, though. Master Brynjar would have made sure of it, so I wouldn't worry. But I *was* surprised to see that he did Kylian's entire sleeve of runes, even the most recent ones."

"Kylian got his runes from a dwarf? Have you met him before?"

"Of course he did." Estrid released my arm. "I told you, we're the ones who discovered rune magic. But I didn't meet Kylian before yesterday. Master Brynjar must have done them in secret."

"But why would a dwarf give magic to Moriath's henchman? I thought you were allies of my parents."

Estrid nodded. "My master said that Moriath had a keen interest in rune magic when they visited. She was fascinated when you two got your *ingwaz* runes and encouraged Kylian to get more. It didn't make up for her aversion to soup," Estrid added with a wink, "but the kings were happy to show off Master Brynjar's work. We didn't know then that she was an accomplished ink spellcrafter herself."

"But you said Kylian had more recent runes?" I asked. "From after Moriath killed my father?"

"The tattoos on his right arm—the Unseelie knots and symbols—are Moriath's work, but I'm sure my master inked his left arm."

"How can you tell so much just by looking at them? You must have—what did Audrey call it—the Sight?"

"Just a bit," she said. "I can't do much other than these." She tapped her finger on one of her own runes. "Not enough to do real spellcrafting. Not enough . . ."

"Not enough to be in the running for queen?" I asked casually. Estrid seemed to have a lot of opinions about what made a good ruler.

She shrugged. "Doesn't matter." The dwarf speared a slice of apple with her knife, eating it off the tip. "Warriors have more fun, anyway." But she didn't look me in the eye when she said it.

"Is your master still around?" I asked. "Maybe he can have a look and see what he thinks is causing my rune to be different."

Estrid shook her head. "Master Brynjar used to take mysterious trips. He'd never bring me along, and he would never talk about it afterwards. Ten years ago, he left and never returned. From your Huntsman's tattoos, I would guess that's when he got the most recent ink done on his arm. We never heard from him again."

"You don't think Kylian . . ." I was unable to put it into words.

She shook her head. "Like I said this morning, I think your Huntsman has been doing his best to keep Moriath from causing as much damage as she would have otherwise. My master must have been helping him."

"He's not *my* Huntsman." I tapped my fingers on the table.

"That's what you're fixating on? Interesting." Estrid ate another slice of apple.

"The only reason I still have this rune is because he's paranoid."

"Sure," agreed Estrid easily.

"So, what do you think happened to your master then?"

"Moriath." She spun her knife on the butcher block counter.

"But I thought you said she wanted Kylian to get more runes?"

"Sure, it's nice to have a powerful minion, but maybe he was getting a little *too* powerful for Moriath's comfort. Not only would he be harder to control, but—" She paused to shrug. "He may not have been born Unseelie, but with his bond to you and the years he's spent here serving her . . ."

"You think she was worried about the crown."

Estrid nodded.

"Why does she care so much?" I asked. "She's *queen*. What difference does it make if she has some crown?"

"Excuse me, Your Highness."

Estrid and I swiveled to see Nora shifting nervously on her goat's feet as she held a tray of golden tarts.

"I don't think you know the truth," Nora continued timidly, "about the Unseelie crown."

Chapter 18

Niamh

GUSTAV NUDGED NORA TO SET DOWN HER tray on the table beside us.

"The tarts have been baked and then cooled to the perfect temperature." Gustav gave a little bow.

"Cooled? How? Small magic?" *Focus, Niamh. The crown.* "Never mind. Thank you, Gustav." I turned back to Nora. "What do you mean? About the crown? Sit down and tell me."

I stood and waved at my stool. Nora stared at me in shock.

"It's fine. I need somebody to try these tarts with me," I insisted.

"You aren't going to argue with your princess, are you?" Estrid teased.

The glaistig blushed. "Of course not." She sat gingerly on my seat.

"Knife, knife. Where's the knife?" I muttered before locating it under a towel and a pile of scraps. "Okay, the crown?"

"The Unseelie crown isn't just a symbol. It's a conduit," said Nora. "The crown is how a ruler channels the power of Faerie. No matter how many people Moriath enslaves . . ." She looked down at her hands. "No matter how many gems she mines or steals, her magic will never compare with the true power of an Unseelie ruler."

I considered this as I sliced the tarts into thin wedges. "So it's not just that it goes to the most powerful Unseelie fae, but it also makes them *more* powerful? No wonder she's cranky."

"My gran said—" Nora's eyes widened as I transferred small pieces of three different tarts onto a plate and slid it in front of her.

"We have to compare them," I said reasonably. "What did your grandma say?"

"Gran always said that the rulers didn't understand—had never understood—what the small folk," Nora said, putting a hand on her chest, "knew to be true."

I dished up a plate for Estrid while I waited for the girl to continue.

"The crown isn't just a link to the magic of the land like the royal bird familiars are," she whispered. "It's a piece of Faerie itself that you can touch. Faerie chooses who wears the crown. It's not just who's the most powerful but who will take the best care of the kingdom. The king or queen needs to be someone strong enough to protect us all, but the ruling family has always passed down knowledge and wisdom with their power. My gran says that when King Fionnbharr and Queen Oonagh were both alive, they each had a crown. The king and queen ruled together for the good of all the Unseelie fae."

"I didn't know there were two crowns." I wished again that I remembered something about my fae parents. "I bet Moriath was mad when she didn't get one after marrying my father."

"Queen Oonagh didn't receive her crown until she had proven her heart to Faerie." Nora blinked back tears. "Moriath, however, might have become queen and bonded with that falcon, but she will *never* wear the crown. Faerie will never forgive her for all that she has done."

I wiped my own eyes as I noticed how many of the kitchen staff had gathered around to listen to Nora. The dwarves still bustled around under Gustav's stern gaze, but the Unseelie refugees clustered near our table. Kylian was right. These people needed a queen who cared for them.

But it wasn't that simple. The more I learned, the less simple it became. My parents might have ruled before Moriath, but I was neither the most powerful fae nor someone who knew how to take care of a kingdom. I knew that in my heart, and the magical land of Faerie was not going to be fooled by me.

Surely, the best hope for these people was to find Maeve, my sister, but my heart broke as I took in their faces. They were so far from home, mere remnants of the villages and families they had loved.

I straightened my shoulders. I would have to trust that the mysterious *land* would find them a good ruler. Meanwhile, they had me, so I'd look after them the only way I knew how. I plated up as many little slices of apple tart as I could and passed them around to the Unseelie kitchen staff.

"Cookies next, I think." I wiped my hands briskly on my apron, ignoring Estrid who watched me with keen eyes as she ate her own slice. "What's your favorite cookie?" I asked Nora.

"Gran used to make this poppyseed shortbread for Imbolc every year. It always makes me think of her."

"Right, then that's what we'll make. What do we need?"

As she rattled off ingredients, Gustav waved at the Unseelie folk to gather the supplies, while I picked up my fork and turned back to the tarts. I had left one bite in each pan for myself.

They were all delicious. But none of them were right.

Estrid dropped me off at my suite of rooms, and I opened the door to find Kylian crouched down, surrounded by chicks. Essie was perched on his shoulder as he shook chick feed out of the container into the dish.

"Big and scary Huntsman." I leaned my hip against the table. "Are you snuggling that chick?"

"They were hungry." He frowned at a chick as it climbed over his foot and into the food dish. "They wouldn't stop cheeping."

"And the one on your shoulder?"

Kylian plucked it off and handed it to me. "It looked lonely," he said shortly, but something made me think that he missed holding the chick.

I looked at him, but he seemed unconcerned as he walked past me to close the door I had left ajar. This wasn't the first time I had gotten a feeling that Kylian's emotions didn't match his words, but how could I tell? I certainly didn't know him well enough to read him, and his body language never gave him away. But I was sure *he* felt lonely, not the chick.

I rubbed Essie's fluff against my cheek and then set her down to eat her dinner with the others. "Sorry for storming out like that." I snagged my green sweater off the table where it had been neatly folded. "I was just a bit shocked by the whole child engagement *situation*. I only met you . . ." I thought for a minute. "One day? Two days ago? I mean, I know I must have known you when I was a kid, but that doesn't count if I don't remember it. And I know that no one's expecting us to get married now, but it's still weird to find out we have this magical connection."

"If it really bothers you so much," said Kylian, "we can have them removed."

Again, he sounded casual, but I somehow knew that the idea made him anxious. It was happening more and more. This couldn't be my imagination.

"You really don't think I'm safe?" I waved my hand around the room. "Even here?"

"I've spent the last two hundred years keeping that woman away from you, and now she knows you're alive. She'll never stop until she finds you."

"But dragons?" I said weakly, gesturing outside.

"Have successfully prevented Moriath from reclaiming these mountains as part of the Unseelie Kingdom. But you're just one person. She doesn't need brute force to get to you."

I shivered. "Fine. I'll keep the stupid tattoo. For now." A wave of relief washed over me, and I looked up at him sharply. "Can you feel that, too?"

"Feel what?" He leaned against the wall and crossed his arms.

"Sometimes I feel things that I know are not how *I'm* feeling." I pointed to my chest. "So I'm guessing they're what *you* are feeling." I pointed at Kylian.

He tilted his head and I watched, mesmerized, as his long locs slid over his shoulder. "That would explain some things," he said.

"So this is not a normal part of the rune bonds thing?"

He rolled up his sleeve and considered his rune. "I don't know anyone else with a bond like this. Unlike the Seelie fae who include a bond in every marriage ceremony," he said with an eye roll, "the Unseelie aren't generally big on bindings. It's more common among the dwarves, but I was told that it's rare to feel anything more than a general sense of the other's location and safety, even after many centuries together. But you do have a lot of power."

"That's what you keep saying." I sat on one tiny chair and propped my feet up on another one. "But I don't feel any different than when I thought I was human. If it wasn't for the whole pointy ear thing, I'd think you had made it all up." I felt the tip of an ear and grimaced. "That and the fact that everyone keeps bowing to me."

Kylian nodded.

"And telling me stories of why they left the Unseelie Kingdom and how happy they are that I'm back."

Kylian looked away.

"I suppose you've heard all the stories. That's what you've been trying to tell me."

"Princess," he said slowly. "I was there."

"You were . . ." He was the big, scary Huntsman. "Of course." I fiddled with the pie plate. "But like . . ."

"But what?" He looked back at me.

"Why didn't you do anything about it?" I whispered.

"I didn't have enough power to confront Moriath directly, not by myself. And I was young and a foreigner. Who would help me?" He sighed. "I did what I could any time she wasn't looking. Never enough, but I couldn't let anyone suspect me. And as time went on, it was easier for people not to trust me."

"You don't have the power to do anything, and you think *I* do? Estrid told me that they haven't ever seen anyone wield rune magic as strongly as you can. What do you think I'll be able to do?"

"You're the one they've been waiting for all this time."

"You mean my sister, Maeve," I cut in. "They all thought I was dead, right?"

"Your people have been waiting," Kylian pressed on, "for the lost princess to come and save them from Moriath. The queen isn't the only one to notice that she doesn't have the true Unseelie crown. It's given the fae hope, and that hope has kept many of them alive."

"Can't you see how terrifying that is? I'm just one girl!"

"You're much more than that."

I sighed. "I'll keep the rune on me for now. And I'll try to help." It wasn't like I could turn my back on them now. "But Aunt Chloe and Amber need to find my sister." I stood. "Because I'm not the queen you need."

I left and locked myself in my room until dinnertime. I pulled out my phone to read a text from Amber. My parents were fine, just worried about me. And like Kylian had promised, most of the wolves had left. Only a sentry or two remained in case I tried to go home. Moriath had no interest in them now that I was gone.

I crawled into bed, overwhelmed with relief but also missing my dad's affectionate teasing and my mom's steady patience and love.

I heard a cheep and saw that Pip had snuck into the room with me. I picked up the little orange and brown chick and snuggled her softness as I flipped to my email app. Audrey had sent me message after message, filling me in on all the adventures she had been having while I baked at the café. I read them twice before my phone warned me it only had a ten percent charge left.

I cried a little then. For the life I'd thought I had, the person I'd thought I was, and the home that was so far away.

CHAPTER 19

KYLIAN

"LJÓSÁLFAR Á MÓTI TRÖLLUM, OR ELVES VERSUS Trolls, as you would call it," explained King Ulf one evening, two weeks into our stay at Nidavellir, "is an exceptional way to learn the strategy you need to be a good monarch."

"If you don't have an opponent who constantly cheats and changes the rules." Ulrik began laying out the pieces of a complex game on the table in the throne room while Niamh and I looked on, seated on cushions.

A castle crafted of dark marble, about three hands high, dominated the playing area, the rest of the table taken up by flat wooden surfaces beautifully painted to represent different types of terrain.

"I never cheat." Ulf stroked his beard. "But if I *did,* it would only add more reality to the game. Who ever heard of an enemy who follows the rules?"

"Who ever heard of trolls who could fly?" grumbled Ulrik, carefully setting out trolls of various types and sizes carved from polished amethyst.

"A monarch must think on their feet," Ulf insisted. "How will Niamh ever learn to be a good queen if all she does is follow the rules?"

"Don't worry about me." Niamh sat cross-legged beside me in the long green dress she had worn to dinner and fussed with the ever-present basket of sleeping chicks by her side. "I'm just here because Gustav won't let me in the kitchen after supper hours. He's informed me that baking pies is not an appropriate evening activity."

She scooped out Clementine and Meringue, depositing them on her lap. The little white chick didn't even wake, and Clem happily snuggled in and immediately fell asleep again. Niamh set Espresso on the knee of my crossed leg. It was easier not to argue with her, so I left the black chick there, choosing not to think too hard about how nice it was to have a small creature feel so safe around me.

"Now, you'll be the elves," Ulf continued, handing me an ornate wooden box. I flipped it open to reveal polished jade elves, each nestled into its own velvet-lined spot, perfectly sized to the different archers, swordsmen, mages, and the king and queen.

"Oooh!" Niamh's arm and leg pressed against mine as she leaned over to pull a tiny jade mage from the box. I didn't breathe until she leaned back with the game piece in her hand. "I like this game. Our adorable tiny elves are gonna take you *down*. Your cute little trolls are all going into our dungeon." She wiggled the mage at the dwarven brothers.

"I don't think we have a dungeon." I examined the two levels of the fortress we were tasked with defending.

"That can't be right." Niamh removed the top level of a tower to inspect. "How will we achieve our ultimate victory with no dungeon?"

"I think we're meant to kill them all." I started setting out the jade game pieces.

Niamh gaped at me with her big blue eyes. "But they're so cute! Have you seen the little tree trolls? They have leaves for hair." She turned to the kings. "Can we switch teams?"

"No," said Ulf firmly. "It's easier for you to learn with the elves."

"What he means to say," called Estrid, entering the throne room from a side door carrying a folding table, "is that it's much easier to cheat when you're the trolls."

The asrai serving girl, Cara, followed behind her with a full tray of tea and fried food.

"How dare you?" Ulf put his hand to his chest.

"You'll see," Estrid told us as she set up the small folding table for Cara.

The asrai girl laid out four porcelain cups and poured tea from a copper teapot.

"I say." Ulrik looked up from the troll he was positioning. "I'm sure I requested mead."

Cara handed me an earthy-smelling cup of tea, careful not to meet my eyes.

Estrid gave each of the kings a stern look. "Doctor Aelfred says no mead after dinner, and that you need to drink your chaga tea if you want to have any hope of keeping your stomach functioning with all the meat you eat. He says you're a medical miracle." She winked at Niamh.

The princess laughed.

"Don't worry, Your Highness." Cara smiled at Niamh. "There isn't any meat on the snack tray."

Ulrik made a strangled noise.

"Thank you, Cara." Niamh gave the serving girl a kind smile.

"Don't be so glum, brother." Ulf chomped on a deep-fried snack. "Not eating meat is more respectful to our little feathered guests, and the fried mushrooms are excellent. What variety is this one, Estrid? I don't recognize it, but it's delicious."

Ulrik's eyes widened in horror as he watched his brother eat. "Ulf. It's green."

"Surely Gustav wouldn't send us moldy mushrooms." Ulf peered at the bite in his hand, then stopped chewing in shock. "What? No. *Estrid?*"

"It's called *broccoli.*" Estrid grinned.

Ulf gawked at his daughter. "My own child has betrayed me."

"Half of them are mushrooms, and half are vegetables, and there's no way to know which is which until you eat them." Estrid patted her father and uncle on their shoulders.

"You taught her strategy well." I inclined my head to King Ulf.

Ulf sighed and sadly popped the rest of the broccoli into his mouth.

"She certainly learned treachery from him." Ulrik picked up an unknown deep-fried object and looked at it as if trying to see through the batter, then sighed. "Let's get on with teaching them the game."

I never did fully learn the rules of Elves Versus Trolls that night. I spent the evening listening to the kings harass each other, while Niamh barreled through the game with hilarious jokes and surprisingly good strategy.

My warriors focused on protecting the jade king and queen pieces from attackers while Niamh's captured amethyst enemies, declaring that if Ulf's trolls could suddenly dig tunnels, then she could have a dungeon.

Finally, the last troll piece was in Niamh's possession.

"We win!" Niamh crowed, throwing her hands in the air.

"I don't even know what game that was." Ulrik stared at his empty battlefield in shock.

"Kylian, we won!" Niamh lunged over and hugged me, causing our chicks to squawk in protest.

I sat there, stunned. The feel of her soft body pressed against mine overwhelmed me, her hair smelling of cinnamon and vanilla. Always vanilla.

"Oh, sorry." Niamh pulled back, eyes sparkling. "I know you're not really a hugger. I get carried away sometimes."

"That's all right." My voice came out roughly.

"I'll try to remember to just give you a good arm punch next time or something," teased Niamh, tucking her little game pieces away like nothing had happened.

And, for her, it *was* nothing. Niamh gave away hugs to the people around her like she did cookies—freely and often, for any reason. It didn't mean anything.

Yet in that moment, I knew that I was in trouble. I would relive that moment with her arms around me for the rest of my days. But I could never, *ever* let her see how she affected me, because this sweet, sunny princess was not for me.

Chapter 20

Kylian

A SHARP KNOCK AT THE DOOR BROKE through my concentration. I wiped the dagger I had been sharpening, my mind still half busy planning tomorrow's training session. Niamh hadn't been able to catch me off guard since that first time almost a month ago, but she still fought with an enthusiasm I admired. Her continuous banter and relentlessly cheerful manner—no matter how hard I pushed her—showed her lack of experience, but there were worse ways to distract an opponent.

I approached the door, dagger in hand, careful to avoid stepping on the chicks milling underfoot. The little birds were sprouting feathers on their wing tips. I prayed they wouldn't start flying anytime soon. I'd have to find a way to keep them off the balcony.

"You know . . ." Niamh poked her head out of her bedroom, dressed in a red silk skirt over a chemise. "It's probably not an assassin. Estrid said she'd find some laces for that bodice of my mother's so I could wear it to dinner tonight."

"Best to be safe." I peered through the window beside the door and saw that Niamh was right. The dwarven warrior held a bundle of silken cord as she waved her free hand at me through the window.

"Kylian, you look extra murdery today," said Estrid, uncowed as ever, as I opened the door. "Niamh, I found the laces."

"Sweet! Let's get me laced up. It's almost dinnertime." Niamh waved Estrid into the bedroom with her.

Since we'd arrived in Nidavellir, every night had been a feast with the kings. If I could have my way, we'd avoid such large gatherings of people. Keeping track of every bit of food and drink, watching every dwarven guest, every server, was an impossible task.

Moriath loved both poison and disguises. But Niamh would be miserable with only my taciturn self for company, and the way she soaked in any story the kings could remember about her parents gave me a strange warm feeling in my chest.

Impossible.

I shook my head as I sat back down at the small table, reminding myself that I was the cold-hearted Huntsman, not the soft princeling I had been when we were children. The prince might have been a good match for her, before everything I had done. But she needed the Huntsman to keep her alive.

I'd been careful to wake early and put the blanket back on my untouched bed every morning after that first time—so that Niamh wouldn't argue with me about sleeping outside her door every night.

She wouldn't understand that I never used a mattress anyway. Niamh was bothered enough by the way I wouldn't eat sweets. She didn't need to know how many other luxuries I had set aside when I became Moriath's Huntsman. I knew it would annoy her that I wasn't using the comfortable-looking second bedroom, but I slept better knowing that any intruder would have to get past me first. Still, in all our time here, there hadn't been a hint of danger.

Suddenly, I heard a soft, strangled gasp. Terrified panic jolted through the *ingwaz* bond, and I shot to my feet.

"Kylian, help!" yelled Estrid.

I slammed the bedroom door open to find Niamh gasping for air, her lips turning blue, eyelids fluttering. Behind her, Estrid's small fingers continued to pull the bodice tighter.

I flipped my dagger with a roar, ready to dispatch the dwarf suffocating my princess.

"Kylian!" Estrid yelled, eyes wide. "Cut the laces!"

Then I saw her fingers trapped in the silken cords. They were growing tighter and tighter all on their own, causing her fingertips to go purple.

In a flash, my wickedly sharp blade sliced through the bodice strings. I flung the garment, strings still writhing, into the lit fireplace.

"Niamh!" I caught the princess by her arms as she collapsed, checking to make sure that the skin underneath the hole I had slashed in the back of her chemise was intact.

Niamh's dark eyelashes fluttered, pink returning to her cheeks and lips. She took one deep breath after another.

"You don't have to grip my arms quite so hard, Kylian."

I carefully relaxed my fingers, which were indeed creating dents in her soft upper arms, and scooped her up to rest on the bed.

"I'm so sorry." Estrid shook her hands. "I don't know what—"

Quick as a flash, I grabbed the dwarf's wrist in an iron grip. She looked at me, her eyes wide.

"Kylian!" protested Niamh, but I ignored her.

"*Perthro,*" I barked. Estrid flinched as I felt the truth rune on my arm flare. "According to the princess, you're Master Brynjar's apprentice, so you know that I'll be able to tell if you're lying."

The girl nodded sharply.

"Are you truly Estrid?" I looked deeply into her eyes.

She nodded. "Yes."

"Was it your intention to assassinate or harm Princess Niamh?" I asked.

"Never," she said. "Kylian, you have to believe me."

I did believe her. Not because I trusted her—I didn't trust anyone—but because there was no hint of a lie. I knew my truth rune was powerful enough to detect falsehoods from even Moriath herself, although I had never been foolish enough to let the queen guess that.

Niamh pushed herself up to sitting. "Estrid is my *friend.* She would never—"

I held up a hand to silence her. "Where did you get those bodice strings?"

"In a box I found with more of Queen Oonagh's things," Estrid stammered.

"Are you certain they were Oonagh's? Did Moriath ever leave anything here?"

"I don't know." She shook her head. "I didn't think of that. Moriath only visited Nidavellir once, over two hundred years ago. There's no way she could have planned this."

I released the girl's arm, and she pulled back. Perhaps now, she would fear me like everyone did. Like everyone *should.*

"What are you thinking, Kylian?" Niamh scooted closer, putting her hand on my arm.

Everyone but the princess, apparently.

"It's not like Moriath could plan this," Niamh said. "No one can see the future."

"If only that were true." I stepped back, and her hand fell away.

"Estrid." I turned to the dwarf, who still flexed her fingers to bring the blood back into them. "I know it's not dwarven magic, but do your kings have a scrying mirror?"

"Of course." Her brows knit in confusion. "A gift from Clíodhna when she visited our newly excavated kingdom."

"I have a theory." I turned back to Niamh, who looked more confused than ever. "But it'll be easier to explain if I can show you."

"You won't get anything out of the kings until they've eaten," Estrid said wryly.

"Then we'd best go to dinner." I started for the door.

"Right behind you," Niamh said, and I turned to see her staring at the smoldering remains of the silk bodice. She tugged her ruined chemise back up her milky-white shoulder. "As soon as I find a less murderous outfit."

I glanced one more time at Estrid, and she gave me a sharp nod. I had met many deceptive people in my life. This girl wasn't one of them. I nodded back and shut the door.

Leaning against the closed door, I slowly exhaled. Seconds more and I would have lost Niamh. I *couldn't* lose her.

I sheathed my dagger and fisted my hands to stop their shaking. Not once during the entire ordeal had I been worried for the fate of the Unseelie Kingdom. I needed to remember that all of this was to put Niamh on the throne. Giving the Unseelie folk a ruler who was truly good and caring, who could set things right, would begin to atone for all the damage I'd done.

If I lost her, it would all be for nothing. But in that moment, when I had seen her ashen face, robbed of breath, I had known that if I lost her . . .

I, too, would be nothing.

Chapter 21

Niamh

"It's just through here. Watch out for that teacup!"

I narrowly avoided stepping on a full cup of cold tea as I followed Ulf and Ulrik into their shared office behind the throne room.

The cozy wood-paneled room was clearly divided down the middle.

A smooth and gleaming marble desk stood on the left half, with a neat stack of papers and a tray holding a variety of quills and ink on the side. Orderly books filled the shelves behind the desk, and the armchairs near the door looked soft and inviting.

The desk on the right side was heaped with papers, open books, and at least five cups in precarious positions. The bookcase had scrolls and notebooks crammed around an array of gemstones, some bottles, and a silver helmet. As for the armchairs, only two taller heaps of books, blankets, and shoes gave away their location.

"My father refuses to let anyone clean his side." Estrid sighed and began stacking dishes. "It drives the head of housekeeping insane."

"Well, he keeps moving my books," grumbled Ulf as Kylian checked the corners of the office for assassins.

"To the *bookcase*." Estrid rolled her eyes.

"Exactly! Why would I look for them there? Put that tea down. I'm not finished with it." Ulf snatched a porcelain cup and saucer from his daughter.

"Now you're just being difficult," huffed Estrid. "This has to be days old."

"It's still good." Ulf narrowed his eyes at her.

"Oh, yeah? Prove it. Drink that tea, and I'll stop cleaning."

Ulf brought the tea to his lips—paused, sniffed, and winced—but opened his mouth.

"Stop being so stubborn. You'll get sick *again*." Estrid grabbed the cup before he could drink and set it with the stack of dishes by the door.

"If you're quite done defending your filth, bring the water." Ulrik pulled a silk cloth off a gold basin etched with gracefully curving mushrooms on a stand between their desks. Behind the fancy birdbath, a tapestry of tall mountains wreathed in clouds took up the wall, hanging to the floor.

"*Filth?* It's been at least two months since we last saw a mouse in here." Ulf lifted a blanket off the floor, dropped it, then peered under a chair before pulling out a large bottle with a cork stopper.

"I can hear them squeaking under your desk." Ulrik accepted the bottle from his brother and began pouring water into the basin. "I think you're feeding them crumbs on purpose."

"Well, I mean, there are the baby mice to think of." Ulf watched the water rise in the gold bowl. "A little more. Stop. *Perfect.*"

Ulrik looked at his brother and added one more glug of water. A few drops spilled over the edge. "Come, Niamh. Look in the mirror."

I stood between the kings and stared down into the water. Instead of the inside of the gold basin, I saw pitch black, perfectly still water.

"I expected something, well, more like a mirror," I admitted. "What does it do?"

"It's mainly used as a way to talk to people over long distances," Ulf told me. "If the person also has a mirror, and you both use it to scry for each other at the same time, you can see the person and talk to them."

"Like a video call," I mused.

Ulf looked to Ulrik, who shrugged.

"You can also observe your surroundings. The more power the user has, the farther they can scry," continued Ulf.

"What about the human realm? Can I see my home?" I asked.

"Well, I'm not sure," Ulf began, then stopped as the water rippled and the farmhouse appeared, bathed in morning light.

As I leaned in closer, Ulf spun away from the mirror. "Wait, put that down!"

Ulrik had joined Estrid in tidying his brother's side of the office and was putting a book back in the bookcase. Ulf snatched it back and started arguing about every item they moved, but I barely noticed the family squabble.

"Show me my mom and dad," I commanded the mirror, but nothing happened.

"It's only been one night in Pilot Bay." Kylian looked over

my shoulder. "The wards are still keeping them safe, but they are also keeping anyone from scrying more closely."

"I suppose that's good." I sighed, then straightened. "Oh! Mirror, show me my sister, Maeve!"

"Moriath's been trying to find her for decades," pointed out Kylian.

"Shhh . . ." I gripped his arm and leaned over the basin. The water grew black again before clearing to show a stone tower in a misty forest. A fae girl who looked about my age—so, she could be eighteen or eight hundred—picked mushrooms and placed them in a basket, her long braid of bright auburn hair topped with a headscarf. Suddenly, she looked up as if startled. When her blue eyes connected with mine, a memory struck me of a pudgy little hand in mine. I had helped her learn to walk in a huge stone hallway with a soft green carpet under our bare feet. I had felt so grown up, only two years older than my baby sister. The memory came and went in a flash before the image in the mirror cut off abruptly.

I stared at the mirror, stunned. My first memory from before Pilot Bay. It had been so short, but there was no question.

"That was really her." I willed the image to return, but the water stayed stubbornly black, and no more memories surfaced. "Maeve."

"I never met her." Kylian shifted, and I released his arm. "But she has the same eyes as you."

I stared at the mirror, feeling a sense of loss. Not just for my sister, but for the memories of her I should have. I took a fortifying breath. I was not going to cry.

"I'll send Amber a text, but I'm not sure if what we saw will be any help," I told Kylian, regaining my composure. What else could I do? "What did you want to show me? What does this have to do with the bodice strings of doom?"

"If you have enough power, and Moriath certainly does, you can scry not just for the present but for the future."

"The evil queen can see the future?" I gulped. "And you want me to defeat her?"

Kylian moved closer. "She can't see everything. Just glimpses of possible futures. But she's very good at using those hints to her advantage."

"But then she should have known you didn't kill me, right?" I tapped my lower lip, trying to understand. "If she set a trap for me here?"

"If she had known that, I'd be long dead," said Kylian. "You being here with the dwarves must have been one possibility she saw long ago and planned for. Moriath is nothing if not thorough."

"And can she still see my future?" I felt unsteady. "How many more traps could she have set?"

"I don't know," said Kylian grimly. "That's why we need to be so cautious."

I squeezed my eyes shut, but this wasn't something I could just ignore. I looked back up at Kylian. "You think I have power, too?"

"I know you do, Princess."

"Then I want to see what she sees," I decided, turning quickly back to the mirror before I could reconsider. Because this had to be a terrible idea. "Show me the future. Show me what happens when I meet Moriath."

"*Princess*. That's not . . ." Kylian trailed off in shock as we both took in the image in the water.

For the first time, I saw Moriath. The woman who had killed my parents and stolen their kingdom stood in front of a stone throne, her pale lips curved up in a smile. A crown of crystals and antlers sat on her white hair, and she wore dozens of gems set in her rings and a sparkling sapphire necklace. But when I dragged my gaze away from her pale blue eyes, I froze.

That was me. In a blue silk dress, lying in what looked like a glass-topped gold coffin. Eyes closed. Chest still.

I wrenched my gaze away and stared at Kylian, the raw terror I felt reflected in his eyes.

"I don't look like I'm breathing!" I grabbed Kylian's hand. "Why am I not *breathing?*"

The dwarves rushed over just in time to see what the mirror showed before the image faded and reformed. But this time, I was nowhere to be seen. Only Moriath.

She leaned closer and smiled. "Niamh, there you are. I've been looking everywhere for you."

"Kylian," I hissed under my breath, still gripping his hand. "Is that the real Moriath?"

"She must have been scrying for you at the same moment. The mirrors thought you wanted to talk to each other," Kylian said in my ear. "You need to break the connection."

"And, Kylian." Moriath's eyes flicked to my Huntsman. "You're looking well. I'm sorry I lost my temper. If you bring me the girl now, I might reconsider. I had to have a Huntsman, so I gave Dylan the tattoos. He *is* enthusiastic, but he lacks a certain something."

"Brains?" I quipped. Snark always seemed to rise up as self-defense with me.

"Power," breathed Moriath. "You just saw how this ends, Huntsman. You've gambled on the wrong queen. She's as good as dead."

Hearing Moriath give voice to the fear in my heart made my resolve snap into place. So what if the vision had looked ominous? Glimpses of *possible* futures, Kylian had said. Who was this woman to tell me I'd lost before we'd even met?

I narrowed my eyes at the woman in the mirror. "You thought you killed me once already. How'd that work out for you? Still wearing that fake crown?"

The smug mirth left Moriath's face as her murderous eyes flashed back to mine. "I'll see you soon, little princess. Best get that coffin in order."

"Well, you better—" The water went black again. "Run away then, I guess."

"The glass coffin, brother." Ulrik turned to Ulf.

"I know." Ulf stroked his beard. "The craftsmanship looked almost dwarven."

I frowned at the mirror. "You know, I don't really like her very much."

"Of course you don't," grumbled Ulf. "Wants to kill you. Doesn't like soup . . ."

"And now knows where Niamh is," Estrid pointed out.

"We'll have to leave," Kylian grimly said.

My heart sank. These past weeks, I'd grown to love Nidavellir. It didn't feel like home, exactly, but I had hoped that I could stay here until the whole Moriath thing just *blew over.* That I could just ignore the queen, and someone else would deal with her.

Because I had no idea how I could take on a powerful fae queen with my sword skills or my pie baking.

"Can we talk about that later?" I flicked the water.

"I'm afraid your Huntsman is right, Niamh." Ulf looked at his brother, who nodded in agreement. "All our wards and dragon neighbors aren't going to be enough now that Moriath's found you."

"We'll always be here for you if you need us," Ulrik added. "Give us a day to think about the best place for you to go next, and we'll meet back here after dinner tomorrow to discuss your options. You might have an easier time learning how to use your magic if you go back to the Unseelie Kingdom."

Ah yes, that magic everyone was so sure I possessed.

"Let's worry about that tomorrow, then," I said. "For now, we should head back to the banquet hall. After all, you were in such a hurry to drag me up here that we haven't had dessert yet."

Kylian stared at me in disbelief. "How can you be thinking about dessert right now?"

"Well, Kylian, not all of us have an unnatural aversion to sweets."

I tried to casually let go of his hand—I hadn't meant to latch onto him like that—but he held mine firmly.

"We just saw you . . ." he started.

"Not breathing," I confirmed.

"Can you not take your safety a little more seriously?" Kylian stepped closer until we were scant inches apart, his face still ashen with fright.

I put my free hand on his chest, feeling his heartbeat hammering beneath my fingers. "You said that the mirror only shows glimpses of *possible* futures."

"Yes, Princess," he whispered. "But—"

"Moriath thought she had killed me when I was little, and you didn't let that happen."

"The coffin," he breathed.

"I know." I patted his chest. "So we change it, you and me. Okay? I'll avoid blue dresses and glass coffins." I thought for a moment. "And Moriath, if I can help it. Although I'm starting to agree that we should do something about her. I really don't like that woman. But do you know what I'm *not* avoiding?"

Kylian reluctantly raised an eyebrow.

"The apple pies I made with Gustav for dessert." I dropped his hand, and this time, he let me go. I tried not to think about how safe I had felt with my hand in his. How I had reached for him when I needed strength. It was just because he was so insistent on protecting me, that was all.

I turned to go. The dwarves had already left with their stacks of dishes, giving us our space.

"I tried a new apple from the cold storage." I kept my tone light as I left the mirror behind. "I have a good feeling about this one."

"Princess . . ." I felt Kylian follow a step behind. "You're . . ."

"Impressive in my dedication to baked goods?" I asked, ducking under the dwarf-height doorway to the throne room.

"Braver than you think," he said softly from behind me.

"I'll be as brave as you like," I called back. "And I'll happily wipe that smug smile off Moriath's evil face. I just won't be your queen."

Chapter 22

Niamh

The day after the bodice incident, I was tripping over my chicks as I attempted to cross my bedroom. They were in an awkward stage of growth, with patches of down and new feathers making my little babies look rather scraggly.

"You can't be hungry already. I just fed you an hour ago." I muttered as I carefully stepped over a surly Pip—now orange with white and black speckles—and narrowly avoided Meringue, the only chick who was still fluffy as she grew into her soft white adult feathers that Silkies were known for.

The little chickens were well fed. Estrid had helped me scrounge more feed from the gem-powered heated enclosure where the dwarves wintered their chickens, but I also caught Kylian feeding them bits of corn and salad from our lunches.

"Hey, I *made* those cookies," I protested as I came out of my bedroom to find Kylian crouched down, feeding Essie bits of soft, cream-cheese-iced gingerbread cookies.

"Are you ready to go down to dinner?" he asked, getting up and brushing the crumbs off his fingers. He didn't even lick the bit of icing off his thumb, instead wiping it clean with a napkin.

Honestly! It was infuriating.

"Are *you* ready for dinner?" I took in his clothes, which were, of course, the same thing he wore every day.

"No one cares what I wear, Princess."

I rolled my eyes. He was probably right, but only because he insisted on lurking in the shadows instead of sitting at the table, no matter how many times the kings tried to convince him that he was a guest, too.

It had been nearly a month now in Nidavellir, and we'd learned that even without guests, every night was a feast night. The kings seemed happy with any excuse to eat and drink the night away.

But now that Moriath knew where I was, this would be one of our last dinners here, so I had decided to wear a strapless dress of purple silk. I didn't care if I was overdressed. It had little embroidered owls flying across the skirt through swirls of crystal. I *had* to wear it. There was just one problem.

"Can you help me?" I turned my back to him. "I found this amazing dress in my mother's trunk, but I can't reach the top buttons. Oh, for a *zipper*."

"Can't you wait for Estrid to get here and help you?"

"Estrid would need a ladder to do these up. Come on, help a girl out." I glanced over my shoulder at him, confused by his reluctance. He looked awfully serious, even for him. "It's only like . . . five buttons. Or maybe thirty. I can't see my back."

"All right, Princess," he relented.

I turned back around, adjusting the bodice as he came up behind me.

"Seventeen." His breath stirred my hair.

"What?" I felt the heat of him at my back as he carefully did up the buttons one at a time.

"Seventeen buttons."

My cheeks suddenly flushed. What was happening to me? This was just Kylian. I had been this close to him every day in our training sessions. So why did I suddenly find it hard to breathe?

He did up the last button, and his rough fingertips brushed the nape of my neck, just under my hair. I shivered, and he froze. I couldn't tell if the sudden wave of longing that swept through me came from me or him. It had to be me, and I tried to shove it down before he noticed.

Then I felt his hand touch my hair, whisper soft, and I stilled, heart pounding. My entire being focused on nothing but that light-as-a-feather touch. If I just turned my head slightly—

A knock at the door made me jump. Between one breath and the next, Kylian was across the room, opening the door for Estrid.

"I'll go ahead and check the banquet room." Kylian was out the door before he finished speaking, never looking back at me.

"I already did and posted extra guards," Estrid called after him. "Is he expecting to find an assassin in the roast potatoes?" She turned to me and her eyes narrowed. "And you're awfully pink tonight. Did I interrupt something?"

"Nothing!" My voice came out higher pitched than I had intended, and she raised her eyebrows. "Um, dinnertime?" I stepped past her onto the walkway.

Kylian was already out of sight. Good. If we didn't talk

about . . . whatever *that* was, we could just pretend nothing had happened. Because nothing *had* happened. He touched my hair. Probably. End of story. Because there was no way I was having thoughts about a fae huntsman who didn't eat my cookies and wanted to make me a queen.

Aunt Chloe would find my sister, and I would go back to the bakery. Simple. There was no room for tall, broody complications.

"More cider!" hollered King Ulrik from the head of the long table heaped with food.

"And ham!" King Ulf held up his tankard. "More ham!"

"In your cup?" Ulrik looked at his brother with horror.

"Of course not. Don't be ridiculous." Ulf slammed down his tankard on the table, and I hid a laugh behind my napkin.

I didn't know how they ate so much. They were half my size, but I had filled up ages ago, and the brothers were once again loading up their plates with meat, fried mushrooms, and potatoes. Nothing green had touched their lips in all the meals we'd shared except the sneaky deep-fried broccoli.

I hoped that Kylian had gotten some food. I couldn't pin down where he was lurking tonight, but I could feel through the bond that he stood close by, like the tug of a thread between us on the edge of my mind.

I rubbed my *ingwaz* rune and tried not to think about our moment earlier. I didn't currently feel anything from him, and I wasn't about to embarrass myself by projecting my own complicated emotions about someone who hadn't even smiled at me more than the occasional smirk during our training sessions. Not even if I had felt his warm breath against my neck when his fingertips had—

I was doing a terrible job of not thinking about it. I needed a distraction, fast. Was it time for dessert yet?

A young dwarf boy in a guard's uniform ran up to King Ulrik and whispered something in his ear.

"What's that?" hollered Ulf through a mouthful of potato.

The messenger ran over and whispered to the second king.

"Oh! Yes! Princess Niamh!" Ulf waved his fork at me.

"Yes?" I asked warily. What could a guard have to do with me?

"There's a present here for you." Ulrik raised his tankard.

"What? From who?"

"It's—" Ulrik began.

"From your subjects, of course," interrupted Ulf, sticking his elbow in his mashed potatoes as he leaned forward.

"Honestly, Ulf." Ulrik held out a napkin, which Ulf didn't notice in his excitement.

I set down my cup. "I don't have subjects."

"That asrai girl. What's her name?" Ulf elbowed his brother, getting potato on Ulrik's arm.

"Kari?" Ulrik wiped his arm and then his brother's elbow with the napkin.

"Cara?" I guessed.

"Cara! That's it." Ulrik pointed the napkin at me. "Her family just arrived from the Unseelie lands."

"Oh! She must be so relieved. I need to meet them later." Before I left for wherever they decided to hide me next.

"Meet them now. They brought you a *gift*." Ulf waved the messenger back over. "Fetch her the gift!"

The messenger whispered something to the king and pointed behind me.

I turned to see Cara standing there with another blue-skinned asrai woman, just as beautiful, with streaks of blue in her long black hair. Behind them, a dozen asrai of all ages gathered into the banquet hall.

"Your Highness." Cara bowed. "This is my mother, Eimear."

Eimear bowed too. "It's an honor to meet you, Princess Niamh." She held out a lacquered wooden box with an intricate pattern of inlaid mother of pearl. "We brought this for you. It's just something small, but . . ."

"Thank you." I knelt by the small woman, and she smiled up at me, opening the box.

Inside, on a bed of velvet, lay the most beautiful comb I had ever seen—the type meant to hold your hair back, not to get rid of tangles. Its teeth were carved from obsidian, and it was topped with frost-tipped roses of ruby and sparkling crystals.

I looked up into the shining eyes of Cara's mother, noticing how slim she looked, how frail. I glanced back at the other asrai people. All of them looked like they needed a good meal.

"I can't accept this." I closed the box. "It must be worth a fortune! You must need the money."

"They'll be well taken care of now that they're here," Estrid murmured to me.

"Please, Your Highness," said Eimear.

It wasn't just the money or the comb. It was the hope in the eyes of these people. Hope I knew I could never live up to. But how could I say that to her—and all her people—in front of the entire banquet hall? Knowing what they'd gone through, telling them that I didn't have any intention of staying to be their queen seemed cruel.

I could always give it to my sister when she was found.

"All right, I accept." I tried to smile. "It's beautiful. Thank you."

"Allow me, Your Highness." Eimear took the comb out and handed the box to Cara.

She motioned for me to lean closer. I felt a spike of alarm from Kylian. For the life of me, I had no idea why. Was he afraid of this tiny lady and her pretty hair accessory?

"Princess, *wait*." I heard Kylian's voice from far away as the woman slid the comb into my hair.

She smiled at me, and I felt a trickle of liquid against my scalp.

"That's strange." I stood and touched my fingers to my hair as the world began to spin and darken around the edges. "So sleepy . . ."

My knees buckled, but I didn't hit the ground before being caught by a pair of strong arms. "Niamh!" I was held tightly against a hard chest. "Stay with me."

The world went dark.

Chapter 23

Kylian

NIAMH'S EYES FLUTTERED CLOSED AND HER BODY went limp, the comb shattering as it fell out of her curls and hit the ground. My heart stopped in my chest.

"Wake up," I commanded desperately.

Her eyelashes fluttered against her pale cheeks, but she didn't open her eyes.

"Call the doctor, quickly!" King Ulrik hollered as he and his brother rushed over to us.

"Guards, restrain that woman! Restrain *all* of them." I pointed at the asrai group, but none of them were trying to run. They simply looked on in terror, and for once, it wasn't fear of me. All their eyes were glued to the limp form in my arms.

A dwarf with a long, braided black beard ran up beside me and felt for Niamh's pulse.

"Weak but steady." The dwarf held out a hand. "I need a wet cloth."

Estrid dunked a napkin in a pitcher of water and handed him the dripping cloth.

"Good, thank you." The doctor wiped the poison out of Niamh's hair and examined the sticky blue liquid on her fingertips before cleaning them as well. "Beithir venom," he pronounced. "Use care when you clean that up," he added to Estrid, who nodded and used another napkin to cover the broken comb, still leaking blue venom onto the stone floor.

My heart nearly gave out again. The venom of the cave-dwelling wyverns was deadly, often used on daggers or arrows to ensure the target died quickly.

The vision from the mirror flashed through my mind again. Niamh, not breathing as she lay in a glass coffin. Would it come true after all?

The kings crowded close. "Will she live?" Ulf asked, wringing his hands.

The doctor didn't answer immediately, and I lost the ability to breathe as he checked Niamh's scalp. Then he leaned back and nodded. "She'll live. The comb didn't pierce her skin. She'll sleep until the venom clears out of her system, but the princess will make a full recovery."

I nearly collapsed with relief. Not for myself. Not from the fear of losing this stubborn girl in my arms. I only worried for the kingdom.

To right all the wrongs I had done, to make it all worthwhile, I had to see her on the throne. Then she would marry some suitable Unseelie boy who didn't make the subjects cower in fright whenever he looked at them. Like the asrai fae who were shrinking away from me right now.

It couldn't be for myself.

"I would never hurt the princess." The asrai woman fell to her knees as the dwarven guards closed in. Her daughter put an arm around her. "Please believe me." Eimear looked up with tears in her eyes. "I would never harm Queen Oonagh's child."

"*Perthro*," I murmured, and the truth rune activated on my arm. I grasped the woman's delicate hand. "Where did you get the comb?" I ground out.

"We met a peddler woman on the road to the mountain. She had many beautiful things, but this comb was all we could afford. She agreed to take fresh fish in payment. I should have known it was too good a deal to be true." Eimear hung her head.

My rune didn't change as she spoke. She told the truth.

"What did she look like? The peddler?" asked Ulrik kindly.

"An old Tuatha Dé Danann crone," said the woman. "She traveled with two large black dogs. For protection on the road, she said."

"Moriath." I gripped Niamh tighter.

The woman shook her head. "She looked too old to be the queen. And they were dogs, not wolves."

"Moriath is adept at disguising herself," said Ulf, and his brother nodded.

The queen did enjoy her glamours. I had seen her take on many forms during my time serving her. The kings asked the woman a few more questions, but it was clear that she didn't know anything more. I turned away, focusing on the princess in my arms. I could see now that she breathed shallowly, her dark lashes twitching as if she were dreaming.

"Cara, take them to the asrai quarters," said Estrid. "We'll keep an eye on them, Kylian," the dwarf girl promised me.

I nodded without looking up. "She can't stay here. Dragons and stone aren't enough to keep Moriath from reaching her. But how can we hide from someone who can scry even into the future?"

Ulrik placed a hand on my arm, and it took all my willpower not to flinch away. "We know a place where no one will be able to find her."

I stood. Niamh stirred in my arms, but she didn't wake.

"Don't say any more." I had relaxed my guard too much. If I were to hide Niamh, no one could know where. "Not here. Show me."

The kings were more somber than I'd ever seen them as they silently led me to their private study behind the throne room. Estrid followed behind and locked the door while Ulf hurriedly moved a stool and a teapot out of the way. Ulrik pulled aside the tapestry behind the mirror, revealing an arched doorway of gems—a smaller version of the Topaz Gate.

"This is our private gate." Ulrik put his hand on a large purple crystal. A ring on his finger flashed, then all the gems on the gate began to glow. "We'll tell everyone that Niamh is recovering in her rooms and that you're guarding her. The tale won't last for long, but it should help muddy the waters."

"While I take her where?" I shifted Niamh in my arms. I hated relying on others, but I had nowhere to hide her where Moriath wouldn't find us.

Ulf dug through a desk drawer. "We could never repay Niamh's parents for how they saved our people, but we did want them to know how grateful we were. They worked tirelessly as rulers, and we thought they could use a place to get away from it all. A secret hideaway, if you will."

"I didn't know anything about this," said Estrid from behind us. "I'm impressed, honestly."

Ulf looked up, offended. "We can keep a secret if we need to. Now, where is that key . . .?"

Ulrik turned back to me. "There's a cottage tucked into a hidden valley west of here. Oonagh and Fionnbharr left the only keys here. They would come on a 'diplomatic visit' and sneak off through this gate to enjoy some peace and quiet." The king gave his brother a pained look. "I should never have trusted you to keep the keys. You've lost them. I know it."

"I have not!" Ulf dumped a drawer on the floor. Paper, rocks, and a fork fell out. "I just haven't seen them in a hundred years or so. Aha!" The dwarf opened a small box that had been sitting on his desk the entire time and pulled out three amulets made of frosted ice, each with a golden leaf in its center. "Found them," he said smugly, dangling the amulets from their leather cords.

"No one knows where this cabin is?" I accepted the amulets from Ulf.

He shook his head. "The king and queen took their own supplies and didn't bring any staff. We set up a spell to keep everything free from dust and decay so they could visit anytime, no matter how long they had been gone, and feel at home. The cabin is warded against scrying, and the gate itself is a twenty-minute walk from the cottage. It was the perfect retreat."

I nodded. "Good. I'll get Niamh settled and then return for food." Though I hated to let her out of my sight.

Ulrik made a face. "You shouldn't have to do this on your own. Can't we offer an armed guard? We can handpick a dozen soldiers to go with you."

I shook my head. "Too risky. I don't want anyone else knowing where we are."

"I'll go." Estrid joined the kings by the gate.

"But who will keep your father from cheating at *Ljósálfar á móti Tröllum*?" protested Ulrik.

"You need someone to help you." Estrid flicked her gaze from Niamh to me, then rested her hand on the dagger at her hip. "Otherwise, who will guard her when you need to get food? You can trust me, Kylian," she added softly.

As much as it pained me to admit that I couldn't take care of Niamh on my own, the dwarven warrior was right. And I did trust her.

I nodded and held out an amulet for her to take, bracing Niamh in my arms. "Come when you've gathered some food."

"We're sorry we couldn't do more to keep the princess safe." Ulf reached up to pat Niamh's limp hand.

"If there's anything more we can do to help, send Estrid," added Ulrik.

"I will." I inclined my head to the two kings and carried Niamh to the gate. "And, Estrid?"

"Yes?"

"Don't forget to bring the chickens."

PART
3

Chapter 24

Niamh

I had the strangest dreams. Sometimes wolves chased me through frozen forests until I changed into an owl and flew away. Sometimes my mother and father teased me about always having flour and cinnamon on my nose, but the bakery grew mushrooms from the ceiling.

Sometimes I thought I woke to large calloused hands gently stroking my hair or putting a cold cloth on my burning forehead, to a low voice imploring me to *please get better, please wake up,* but my eyes always drifted shut again. I was just so tired.

"Who are you?"

I jolted awake at the sound of the girl's voice. But no, I couldn't be awake. The garden I stood in had a dreamy quality. Huge rose bushes climbed on stone walls, pale pink blooms peeking out from sharp black thorns as long as my hand.

"How did you get here?" the voice insisted.

I spun around to see a tall brown-skinned girl in a gold-embroidered pink dress standing in front of me.

"I must be dreaming," I said.

"Obviously." The girl flipped her shining black hair over her shoulder. "But how did you get into *my* dream?"

"I think I was poisoned?"

"Interesting." The girl paced as she examined me with her gold-flecked brown eyes, her full silk skirts swishing as she walked. "But who are you?"

Who was I? I struggled to remember my name. "I'm the Unseelie princess." I was pretty sure that was true.

The girl tilted her head. "I could say the same thing," she said. "Not very helpful."

"Oh! I'm *Niamh*." Memories rushed back at me. "Who are you? Did Moriath poison you, too?"

The girl tilted her head. "I don't think so."

"Niamh!" another voice called.

"Kylian?" I looked around, but I didn't see him.

The garden began to fade around me, pale rose petals blowing around us, curling vines disappearing into puffs of smoke.

"Wait!" the girl cried, reaching out her hand. "Don't leave!"

I reached out, my fingers brushing hers just before whatever wind had brought me there blew me away again.

I slowly opened my eyes, for real this time. The sunshine slanting through a diamond-paned window told me I wasn't in my dwarven bedroom in the mountains. The wall with the large window was made of stone, and the other three had been papered in wide, pale, mint-green stripes. The planks on the ceiling and floor were painted a bright white, and the furniture was a warm, golden wood.

I tried to sit up and failed, pinned down by a weight on top of me. *What?*

I looked down and saw a dark brown arm, covered in black tattoos, wrapped around my waist. I wasn't alone in the bed. I was tucked up against a warm body.

Alarmed, I yelped. Kylian jerked awake and fell off the side of the bed, tangled in the quilt.

I bolted up as Kylian scrambled to his feet.

"You're awake."

"What happened?" I felt my cheeks heat. "And, um, why were we cuddling just now?"

"You were burning up, and then you couldn't stop shaking. I needed to warm you up."

Well, that explained it. Nothing but duty would have made Kylian a snuggler. The king of personal space had never reached out and touched me of his own accord. Except for that moment in our rooms before the feast, but I was almost convinced I had imagined it.

"The feast with the dwarves," I remembered. "Cara's mother put that comb in my hair."

"Poisoned," said Kylian grimly. "Not by her. Moriath. Here, you need to rest." He added another pillow behind me.

I touched my head gingerly, but it felt normal. "How long was I asleep? I dreamt that I met someone. Something about roses?" I shook my head, the dream already fading.

"You slept for nine days, ten hours, and thirty-six minutes."

"But who's counting?" I gave him an amused look. The Huntsman must have really been worried about losing his precious future queen.

He ignored my comment and tucked the quilt back around me.

"The chicks!" I threw back the quilt and swung my legs over the side of the bed.

"Lie back down. The chicks are fine. They're outside."

"In the *snow?*" I tried to stand, but my legs crumpled under me.

Kylian was there before I could hit the ground, one arm under my knees, the other at my back. "You need to rest, Princess. You can't just wake up and start running around."

"She's awake!" Estrid's head popped inside the door. "That was a long nap."

Kylian grunted and put me back on the bed, tucking the quilt firmly around my legs.

Estrid jerked her chin at Kylian. "This one, here, was going out of his mind with worry."

Kylian frowned at the dwarf. "She nearly died."

"That's true," Estrid allowed, climbing up to sit on the foot of the bed.

"What is this place? How did I get here?" I asked, looking around the snug room. I plucked at my nightgown's sleeve of soft lace. "And where did this come from?"

Estrid stretched out her arms. "This was your parents' secret romantic getaway cabin. Your mother had more clothes packed in a trunk here."

"Oh." I made a face.

"You don't like it?" Estrid asked.

"It'll be fun to see more of her things." I leaned back against the pillows. "But so far, nothing has helped me remember her, and I miss my own clothes. I spent a lot of time tracking down vintage dresses in my size, and I guess I just miss feeling like myself, you know? But the cottage seems cute."

"You'll be safe here." Kylian covered my legs with another quilt. Was he trying to restrain me? "We have the only keys to the closest gate, and it's a twenty-minute hike from the cabin."

"Which is a long way to carry seven chicks, by the way," added Estrid. "They don't fit in your backpack anymore."

"Thank you for bringing them!"

"Of course," said my friend. "We didn't want you to worry. I know how you are about those chickens."

"Can I see them?" I pleaded.

"Can you walk?" asked Estrid. "Because you don't look like you can walk."

"Maybe?" I said. "I might have regained my strength in the past five minutes."

Kylian sighed and left the room. A minute later, he returned with his boots on and scooped me up, quilt and all.

"Hey, I'm not a toddler," I protested.

"Do you want to see your chickens?" Kylian adjusted me in his arms.

"Yes," I said meekly. I leaned my head against his shoulder, too tired to pretend that I wasn't soaking in the feeling of his arms around me.

"Then let's go see them."

"I'll find some lunch." Estrid exited the bedroom. "And yes," she called back, "making sandwiches *is* now one of my duties."

Kylian carried me through the coziest cottage I had ever seen. It looked like something straight out of a fairytale with pink floral wallpaper, brass chandeliers, and flower-shaped wall sconces that lit automatically as we walked past. Paintings in gilt frames lined the walls of the hallway.

"Wait." I craned my neck. "Is that my parents?"

Kylian stopped in front of a portrait of a man with curly red hair, a matching beard, and blue eyes. Beside him, with her hand on his arm, stood a woman with long black hair, gray eyes, and rosy cheeks. She was soft and curvy, just like me, with a round face and full red lips tilted up in a smile. They each held an owl perched on their free hands, his large and white, hers little and gray.

I reached out and touched their faces, then leaned back against Kylian as my eyes welled with tears.

"I'm sorry," I sniffled. "I'm just so tired."

"Don't be sorry." Kylian's voice rumbled in his chest. "I never saw a portrait of your mother. Moriath had them all removed. You look just like her."

"She was beautiful." I blinked back tears.

"Exact—" Kylian cut himself off and carried me farther down the hall. "Look at these."

Had he just called me beautiful? Before I could follow that train of thought, I saw the matching pair of gilt oval frames, each with the painting of a small child. A little girl with dark curly hair and an even younger girl with wavy red hair.

"I really *was* here, wasn't I?" I whispered. "In Faerie."

"You still doubt it?" Kylian carried me through an airy main room with green-painted cupboards along one wall, framing a fridge and a sink. A large red pot sat on a stove of dwarvish design.

A wooden table and chairs with a stained-glass pendant light overhead divided the kitchen side of the large room from a sitting area on the opposite wall. Two cozy armchairs and a velvet upholstered sofa sat on a braided rug, flanked by a large bookcase and end tables topped by lamps with silk shades. A stone fireplace with a crackling fire took up the corner.

"I believed it in my head, but seeing those paintings makes it seem *real*." I scrubbed my eyes, trying to regain my composure.

I wished my human parents could be here. Dad would love the tidy kitchen and gem-powered appliances, and Mom would swoon over the lamps and wallpaper. And me? I could really use a hug from them. A reminder of who I was.

Kylian continued through to a coat room, then stopped at a mint green door topped with a stained-glass half circle featuring apples and leaves. He braced me against his chest with one strong arm while opening the door to a path neatly shoveled through waist-high drifts of snow that sparkled in the sun.

The snowy path led to the most beautiful greenhouse I had ever seen. The green-tinted glass shone in the sunlight, the vaulted copper frame rising higher than the roof of the cottage. A weathervane with a bright copper owl sat atop its pitched roof.

"We didn't want to keep them in the house," Kylian explained as he carried me down the snowy path. "We had enough to worry about with taking care of you. I wasn't going to clean up after chickens at the same time."

"I wonder if I should make them diapers?" I snuggled against Kylian for warmth as a gust of wind sent snow scattering around us.

"I'm not changing chicken diapers." Kylian opened the greenhouse door, and I could immediately see that I had nothing to worry about.

The greenhouse was a chicken paradise. The space looked huge, with a floor overgrown by grass and moss. Raised beds full of tangled flowers and herbs surrounded the indoor meadow. The air felt more pleasant than I would have expected in the winter, even inside with the sun shining through the glass. There must have been dwarven spellcrafting involved to keep the place running all this time.

The chicks, bigger now, scratched happily in overgrown garden beds. As soon as Kylian stepped inside, they perked up and came scurrying over.

"Just a minute, you little vultures." Kylian kicked the door shut behind us.

I smothered a laugh at his grumpy tone, then gaped as he carried me to the center of the greenhouse. A beautiful tree dominated the space, its curving branches reaching out and up toward the vaulted roof and spreading to fill the top of the glass structure. Pale pink flowers bloomed among the leaves, but beautiful, perfectly ripe, glossy red apples also hung heavily from its branches. Magic. The scent of apples filled the air, dancing at the edge of my memory.

Kylian set me down on a grassy spot between the tree roots, my back against the mossy trunk. It was surprising how forlorn that made me feel. I had no business enjoying being in his arms that much. He tucked the quilt around my legs as the chickens climbed over his feet.

"The apples!" I reached my hand up, and Kylian plucked a fruit from a low branch.

"I know. The chickens won't stop eating them off the ground." He handed me the apple and then picked Latte up, dropping the silver hen into my lap before stalking off to a corner of the greenhouse. He muttered to the chicks darting around him, "And that's how I know you ungrateful creatures aren't actually starving. It's only been three hours since you were fed." He sighed. "Yes, yes, come and get a snack."

I took a bite and juicy sweetness, balanced with just the right amount of tart, filled my mouth. I closed my eyes, and as I chewed, a memory emerged from the depths of my brain.

"No more sneaking apple slices." My mother bopped me on the nose with a flour-covered finger.

"But I'm so hungry!" My little fingers—still chubby enough to end in dimples on the back of my hand—reached for another slice of fruit.

We were baking in the green kitchen of the cottage. I loved it when we came here and it was just the four of us. Just our family together.

"Well, you certainly worked up an appetite chasing your father all morning and climbing the apple tree, but if you eat any more, I won't

have enough left for the pie." Mama's glossy black hair shimmered in the sunlight from the window as she shook her head at me. "No more slices. Grab a whole apple."

"But these are yummier," I said, my mouth full of apple, "because you already put love into them!"

"Niamh, are you all right?"

The memory drifted away. I wiped the tears from my face with my free hand as Kylian sat down next to me. Essie immediately crouched on his knee while Clem and Snickerdoodle curled up against me.

"I'm fine." I smoothed Latte's soft silver feathers for comfort. "I just . . . Since that brief memory of my sister, I haven't been able to remember anything else from before you took me to the Klassens."

Kylian nodded. "That was part of the protection spell Clíodhna put on you. It might be fading now with the glamour. Did you remember something?"

"My mother."

"These are her apples?" Kylian snagged a fruit from the ground, and Essie pecked a bite.

"Yep, I finally found them." I examined the fruit. The flavor reminded me of a Honeycrisp but lighter and brighter. The apples were on the small side, with pink speckling the bright red.

"You're in no condition to bake a pie right now."

"I know." He was right, but my whole being itched to bake my mother's pie. Would I remember more if I did? A tear rolled down my cheek. "I'm just so tired."

"Right, so we'll go back inside." Kylian removed Essie from his knee with a pat on the black chicken's head then scooped me back into his arms, carefully rearranging the quilt to keep me warm for the walk back. "And you're going to lie down to rest."

I nodded, more tears welling up.

"On the sofa," he continued, "while you tell me how to bake this apple pie."

"Really?" I sniffled. "But you don't even eat sweets."

"Be that as it may, Princess, I'm yours to command. Don't you have some sort of recipe in that notebook you're always scribbling in? I put it on the desk in your room."

"Yes." I wiped my cheeks as he carried me to the greenhouse door.

"Then that's what we'll do." He nodded, then looked down at the chicks following underfoot. "And you will all behave, or you won't get any treats with your breakfast tomorrow."

Chapter 25

Niamh

"You certainly seem to know your way around this kitchen," I remarked from my pillow-heaped sofa, apple in hand, quilts once again tucked around my legs. I felt like a tattooed burrito.

Kylian raised an eyebrow at me as he grabbed a glass mixing bowl and wooden spoon from one of the lower cupboards in the cozy little kitchen.

"Who do you think has been keeping us fed this past week?" Estrid leaned against a smaller version of the steam-powered stoves I had seen at Nidavellir. "You've seen my kitchen skills. I only assemble sandwiches and salads."

"I assumed you ate, like, raw apples and chunks of meat or something like that." I took a bite of my apple.

Estrid nodded at Kylian, who continued arranging flour, sugar, and butter on the table. "*This one* can make a mean omelet, and he kept that mushroom broth simmering on the stove day and night to keep you alive. Which he fed you in little sips."

"You should have some before you eat any pie." Kylian filled a yellow ceramic mug with broth from the red pot on the back burner of the stove. "The dwarven doctor gave me a recipe," added Kylian, setting the mug on the end table beside me. "Don't worry, it didn't have meat in it."

I just stared at him with my mouth open, stunned by the care he had taken to nurse me while I'd slept.

"You'll drink that when you're finished with your apple." Kylian pointedly looked at me.

"Yes, *sir*," I said brightly. I waved my hand at the table covered in baking ingredients. "But you can't tell me this cabin had a fully stocked kitchen when we arrived." I continued munching my apple.

"*I* carried it all over from Nidavellir when I went to restock yesterday. Kylian would *not* leave you alone until you woke up." Estrid rolled her eyes. "He told me to grab baking supplies."

"Why?" I finished up my apple, and Kylian plucked the core from my hand and tossed it in a bowl on the table before passing me the mug of broth.

"It's my job to take care of you. And you need to bake to feel better. What's the first step?" Kylian opened my notebook and held it out.

I stared at the big man, his brows furrowed as he looked down at me, and my eyes welled up with tears again.

Kylian leaned down and tapped the notebook. "Focus. What do I do first? Something with cinnamon?"

"You could read my notes if that's easier." I took a sip of the warm, savory broth.

"No, it is not, Princess. Have you seen your handwriting?"

"Hey!" I looked over at the scrawl of writing on the page. Many of the lines were crossed out with arrows pointing to other sections where I had written more notes, everything covered in a thin smear of butter and cinnamon. "Okay, you might have a point. To be honest, I don't look at my notes very often anymore. I just like to be able to remember what I've tried before. I can tell you what to do?"

Kylian nodded and shut the notebook before placing it on the end table.

"I will peel the apples," announced Estrid. "I am now an expert apple peeler."

The dwarf grabbed a fruit from the bowl on the table and unsheathed a dagger at her hip.

"Are we worried about the apples attacking?" I asked.

"Better to be safe than sorry." Estrid began removing a long spiral of peel, cursing under her breath when it broke before she finished.

"And the pastry?" asked Kylian, who was tying up his locs in a neat ponytail.

"Are you sure you don't need an apron?" I smiled to myself, imagining the deadly Huntsman in something frilly and pink over his practical black attire.

"These clothes repel dirt, sweat, and—"

"Flour?" Estrid set down her dagger and reached into the flour tin.

Kylian didn't look at her as the flour hit him and slid to the ground. Not a speck of flour stuck to his shirt, but a white dusting graced his left cheek. "You're sweeping that up. How much flour, Princess?"

"Two and a half cups. A teaspoon of baking powder and a pinch of salt. Then cut the butter into really small pieces and mix it into the flour."

"Why don't you just *melt* the butter? Wouldn't that be easier?" asked Estrid as Kylian chopped the butter into much smaller pieces than I ever had the patience for. Estrid threw another broken peel spiral onto the table. "So close!"

"You want tiny pockets of butter in the pastry. They melt in the oven and make the crust flaky instead of chewy," I explained. "And, Estrid, are you sure you don't want a paring knife?"

"I laugh at your tiny paring knives." She unsheathed an even larger dagger from her belt and continued peeling. "Who knows when they were last sharpened?"

Once Kylian had cut the butter into the flour—my mother had left a fully equipped kitchen, pastry cutter and all—it was time to add liquids.

"Do we have any vinegar?" I asked before drinking more broth.

"Nope." Estrid looked up from her peeling. "Why would we need vinegar?"

"It's just a trick to keep the pastry tender, but that's fine. We can skip it. Crack an egg into the cup," I directed Kylian, "and then fill it halfway up with cold water."

"How cold?" asked Kylian, eyeing the kettle on the stove.

"Very. It helps with the butter-pocket situation. You can add some snow to the cup if the water isn't cold."

Kylian nodded and wandered out in search of snow while I finished drinking my broth.

"Success!" Estrid crowed, holding up a long spiral of apple peel. "Paring knives," she scoffed. "Is this not the most beautifully peeled apple you ever saw?"

"It's gorgeous," I told her. "Stunning. Peel three more and slice them. Then toss them into a bowl with the sugar and cinnamon."

Kylian returned with a cupful of snow and Meringue, whom he deposited on my lap before taking my empty mug.

"I thought you didn't want to clean up after chickens?" I stroked the fluffy white chick, who sighed and promptly fell asleep on me.

"You looked like you needed one." Kylian washed his hands and continued making the dough.

I gave a happy little sigh and closed my eyes to rest for a moment. It was just so peaceful with Meringue sleeping on my lap, the fire crackling in the hearth, and Kylian and Estrid bickering about the proper width of apple slices. I drifted off to sleep in a place I'd never seen before this morning, in a land far from anything I had ever known, with people I'd only met a month ago . . .

And wondered when it had all begun to feel so very much like home.

I woke to the smell of my childhood.

"*You* are going back to the greenhouse," said a rumbling voice.

I opened my eyes to find Kylian wiping the floor with a rag in one hand and Meringue tucked under his other arm.

"But . . . fluffy baby!" I reached out my arms.

"You're awake. Good. I'll get you another one." He held the Silkie up to eye level, and she cheeped happily. He raised an eyebrow at it. "This one needs to run around."

Kylian disappeared out the back door and returned a moment later with a disgruntled-looking Pip. Using his free hand, Kylian helped me scoot back to sitting, plumping the pillows before handing over the orange chick with black speckles.

"Are you hungry?" He washed his hands in the kitchen sink and then pulled out a plate from the cupboard.

My stomach growled loudly.

"All right, then." He cut me a large wedge of steaming pie and handed it over before sitting in the armchair by the fireplace.

I paused with my first bite halfway to my mouth. "Aren't you gonna have a piece? You made it, after all."

Kylian gave a short shake of his head.

I rolled my eyes and took a bite.

If the raw apple had brought me to tears, the taste of the finished pie enveloped me like a warm hug. I sat there, eyes closed, the perfectly balanced flavors of butter, cinnamon, and apple filling my senses.

"Did we do a good job?" asked Kylian.

"You *have* to try this," I moaned.

"No."

"But you did such a good job on the crust!" I broke off a little piece and fed it to Pip before taking another bite. "It's honestly even flakier than mine. I never have the patience to get the butter chunks that small. Just have a bite." I held up a forkful.

"No," he said again. But his eyes tracked the bite as I put it in my mouth.

"Oh, come on." I waved a hand at him. "One bite won't ruin your—admittedly impressive—physique."

"I know." Kylian shifted in his seat.

"Just take a bite."

"No." Now there was an edge to his voice.

"Are you allergic to sugar or something?"

"I am not."

"Then why won't you just try it?" My voice rose. "I know

it's just pie, and it's stupid, but this is really important to me. I don't want to sit here and eat it by myself."

Kylian gripped the armrests of his chair, his knuckles paling. "You're right. You shouldn't eat this alone."

I perked up.

"*Estrid*," he called. "Come in here and try a piece of pie."

I shot daggers at him with my eyes.

"You could not pay me a million diamond chips to go into that room right now!" yelled Estrid from the other end of the cabin. "I'll have some later. When it's safe, thanks."

I glared at Kylian.

He glared back.

Something broke in my chest, and all my anger shifted into hurt. I knew it was irrational, but I suddenly felt so alone.

"I don't understand!" My eyes welled with tears. "This little pie represents years of testing and research. It represents the childhood that I lost. My mother, who was taken from me. And you're rejecting it. Why won't you take a bite? Why won't you share this moment with me?" I was crying now.

Kylian closed his eyes. "I don't deserve it," he said quietly. "Not anymore."

"Then neither do I." I poked my pie with the fork. "All I've done is hide and get poisoned. I just make things harder for you."

Kylian surged to his feet. "You deserve *everything*. You deserve a kingdom. Friendship." He pointed in the direction where Estrid was hiding. "You deserve a family and every happiness, and I will do everything in my power to give it to you. *You* . . ." He pointed a finger at my plate. "You deserve apple pie."

"But you don't?" I looked up at him.

"No," he bit out. "Not anymore. Not after everything I've done. Don't look at me like that, Princess."

My heart clenched. *Princess* had been starting to feel like an endearment, but he held it between us like a shield. Like a reminder not to get too close. But it was too late for that, I realized suddenly. At least for me. I had been trying to ignore them—these feelings for someone who would only tie me to a kingdom I had never asked for—but I didn't have the strength to keep pushing them down.

I knew he could probably feel all of that through the bond, but I didn't care. Not when I looked him in the eyes and felt the pain echoing from him. I hadn't imagined the heat he'd tried to hide when he looked at me, or the touch of his fingers against my hair. Something had been growing between us, and we were both too raw in this moment to lie about it.

But that honesty hurt all the more when he tore his gaze away, clenching his jaw.

"Save your tears, Princess. Save your sunshine and your warmth and your apple pie. Save them for someone who deserves you."

"I think you do." I wiped my cheek. Suddenly, it was like I could see twelve-year-old Kylian standing in front of me. The boy he had been when we'd first met. Lanky and tall, his hair a mop of black curls, his eyes containing a sparkle that this current version was doing his best to stamp out.

I blinked, and the vision disappeared. Adult Kylian looked back at me, his face blank as he turned to leave. "That's what you think now, but it's my job to protect you, Princess."

"Even from you?"

"Especially from me."

Chapter 26

Niamh

KYLIAN DISAPPEARED FOR HOURS AFTER OUR ARGUment, leaving me in Estrid's care. When he got back, I didn't try to make him eat pie again, and we both pretended the conversation had never happened. But the tension between us persisted.

The next morning, I opened the wardrobe in my cottage bedroom expecting to find my mother's clothes that I had been wearing since arriving in Faerie. Instead it was filled with my own vintage dress collection from home. All my knee-length floral and polka-dotted dresses crowded the practical training clothes and one or two fancy gowns from Nidavellir.

Kylian had gone to my home and gotten my things for me, risking whatever wolves Moriath still had watching the area, just so I could feel more like myself again. And yet, he was still convinced that he was the villain.

I sat on the floor by my dresses and cried, alarming my caretakers, who forced me back into bed for the rest of the morning.

While I regained my strength, Estrid tried to lighten things up with dagger-throwing tournaments in the greenhouse—Kylian kept the chickens shielded—and Estrid always won. She also read aloud to me with dramatic flair from books in the sitting room.

I got the occasional message from Audrey when I powered up my phone to quickly check it without using too much battery. She was back at Liadan's with Gavin, trying to figure out a teleportation device like the one Dylan had used, but was frustrated with her lack of progress. Apparently, teleportation without blood magic wasn't working, although I had no idea why. The more Audrey explained, the less I understood.

She wasn't telling me everything they were up to, though. I could feel it, and I felt more than a little hurt that, even now, she still kept secrets from me.

Amber texted me, too. They still hadn't found anyone who knew where Maeve was, even with my short vision of her. Aunt Chloe planned to take Amber to Rahivea next to update the Seelie king and queen on my situation. She said that Moriath hadn't made any friends with the Seelie Kingdom, so they would be good allies for us.

I knew a conflict with Moriath was inevitable, but I felt less equipped than ever to deal with it. And if we defeated her, what then?

Everyone seemed to be busy but me. Yes, I was recovering, but then what? My whole mission was to stay alive, and honestly, I had nearly failed at that twice now. The thought of being queen terrified me, but I wanted to do *something*. The refugees in Nidavellir were never far from my mind.

I felt strong enough after a few days to become restless, so after examining all the paintings in the cottage, I wandered into the sitting room to find Kylian reading in his favorite armchair.

"*Daggers and Doughnuts,* the sixth *Phouka Knitting Club* mystery," I read aloud. "Have you read books one through five?" I picked up an afghan from the sofa and wrapped it around my shoulders. The cute pink floral dress I had chosen for today was not really a winter dress, but it had made me smile.

"I have." He didn't look up from the book in his hands.

"Huh. I thought you'd be into something a little more . . ."

"Yes?"

"Huntsman-y."

"That's not a word." Kylian flipped a page.

"I'm sure it's a genre. Like *How to Hunt Wolf Boys Across Realms*, or *Axe Throwing for Beginners*." I peered at the cover. "And now I want doughnuts. I should make some. Do we have any oil?"

"Put it on the list in the kitchen. Also, I already know how to hunt wolf boys across realms, and my axe throwing is expert, thank you very much. What I *don't* know is who murdered the piskie innkeeper's cantankerous old aunt, so if you don't mind . . ." He flipped another page.

"Are they good? Should I read them? Where's book one?" I wandered over and inspected the bookcase under the sitting room window. "I don't see it."

Kylian closed his book with an exasperated sigh, his finger marking his spot. "The shelf is connected to the Royal Seelie Library system."

"I thought we were Unseelie." I scanned the variety of titles.

"The Unseelie don't have a system like this. Or many systems at all, really. The Seelie like to come up with all sorts of nonsense, but this one is . . ." Kylian searched for a description. "Nice," he finally said. He leaned over and tapped a shelf. "There is a selection of different genres here, and if you take a book, a new one in the same genre will appear on the shelf in its place."

I peered in and found *Baking with Cockatrice Eggs.* I pulled it out, but a quick scan told me it was not going to be of any help to me as I did not have a cockatrice. When I looked back to the shelf, I saw that Kylian was right. The spot where the book had been sitting now held *Soup for Piskies: How to Cook in Thimbles, Acorn Cups, and More.*

"How do they know what you like? Is it just random?"

"If you put the book back on the shelf with the spine facing in, they'll send you something completely different. If you put it back spine out, they will pick the next book in the series or, if there isn't one, a similar book that they think you'll like. You can also leave a note in a book if you're looking for something specific."

"There's actually someone picking out the books?"

"Of course. The Royal Seelie librarians."

"Huh." I flipped open the piskie soup book to find beautiful illustrations of tiny winged people making soup. "You know a lot about this."

"There's a library bookcase at Skyretaine. I moved it to my room when—" He paused. "I didn't think it was something Moriath should have access to. I don't read a lot of nonfiction." He picked up his book again. "And I like to read when I have the chance. When it's *quiet,*" he pointedly added.

"Okay, okay. Guess all I needed to do to see the *Big, Scary Huntsman* was to interrupt his reading." I slid the cockatrice cookbook back on the shelf spine out, hoping for another baking book, and it vanished. A moment later, the shelf rewarded me with *Favorite Cookies of the Fourteenth Seelie Queen and Her Pet Dragon.* Promising. I opened the book to see if the Seelie queen had good taste in cookies. There'd better not be any raisin-chocolate-chip combos in there.

On the first page, I was surprised to see a painted illustration of Amber's friend Ella—who had graduated a year ahead of me from Pilot Bay High—with a Japanese dragon the size of a lapdog. Come to think of it, Amber *had* said something about her best friend being the Seelie queen.

"So that's why I haven't seen her at the café for months."

"Shh," said Kylian.

"You won't even know I'm here," I whispered, turning the page. Oh, those ginger cookies looked pretty good. "Kylian? You didn't happen to bring any molasses, did you?"

"Put it on the list." Kylian didn't look up.

"Okay, okay." I ran over and scrawled *molasses* under Kylian's neat list of food items.

Sitting down at the table with my book, I flipped through a few more recipes. "What about semi-sweet chocolate chips?"

Kylian shut his book with a sigh. "I'm never going to find out who killed the aunt, am I?"

"I'm sorry." I squirmed in my seat. "I just spent the last two weeks mostly in bed, and I'm bored."

He narrowed his eyes at me. "I can give you something to do."

"You're not going to tell me to clean my room or something, are you?" I asked suspiciously.

"If you're well enough to be bored, then you're well enough to get back to training."

"Yes! *Perfect.* I'll go change." I shot to my feet, dropping my afghan shawl in a heap.

"Don't rush," Kylian said as I left the room. "I still have five pages left in this chapter."

I met Kylian in the greenhouse once I had changed into my leather pants and tank top, and he had finished reading his chapter. He had cleared the tall weeds and overgrown potted plants in front of the apple tree to make space for a grassy sparring ring.

Snowdrifts piled against the green glass outside, but it felt as warm as a spring day inside.

"What's it gonna be?" I bounced on my toes. "Swords? Knives? Swords and knives? Expert axe throwing?"

Kylian crossed his big tattooed arms. "Can you even lift that axe?" He nodded at his ever-present weapon leaning beside the greenhouse door. "Pick it up and we'll see if you can throw it."

I eyed the weapon dubiously. "I need more pie before I can do that."

Kylian raised an eyebrow.

"For *strength*, obviously. *Plus twenty stamina*, as Audrey would say."

I rolled my shoulders, loosening up, and noted how his dark eyes tracked the movement. Excellent. He might have been trying to stay away from me for some form of self-loathing practicality, but I hadn't agreed to his plan. I stretched my arms up overhead and to the side, knowing that it caused my shirt to ride up from the waistband of my leather pants.

His eyes narrowed.

"Just stretching." I smiled innocently. "I wouldn't want to pull something."

Should I touch my toes? Too much? I stepped back into a lunge and nearly fell over when my back foot connected with a small orange, speckled chicken, who clucked in annoyance. "Jeepers!" I flailed for balance. "Sorry, Pip."

"Focus, Princess," Kylian said. "I know it's difficult for you."

I made a face at him.

"You need to get your strength back, so we'll stick with hand-to-hand today."

"Perfect." I winked at him.

He ignored it.

"Come at me." Kylian widened his stance. "Left hook, right elbow, left leg sweep."

"Left, right, left. Got it." After checking to make sure no chickens were underfoot—they'd all gone back to happily munching the grain mix Kylian had been spreading out for them when I'd arrived—I threw my left fist at the mountain of a man.

"Don't hold back," he said, "or you won't be able to use your full force when you need to."

I quickly slammed my elbow up, using all the force of my rotation. Kylian, of course, expertly blocked—his arm so hard that it almost made me wince—but I used my momentum, as he'd taught me, to spin and hook my leg behind his knees.

I knew he was letting me take him down. I could never overpower someone of his size and skill without the element of surprise firmly on my side. But it still felt good to hit the ground with my knee on his chest and my arm across his throat.

"Good," he breathed.

"How good?" I quirked an eyebrow and caught an answering flash of heat in his gaze.

His eyes flicked to my mouth and back, then he cleared his throat. "Your turn to defend." He rolled up and set me down as if I weighed nothing.

"Okay." I gave my head a shake and collected myself into a ready stance.

The chickens circled us curiously.

"All right, come at me." I smirked with a beckoning hand. "Try to dodge the leg sweep so you don't fall."

Too late for that, I thought ruefully.

Kylian's fist came up without warning, but I managed to get my hand up in time to stop the punch, my other arm crossing over to block the elbow. He shifted his weight, telegraphing which leg he would be attacking with. And then . . .

Apple?

What—?

Kylian's leg hit me like a freight train to the shins, and I crashed down.

"Niamh!" He dropped to his knees beside me.

I blinked, feeling dazed from the wind being knocked out of me. "Did you hear that? Someone else is here."

"Are you all right?" Kylian's eyes widened as he processed what I had said. "Where?" He looked all around, his hand going instinctively for the dagger on his leg.

"I heard someone." I pulled myself up to a sitting position. Oh, that was gonna hurt tomorrow.

Kylian helped me to my feet, and I didn't even try to make my hand linger in his, I was so distracted.

More apple?

"There it is again!" I peered around the greenhouse, but I didn't see anyone.

Mama has more pie?

Latte butted against my leg, and I picked her up absentmindedly, still looking around.

Maybe bread?

Latte looked right at me, and I looked back. The silver chick blinked.

More black mush?

I stared at the little chicken. I had burned the bottom of the oatmeal this morning, distracted by searching the cupboards for more clues about my parents.

"Kylian," I whispered. "It's the chickens."

"What?" Kylian was still scanning the greenhouse.

"The voice I heard." I held Latte up in front of Kylian's face, her feathered feet dangling.

Daddy!

"Can you hear her? Kylian . . . They're talking."

He looked from me to the chicken. "Are you sure?"

"It finally happened," I said faintly. "I'm losing my mind. Am I even here? Maybe I hit my head while I was doing dishes in the kitchen at home."

Kylian stared at me, trying to keep up. "You're hearing the chickens talk?"

"You're concerned." I hugged Latte tightly. "Me too."

The chickens on the ground milled around our feet, asking for treats. We both stared at them.

"Kylian?" I rested my cheek on the little chicken in my arms for comfort.

Mmmm, nice.

"Are you not a bit freaked out by this? Talking chickens is weird, right?"

Kylian took a deep breath. "The monarchs in Faerie have always had a strong connection to the land and the inhabitants in it. Especially," he added, picking up Essie, who'd been sitting on his foot, and holding the little black hen up to his narrowed eyes, "birds."

"Why? How does talking to chickens make someone a better *ruler?*"

"Well, most of the rulers use birds as messengers and spies, which is quite helpful. Moriath has her falcon, Ránach."

"I suppose," I conceded.

"And each monarch has had a special connection to a certain species of bird." His eyes flicked to my tattooed shoulder. "Generally owls, in your family's case."

"I guess I should have gotten a chicken tattoo instead." I tucked the silver chick under my chin. She sneezed.

"Most of the rulers only get basic images from their familiars, though." Kylian paused. "Except for your father. He could speak with all the animals in Faerie. So I don't think the chickens are specifically your bird." He paused again. "I think it's more likely that you can speak with any animal in the kingdom, like your father could. They say it helped him with hunting."

"Ew!" I said. "How can you kill something you can talk to?"

Kylian shrugged."He didn't ever discuss it with me."

"So, there hasn't been a mistake then." I sank down to the ground, and the chicks climbed around my lap with chirps of *Mama!* and *Treats?*

"What do you mean?" Kylian crouched beside me and tried to hand me Essie, but she protested until he sat and set her on his knee.

"You kept talking about these powers I'm supposed to have. But none of them had shown up yet. So, I thought that maybe you had made a mistake. That my sister was the powerful one, and the magic had skipped me."

Kylian held his tattooed wrist against mine. "This level of bond doesn't happen without magic."

"Yeah, I know." I sighed. "It was a long shot, but . . ." I perked up. "Maybe this doesn't mean anything. Maeve can probably talk to animals too. She might even have the crown *already*. I wouldn't even have to leave Faerie." I glanced around the greenhouse. "She can be the queen, and I will be the . . . the royal baker and chicken keeper! My parents could come live at the castle, and you can keep the chickens safe from predators with that giant axe of yours. I think they're starting to like it here," I added wistfully.

I looked up at Kylian, and for a second, something that felt suspiciously like longing flashed through the bond before he firmly set the chicken down and stood.

"That's not how this works, Princess."

"Says who? Anyway, you don't even know if I can talk to other animals. I could just have a magical connection to my chickens. Not really *queen* material after all."

He tapped his chin. "You could be right."

"Really?"

"No."

I scowled at him. "Prove it."

"That's a good idea. I think it's time you saw more of your kingdom, Princess."

Chapter 27

Niamh

As eager as I was to leave the cottage and *do* something, falling asleep on the couch after lunch hadn't done much to convince Kylian or Estrid of my regained strength.

"I can't stay here forever," I grumbled that evening while eating my portion of Kylian's excellent lentil and carrot stew with some bread I had made the day before. "You're the one who wants me to be queen." I waved my spoon in Kylian's direction. "What kind of queen would I be if I stayed in a cottage for the rest of my life?"

"You were willing to stay in Liadan's tower for the rest of your life," he pointed out.

"Yeah, but I wasn't *bored* then."

"You would think that being poisoned would be enough excitement for the month," commented Estrid, who had stolen the two largest books from the library shelf to make her seat the right height for her to reach the table.

Yes, you would think that. I couldn't explain it, but after spending a lifetime barely leaving the limits of Pilot Bay, I was curious to see more of the world. Besides, traveling in Faerie sounded much more exciting than traveling in the Kootenays. No offense to the mountains.

Kylian tapped his spoon on the table, thinking.

"You mentioned that you were interested in rune magic." Estrid rolled up her sleeves and eyed her runes. "We can't do too many runes—not in the condition you're in—but we could do one or two. Maybe *thurisaz*?" She looked over at Kylian. "The shielding rune would help keep her safe while we wait for her to fully recover."

"And *uruz*," he agreed after some thought.

"Really?" I sat up straighter. "Let's do it!"

"I don't have my equipment." Estrid scraped up the last of her stew with her bread. "I can pick up the gold dust and my ink and needles tomorrow."

"And molasses." I took a bite of buttery bread.

"Do they use molasses in tattoos in the human realm?" Estrid looked up skeptically.

"No, no. I just want to make cookies."

"I'll get it for you, but it might be a day or two before you're recovered enough to bake again."

"I've gotten a tattoo before," I huffed.

"I know." She slid off the chair and cleaned up her dishes. "But not like *this*, you haven't."

The next day, I sat cross-legged on my bed while Estrid arranged her tattoo kit and Kylian leaned against the doorway.

"What were you thinking of, for placement?" Estrid set a bottle of gold paint on the bedside table. "Your right arm?"

I looked at the milky skin of my arm. I had been thinking of getting something done there. But . . .

"Do I have to see the runes for them to work?" I asked.

"It can be helpful," said Estrid. "But no, you just have to visualize the rune. Most people prefer to see them until they get them memorized, though."

"Why do you ask?" Kylian examined a bottle of shimmering gold dust suspended in black ink.

"It just seemed like it would be an advantage to not announce that I have the runes."

Estrid looked thoughtful. "I suppose I could write them out for you to look at until you get them memorized. And put that down." She waved a needle at Kylian. "I mixed it myself this morning. It's not poisoned."

Kylian shrugged and set down the ink. "That's a good idea." He looked at me. "If you can pull it off. Any advantage in combat is helpful. For me, the advantage of having the runes visible is intimidation. But part of your strength lies in the fact that no one who looks at you expects you to be the deadly creature you are."

I preened. "No one's ever called me a deadly creature before." I turned to Estrid. "My back then. Down my spine."

"That will hurt more than your arm did," warned my friend.

I shrugged.

"Brynjar did mine with a needle attached to a stick." Kylian inspected Estrid's tattoo gun suspiciously. It reminded me of the machine my local tattoo artist used, but Estrid's was gold plated and wireless with a topaz bracketed into the end.

"It's my own design," Estrid told him proudly. "I researched equipment from other parts of Faerie as well as the human realm to come up with a system that's faster and less painful than the traditional stick-and-poke method."

"Huh." Kylian set the tattoo gun down.

"All right. Off with you, then." Estrid waved at the door.

Kylian looked up from the row of needles he was inspecting.

"Unless you want to stick around while I take my shirt off." I smiled sweetly.

Kylian blinked. His face didn't change, but if emotions could blush, I swear that's what I felt through the bond.

"I'll be in my room." He disappeared in a flash.

Estrid laughed. "I don't know exactly what's going on between the two of you, but it is entertaining."

"He thinks he knows what's best for me." I pulled off my tunic. "But I'm more stubborn than he is."

"Ah, young love." Estrid chose a needle from her kit and fitted it into her machine.

"Isn't he older than you?" I spread out a bath towel to protect the bedspread.

"Anyone under three hundred is young in Faerie. Lie down and we'll get started."

I unhooked the short stays they wore in place of a bra here—surprisingly comfortable—before lying face down on my bed while Estrid cleaned my back and then painted a rune on a piece of paper and handed it to me.

"This is the rune for protection. Its name is *thurisaz,* and it creates an invisible shield around you. I'll paint it on in gold and then ink it into your skin with this mixture. I've enchanted the gold to help set the spell."

Estrid held up the bottle of gold ink and whispered something over it in dwarvish. Bits of gold light swirled around the vial, but not in a recognizable pattern like Audrey's magic code had been. This felt more like *potential.*

The brush slid across the spot between my shoulder blades as she painted the gold rune.

"Now, think of things that make you feel safe, and use that feeling to build an imaginary shield around you. That will help the rune to know its job." She paused, and I could feel the needle resting against my skin. "Casting runes uses your magic. Well," she amended, "the magic you have access to. Everyone has some magic potential, and we store some in the rune with the gold, but it's stronger if you can channel more of Faerie's magic."

"That's why Kylian's are so strong?" I asked. "Because of his magic?"

"Yes, he has a lot of personal power, but it honestly still doesn't account for all the stories I've heard," she said. "It takes magic to set the rune, which is why most people need a day or so to rest, to regain their strength."

"Okay, got it." I was tired of being tired, but it would be worth it if this meant Kylian would let me go out and about with him.

"All right, let's begin. Safe thoughts."

As the first sharp tap hit my skin, I thought of my parents. Of the farmhouse where I had always felt safe. I now realized that safety was in no small part due to the wards Aunt Chloe had put around it. My godmother, my parents, and even Kylian had been protecting me for the past fifteen years. I held on to that thought as Estrid continued to ink her way through the rune.

I thought of the dwarven kingdom and the strong mountain walls surrounding its people. The Unseelie refugees, too—Cara and her family and the rest of the kitchen staff.

Something welled up inside me. A desire to protect not just myself or the chicks, but the Unseelie fae. The kingdom needed a shield.

I might not be a good choice for queen, but maybe I could still offer some form of protection. Maybe Maeve and I could work together. The tingling feeling of the needle grew stronger, spreading throughout my body. A humming vibrated my bones, and I gasped as it flared almost painfully.

"Whoa." Estrid wiped my new tattoo with a cloth.

"What's happening?" I panted through another wave before the feeling gradually faded.

"I've never seen this much power go into a rune before." She leaned back. "It's actually glowing. And it's healing on its own. I usually have to use a bit of my own magic to heal a new rune. How do you feel?"

I sat up, wincing at the feeling of the fresh tattoo on my spine, but it already felt more itchy than painful. Other than that . . .

"I feel amazing." I did. I felt stronger than I had before being poisoned. Before *ever*.

"It's really true then," Estrid whispered.

"What?"

"The power in that rune." Estrid handed me my shirt.

"People keep telling me I have power, but I thought it might just be talking to chickens." I pulled on my shirt as the pins-and-needles feeling slowly faded from my body.

"This time it wasn't your power, Niamh." Estrid looked at me solemnly. "That was the land's power. That was the power of Faerie."

Chapter 28

Kylian

After the success of the shield rune, Estrid and I decided that she should keep going and give Niamh *uruz* for strength and *sowulo* for healing. Instead of being drained like I had always been after getting even one new rune, Niamh finished with enough energy to throw the kitchen into complete chaos, baking bread, muffins, and cookies all at once. Her burst of energy seemed to disappear when it came time to do the dishes, however.

But, even with all the magic that had gone into her runes, *using* them was another story.

"Focus," I growled as we trained in the greenhouse the next day. I couldn't see Niamh's shield the way I knew she could, but I could feel her lack of power through our bond. I tapped the air in front of her and felt the weak barrier break apart under my light touch.

"I'm *trying*," Niamh protested.

And she was. I could see the sweat on her forehead as she focused, but the connection to the power of Faerie that she had tapped into while the *thurisaz* rune had been inked continued to elude her.

"Just take her out into the kingdom like we discussed," advised Estrid, dodging the chicks, who were taking advantage of her shorter height by jumping and flapping for the ginger cookies she was snacking on. "You know it's harder to use the runes in controlled conditions. A little adrenaline is what she needs. *Stop* it. Niamh, help!"

Niamh leaned her sword against the apple tree and snagged Snickerdoodle mid-jump, giving the rooster a stern look. "Cookies are not for chickens. It's your fault for spoiling them," she shot at me.

She was right about the chickens, but that wasn't the point. I crossed my arms and considered Estrid's suggestion. She wasn't wrong.

I hadn't learned to use rune magic in the comfort of a cottage greenhouse. I had been thrown into battles and used my magic to survive. But Niamh had only just recovered, and beyond the battle with the faoladh outside her home, she hadn't done more than train, even though she was skilled. And I *did* want her to see more of her kingdom, to see why it needed her.

Was she ready?

"It's not a battle or anything. We're just gonna talk to some animals, right?" Niamh snuggled her rooster. "To see if I can communicate with more than just chickens?"

Reluctantly, I nodded.

"Yes!" Niamh bounced on the spot, causing Snickerdoodle to squawk in protest, his feathered crest flopping.

"Where are you thinking of taking her?" asked Estrid.

"Huath Forest," I decided. Maybe the time had come to start fixing some of the trouble I had brought to the Unseelie Kingdom. Or at least make sure it didn't get any worse.

"Oh." Estrid's eyebrows rose.

"Oh, what?" Niamh asked, setting her rooster down and retrieving her sword.

"She'll be safe enough," said Estrid.

"Totally. I have my strength back now." Niamh twirled her sword in a flashy motion and, amazingly, didn't fumble it. "Is there something I can help with?"

As much as I wanted to keep her safe and away from Moriath's scrying arts, we couldn't stay hidden forever.

I nodded. "Put on something warmer, and we'll leave."

"Do you want me to come with you?" asked Estrid.

I tilted my head, considering. "We need to relocate the herd to somewhere outside the Unseelie Kingdom where they'll be safe. Can you use the mirror at Nidavellir to contact Kilinaire first and let the Rose Prince know that we'll be on our way?"

Estrid nodded. "Do you know numbers?"

"Maybe ten young ones." I tried to keep from dwelling on the details since Niamh would be able to feel my emotions. "Five elders? I'm not sure."

"Young and elder what?" Niamh asked, intrigued.

"*Aonbheannach.*" Estrid finished her ginger cookie.

"What?"

"Unicorns, Princess." I grabbed my axe and headed for the door.

Niamh squealed.

We each packed some food and water, and I helped Niamh with the baldric Estrid and I had prepared for her to carry her sword on her back. It didn't allow for as fast a draw as her usual waist belt, but with the distance we were traveling, it would be more comfortable, even with the small pack.

After bundling up in cloaks and fur-lined boots, we snowshoed out to the gate. Niamh was able to keep a fair pace. Good. She really was back to full health.

The forest looked beautiful. The sun shone between the branches of towering evergreen trees, and the smaller trees were heaped with pillowy soft white snow. How long had it been since I had actually enjoyed spending time in the kingdom I was trying to save? Niamh's sunny nature must be rubbing off on me. Was that good or bad? I couldn't afford to lose my edge, not now.

"Do you see any birds? Rabbits? I want to see if I can understand them. *Ooof!*"

Niamh collided with my back when I stopped. She must have been looking at the trees instead of the path. I shook my head. No survival skills. There was no way I was letting her out of my sight.

"This is the Frost Gate." I pointed ahead.

Niamh stomped in her snowshoes to my side and gasped when she saw the beautiful ice structure in front of us. Symmetrical fractals of curling, feathery frost blossomed out from an arch of golden ferns and sprigs of red berries coated in ice. Lazy little specks of frost danced in the wind, making the whole structure glow with sparkling motes of light.

Niamh reached out her hand, and a tiny crystal snowflake landed on her mitten-clad fingers.

"King Ulf told me that your mother made the Frost Gate." I watched her face as she stared up at the gate. "Her magic with ice wasn't as powerful as Moriath's, but she loved crafting. This might be the only work of hers that escaped her sister's jealous destruction."

"It's so beautiful." Tears welled up in her eyes.

"Do you miss her?"

"I want to," she sighed. "Do you miss your family?"

"I wish I had seen my younger siblings grow up," I admitted.

"You have more siblings?" Niamh looked surprised, and I remembered how much she didn't know about me.

I nodded. "There were—*are*—five of us. Safiya and I were inseparable when we were children, and our two little brothers were always tagging along after us. We also had a baby sister. I barely had time to get to know her before I left. I sometimes wonder what they are like now. If they have families of their own."

"Safiya is the twin sister you said was traded to the Seelie Kingdom? Have you ever tried to visit her?"

I shook my head. "I know she's safe and the new Seelie King's foster sister. She has a good life there." A good life that didn't need to be complicated by a brother who had been her kingdom's enemy for countless years and battles, no matter what my intentions had been. How many of her allies—friends even—had she lost because of me?

Niamh nodded and I wondered if she was thinking of her own sister. At least I could remember my siblings.

"But you don't miss your parents?" she asked after a moment.

"I did at first," I admitted.

"Not anymore?" she asked quietly.

"They traded my sister for safety and me for power. It's hard to miss people who would do that to their children."

"Did they have a choice?"

"There's always a choice, Princess." I dug in my pocket before handing her the third gate key.

Niamh admired the frozen amulet. “It’s not even cold,” she marveled.

“That will allow you through the gate. Estrid and I each have one. No one gets through the gate without a key.” I tugged off my glove and offered her my hand.

“Oooh, have we moved on to the hand-holding stage of our relationship?” she teased as she slipped the necklace over her head.

I huffed in exasperation. “Unless you know where Huath Forest’s gate stands?”

She pulled off her mitten and put her palm on mine. I resisted the urge to thread my fingers through hers, to press my palm against the one brushing mine. I just needed contact to bring her safely through the gate with me. Nothing more.

Still, the infuriating girl winked at me. “Lead on, Huntsman.”

Chapter 29

Niamh

HAND IN HAND, WE STEPPED THROUGH THE Frost Gate into a cold and misty forest, unlike the sparkling evergreen Narnia we'd just left. This forest was leached of color, the bare branches of the trees tangling overhead, the odd dead leaf blowing from a twisted point. A dense fog hid the sky from view.

I glanced back to see the gate we'd come through. It was little more than an arch of dead branches with a gold plate stamped with a swirling knot symbol attached to one piece of wood.

"This way." Kylian dropped my hand abruptly and put his glove back on. He avoided my eyes, looking distantly through the trees before setting off.

Our snowshoes crunching on the hard-packed snow made the only sound. No birds or animals broke the empty silence.

"Not what I pictured a unicorn forest looking like." I wrinkled my nose.

"It didn't always look like this."

"What happened to it?"

"I did."

"What?" I stopped in my tracks.

"Keep up, Princess." Kylian didn't slow down, and I struggled to catch up, nearly tripping over my snowshoes.

It was almost like he was trying to avoid further questions, but even when my breathing went back to normal, I didn't pester him. Something about this place didn't encourage conversation.

We hadn't walked for more than fifteen minutes when the forest began to come alive. At first, it was just the odd patch of moss on a tree trunk or a distant rustling. Then the snow got thinner underfoot, and little clusters of snowdrops and blue flowers shaped like stars appeared around the trunks of larger trees.

When the snow thinned enough, we stopped to remove our snowshoes, and I noticed the branches overhead had just a hint of green budding on the tips. It was like we were walking into spring.

"Are we that far south from the cottage?" I asked.

"We aren't." Kylian tied his snowshoes to the back of his pack and motioned for me to do the same. "It's not the climate. It's the unicorns. They're a natural conduit for the magic of Faerie, and that magic brings life wherever it goes, no matter the season. When the herd was larger, they infused the whole area with magic."

"That's amazing." I reached down and touched the bell of a white snowdrop blossom.

"They're not the only ones. Look back." Kylian nodded to the trail behind us.

It took me a minute to see what he meant. At first I had to squint to make it out, but the path we had walked along had noticeably more bits of green than the rest of the gray forest.

"Is this like the talking-to-animals thing?" I ran my finger across a little cushion of moss and jumped when it spread under my touch.

"Animal speech is your own personal magic. You would have that regardless. It was just smothered by the glamour." He waved a hand at the flowers behind us. "*This* is because you're the rightful queen, and the land knows it."

"It's barely a hint of moss. Maybe four tiny flowers."

Kylian just nodded. "Think of what it *could* be." He met my eyes. "If you stop fighting it."

I brushed the moss again and it almost seemed to glow, just for a breath. But it didn't feel like I was doing it. More like the forest was happy to see me. "I don't know how."

"What don't you know?"

"You say the kingdom needs me. But what it really needs is someone who knows what they're doing. Someone who grew up here."

"Like Moriath?"

"Well, maybe a little less murdery," I conceded.

"What this kingdom needs is someone who loves it and is strong enough to fight for it."

"Obviously." The shimmering moss flickered and faded to a dull green. "That's not me, though."

"Come on, Princess." He nodded at the trail, and I followed him deeper toward the green heart of the forest.

It wasn't long until we were in full spring, the fog disappearing under the warm sunshine. I stopped to breathe in the fresh scent of new growth. "It's so beautiful."

The trees' buds had unfurled into full green leaves, the

swirls in the bark glittering with gold that pulsed like a heartbeat. Shimmering white petals drifted down from tall, slender, flowering shrubs. Bluebells carpeted the forest floor, and my boots disappeared into a sea of flowers. Motes of golden light danced like tiny fireflies above the blooms.

All around, birds sang sweetly in the trees, and I realized I could understand them as they called to impress potential mates or announce their territory.

"You need to find the herd from here."

I turned to find Kylian watching me, his gaze as dispassionate as ever. But, through the bond, he almost felt *wistful.*

"You aren't coming with me?"

He shook his head. "You won't get near the herd if they see me. I'll meet you back at the gate. Tell them that you're taking them somewhere safe. Kilinaire is in the Seelie Kingdom, out of Moriath's reach. It has fields and orchards, perfect for them. Moriath has had me scout it more than once. It's close to the mountains that divide Tír na nÓg, and she's been annoyed that it's so well protected. Tell the elders that Moriath is planning to capture the rest of the herd. She was never happy with me for only bringing her the strongest unicorns, and now that *Dylan* is her Huntsman, he'll happily do anything she asks." He made a face.

"What happened here?" I crossed my arms. "What happened to the rest of the herd?"

"I told you that unicorns are natural conduits for magic. If there's one thing Moriath can never get enough of, it's power. She discovered a way to channel their power into gemstones to increase her already-formidable resources."

"Are they dead?" I whispered.

He shook his head sharply. "They're much more useful alive. Now go ahead, Princess." He pointed in the direction where the plant life grew thickest, then whispered "*ansuz*" to activate his silence rune before soundlessly slipping behind a large tree. He made no noise, even when I saw him step on a twig.

"Oh, I want that one too!"

Later, he mouthed at me. *Go.*

Birds were still twittering overhead as I reluctantly left Kylian and walked deeper into the mossy green patch of forest. Suddenly, their distant calls shifted.

Intruder! twittered a bird in the tree, causing a flurry of activity.

Looks friendly? called another one. *Investigate!*

"Um, hi." I waved nervously as the trees around me filled with curious birds in shades of browns, yellows, reds, and blues. There was even a large white owl with black speckles and three fluffy owlets blinking sleepily on a branch just above me.

"I'm just here to visit the unicorns," I said. "It's not safe for them to stay here."

The white owl looked down from the high branch. *The forest will go back to sleep without the aonbheannachs,* she said.

"I guess?"

If the forest sleeps, so does the food, continued the owl, her black ear tufts stirring in the breeze.

"Oh." I thought about the silence we had walked through. There had been no scuttling small creatures, no berries or seeds.

"Kylian says Moriath wants to come back and capture the rest of the herd," I told them. "They need to leave. We have a safer place for them to stay."

The birds chattered amongst themselves, too fast for me to keep up with their lilting conversation.

Very well, said the owl at last. *We'll come with them.*

"I'm sorry that you have to leave your home."

The owl blinked gravely. *It's only temporary. You'll repair the forest when you become queen.*

"Well . . ."

Fluffy. The owl nudged a white puffball about half her size on the branch next to her, startling it out of a nap. *You will go with Princess Niamh.* She rotated her head back to me. *He'll help you find the unicorns.*

The owlet yawned in response.

"You know my name?"

You think we owls don't know our own monarchs? Off you go, now! The mama owl bumped the owlet off the branch.

I yelped and thrust out my arms to catch the baby owl as he plummeted sharply, taking my heart with him. At the last minute he opened his wings and banked to land on my hand. I winced as the surprisingly large talons gripped my fingers. The owlet blinked up at me with sleepy golden eyes.

We will ready the others, the mama owl said as she launched off the branch.

The other owlets fell back asleep while the rest of the birds took off in a flurry of wings, scattering in every direction.

Why did you come in the middle of the day? asked Fluffy blearily. *Don't you sleep?*

"Sorry?" I lifted the owlet, and he wobbled but held on. "Can I pet you?" I whispered. He looked so soft.

That's not very dignified. The owlet shifted on his feet. *But if you must.*

"Thank you!" I ran my hand over the cloud of downy feathers.

It felt even softer than I had imagined. The little owl closed his eyes and leaned into my touch, then opened them wide again and straightened.

If you are quite done, he groused, *the herd is that way.* He leaned forward and to the left.

I looked around for Kylian, but the Huntsman had disappeared. I could sense him following from a distance while Fluffy guided me through the bluebells. Then the forest around us opened up into a meadow of green grass and scattered wildflowers, containing the most beautiful creatures I'd ever seen.

Chapter 30

Niamh

I'D ALWAYS THOUGHT OF UNICORNS AS JUST horses with horns on their foreheads, but that didn't begin to describe the graceful white, black, and silver animals grazing happily on the grass and wildflowers. They were smaller than I had expected, the largest ones maybe waist-high, with delicate legs and soft coats that curled on the backs of their legs.

They reminded me as much of goats as of horses. Some even had curly little beards, and their hooves and horns glowed with a pearlescent sheen.

The herd startled and froze as Fluffy clambered up my arm, talons gripping my cloak.

Here they are. Good night. The baby owl climbed into the hood of my cloak. I could feel his soft down against my neck.

Please leave, whinnied an adult unicorn with the voice of

a grandpa. White hairs peppered the black coat around his muzzle and eyes.

"I'm Princess Niamh. I'm here to tell you that you're in danger. I can take you somewhere safe." I sat down to appear less threatening, shrugging out of my backpack and baldric to lay my sheathed sword on the ground behind me.

The crown princess was killed long ago. The black unicorn narrowed his eyes at me.

The unicorns all took a step back, the little ones hiding under the legs of the adults.

Apparently, whatever connection the owls had to the royal family, they kept it to themselves.

"They hid me away in the human realm when I was little," I told the unicorns. "But I'm back, and I want to help you."

The herd just stared at me.

"Um, would you like a cookie?" I reached for my backpack.

What's a cookie? murmured Fluffy from my cloak hood.

"Shhh, I'll show you later," I whispered.

Okay . . .

He didn't say anything more as I pulled my lunch out of my bag. I'd packed slices of freshly baked bread with cheese, two apples, and a bag of cookies. Did I really need a whole bag of cookies for my lunch? Probably not, but it was always better to be safe than sorry. What if I made a hungry friend?

Is it sweet? A little silver foal no taller than my knees danced forward, ears up.

Back up, child, huffed the grandpa unicorn. *It could be Moriath, here to steal you away.*

His caution made sense from what Kylian had told me about the queen and her love of disguises and tricks. What could I do that Moriath couldn't? *Oh!* I was doing it right now.

"Moriath can't communicate with you like this." I smiled. "It's a gift I inherited from my father, the last Unseelie king."

There are others with that gift. The unicorn shook his mane. *You could still be working with her. Or she could have found a way to steal that magic like she's stolen so many other things.*

"I'm *not* Moriath," I said. "But if you stay here, she's going to come for the rest of you. Soon."

Prove it, said the grandpa. *Prove that you're really the princess.*

If they didn't believe me just by the fact that I could understand them, I didn't know how to convince them.

"I can't . . ." *Wait.* The glowing moss earlier. How had I done that?

I set the food on my lap and rested my hands on either side of me, digging the tips of my fingers into the soft soil. Closing my eyes, I tried to remember the feeling that had washed over me when I had gotten the runes. That sense of connection.

Nothing.

Please, help me protect them, I pleaded with the magic. Still nothing.

Then I felt it. A tingling in my fingertips that spread through the rest of me. I could feel a warm glow through my eyelids, like when you're lying down on the beach, face to the sun with your eyes closed.

I felt shining bits of potential scattered around the meadow and sent that warmth out to them. The unicorns stomped their feet and whinnied excitedly.

I opened my eyes to watch green shoots push up out of the ground before sprouting leaves as they grew taller. Little pink fairy bells blossomed in clusters along each stalk. Motes of golden light spun around each plant as it grew, then dispersed like dandelion seeds in the wind.

She really is *the princess,* whispered the little silver unicorn.

All the elderly unicorns bent their front legs and bowed their heads, but the young ones danced closer, bits of golden magic sticking to their tails and manes.

Tell us more, said the little silver one. *About cookies.*

The unicorns made short work of my cookies, and soon, I had the little silver one in my lap and three more snuggled against me. Truly, nothing in the world helped make friends like fresh cookies. Unless, of course, you were trying to make friends with a grumpy, axe-wielding fae. Where was he hiding, anyway?

Will you reclaim your throne? asked the grandpa unicorn. *If you need our help with that goal, I'm afraid you'll find our power much diminished.*

"I'm not sure what I'll do," I said. "But I do know that Moriath plans to send her wolves for the rest of you soon. I'm here to take you somewhere safe."

To be with Mama? The little silver unicorn lifted up her head.

I looked around at the herd. There were maybe twenty-five foals of various ages—but none more than half grown—and five adults, all with white around their muzzles, who were slow and careful in their movements.

"What happened?" I asked the grandpa unicorn.

The Huntsman came, he spat. *With his wolves. He slew our leader, my daughter,* he added more softly, *with that silver axe of his.*

That explained Kylian's shuttered face since we had arrived here.

Then he ordered his wolves to separate out the strongest of our herd.

The baby unicorn whimpered in memory, and I stroked her silver mane while I listened.

We tried to stop them. The elder unicorn lowered his head to reveal scars like claw marks across his neck.

All the adults, I realized, were not limping just from age, but from old injuries. *We slew three of them,* he continued, *but they still took the rest through that unnatural arch in the woods.* He shivered. *And we've heard nothing since. We don't know if they're dead or alive.*

"They're alive," I said quickly.

The baby looked up, hope sparkling in her eyes. *Will you take us to them? To Mama?*

"No, sweetheart." I ran my fingers through her soft mane. "Not today. But I will. I'll reunite your herd. I swear it."

The earth trembled and the glow of magic flashed before disappearing again. I got the impression that vowing meant something more in Faerie than it did back home. I didn't care. I meant what I'd said. Kylian would know where the rest of the unicorns were being held. I was sure of it.

"The place I'm taking you to now has beautiful fields to run in with delicious grass and fruit trees. Nothing will hurt you there. And, if you're patient with me, I'll find all your mommies and daddies and make it safe for you to come back to your forest together. Does that sound good?"

How big is the field? asked the foal. *Grampa won't let me run too far away.*

"It's so safe there that you can run until your legs are tired." I looked up and saw the elder unicorn blink away tears.

Very well, Princess, he said. *How do we get to this magical field of yours?*

"I'm afraid," I said, "that we're gonna have to go back through the unnatural gate."

I didn't see Kylian as I led the unicorns back along the trail of green I had sprouted on the walk over, but I could sense his presence close by, guilt and self-loathing radiating off him. I looked at the unicorns skipping around me and wondered how I would feel if I had killed one of their parents and led the rest into captivity. Probably about the same.

It's not your fault, I thought desperately and felt an answering disagreement. Wait, could he sense my thoughts? If so, that would be pretty handy about now because he was right—the unicorns were afraid of him. If we met him at the gate like he had planned, they might think I'd betrayed them.

But I didn't think he could actually go invisible, and if I wasn't touching him, how would I take us to somewhere I'd never seen? I'd never even gone through a gate on my own.

Kylian! I thought as loudly as I could.

Niamh?

I inwardly cheered that I had startled him enough to use my actual name.

I don't know where we're going, I thought at him. *I need you to help me through the gate.*

I don't think I should reveal myself, after all.

I know. I hated that. But it had been hard enough to get them to trust *me*. And he didn't even have any cookies.

Close your eyes.

I stopped and did so, unicorns clustering around me impatiently. A flash of something crossed my mind before it disappeared.

Did you get that? he asked.

Go slower, I answered. *I couldn't see it properly.*

He tried again. This time, I could see a drawing of a forest. He was remembering a map. Then my view panned down across a mighty mountain range to a little gold star.

Got it? he asked.

The star?

Yes. That's Kilinaire. Picture it in your mind as you step through. Keep the unicorns close. They need to be touching each other, and you need to touch one of them.

Okay, I'll meet you there.

I'm not sure—

Good, it's settled.

All right, Princess.

I opened my eyes. We were almost to the rough forest gate.

"Here's what we need to do." I turned to face the unicorns. "Everyone line up. We all need to be touching, so your nose needs to be against the flank of whoever's in front of you."

While the unicorns arranged themselves, I heard a flurry of wings. Birds of all sizes flew in and landed on the unicorns, who seemed to accept their lot as perches.

The white owl landed gently on the black unicorn, her two owlets hopping up with a flap to join her. *We are ready to go, Princess.*

"All set?" I asked the group.

The little silver unicorn bumped my leg with her nose, upsetting a chickadee perched beside her ear. *I'm scared.*

"Come here." I picked up the silver unicorn. "I won't let anything happen to you," I promised, holding her tightly against me.

I pictured the star on the map that Kylian had given me and rested my free hand on the neck of the black unicorn.

You'd better be right about this place, I thought at the Huntsman before I stepped through the gate and into a rose garden.

CHAPTER 31

NIAMH

I KEPT WALKING FORWARD TO ALLOW THE rest of the unicorns to follow me through the gate. My feet crunched on a snow-covered path surrounded by neatly trimmed hedges, bare and thorny in the cold. Ahead stood a beautiful castle of white stone, its towers shingled in blue.

A fae man dressed all in black strode down the garden path, his dark hair caught neatly at the back of his neck and a patch covering the eye on the scarred side of his face. At his side in a pink, fur-trimmed cloak was . . .

"Isobel Watson?" Surprised, I set down the little silver unicorn.

"Hi, Neve! Princess Isobel of the Rose Court now," said the dark-haired human girl, mischief dancing in her brown eyes. "I've been the Rose Princess for . . . four years, Leith?"

She turned to her husband, and I noticed the swell of her belly under the yellow silk of her dress.

"Three and a half," he said. "Four years in *Duir.*" He kissed his wife's cheek fondly.

I blinked, trying to catch up. Isobel Watson had graduated a year ahead of me and then had spent the next two years in Pilot Bay living with her sisters. It must be that Faerie time versus human time thing again.

"You've been having adventures, too, I see," Isobel said with a laugh.

The entire unicorn herd clustered around me. The birds flew off in all directions, but the white owl and her owlets stayed on the back of the black unicorn.

"Something like that," I agreed.

She gestured at the unicorns. "Well, why don't we take these guys to their new home, and then we'll have some tea and you can tell me all about it? Amber mentioned something about you being a princess? Oh, speaking of Amber . . . Falkor!"

A smokey-blue Japanese dragon the size of a cat appeared with a *pop* in front of Isobel, and the princess caught the creature in her arms.

"Falkor, please find Amber and tell her that Neve's here."

The dragon squeaked and jumped out of Isobel's arms, disappearing again in midair.

I watched with wide eyes. How had a girl from Pilot Bay ended up a princess with a pet dragon?

Isobel winced. "You're very wiggly today," she accused her belly.

"You go inside and tell Ena to start making tea, and I'll take them to the back pasture," suggested Leith.

"Are you sure they'll be warm enough back there?" asked Isobel. "It's cold this time of year."

"Well, from what I've seen today, the unicorns should take care of that." I looked around us.

"Oh!" Isobel exclaimed, noticing the rose bushes closest to the unicorns starting to sprout green leaves and dark red roses. "Interesting." She bent over to examine a rose and winced.

Leith turned Isobel toward the door and gave her a little nudge.

"Okay, but," she said, pointing a finger at me, "promise you'll come inside to visit. I want to hear everything."

I promised, and Leith watched her go back inside with a little smile on his face.

"How far along is she?" I asked as he led me through the snowy garden, unicorns trailing behind.

"Seven months."

"Nearly there, then." I stopped abruptly. "She *is* nearly there, right? Living to a thousand doesn't make pregnancies last for years, does it?" I already felt iffy on the idea of kids. That would take them right off the list for me.

"No." Leith glanced back with an amused look. "That's not how it works. It's nine months, the same as in the human realm."

I followed the prince around to the back of the castle and through an apple orchard—I wondered what variety they grew here—to a low stone wall. Past the wall, vast snowy fields stretched out, edged by an evergreen forest.

"We moved the aurochs closer to the castle." Leith pointed in the direction of the biggest, shaggiest cows I had ever seen. "The unicorns can have the pastures on the left that include a forested section." He patted the waist-high stone wall. "This shouldn't be a problem for the adults to get over, but hopefully it'll keep the little ones contained."

"What do you think?" I asked the black unicorn once I had translated.

It's perfect, he whinnied. *Thank you, Princess.*

Leith and I scooped the little unicorns up and over the wall. They immediately began running through the snow, leaving hints of new grass growing in their hoofprints. Once they were all settled in, the prince went inside to check on his wife.

"And you?" I asked the mother owl, who watched the unicorns from the wall. Her owlets had hopped into a shrub growing over the wall.

This looks like a good place. The owl swiveled her head to look around. *Many rodents scurry through that field, and the forest will be good for all of us. Fluffy!* she called.

Mama? The owlet popped out of my hood, making me jump.

I had forgotten all about my passenger.

Are you coming with us or are you staying with the princess? asked the mother owl.

I'll stay. Fluffy clambered out with a hop and a flap down my arm. *I think she needs me.*

"Do I need you, or are you just curious about cookies?" I lifted my arm to bring Fluffy up to eye level.

Both things can be true at the same time, Fluffy said wisely.

Very well, little one, said the mother owl approvingly. *Behave yourself, and remember that most fae have terrible taste and don't enjoy dead mice as much as we do.*

I'm sure that's not true. Fluffy looked up at me.

"Unfortunately, it is." A thought struck me. "Wait, you don't eat chickens, do you?" I trailed off at his look.

Noooo . . . Right? Fluffy looked at his mother, who widened her eyes and shook her head. *I do not*, he told me confidently.

I was skeptical, but surely he was too young to take on the chickens at their awkward teenage size. "Why don't you stay with your mother while I visit inside, and then I'll come get you before I leave?"

Oooh, I'll find you a present! The baby owl hopped off my arm and glided down to the field.

No mice, his mother reminded him.

Right, I was thinking a vole, said Fluffy.

Better, agreed the mother owl, joining Fluffy in the field to search.

I sighed. Hopefully there wouldn't be too many dead rodents in my future.

Closing my eyes, I tried to sense if Kylian was nearby before I went back to the castle. Nothing. I knew he'd keep his word to meet me here, but I wasn't really surprised that he was taking his time. As much as I wanted to see how he was doing—to try and cheer him up—I knew he needed space today.

After one last scan of the area through our bond, I hiked back through the orchard and around to the front door of the castle. I stared at it for a moment, trying to decide what I would say to a former schoolmate who was a current faerie princess, when the door creaked open.

"Come in, my dear." A woman about three feet tall with mottled brown skin and pointed ears, wearing a neat linen dress and apron, held the door open as I entered the castle. "I'm Ena, the housekeeper. I'll just take your things. Princess Isobel is waiting for you in the sitting room."

"Thank you." I stripped off my backpack, cloak, and sword.

"The sitting room is down the hall, second door on the left." The little woman, a brownie if I remembered correctly from my book, hung my gear on low hooks by the door.

I followed her instructions and found Isobel lounging on a blue velvet sofa, wearing furry slippers and wrapped up in the most atrocious knitted afghan I had ever seen.

"I know, right?" Isobel laughed at my expression as I took in the blanket. "Ena has been trying to find a way to quietly burn it."

"I can't imagine why." I aimed for politeness and failed, perching awkwardly on a chair across from the princess.

"My older sister, Lily, made it. She says she's practicing to make things for the baby." She rubbed her belly. "You will look very ugly in them," she crooned to her unborn child. "But very loved. Help yourself to some tea and cookies," she added to me. "They're almost as good as yours. And tell me what it's like finding out you're the lost Unseelie princess."

I laughed, relaxing a little, and took a bite of a cookie to fortify myself while I considered my answer. It was lavender shortbread, and the butter melted on my tongue.

"I don't know how I feel, honestly. I had a plan, you know?"

"Oh, yes, I remember having plans." Isobel took a sip of tea, balancing her plate of cookies on her belly.

I smiled. "I was happy at the café, working with my parents, and then this obnoxious man with an axe burst into my life. And then there were the wolves . . ."

"Oh, yes. You're the reason why there were so many wolves in Pilot Bay." Isobel took a bite of shortbread. "They almost ate me, you know."

"Oh. I'm sorry."

"It worked out." Isobel waved her hand around the room. "Just like it will for you."

"I'm not so sure about that. Kylian thinks Faerie needs me to be some sort of powerful queen to take down Moriath. I haven't even met her in person, and she's already tried to kill me. Twice."

"I've met her," said Isobel.

"What's she like?" I leaned forward.

"Terrifyingly powerful. Likes to curse people." Isobel took a bite of her cookie. "She's destroying the Unseelie Kingdom," she continued more somberly. "The unicorns aren't the first creatures we've had come through looking for a new home. The land is going to reach a breaking point soon. A Faerie ruler was never meant to suck and suck the magic out of it." She looked out the window at the dormant rose garden. "I don't know what will happen if someone doesn't stop her soon."

"Why would that someone be a twenty-year-old baker from Pilot Bay?" I asked desperately. "I never wanted this."

Isobel tilted her head. "Is that true? If you really don't want the crown, that's one thing, but I think you do."

"You clearly don't know me. My life's ambition was to help run Pie in the Sky and perfect my apple pie recipe."

"People who don't care generally don't show up with arms full of baby unicorns on my doorstep."

"What are we discussing?" asked Leith from the doorway.

"How tired my feet are," Isobel pouted.

The prince raised an eyebrow at his wife before sitting beside her on the couch and lifting her slippered feet onto his lap.

"I'm just not sure I'm cut out to be the Unseelie queen." I poured myself a cup of tea.

Leith looked at me thoughtfully. "I certainly didn't feel cut out to be the Rose Prince when my parents died."

"But everything turned out fine?" I asked skeptically. "You're going to tell me to just give it a try?"

"It was a disaster." Leith pulled off Isobel's slippers. "I got us all cursed. And my sister . . ."

"That wasn't your fault," protested Isobel. "That was Moriath."

"If I hadn't been so eager to run away, it never would have happened." Leith began massaging Isobel's foot, and she groaned happily, falling back on her stack of pillows. "The point I'm trying to make is that I had to learn that I couldn't do it on my own."

"So I need to get married? I can't even get him to kiss me," I grumbled under my breath.

Leith tilted his head, but didn't ask. "I'm not saying you need to get married. Tiernan, the Seelie king—"

"Is married," pointed out Isobel, her eyes closed.

"Yes, but he also has his fianna, is what I was going to say."

"Fianna?" I sipped the tea.

"A group of warriors." Leith switched to massaging Isobel's other foot. "But in this case, they're also his adopted family."

"I currently have one dwarven warrior tattoo artist, seven chickens, a baby owl, and a grumpy axe-wielding bodyguard who believes I'm the chosen one. Which is ridiculous."

"I'm not sure the unicorns would agree with that sentiment." Isobel opened her eyes and fixed me with a serious look. "Your Aunt Chloe once told me there's no such thing as a chosen one."

"Exactly." I sipped my tea again.

"But," continued Isobel, "she said that doesn't stop you from being the right person at the right time to change things for good."

"Ugh, that sounds like Aunt Chloe."

"I guess what it comes down to is that it doesn't matter if you have some sort of great destiny or if you're *meant* to be the queen of the Unseelie fae. What matters is do you have the power to save them, and are you willing? If not, are you really able to ignore the problem, now that you know what Moriath is doing?"

I thought of my vow to the unicorns. "You make it sound so simple."

"It is simple. But it's not easy."

The smoky-blue dragon appeared out of nowhere and landed on Isobel's lap.

"Falkor!" The princess scratched his head between his little silver horns, and the dragon cooed.

Isobel unrolled a scrap of paper and quickly scanned it. "Amber can't come right now. She refuses to explain why. Miss Chloe is a terrible influence on her," she groused to Leith, who chuckled. "She says she tried to text you, Neve, but it didn't deliver. She wants an update on you and the hottie Huntsman." Isobel raised her eyebrows.

"My phone is officially out of battery. Audrey couldn't make me a charger in time." I finished my tea. "And no comment."

"Speaking of which." Leith slipped Isobel's slippers back onto her feet. "He's in the back pasture."

"Kylian?" I set down the teacup.

"He came through the gate like one who wished to go unnoticed, so I didn't invite him in," said Leith. "But sneaking into the Rose Court isn't possible, no matter how many runes you have."

"I should go." I stood, snagging another cookie for the road. "Thank you for the tea, Isobel."

"You can return the favor someday." The princess smiled at me. "Maybe when you're living in that fancy ice castle."

"Maybe," I agreed. "If you bring me some of your apples."

"Oh yeah, you had a new apple pie every week! You were trying to get your recipe perfected."

"I finally figured that out," I said.

"You'll figure this out, too. I know it." Isobel stood to give me a hug, dumping Falkor into Leith's lap. The little dragon complained until the prince gave him a cookie.

"Does Kylian know?" Leith asked before I could leave the room. "That his sister is living here, in the Seelie Kingdom?"

I turned back, surprised. "Do you know her?"

Leith nodded. "She's a good friend."

"He'll be glad to hear that she's doing well," I said, carefully. I wanted to grill the prince for more details, but it wasn't really my place to be nosy. I'd wait for Kylian to tell me more himself.

As I left, I heard Isobel ask quietly, "Should we tell Saoirse about her brother?"

"Not yet," murmured Leith. "He'll reach out when he's ready."

I pushed my curiosity aside and retrieved my gear.

I had a huntsman to go find.

Chapter 32

Kylian

I FELT HER THROUGH THE BOND BEFORE I saw her. Glowing along the edges of my senses like the sun breaking through dark clouds. Niamh swung her legs over the stone wall and settled next to me, so close that her arm brushed against mine. I knew I should move away, but I couldn't bring myself to.

We sat on the wall in silence, watching from the cover of a shrub while the little unicorns chased each other around a field that was quickly becoming green, with little pockets of field flowers popping up through the grass.

"You understand now." I clenched my fists where they rested on the wall.

"What do I understand?"

She was really going to make me say it.

"What a monster I am," I ground out.

"You just helped me save them." Niamh waved her arm at the herd of unicorns. "Oh no, they're so happy! Such a monster."

I clenched my teeth. Why was she so stubborn? "They wouldn't need saving if it wasn't for me. Their parents wouldn't all be in captivity being used as some sort of magical battery for Moriath."

"She would have just sent someone else," Niamh pointed out. "Was it your idea?"

"Of course not. But I killed their leader. She was a peaceful creature who didn't stand a chance against me."

How I had scrubbed my hands after that. Even now, I felt like the silver blood had left tattoos on my skin as surely as the ink on my arms.

"What would have happened if you hadn't done that?"

I closed my eyes. "She would have rallied the herd against us."

"Would they have won?"

I shook my head. "Not a chance."

"So *more* unicorns would have died."

"Don't make me out to be some sort of hero, Princess. Killing that unicorn is only one of the terrible things I've done."

"Because you were trying to protect me. So don't I bear responsibility for it, then?"

I glared at her. "Don't you dare take this upon yourself. My actions were mine alone."

"Do you regret it?"

"I regret every bit of it. But I would do it all again to keep you safe."

"So you say." Niamh pierced me with her icy blue eyes.

"But it wasn't for *my* sake that you didn't bring back the elderly and baby unicorns, even though you knew Moriath wanted them all. You were protecting *them*."

"Of course I was."

"For two hundred years, you've protected this kingdom from Moriath in the only way you knew how. Stop trying to make me hate you for it." Niamh laid her hand over my fist, forcing her fingers between my knuckles until I relented, allowing her fingers to twine with mine. "You're trying to make me love this kingdom and still hate you for doing everything you could to hold it together."

"If you learn all that I've done, you may feel differently," I warned.

She shook her curly head and leaned it against my shoulder. I felt something start to thaw deep inside my chest.

"Stop trying to scare me away," she said.

I didn't have it in me to argue more. Not today. I left her hand on mine and basked in her warmth as we watched the unicorns.

A few minutes later, the majestic white owl I had seen talking to Niamh earlier flew up and landed in the shrub beside us, her owlet hopping and flapping along behind. His downy wings weren't ready for proper flight yet. Instead of landing by his mother, the little one hopped right up to Niamh and perched on her hand, looking up at her with blatant adoration.

I understood the sentiment.

"You're sure you don't want to stay with your mama?"

The owlet chirped happily and climbed up her arm to nuzzle into her hair.

I was *not* jealous of a baby owl. Not even when Niamh pulled her hand off mine to scratch his head. Not even when I suspected her hair smelled like vanilla and apples.

"We'll be back to visit when we can," Niamh told the mother owl, who nodded in reply and flew off.

"I even snagged a cookie for you." The princess shifted and pulled a cookie from her pocket, snapping off a small piece for the owlet. "None for you, though," she sniffed at me.

"Oh no?" I watched the little owl gobble down the cookie crumb and beg for more. "I thought you were deeply offended by my refusal of baked goods?"

"Oh, I am, but the first sugar you eat in two hundred years is not going to be something I didn't even make."

I couldn't help a rumbling laugh from escaping at the snooty look she gave me.

"Why, Huntsman. Was that a *giggle?*"

"I don't know what you're talking about."

"Sure, sure, whatever you say. Well, let's go home."

As she stood, something warm stirred in my chest. Home. When was the last time I had felt like I had a home? Not since the king had died. Maybe not since my parents had traded me away. But home wasn't a little stone cottage in the woods, no matter how cozy. Home was wherever this smiling girl and her increasingly large flock of birds led me.

I would need to leave her when the time came. Nothing had changed. If anything, today's excursion only reinforced Niamh's need for a future king whom the Unseelie fae would love and trust like they did her. But, for today, I pushed those thoughts down and followed my princess home.

The unicorns were only the beginning. We went on more excursions and began undoing some of the damage I'd brought on the Unseelie fae as Moriath's Huntsman. Sometimes just the two of us, but usually with Estrid's blade at our side.

We relocated a peiste Moriath had ordered me to set on an asrai village. Niamh's ability to talk to the giant water serpent allowed us to locate the peiste's family and bring them home as well. We brought supplies to a tribe of grogachs whose forest I had watched be trampled by giants, and threatened a swamp full of sheerie who had taken to leading travelers into Moriath's traps.

I avoided bringing Niamh into any situations that were too dangerous, but I wanted her to see more of the kingdom. So she could see how much it needed help, but also how beautiful its mountains and forests were and how varied and interesting its inhabitants.

Between missions, Niamh collected more tattoos. Estrid inked runes for speed, silence, stamina, and night vision onto her spine, but even after two months of training, her use of them remained inconsistent.

"You're still relying on your own magic." I circled the princess in the greenhouse. Spring was approaching, but the snow still reached up to my knees outside. Her owl ignored us and slept in the apple tree.

"Isn't that what *you* do, oh fearsome Huntsman?"

I pressed against her weak shield, grunting as my hand broke through the barrier. "I have an affinity for runes." I pulled my hand back and the barrier shattered. "You have an affinity for animals, which is impressive, but won't stop a blade coming for your throat. You need the magic you can channel from Faerie to protect you."

Narrowing my eyes, I considered for a moment, then tossed a dagger at the white hen watching us.

"*Thurisaz! Raidho!*"

Before my brain had time to register the movement, Niamh had a dagger pressed against my throat.

Better.

"How *dare* you," she seethed.

"I wouldn't hurt your chicken, Princess. Trust my aim better than that." I gently pushed her dagger down and stepped past her to inspect the shield around Meringue. The fluffy white hen pecked at the ground, unconcerned by my lazily thrown blade. "This is much better. You could fend off a fomóire with this. A giant," I added at her confused look. She still had so much to learn about Tír na nÓg.

Niamh stalked past me to scoop Meringue into her arms, the downy white chicken clucking happily. She cooed at it while glaring daggers at me.

I sighed. "I just wanted to remind you of how much power you can draw from the land if you are properly motivated. And I would appreciate it if you were as motivated to protect *yourself* as you are the birds."

Espresso looked up at me from underfoot, so I picked up the brown and black hen. Even nearly full grown, she was a small bird. I pulled an oatmeal cookie from my pocket for her.

"You know I don't make those cookies for the chickens," Niamh grumbled.

"You told me they were healthy," I said innocently as the bird pecked the oatmeal crumbs out of my hand.

"I was trying to convince *you* to eat one, and you know it."

I shrugged, not interested in having this argument again. "Use a proper shield around *yourself* and not a chicken, and I'll eat a cookie."

"I don't think you know how bribery is supposed to work," grumbled Niamh.

"That's the deal."

She set down the chicken and went back to training with renewed—if grumpy—enthusiasm. But it still wasn't enough motivation. She learned to use her other runes beautifully in a matter of days, but the shield eluded her.

And so another week passed without sweets. But as I watched Niamh train, I had to admit that cookies were the least of my temptations.

Chapter 33

Niamh

"KYLIAN! NIAMH! YOU NEED TO—*AH!*"

I paused in my mixing at the sound of squawking chickens and dwarven curses.

"I thought the chickens weren't allowed in the house?" Estrid stumbled into the kitchen, Pip and Snickerdoodle weaving underfoot. She stopped and stared at me. "Seriously?"

"What?" I fed a dried cranberry to Latte, who was perched on a stool beside me.

"Even *you?*" Estrid threw a shocked look at Kylian reading on the sofa with Essie asleep on his lap. The little hen was looking beautiful with her adult black and copper-laced feathers now fully grown in.

"It wasn't my idea." Kylian continued reading as if he hadn't lured his favourite hen over with a slice of sourdough bread.

"I talked with them, and they agreed to no pooping in the house. So there's no problem." I gave each of the chickens on the floor a dried cranberry. "Is there, chickies?"

"Honestly." Estrid pinched the bridge of her nose. "Whatever. This isn't important right now. My father received an urgent message from one of our outposts while I was there. Moriath has set an ellén trechend made of ice on the piskie city at the edge of Nidavellir's mountains." She unloaded her backpack of supplies onto the counter.

"A what?"

"It's a giant three-headed bird," she told me. "One large enough to take down a Tuatha Dé Danann town, never mind a city of fae the size of butterflies."

"But this is a construct?" Kylian set down his book and sat up straighter, causing Essie to wake with a disgruntled squawk.

"Yes," confirmed Estrid. "One of Moriath's ice-crafted monsters."

"Is it near a gate?" I pulled off the apron protecting my striped knee-length dress, wiping my hands on a towel.

"Princess," Kylian warned.

"Yes." Estrid's eyes flicked from me to Kylian. "It's a small gate, but even *he* should be able to fit through it."

"Great." I covered the bowl of cookie dough with a towel. "Let's go."

"Princess," said Kylian again.

"What are we waiting for? I'll change into pants, and we can be out of here in two minutes."

"*Niamh*," said Kylian, finally gaining my whole attention.

"What?" I said, exasperated.

"This is likely a trap."

"And?"

Estrid started putting groceries away, watching us out of the corner of her eye.

"*And* Moriath has nearly killed you twice," he pointed out.

"Is it your plan for me to stay in this cabin for the rest of my life?" I asked. "Do you not want me to confront her? Ever?"

"Not on *her* terms."

"Kylian. If you think I'm just going to sit here and bake while a giant three-headed ice bird takes out a city of . . . How many piskies?"

"About two thousand," Estrid said quietly.

"Two *thousand?*" I turned to Kylian. "Get your axe."

"She wants you dead." Kylian set Essie down on the ground.

I could feel how conflicted he was through the bond, but it was *his* fault that I was so worried about the Unseelie fae.

"Well, then, you'd better come along to keep me safe because I'm not letting her destroy any more Unseelie lives. Not if I can help it, and certainly not if I'm the cause of it. Two thousand fae, Kylian. Could you really live with yourself if you didn't stop her?"

He clenched his jaw. "Fine," he ground out. "Get your sword, Estrid."

She nodded and dashed into her room.

"I am *done* letting Moriath destroy my kingdom, Kylian." I slammed my fist down on the table and saw a matching fire flash in his eyes.

"All right, Princess," he said. "Let's save some faeries."

"You'll need to crawl through the middle." Estrid sketched an arch with her hand as we stood in front of the Frost Gate. The icy gate still glittered with drifting flakes of frost in the early spring warmth, and a chill radiated from it, like if someone had left the walk-in freezer at the café open.

Kylian grimaced but nodded.

I lifted my leather-gloved hand to where Fluffy—no longer a little puffball but a beautiful white owl with black-tipped feathers and majestic ear tufts—blinked at me.

"Fluffy," I began.

I wish you wouldn't persist in calling me by my baby name. I'm Frederick Otus Sharpbeak the Third. No one calls me Fluffy anymore.

"Your sisters called you Fluffy when we visited them."

The owl just stared at me.

"Well, you won't let me call you Freddy, so you're just going to have to deal with it. Also, you'll need to go through the gate with Estrid," I told the bird.

He continued to stare, unblinking. *But I'm* your *owl. I'm supposed to make you look more heroic when you smite your enemies.*

"I know, but if I'm crawling, I can't carry you, and we only have three keys. It's Estrid, or you ride on my foot while I crawl."

That's not very dignified, complained Fluffy, ruffling his feathers.

"I know," I said. "But saving a city of fae will be very heroic."

That's true, mused the owl.

"And I'll bake cookies when we get back," I promised.

Fluffy tilted his head. *Oatmeal raisin?*

"You got it."

Fine, I'll go with the dwarf. This once.

I turned to Estrid. "We're ready."

Estrid—who of course had understood only my half of our conversation—nodded, checking the sword on her back before reaching out an arm for Fluffy.

The owl sighed and glided down to her. He turned his head to give me a look of long-suffering as Estrid ducked her head and disappeared through the gate.

"I'll be at your back," said Kylian.

I nodded. "I know."

With a sigh, I dropped to my knees in front of the gate's center. Fluffy was right, this *did* feel undignified. But a moment later, I emerged through a mossy hollow log covered with delicate fairy bells crafted in gold.

The bells hung from golden vines with fanciful curls and leaves crafted in such exquisite detail that they had to have been made by very small hands. As I crawled through, the bells jingled, the little crystal stamens tinkling inside the golden flowers.

As soon as I was through, I stood, and Fluffy immediately landed on my shoulder. I stepped aside as Kylian squeezed through the tiny gate. Estrid peered up at a giant oak tree, its leaves bright green with the first spring growth. But, as huge as the tree was, that's not what captured my attention.

Tiny houses covered the entire tree, some built of twigs and moss, some woven from grasses and hanging from branches. Some were carved into the tree itself with little balconies and miniature gardens of mushrooms, flowering moss, and tiny wildflowers. There were no staircases or ladders, because the piskies didn't need them.

Tiny faeries, no taller than my hand, flew every which way with wings like butterflies in every color. As beautiful as the city was, the faeries were clearly terrified, scooping their children into houses near the trunk of the tree and arming themselves with tiny swords the size of sewing needles.

"It's the Huntsman!" shrieked a piskie, and the faeries scattered in fear.

"Wait, we're here to *help*," I called.

Most of the faeries disappeared into the tree, but a little man with tiny orange wings, sparkling silver armor, and a crown carved from a gleaming acorn cap landed on a branch near us.

"I am Prince Darach." The piskie drew his sword. "If you've come to command that ice creature—"

"It hasn't attacked yet?" I interrupted.

The prince shook his head. "Who are you?"

"I'm Princess Niamh." Funny how easily that came to me now, but introducing myself as a pie baker here to save them didn't have the same ring to it.

Darach peered at me. "The crown princess. Not dead after all. I have heard rumors of your return. Why are you with *him?*" The prince pointed his sword at Kylian, who scanned the forest surrounding the tree.

"He's on our side," I said. "I know it's hard to believe, but he always has been."

"Where's the beast?" Kylian asked.

Darach looked from Kylian to me.

"I serve the princess," Kylian said shortly.

Prince Darach considered, then nodded. Apparently, when your city was in danger, you were willing to let some things slide.

"And this is Estrid," I introduced my friend. "Her father, King Ulf, received word of the ellén trechend from his sentry, and we came as quickly as we could."

"But it still hasn't attacked?" pressed the dwarf.

Darach shook his head. "It's been making passes overhead, but it hasn't landed. We don't know why."

Kylian looked sharply at me.

"Fine, yes, it might be a trap." I squinted up into the trees.

"Trap?" Darach asked.

"Moriath may have sent the bird thing for me," I confessed.

"She definitely did, Princess," rumbled Kylian.

"Do you think she's close by?" I asked him.

"No, she'll be watching through her mirror from a safe distance. She's testing you."

I made a rude gesture at the sky.

"Very mature, Princess," said Kylian wryly.

I smiled sweetly at him.

"Anyway, Prince Darach, don't worry. We'll keep your city safe." I lifted my arm, and the piskie prince drew back as Fluffy flapped his wings. "Fluffy, can you please fly up and see if you can locate the bird monster?"

Fluffy blinked at me.

"Hero, remember?" I coaxed.

They'd better be exceptional cookies, grumbled the owl.

"Oh, they will be," I promised.

With beetles this time.

"Gross," I told the owl, who just stared at me with big golden eyes. "Fine, but I'm not catching them."

You never appreciate my culinary input, groused the owl as he launched himself above the treeline.

"If it's after *me*, maybe we can draw it away from the city," I thought out loud.

Estrid looked at Kylian, who shook his head.

"Why not? It's me she's after."

"She'll still attack the piskies," said Kylian. "Moriath would rather keep you busy trying to protect innocent lives. It will make you more vulnerable to attack."

"Well, that's not very nice," I huffed.

"She's not interested in a fair battle, or she wouldn't have poisoned you," he pointed out.

"Maybe if Fluffy can locate the ice construct, we can sneak up on it." Estrid tapped her fingers on the hilt of her dagger.

"We're at your command," proclaimed the piskie prince as a group of about a hundred tiny armored knights landed on the branch beside him.

"Thank you." I silently vowed to do anything I could to keep these tiny fae out of combat. I couldn't imagine their swords, however sharp they might be, having any effect on a giant creature created from ice.

I found it! shrieked Fluffy, dropping through the overhead leaves.

I held out my arm for the owl as he landed. "Great. Where is—?"

Shards of ice crashed to the ground as a giant three-headed vulture dropped down in front of us, flattening a copse of small trees.

"Never mind."

The construct stood taller than the oak tree, with talons as thick as my arms. Spikes of jagged icicles protruded from its beaks and ran down each of its long necks, to become tall, wickedly sharp spines on its back. I could vaguely see the forest through the beast, warped and blurred by the ice. It lashed its barbed tail and opened its enormous middle beak to unleash a scream like shattering glass.

CHAPTER 34

NIAMH

I BRACED MYSELF FOR AN ATTACK, THEN stared in shock as the sound of beating wings surrounded us. Falcons crafted from ice poured out of each of the giant creature's beaks, hurtling through the air toward us.

"*Runes*, Princess," ordered Kylian.

I hurriedly squeezed my eyes shut, picturing the runes for strength, speed, and shielding. Estrid and Kylian shouted the Dvergr words along with me as the birds swarmed from the frozen monster.

Prince Darach roared, and his butterfly-winged knights followed him into battle, surrounding the closest falcon with their tiny silver swords.

The ellén trechend just watched. Was Moriath toying with us? Testing how we responded to the smaller attackers?

Finally, an epic battle. Fluffy launched off my arm, and my heart clenched as he tangled with a flying construct in an explosion of feathers and frozen crystals.

"Focus!" Kylian yelled as an ice falcon hit my pitiful shield.

The barrier flickered and failed like all my previous attempts at shielding, but I got my sword up in time to cut through the creature's crystalline wing and send it crashing to the ground.

"Yes!" I cheered. "Wait, what?"

The falcon struggled to its feet, a new wing of frozen crystals rapidly growing out from its shoulder, before it launched at me again with a cry of rage.

Kylian crashed through the bird with a swing of his silver axe. This time, the construct burst in a shower of tiny icicles, and something fell with a thud.

"You have to destroy the power source." Kylian pointed at two halves of a feather crafted from gold, lying in a pile of frost.

"You've fought these before?" I raised my blade as more birds flew at us.

"I've fought alongside them, Princess," Kylian reminded me grimly.

I didn't have time to consider his words as a cry overhead grabbed my attention. I glanced up to see a tiny knight scream in distress, caged in icy talons. My breath caught in fear for her, but then a group of piskie knights mobbed the bird from behind in a coordinated attack. Their silver blades pierced the ice, cleaving through the power source. The bird burst into sparkling dust, and the rescued piskie grinned at her team. "Good work!" she yelled. "Let's get the next one!"

"They'll be fine. They're warriors." Kylian grabbed my arm, spinning me around to position my back to his as the sparkling falcons surrounded us.

"But, Estrid and Fluffy!" My friends were both locked in battle with the winged attackers.

"They can take care of themselves. You need to do the same."

I had no choice but to listen as more falcons descended on us. When I raised my blade, a deadly calm replaced my fear, and my head emptied of everything but the fight. Months of training with Kylian, augmented by the speed and strength runes, had my body moving like it never had before, my sword an extension of my arm.

I could feel Kylian at my back through the bond, our movements perfectly in sync as we took down one enemy after another, our friends fighting around us. Together, we kept the birds from reaching the piskie tree behind us.

That's the last one. Fluffy swooped down to land on my shoulder.

Sure enough, the sky was empty. But there wasn't time to do more than glance around to check that my allies were all still safe and uninjured before the ellén trechend screamed again. How many birds could fit inside the beast? But, no. Instead of winged attackers, this time giant icicle spears exploded out of the creature's mouths, aimed straight for us.

Kylian stepped in front of me. "Princess, *back*. Estrid!"

"Thurisaz!" my companions yelled together.

A shield snapped into place in front of us. The force of the shards made Kylian stumble back beside me, but nothing got through the glittering golden shield.

The creature flapped its giant wings, two of its heads craning higher this time. My heart jumped into my throat as I saw where they were aimed.

"Kylian!" I yelled frantically.

"We can't make a shield that big, Princess." He kept his eyes locked on the monster. "But you can."

"I can't," I whispered. Not once had I made a shield even half as strong as his.

"Then they'll die," he said.

The bird screamed again, and another barrage of ice, wider and higher this time, erupted from its icy maws.

I had to do this. I closed my eyes. *"Thurisaz!"*

The rune on my back flared, and I felt magic rush through me in a tingling wave.

The ellén trechend screeched in frustration, and I opened my eyes to see the massive frozen shards crashing against a shimmering golden barrier surrounding the tree.

"I did it!" I punched my fist in the air. "Kylian, *look*."

"I see it," said the Huntsman tersely. "Maybe next time, you could create the shield in *front* of you."

I grimaced. "Oh, yeah."

"Get her behind her shield," Kylian ordered Estrid. "I'll take care of this."

"Take care of what?" I stared at Kylian as Estrid dragged me back behind my shield. Fluffy flew up into the piskie tree. "Take care of *that?* The giant three-headed *monster?!"*

"Focus." Estrid let go of my arm. "Keep the shield up."

The shield flickered, and I tried to concentrate as the monster screamed again, its ice spears embedding in my weakened shield. But Kylian ran toward the beast, shards crashing off his smaller shield.

"He'll be fine." Estrid almost sounded like she believed it. "He's the strongest fighter in the Unseelie Kingdom. Focus."

I took a deep breath and reinforced the shield. The frozen chunks pushed out to shatter on the ground in front of us, but I kept my eyes glued on Kylian.

"We have to *help* him."

"Can you do that and hold the shield at the same time?" she asked.

I could not. It was taking all of my concentration to keep the golden shield up as yet another barrage of shards crashed against it. Small folk in the tree were screaming.

"He's stronger than you think." Estrid gripped my arm. "And he has his runes."

He did. I could see them flaring on his arms as he ran toward the ice monster, determination shining through our bond as he reinforced his runes for speed, strength, and accuracy. Then he ran up a rock and leapt toward the bird's middle neck.

I held my breath.

Kylian flew through the air, swinging his silver axe down. The construct screeched as shards of shattered ice burst from the hit.

The giant bird staggered, and for a second, I thought Kylian had defeated it. Then the monster suddenly spun and slammed into my huntsman with a frozen beak, sending him flying.

"*Kylian!*" I screamed as he crashed into a tree and collapsed on the ground, shield faltering.

The huntsman scrambled to his feet, shield back in place, but I could tell that he was favoring his right arm.

"Estrid, we need to help!"

My friend had blanched. "What can we do?" Her voice broke. "I want to help, too, but he is the strongest warrior in the kingdom, and he barely made a dent on it. Moriath must have poured a lot of magic into that construct. We need to find its power source."

"I can't see anything." Unlike the falcons, the ellén trechend was so big that the ice warped our view inside it. The power source could be anywhere in its giant body.

The construct opened its beaks to shriek again.

"*There*," I yelled, pointing. "The right head. I can see the gold through its mouth."

"Got it." Estrid nodded. "Inform Kylian through that bond of yours."

The dwarf squeezed my arm and dashed toward the ice monster. One of its heads spun to track her.

"Estrid!"

But she was already through my barrier, her shield glittering faintly around her. She wasn't as strong as Kylian. How many hits could her shield take before breaking?

"Over here!" Estrid dodged as the beast let out another barrage of ice. It now watched her with two of its vulture heads.

I narrowed my eyes and kept my shield solid this time, the frozen spears shattering on impact.

"Over here, bird brain!" shouted Estrid.

I didn't know if the construct understood her taunts, but it turned all three heads in her direction with a shriek. We had to act fast.

Kylian, the power source is in its right head, the one farthest from you.

Kylian glanced back at me and nodded. He turned toward the construct again, rolling his shoulder, which looked a little better. He must have used his healing rune.

"This way, you feathered *popsicle,*" Estrid taunted the creature, and it continued to track her movement as she ran closer.

Kylian circled behind the giant vulture, readying himself for another leap. As much as I admired his skill, I couldn't help wondering what good it would do. He had already attacked with his full strength, and his axe hadn't sunk nearly deep enough to reach the construct's golden power source.

It's okay, Princess, said Kylian down the bond. *Don't worry about me. Just keep them safe.*

Don't *worry* about him? Stupid man. I bit my lip in thought. Could I extend my shield to protect him without also putting the construct inside the barrier?

I could feel his determination to protect me at all costs, but I was the one who had brought us out here. Yes, to protect the piskies, but was it worth losing *him*?

The giant vulture snapped one beak at Estrid, then another. She barely rolled out of the way in time. What could any of us do against that kind of power?

Power. Kylian had the skill, but he needed *power*. I looked up at the giant barrier fueled by the magic of Faerie.

"Please do this for me," I murmured to the magic running through my body as Kylian ran up a broken tree and launched himself toward the construct. It screamed and whipped its head toward the Huntsman. "*Uruz!*" Strength.

I pushed my magic through our bond to Kylian. The *ingwaz* rune on my wrist flared, along with the *uruz* on my back, just as Kylian's axe connected with the vulture's right skull.

The forest rang with the sound of ice shattering as the construct exploded. Shards crashed against my shield, but I was already running through the splinters, dropping the barrier as soon as the shards fell safely around the piskies' tree.

"Estrid! *Kylian!*"

"I'm fine," Estrid hollered from behind a boulder. Pieces of melting icicles surrounded her, but her shield looked intact. The rock had taken most of the blows.

"Kylian!"

He didn't answer as I ran to the heart of the icy shrapnel, where he had hit the construct. Kylian lay on his back, eyes closed, a huge shard of ice through his shoulder. Another protruded from his knee, while smaller ones peppered his side.

"No, no, Kylian." I dropped to my knees beside him, only breathing when I saw that he did. His eyes fluttered open, and I felt a flicker of pained amusement through the bond.

"Could you be any more *reckless?*" I shouted at him, yanking the icicle out of his shoulder. He grunted in pain, and I slapped my hand over it. "*Sowulo!*" I activated my healing rune before shoving it through the bond.

"Princess," he said.

"We could have come up with a *plan*." I pulled the shard out of his leg, roughly healing that one as well.

Kylian grimaced. "You have such a gentle touch."

"You don't get to make jokes!" The other shards were already melting, but I healed those as well with another shove of my magic into him.

"Princess." He smiled at me as he pushed up to a sitting position.

"You could have *died*. You almost did. I am tired of you thinking your life isn't worth anything!" I hit him on the shoulder.

Kylian caught my hand and pulled me down onto his lap. "*Niamh*. I'm okay."

"An icicle could have gone through your heart! And don't joke that you don't have one. Don't you know what that would do to me? Do you know what would happen to me without you? Do you know—?"

Kylian tangled his hand in the curls at the back of my neck, wrapping his other arm around my waist and pulling me against his chest. And then his mouth was on mine.

I gasped in surprise. He started to pull back, but I wrapped my arms around his neck and kissed him back. No way was I stopping before he knew how much I needed him. His lips were soft and warm and so right against mine. I knew in that moment that my heart belonged to him. Like it or not, I was never letting him go.

He pulled back, his forehead resting against mine. "I'm okay, Niamh. You saved me."

My cheeks were wet with tears. "I can't lose you."

"You won't. I'm here for you. I've always been here for you. Okay?"

I nodded, scrubbing my wet cheeks. Kylian gathered me against his chest, his chin resting on top of my curls.

My racing heart gradually began to slow.

"What kind of cookies do you want?" I said into his black shirt.

"What?"

"Or pie? Cheesecake?" I sniffed. "I make an excellent berry cheesecake."

"I don't—"

"Didn't you see that shield? We had a deal. You promised to eat my baking."

We both looked in the direction of the piskie city. Unharmed. The tiny people flew toward us with cheers.

Kylian chuckled. "It's been so long that I don't even know what I like."

"Well, then." I threaded my fingers through his scraped knuckles. "I guess we'll find out together."

Chapter 35

Kylian

THE PISKIES INSISTED ON THANKING US WITH a feast, giving us no time to talk privately about the kiss. Admittedly, I felt grateful, as I hadn't sorted out my own feelings. All the reasons why us being together was a bad idea still existed. She deserved someone without my issues, and the kingdom needed someone they could love ruling by her side. And even though the piskies, who had fled from me earlier, were now weaving garlands of wildflowers, leaves, and iridescent beetle shells for us, I couldn't help but note how the mothers still kept the little ones away from me as they offered their thumbnail-sized babies up for a kiss from the princess.

Despite all that, I couldn't bring myself to regret giving in to my impulsive need to prove to her that I was all right, to quiet the panic I felt through the bond. And the way her eyes had flashed when she was angry, the pink that rage had brought to her cheeks? Well, I hadn't been immune to that either.

While Niamh laughed and cooed at the tiny infants too little to receive their wings, her hand found mine, resting between us on the mossy log serving as a bench. I didn't pull away. Instead, I ran my thumb along her knuckles and enjoyed her little shiver. She glanced at me, and I became very interested in examining the feast in front of us.

The low, flat rock was bedecked with flowers. Acorn caps and leaves lay heaped with roasted mushrooms, nuts, and even tiny iced cakes. The faeries had given us their largest cups of mead, which were about as tall as my little finger and, I suspected, were actually full kegs with the tops removed.

Niamh laughed at something the piskie prince beside her said. I picked up a tiny black something with my free hand and squinted, trying to guess what it was.

A piskie woman flew over, noting my curiosity. "Roast cricket, my lord."

"Cricket!" Niamh glanced over. "Audrey says they're an excellent source of protein. Gavin bought this big box of cricket protein bars on sale, and they ate them while they were running around in Paris." She paused. "Although, now that I think about it, they were probably here, not Paris."

"So, she liked them?" I asked.

"Well, I don't know if I'd go *that* far." Niamh tilted her head, remembering. "I seem to remember her saying that the carrot cake flavor tasted . . ."

I looked at her.

"Not great," she finished.

"Who would make desserts out of crickets?" The tiny cook looked aghast.

"So this is not cake flavored?" I asked the cook.

"Certainly not! This is prime aphid-fed cricket, citrus brined and seasoned with rosemary and garlic."

Well, that sounded pretty good. I shrugged and popped the bug into my mouth.

The cook, Niamh, Estrid, and even Fluffy watched intently as I chewed.

"Crunchy," I said. "And delicious," I added to the chef, who nodded proudly. I ate another one. "You're not going to try them?" I offered a cricket to Niamh.

"Oh, no." She held up her free hand.

The piskie cook popped her hands onto her hips and stared at her.

"Oh, I'm just . . . I'm a vegetarian," she explained. "I don't eat meat."

"Do crickets count as meat?" I waved a bug her way.

"Yes," she said firmly. "I think."

"Of course they're meat," huffed the cook. "We raised the herd ourselves in the west pasture." She pointed at a clump of clover near the edge of the meadow. "Never you mind, Princess. Try a cake."

Niamh gingerly ate a pink confection the size of her fingernail. "Oh, it's delicious!"

While the cook and princess discussed piskie baking ingredients, I made a mental note to see if the piskies needed any supplies. Providing a feast for people as large as we were had to take a toll on their larders.

Estrid nudged me with her elbow. "So . . . things are going *well?*"

She smiled and waggled her eyebrows.

"I don't know if I would say that," I said cautiously.

Estrid nodded with a smirk. "I'm sure I just *imagined* you making out with Niamh after defeating the ice monster then."

I attempted to extract my hand from Niamh's, but she held

on firmly. So firmly that I wondered if she still had residual Faerie magic giving her strength.

"Well, I'll be sure to give you some privacy when we get back so you can talk about *nothing*. I need to get some more ink anyway if we're going to finish the *perthro* rune."

Niamh looked over. "Speaking of tattoos, I've been meaning to ask if you have any colored inks. Reds or pink—"

A sudden avian cry overhead interrupted her, followed by a shouted, "Falcon!"

I surged to my feet, peering through the leaves overhead.

"What is it?" Niamh asked.

"Moriath," I said grimly.

"Are you sure?" The princess stood, too.

"No, I need to see the bird."

"Fluffy, go with the piskies and take a look for me. I'll give you a cake," she coaxed as the piskie knights banded together and took off in the direction of the noise. "And show me what you see."

The owl flew up out of sight.

I stared at Niamh. "He can send you visions from a distance?"

"We've been practicing." She shrugged as if she wasn't the most powerful Unseelie fae in generations. "Got it," she said a moment later, closing her eyes.

I did the same as the image of a slate-blue bird with a dark head and pale, speckled underside appeared in my mind. She could be any peregrine but for the golden glint in her clever eyes. "Ránach," I said. "Moriath's familiar. She must have sent her to check on the ellén trechend. Who knows how long she's been spying here."

Niamh shivered. "I wish we could help."

"They seem to have it well under control," I pointed out as the cries grew louder.

The small knights and Fluffy came into view as they attacked the falcon with swords and talons. Ránach shrieked again, landing a swipe on the owl before disappearing through the branches, Fluffy in hot pursuit.

The prince and his knights landed on the table to accept the fussing of the piskie folk, but none of them seemed injured. Soon after, Fluffy also returned, looking disgruntled. The owl scratched at a spot on his wing, and Niamh examined it, spreading the feathers.

"You look fine." She paused, listening to the owl in her mind. "I'm sorry it itches, but I don't see anything. Wait, maybe there's a bit of gold . . ." She narrowed her eyes and then shook her head. "Nope, nothing. Just a scratch from that nasty bird of Moriath's."

The owl made a pitiful noise.

"I know," Niamh said soothingly while feeding him a tiny cake. "It's not your fault. You're not built for speed like she is." Fluffy looked up at the princess mournfully, and she laughed and gave him another cake.

"Moriath is not going to be happy." Estrid stared in the direction Ránach had flown.

"No," I agreed.

"And she was soooo happy before." Niamh rolled her eyes. "How does this make a difference?"

"Before," I said, "you didn't have the power to destroy a giant ice construct."

"We did it together," she countered. "The three of us."

"We did," I agreed. "But I and everyone here would be dead without you."

"Say you're right. What do we do now?" She sighed. "Back to hiding?"

"Is that what you want?"

"She'll just do something like this again, won't she?" Niamh shook her head. "Or worse."

"Probably," I agreed.

We watched as the little piskie children shook off their mothers' clutches and began playing again, racing around the glen on tiny wings.

"It's time," Niamh said. "The best way to protect the Unseelie folk is to take the fight to Moriath."

"Yes! *Finally.*" Estrid punched her fist in the air.

My insides clenched at the thought of putting Niamh purposely in danger after all these years, but as she stood strong and fierce beside me, I knew she was right.

I nodded. "It's time to plan our offensive, Princess. Time to claim your throne."

CHAPTER 36

NIAMH

I HUMMED TO MYSELF AS I TIED on my apron. Kylian sat across the table from me with his latest mystery novel.

We had returned from the piskie tree late last night—those tiny people really liked to party—and Estrid had left after a late breakfast to talk with the kings about our plans and to pick up the inks to finish my runes. I'd asked her to grab some colored ink, too. So now it was just me and my Huntsman.

Apple?

And our seven chickens. I fed Pip an apple peeling, and she gobbled it down happily.

The spring breeze drifted through the open back door, and the chickens wandered in and out as they pleased. Fluffy didn't enjoy the indoors, even if there were cookies, and he couldn't understand why the chickens didn't want to soar above the treetops with him. I had explained that they were very fat, but he still kept trying to convince them.

In the back of my mind, I knew I should be more concerned about Moriath, who was undoubtedly coming up with more plots to do me in, but we'd talk about that later with Estrid.

Right now, it was a beautiful day, I was getting ready to bake, and I had fallen asleep last night with the memory of Kylian's lips on mine. I couldn't bring myself to worry today.

"So, you really have no idea what you like?" I asked Kylian.

"I told you. It's been a long time." He tapped the table.

"Is there anything your mother made when you were younger?"

"She didn't cook."

"That's so sad." I took the lids off a few bottles of spices and lined them up.

"Most queens don't bake, Princess," he reminded me.

"Niamh," I corrected him. "We've kissed. Surely you can call me by my name now."

"Niamh," he said softly, and I felt my cheeks flush.

"And I just meant that . . . Well, I'm sorry you didn't have someone to take care of you."

"I took care of myself."

"I know. But I'm going to take care of you from now on, okay?"

He opened his mouth, doubtless to say something about how we couldn't have a future together because I should be with some boring, *nice* Unseelie noble, so I cut him off.

"So now that we've settled that, smell these and tell me which ones you like." I pushed the spice bottles across the table. Kylian's fingertips brushed mine as he took the last bottle from me, and I felt a spark from him through the bond that matched the little shiver I felt at the contact.

Kylian read the labels on each bottle before obediently sniffing the spices, sneezing when he hit the ginger.

"Smell, not *snort*," I chided.

"I like that one, though, I think." Kylian squinted at the golden powder.

"Okay, that's a good start." I tapped my lip. "And you like coffee . . ."

"When no one's trying to kill me with it, yes."

"Who would do such a thing? How about chocolate?" I passed him a bowl of dark chocolate chunks, and he handed one to Essie before trying a piece.

"No more chocolate for the chickens!" I protested.

The black and copper hen gave me a sad face.

"It's for your own safety," I told the black hen sternly. "Good?" I asked Kylian.

He nodded and took another chunk.

"Strong flavors, then." I scribbled some ideas down in my notebook. "I bet you'd like molasses too. I wonder if I have any left. For today, I'll make a salted double chocolate cookie."

"Salted? I thought you were convincing me to eat sweets?"

"The salty makes it sweeter."

Kylian looked dubious.

"Much like my personality." I batted my eyelashes at him and actually got a rumbling laugh. *Winning!*

But then his look turned serious again. *Boo.*

"We need to talk," he started.

"Is it about cookies?" I took the lid off the butter dish and sliced a cup off the pound of butter.

"Niamh," he said.

"Chickens?" I slid the butter into the mixing bowl.

Kylian glanced at Essie, who nudged his hand for pets. "Not exactly."

"Those are the only two subjects I'm currently interested in talking about." I carefully measured sugar into the bowl and pushed it across to Kylian. "Cream this."

"You know what—"

"That means mix them together until they're fluffy." I handed him a wooden spoon, then pulled out another bowl and measured out the flour.

"The kiss—"

"If you dare call that kiss a mistake, I will . . ." I searched for an appropriate threat. "Mix raisins in with the chocolate chips in these cookies."

"What?"

"Chocolate chip raisin cookies are an abomination. Is it a raisin or is it a chocolate chip? No one knows until they take a bite. Anarchy!"

"It's just that you'll be queen, Niamh." Kylian mixed the butter. "And whoever you marry . . ."

"I'm sorry." I set down the cocoa and stared at him. "Not only have we not actually settled the whole me-being-queen thing, but did you propose marriage to me? Did I miss something?"

"Well . . . no."

"Did I propose to you?" I picked up Pip and looked the speckled orange hen in the eyes. "Tell me honestly. Am I that forgetful?"

Apple? She tilted her head, fluffy head feathers sticking out.

"You ate it all. I might have some carrot peels around here, though." I set the chicken down and found the scrap bowl.

"This is serious, Niamh. Whoever you marry will be king. That can't be me. I never should have kissed you."

I closed my eyes and reminded myself to remain calm. He wasn't rejecting me. Not really. If anything, he was rejecting himself.

I took a deep breath and added baking soda to the bowl, along with a pinch of salt.

"First of all, I know you think you'd make a bad king, what with how you've spent Moriath's reign—"

"Terrorizing the kingdom?" Kylian kept stirring.

"I was going to say *protecting*. Potayto, potahto."

"Your subjects don't see it that way." Kylian didn't look up.

"Well, they don't know you like I do." I leaned over the table. "No one cares as much about the Unseelie folk as you do. And secondly, who says you have to be king? If I should happen to become queen, there could be a consort situation. Until I convince you to rule with me, but that's a secret. Don't tell."

Kylian gave me a look of long-suffering.

"And thirdly, I'll get married when I want to, and as pointed out, no one has proposed to anyone yet. Stop borrowing trouble and enjoy the moment. After all, this is an excellent moment." I set down my spoon and walked around the table to Kylian.

"Oh?"

"Yes." I dipped my finger into the bowl and stole a bit of creamed butter and sugar. "This is the best part of baking cookies. Try a bit. Not too much or you'll throw off the ratios, but you can't make cookies and not try the creamed butter and sugar."

Kylian looked skeptical as he scooped a dab of butter, but his eyes widened when he tasted it.

"See?" I leaned in and kissed his cheek before whispering into his ear, "It's okay to just be happy. All right?"

I leaned back, but Kylian stood and caught me around the waist, pressing me back against the table. Essie left with a jealous squawk.

"All right," he whispered against my lips before kissing me softly.

I sighed happily into the kiss, wrapping my arms around his neck.

When we broke apart, I said, "No more freaking out?"

He rested his forehead on my shoulder. "No promises, but I'll try."

"Good, because I'm not that easy to get rid of." I straightened. "Did you hear a popping noise?"

We both turned to see a tiny smoky-blue dragon appear in the air and land on the table.

"Falkor?" I crouched down to eye level with Isobel's pet, who held a small package wrapped in a dainty handkerchief in his mouth.

The little dragon dropped the parcel, stole a chunk of chocolate from the bowl on the table, and then disappeared.

"Huh." I reached for the package, but Kylian snagged it first.

"I don't think Isobel sent me a handkerchief bomb." I held out my hand for the package.

Kylian ignored me and examined it before carefully unwrapping the delicate cloth and revealing a small gold device with a note. I snatched the paper before he could protest.

Neve, I'm passing this along from Audrey, who sent it to Miss Chloe, along with the message: Charge your dang phone and call me.

Hope to see you soon for tea and pie!

- Isobel

"It's a charger!" I grabbed the device and dashed to my bedroom.

Now, where was that thing? I pulled open the drawer of my end table, pushing aside notes, cookbooks, and a pair of gloves to reveal my forgotten phone. The golden charging device had a familiar-looking cord on one end. I plugged my phone in and bounced on my toes, waiting as the screen reluctantly flickered to life.

I ignored the missed-call notifications and the wall of texts, hitting the call button and choosing the first name on my contact list.

Kylian leaned on my door frame as I waited for my friend to pick up.

"Neve!" Audrey squealed. "I've been trying to get a hold of you all week! I sent like ten texts."

I heard a muffled noise in the background.

"No, I will not ask her to make you cheesecake, you greedy wolf!" Audrey said away from the phone. "Sorry about that. How are you?"

"Good," I said slowly, glancing at Kylian.

"Mmmm, *how* good?" she asked with a laugh. Audrey could always tell when something was up with me. "Actually, no, tell me in person. We need to talk."

"Aren't we currently talking?"

"I heard about the ice constructs. Sounds like Moriath is stepping up her game. You need to make a plan, hun. We should meet up."

"How do you know that?" I felt Kylian behind me and switched over to speaker so he could listen in.

"Liadan's been scrying." Audrey's voice was joined by male voices talking to each other in low tones in the background.

"Who's there with you?" I asked.

"I'll tell you everything when you get here. We're at Liadan's tower."

"It'd be safer to bring her here," Kylian suggested to me.

"Did you catch that?" I asked Audrey.

"Yeah, um, that would work," she agreed. "But I don't know where you are."

"I'll go get her when Estrid gets back." Kylian glanced out the window.

"Okay, sounds good! We'll get Liadan to set up the gate. I have to take care of something, but text me when he leaves. Okay, Neve?"

"Got it." I hated to hang up. I hadn't realized how much I missed my friend until I heard her voice. "Love you!"

"Love you, too. See you soon!"

I hung up and set my phone down.

"This is good," said Kylian. "They can help us plan our next move."

"Yes. But first . . ." I grabbed his hand.

Kylian gave me a half smile. "Cookies?"

"Always." I laughed, tugging him back into the kitchen.

Chapter 37

Niamh

"Oh, THAT'LL BE ESTRID." I SLID A tray of cookies into the oven as the front door creaked open.

"I'll go get Audrey and Gavin." Kylian set down his book.

"Not so fast! These should be cooled enough to eat now." I poked a cookie on the cooling rack. "Estrid! You're just in time to watch Kylian eat a *cookie*."

"Kylian doesn't eat sweets." The dwarf wandered into the kitchen, eyeing Meringue suspiciously. The white chicken gave Estrid an equally suspicious look in return.

"Right, but he agreed to try some, remember? And no boots in the kitchen, you know that."

Estrid harrumphed and pulled her boots off.

"You're in a mood," I said, peering at her. "Did things not go well with your dad?"

"I'll tell you later." She set her bag of inks on the table.

"Oookay. Anyway, your bad mood will be defenseless in the face of salted double chocolate cookies!" I handed one to Estrid and then took my time selecting the one I deemed most perfect from the rack. I finally decided on one with a beautiful sprinkling of salt on top that I could tell would still be a little gooey in the middle. I carefully picked it up and presented it to Kylian.

"You're going to stare at me while I eat this, aren't you?" He took the cookie from my hand.

"Yes, I am."

He sighed and then took a bite.

His eyes widened and I felt a wave of emotion through the bond. It was as if allowing himself this little luxury had broken through another walled layer he had built around himself.

"It's amazing, right?" I said smugly.

"*You* are amazing." Kylian leaned forward and kissed me, his lips tasting of chocolate.

"I know," I said happily. "They're good, right?" I asked Estrid, who watched us with the strangest expression on her face as she ate her cookie.

"*Now* you can go get Audrey." I took a bite of my own cookie. Excellent. I'd have to write this one down.

"I won't be long." Kylian grabbed his boots and tied them up. "Keep a close eye on things, Estrid. It's been too quiet today. I expected more from Moriath after the ellén trechend incident."

"You're probably right," said Estrid.

Kylian strapped on his harness and slid his silver axe into place.

"See you soon." I kissed him goodbye—any excuse, honestly—and watched him head down the trail. I shivered as a shadow flitted overhead. Probably just a random bird, but still . . .

"Fluffy!" I called.

My owl flew down from his perch in a nearby tree.

It's the middle of the day. Fluffy yawned as he landed on my arm.

"I know. I'm sorry. But I saw something falcon-ish fly overhead just now. Could you go have a look?"

Fluffy blinked at me.

"Kylian thinks Moriath will try to figure out where we are." I pulled one of his favorite oatmeal cookies out of my apron pocket. I always kept a couple around just in case I had to wake him up.

All right, all right. Fluffy took a bite of the cookie. *Save the rest for when I get back,* he said, beak full of oatmeal, and then shot up into the clear blue sky.

"Thank you! I'm sure it's nothing," I added to Estrid as we went back to the kitchen, "but Kylian's worries are rubbing off on me."

"Well, you never know." Estrid held up the bag she'd brought. "Shall we get started? Were you wanting the rune first, or do you have a plan for the colored ink?" She opened up the bag, examining the vials of pink, red, and green nestled in with the black rune ink.

"Just a minute." I dashed for the greenhouse, scooping up my fluffy white hen on the way out. I didn't need any chickens distracting Estrid while she worked.

Estrid strange, said Meringue as we ran up to the apple tree.

"I know. She's in a mood," I agreed with the bird as I set her down in the grass.

Smells funny.

"Well, that's just rude." I examined the tree before picking the perfect apple, red with a blush of pink.

Apple? asked Snickerdoodle, tilted his feather-crested head.

I grabbed a couple more apples off the tree and tossed them down to the waiting chickens before heading back inside.

I set the apple down on the table, and then sniffed.

"I think your cookies are burning." Estrid was still rooting through her bag.

"Ah! I forgot to set the timer!" I grabbed a tea towel and pulled the last tray of cookies out of the oven. It was a good thing I'd already given Kylian a cookie. These were barely edible, let alone the way to break a two-centuries-long sugar fast.

"What's the apple for?" asked Estrid.

"That's what I want you to tattoo." I picked up another perfect cookie for comfort. Poor burnt cookies.

"I see." Estrid tilted her head. "Where do you want it?"

"On my arm." I untied the apron I wore over my sweater.

"I'll get set up." She set a jar of ink on the table.

"Out here?" I furrowed my brow. Estrid was always such a stickler for hygiene. "Is it clean enough?"

"I'll wipe up. It's easier to do your arm this way," she explained.

"Oh, sure. That makes sense." I ran off and changed into a sleeveless dress, buzzing with excitement to finally complete my sleeve and to have the memory of my mother to carry with me everywhere.

"Have a seat on the chair." Estrid examined the apple, turning it to find her favorite angle.

"You don't need to sketch it first?" I asked as she loaded up the black ink, squinting for a moment at the tattoo gun before turning it on.

"So you were saving this spot for an apple?" she asked, ignoring my question.

"Yeah. This whole time, I was looking for *these* apples. And, well, what I was really looking for was my mom." I sighed.

"I know that she's gone, but with everything that's going to happen now, what with confronting Moriath, I just wanted to have a little bit of her with me, you know?"

"Hmm." Estrid set the needle to my skin.

"You never talk about your mother. Was she a runecrafter like you?" I winced a little. She usually used a little magic to take the sting off, but she must have decided that an arm tattoo wasn't painful enough to bother.

"Her magic was a lot like mine." Estrid inked the outline of the apple.

"Were you close?"

"When I was younger, I thought we were," mused Estrid. "But I was never more than another tool to her."

"What happened?" I asked softly.

"She had a bad fall." Estrid didn't elaborate, and I didn't press her. She clearly didn't like talking about it.

"That's looking great!" She had outlined the apple perfectly. "You're so fast. Runes must take longer."

Estrid hummed in agreement, searching for the pink to fill the apple, before shading it with a deep red.

I admired the design. "That almost looks like you could reach out and touch it."

"I have an idea for a design to tie it all together. Do you trust me?"

"Of course."

She picked up the vial of gold ink and gave it a little shake. I thought I saw some specks of black, but when I blinked, they were gone. Must have been my imagination.

"Wow, that's pretty. How is the gold so shimmery?" I asked as Estrid filled in the space around the apple with deft strokes, creating a design of Celtic knots.

I blinked, suddenly feeling a bit tired. Maybe yesterday's battle was catching up with me.

"Thank you, child. It's an ink I've been working on for years now."

Child? I shook my head. Why would Estrid call me that? Something felt off, but I couldn't seem to collect my thoughts. Everything was fuzzy.

Estrid pricked her thumb with the needle, a bead of blood coating the tip.

"What are you doing?" Alarmed, I tried to pull back, but Estrid clamped her hand on my arm, holding me in place more firmly than her size should have allowed. Or was I suddenly feeling weak?

"Almost done," she said, but the low, husky voice didn't quite sound like hers as she put the needle to my skin for the final stroke. "There."

I stumbled to my feet and swayed, my head spinning. "You're not Estrid."

"No, little niece, I'm not." She pulled out a gold necklace that had been tucked into her tunic, a lock of auburn hair looped around the flashing gem. "Sorry about this, but it's really your mother's fault." She unclasped the necklace, and I shook my foggy head as she doubled in height, her freckles replaced by pale skin, her red hair lightening as it rolled down her back into waves of snowy white. "If Oonagh hadn't stolen Fionnbharr and the crown from me, along with our parents' love—and everything, really—it wouldn't have come to this." She looked thoughtful. "Although I suppose you wouldn't have been born at all then."

"Moriath," I whispered as everything began to grow dark around me.

My aunt placed a cold hand on my forehead.

"You don't look so well, little Niamh. Maybe you should lie down. It wasn't easy to find you, you know, even with the tracking spell Ránach put on your little bird. Still, it seemed right that I come here myself. I thought we should see each other face to face one more time before . . ."

"One more time before what?" I felt myself falling.

Moriath caught me and eased me onto the sofa, arranging my hands on my chest.

"Before you die, child."

"But I'm . . ." I could barely keep my eyes open. "I'm your niece."

"It's true. But I've already killed my sister and my husband for those blasted icicles."

Icicles? My eyes were so heavy. Maybe I would just rest them for a minute.

"I'm not about to give up now, no matter how well you bake cookies, child."

She smoothed my hair as I drifted into darkness.

"It's nothing personal, but I need that crown."

PART 4

Chapter 38

Kylian

"So if someone could just yank that amulet off Dylan next time we see him," Audrey prattled on as I brought her and Gavin through the Frost Gate, "I bet I'd have an easier time reverse-engineering the portable portal. Portalable?"

I dropped my hand from her arm. Something felt off. A flicker of sensation through my bond with Niamh.

"I mean, I'm not sure I want to actually touch it. That blood magic looked pretty icky. Obviously I need a different angle, but I'm not coming up wi—"

"Shh." I froze. Before I could probe the bond further, I heard a faint crashing noise.

"Sorry, I know I'm very chatty. Gavin says—"

I held up my hand to the girl. "Do you hear that?"

Gavin cocked his head to the side and nodded. His wolf-enhanced hearing was even better than my hearing rune.

Audrey looked between the two of us and shrugged.

I unhooked my axe and followed Gavin through the forest, squinting past the shrubs and ferns. The wolf boy stopped, then corrected his direction before coming to a halt in front of a battered white owl.

"Fluffy." I knelt, trying to pick up the owl. He evaded my hands and hopped along, attempting to fly with his bloody wing outstretched. "I wish I could talk to him like Niamh does." I reached for the owl again.

"Neve talks to animals?" Audrey trailed behind us.

"Yes, and this is her familiar," I said. "I'm sure she'll tell you all about it when you see her. I don't know why he won't let me pick him up though. I need to get him back to the cottage and have a look at that wing. Maybe I can get Niamh to meet us out here. Just a minute. I'll call her through the bond." I closed my eyes.

"We've obviously missed quite a bit," Audrey muttered.

Niamh, can you hear me? I need help with Fluffy.

Silence.

I tamped down my worry. Maybe she was just taking a nap. I probed deeper and realized I could barely feel the bond between us.

Niamh, I called again.

Nothing. Just blackness. The hair rose on the back of my neck.

"Moriath." A chill washed over me. I needed to get back to the cabin. Niamh would want me to rescue Fluffy first—she loved that bird—but—

"Over here," called Gavin, hoisting an unconscious Estrid into his arms. "I think the owl was leading us to her."

"She doesn't look hurt, just unconscious. I can see remnants of a sleeping spell." Audrey checked the dwarf over. "Who is this?"

"The person who should be guarding Niamh." I turned to run.

"*Raidho.*" I flew down the path as quickly as my speed rune could take me before smashing into an invisible shield just inches from the cottage. I slammed my fist into the shield, but unlike Niamh's training shields, this one was perfect.

Audrey skidded to a stop with Fluffy in her arms, Gavin carrying Estrid behind her.

"Whoa, that's some shield." Audrey carefully set Fluffy down before she peered at the shield. Without the Sight, it was invisible, but I knew that the apprentice spellcrafter could see the magic that made up the shield. She ran her fingers along its surface as if reading a book. "It's huge. It covers the entire cottage." She pulled her fingers back, examining the air in front of her face. "Moriath," she said grimly.

"How did she find us? *Uruz!*" I activated my strength rune and hit the shield again, but I was still no match for the barrier.

"The owl has a tracking spell on it. It's nearly gone now, but Moriath's signature is all over it."

I cursed. I should have thought to check Fluffy after his skirmish with Ránach.

"We have to get through it," I gritted out.

"I know, I know. I'm looking for a weak spot." She paced frantically around the cottage, trailing her hand along the invisible shield.

I followed the girl, using all my willpower to give her space to study the shield, while Gavin laid Estrid down in the grass beside the still-agitated owl and checked her over again. We reached the window to the sitting room, and I froze.

Inside, Niamh was lying on the sofa. She was so still that I couldn't even see if her chest moved. On a chair next to her, holding her hand in an almost tender manner, sat the false Unseelie queen.

Ice clenched around my heart.

Moriath lifted her head and smiled at me. Her smug expression mirrored the one in the vision. I couldn't hear her through the window, but I saw her lips move.

You're too late.

I roared with anger, slamming my fist against the shield. The queen just laughed and looked down at the princess again.

"Over here!" yelled Audrey.

I ran around the side of the house to find her concentrating on the space under her outstretched hand.

"I can only weaken it," she warned. "And only for a moment."

"Do it." I adjusted my grip on my axe.

Audrey placed both her hands on the shield, staring at something that only made sense to her, before stretching her fingers wide apart.

"Quickly," she said. "Go between my hands."

I poured all my energy into my strength rune and ducked under the girl's arms, shoving past the resistance until I staggered through to the other side.

"Thank you." I ran to the back door.

"Just save her," Audrey called after me.

I shoved the door open and lunged into the sitting room, axe already swinging, only to be frozen midair.

"Kylian, so nice to see you." Moriath smiled, her cold eyes glinting with happiness. A green gem flashed on her ring as she held me in place.

"I will *kill* you," I growled, struggling to move.

"No, I don't think you will. On the other hand, I'm not sure I should let *you* leave here alive. You're causing so much trouble. Honestly, Kylian, you couldn't just let me have the unicorns?"

"I was surprised they were still there. Dylan not up to doing your dirty work?"

"Hmm." Moriath pulled a jeweled dagger from her belt. "He's eager to please but just not cut out to be the Huntsman you were. After all, he couldn't even finish you off." The queen looked down at Niamh, so still on the cushions. "The poison almost has her, but maybe I should slit her throat just to be sure . . ."

Something snapped inside me. I roared, pushing against the queen's hold on me. The runes on my silver axe flashed, sharpening the blade and shoving against her enchantment.

The queen's eyes widened, and I saw fear fill them for the first time in two hundred years. She stumbled back, knocking over the chair as she pulled an iron amulet from her pocket.

"It doesn't matter," she gasped. "Three more heartbeats and that crown is mine."

In the next breath, Moriath vanished, and my axe swung through empty air.

"The shield's down!" I heard Audrey yell.

I fell to my knees in front of Niamh and placed my hand on her forehead. So cold. I fumbled for a pulse as I leaned over her pink mouth. I couldn't feel breath stirring against my cheek, but I repositioned my fingers. Was that a faint heartbeat?

Audrey burst into the room, taking in the scattered bottles with her Sight. "Iron ink." She cursed and knelt beside me.

"She's not breathing," I said in a panic.

"Focus, Kylian." Audrey looked Niamh over. "Does she have any new tattoos?"

"We've been working on—"

"Since you left," she clarified. "Moriath loves tattoos, as you know."

I took a breath, nodded, and helped her examine Niamh.

"*Here.*" I touched the apple on her arm, the ink still raised and fresh, surrounded by faintly glowing knotwork inked in gold flecked with black.

"Step back," said Audrey.

Reluctantly, I moved over enough to give the girl access to the tattoo.

"This is bad." Audrey hovered her hand over the apple. "She's slipping. You said you have a bond. Can you feel her? Can you talk to her?"

Niamh, I tried again. *Please, Princess.*

I felt the faintest flicker in the blackness.

"She's fading," I said desperately.

"Hold on to her." Audrey looked up at me with wide eyes. "I need her to hold on long enough for me to untangle this."

I closed my eyes again.

Niamh.

I felt for that flicker and focused on it with everything in me, wrapping myself around that tiny spark.

Princess, please stay with me.

Chapter 39

Kylian

In a blink, I stood in a meadow of wildflowers. Warm sunlight filtered through the leaves overhead, and pale pink blossoms drifted down from the flowering hawthorn trees. I recognized the unicorns' meadow, but it looked empty today except for the distant call of birdsong.

"Why are you telling me to stay?"

I spun to see Niamh standing beside me in a long, flowing dress of deep rose, her dark curls tied back with a matching satin ribbon.

"Honestly, that's a bit rich, coming from you." She reached up to pluck a hawthorn blossom from a waving branch.

"What do you mean?" This had to be a dream, but I could feel Niamh so strongly through the bond. She felt so real. Had I slipped into her dreams somehow?

"Why do you want me to stay," Niamh repeated, "when you're just going to leave anyway?"

"Is that what you think?"

"I know it." She twirled the flower between her fingers. "You'll make me queen, and then you'll leave me. You're always saying that I should marry some Unseelie noble boy."

"It would be best for you," I agreed reluctantly.

Niamh sighed. "And there it is. You still don't think that *I* know what's best for me?"

She reached for my hand, and even though the meadow still looked like something out of a dream or a memory, her hand in mine felt as solid and real as it had when she had held it yesterday.

Her pale blue eyes were fierce as she looked up at me. "You think you know what I need? I need you. The *kingdom* needs *you*." Niamh gripped my hand more tightly. "You think you can protect me by breaking my heart? Or protect the kingdom by letting someone who you *know* won't care for it as much as you do rule by my side?"

"Niamh." My heart ached.

"I thought . . ." She looked away. "I thought you might love me as I love you," she whispered.

I stood there, overwhelmed by her confession, unable to speak.

When I didn't answer immediately, she gave a rueful laugh. I could hear the tears in her voice as she said, "I see."

"No, no. Niamh." I cupped her cheek and pulled her gaze back to me. I let her see everything I had been holding back. Everything I had been trying to deny. How I would *break* if I lost her.

I prayed that Audrey was somehow saving her back in the cottage, but either way, I didn't want another moment to go by without Niamh knowing how I felt about her.

"I love you." I stroked her cheek, brushing away a tear with my thumb. "I didn't believe it at first. I thought my heart had turned to ice inside me long ago. Then you came back into my life with your chickens and your pies and your smile like the sun shining through the clouds, and I don't know if my heart of ice melted or shattered." I kissed her on the forehead. "But I do know that it's yours."

"Then why do you still pull away?"

"I'm afraid," I answered hoarsely. I looked down at her small, smooth hand in my scarred one.

"Am I so fearsome?" she whispered.

"I'm scared," I said, "that I'll fail this kingdom. This kingdom has become my home, but I have caused it so much pain while I've tried to protect it. I'm scared that I'll fail you, who brings light and joy to everything you touch. What if I dim that light? I would never forgive myself."

"Oh, Kylian," Niamh sighed. "You may have the jump on me in experience after stashing me in the human realm, but I can see there's still something I can teach you."

"What's that?"

She leaned in and whispered in my ear, "People don't need to be the same to make a good team." She kissed my cheek before pulling back to fix me with another fierce look. "You think you can dim my light? I think I've never shone brighter than I have since I met you. I've been fighting and fighting you because I've been so afraid of what I'd be like as a queen."

"Niamh," I protested.

"No, it's true." She laughed. "It could be a disaster! No one would get punished. Everyone would just get cookies."

I couldn't help a small smile.

"But I've been learning from you how to be strong. You've shown me how much more I can be than just *sweet.* I *will* be the strong queen the Unseelie fae need."

Niamh's hair swirled as an invisible wind blew motes of magic around her, but she didn't seem to notice as she pressed on.

"*You* taught me that. Please don't leave me to do it alone." Niamh squeezed my hand. "I don't want someone more like me. I want *you*. We're stronger together. Can't you feel it? Not just here." She tapped my bond rune with a finger. "Here." She rested her hand over my heart. "Let's take down Moriath and rule this kingdom. You and me."

I covered her hand with my own, and the last bit of frost surrounding my heart melted under the weight of her smile.

"How do you make me believe anything's possible?" I whispered.

"Because we're unstoppable together. Agreed?"

"Agreed." I leaned down and rested my forehead against hers.

"So, no more talk of leaving me or of making me rule alone—or with some imaginary, but foolishly happy, boy."

"No more leaving," I promised, my lips brushing against hers. "You win."

She smiled against my mouth. "*We* win," she corrected me.

Then my princess released my hand to wrap her arms around my neck, pulling me down for a deeper kiss. Her warm body fitted against mine, like the part of myself I had always been missing, and I knew she was right.

"We win."

Chapter 40

Niamh

I KISSED MY TRUE LOVE AGAIN IN a meadow of flowers, my heart full. I could do this. I could be the Unseelie queen. I could do anything with Kylian by my side.

"Yes! I think that's doing it. Keep kissing!"

Audrey? Where was that voice coming from?

The dream drifted away, and my eyes fluttered open. Kylian brushed his lips against mine a final time before pulling back with a smile.

"Good morning, Princess." Relief filled his eyes.

"What happened?" I blinked, trying to remember. "Estrid was tattooing me, and . . . Did I fall asleep? And then there was this meadow, and . . . Were you there with me?"

"I think it was a dream, but I was there too."

"It was real?" Relief swept through me, and happiness filled my heart. He *loved* me.

Kylian nodded. "Somehow, the bond must have—"

"Success!" yelled Audrey. "Now, what did she do here? I really need more examples of spelled tattoos to practice hacking . . ." Her voice trailed off as she pushed up her glasses and examined my arm.

"Audrey, you got here!" I pulled myself to a sitting position, gently moving one of the seven chickens snuggled around me. "Were you worried?" I asked Pip. "How long was I asleep?"

Mama! Treat?

"Well, unless Kylian ate all the cookies, there should still be some. What?"

Kylian stared at me, open-mouthed.

I reached up to feel my nose. "Do I have flour or something on my face?"

"Hold still." Audrey frowned at my shoulder in concentration. "I've almost got it, but we don't want Moriath's spell to kick back in the next time you take a nap."

"Moriath!" I straightened. "She poisoned me. Or cursed me? She looked just like Estrid. Where's Estrid? Is she okay?" I turned my head and winced. "It must still be affecting me. My head feels so heavy."

"Estrid's fine." Audrey didn't look up. "She woke up when Moriath took off. She and Gavin are outside taking care of your owl—who's also fine."

"Are you sure I'm okay?" I reached up and pressed my fingers to my temples.

They touched something cold and hard. *Ice.*

"Kylian."

He was still staring at me, wide eyed.

I felt another icicle form.

"What's on my head?!"

"The crown," he whispered.

"And that does it!" Audrey cheered. "No more sleeping death spell. You should be as awake as an—" She looked up at me. "Holy *crap*. Well, that's new."

I shot up, dumping indignant chickens on the ground. My balance wobbled, thanks to the weight on my head, and I steadied myself with a hand on Kylian's shoulder.

"I need a mirror." I staggered down the hall toward my bedroom.

"Wait!" yelled Audrey.

I skidded to a halt in front of the bedroom doorway.

"You'll need to duck," she called.

"How tall is this thing?" I felt off-balance as I reached up again. "Do I have *antlers?*"

I turned to see Kylian following me. "You didn't warn me it would be *attached to my head*."

His eyes were still wide. "I didn't know. I've never seen it close up," he said. "Your father didn't wear it very often."

I sighed and ducked as I carefully went through the doorway to stare open-mouthed in front of the full-length mirror in my bedroom.

For the most part, I still looked like myself. Everything was the same. Same knee-length floral dress I'd baked cookies in this morning. Same ink up my arm. Oh, wait. The apple was new. And she might be evil, but I had to admit that Moriath had talent with a needle.

But then there was my head. Through my sleep-mussed black curls rose a circlet of icicles, faceted and sparkling like diamonds, alternating between the length of my thumb and hand in height. But that wasn't the crazy part. Rising from my head were two graceful, pale gold antlers. I ran my fingers around the base of one. By all indications, they were actually growing out of my skull.

"I'll never fit through doorways again," I whispered.

"That explains why all the ceilings in the palace are so high." Kylian had gotten over his shock, coming to stand behind me.

I met his eyes in the mirror. "I look insane."

"You look like a queen." He put his hands on my shoulders.

I laughed sharply. "I do not. Shouldn't a fae queen be . . ." I waved toward the mirror. "I don't know. Graceful? Ethereal? Cate Blanchett could totally pull off this crown," I muttered under my breath.

"I don't know who that is," said Kylian. "But she could not look more queenly than you do."

"I feel like a baker playing dress-up."

Kylian tipped my chin up, meeting my eyes in the mirror. "You're the daughter of the strongest, most beloved Unseelie queen in history."

"I'm pudgy and ordinary," I grumbled, running my hands over my full hips.

Kylian settled his hands on my waist. "You're perfect. And beautiful, but that doesn't matter."

"No?" I shivered as his thumb made a little circle on my waist.

"What matters is that you're strong and brave. You think some pretty little waif has a better chance at taking down Moriath than you?" He ran a hand down my arm. "You're beautiful, but you're not decorative. You're a weapon. A shield."

I took a deep breath. "So you don't think I look ridiculous?"

"I've never seen anyone look more like a queen." His eyes glinted in the mirror. "Want me to get down on my knees to prove it?"

"Don't you dare," I warned, inhaling another deep breath. Queen. Okay. "I guess you can't call me your Princess anymore."

"Not a princess." Kylian shook his head, then kissed my temple. "I'll just call you *mine*."

"Okay, let's take a closer look at this."

I sat on the rug in front of the sofa while Audrey examined my head. She wiggled an icicle, and I whimpered.

"That's really like . . . fully attached," she said. "No, no. Don't worry! First of all, you look amazing. Doesn't she, boys?"

"It's a killer crown," agreed Gavin as he stirred a pot on the stove.

Kylian, sitting at the table with Essie on his lap, just winked at me, making me blush.

"I look like a *deer*," I wailed.

"I think you look like an epic druid queen." Audrey tapped an antler. "Very night elf. But without the eyebrows. I wonder if there's a way to turn this on and off," she mused. "There's gotta be a way to turn it off. I mean, it *is* a disappearing and reappearing crown."

She looked at the group in the kitchen. "Any thoughts?"

Gavin shrugged, pouring hot chocolate out of the pot into a mug and sliding it over to Estrid. Kylian looked thoughtful but said nothing. The three chickens milling about ignored me, and Estrid just stared morosely into her cup of hot chocolate.

"Estrid," I said. "It's okay."

The dwarf shook her head. "I failed in my duty to protect you."

"There wasn't anything you could do," I told her.

"I didn't even see her coming."

"That's not your fault," I insisted. "Moriath is pretty powerful."

"Then what was the point of me even *trying?*" wailed Estrid. "I should just go home and be confined to my quarters where I can't hurt anybody."

I pointed at her. "You will not. Gavin, give her more sugar."

The wolf boy handed the dwarf a cookie.

"I don't deserve it." Estrid rested her forehead on the table.

"Nope! No more of that. Eat your cookie. That's a royal order."

"Give her a crown and she gets so *bossy*," grumbled Estrid, but she took a bite.

"No one is going anywhere," I said, "and everyone deserves cookies—Ow! Is the hair pulling really necessary?"

"Sorry," muttered Audrey. "But I think I figured it out. Get up here."

I climbed up and sat facing her on the sofa.

Audrey leaned forward, showing me a little bit of golden magic dancing in front of her hand. "You see? Right here." She pointed at a swirl.

"That's a swirl," I agreed.

"This part." She pointed again.

"Also a swirl," I said. "Just because I can see the magic doesn't mean I know what it does."

"Oh, right." Audrey spun her hand, and the magic disappeared in a small shower of sparkles. "It's tied to your will. You're wearing the crown because you want to."

"How is that possible?" I wobbled my head, feeling the weight of it. "I did not ask for this, and it won't go away."

"Okay, yes. It's not quite that simple." Audrey tipped my head to the side and hummed. "The crown is made of pure magic. It's a physical manifestation of the magic of Faerie. Specifically the magic that runs through the Unseelie Kingdom."

"So, they aren't real antlers?" I asked.

"Well, yes and no." Audrey took off her glasses and cleaned them with a corner of her t-shirt before putting them back on. "You are not part deer, nor were they harvested from a deer. But . . ." She tapped one antler. "The magic has taken physical form."

"How do I make it un-take physical form?"

"Have you tried telling it to go away? Nicely?"

"Dear crown," I said. "Please go away."

Nothing happened.

"Estrid, is there some sort of rune for this?" I asked my dwarven friend.

She shook her head. "I don't think so. I've never inked anything that would help with a magic crown."

"You do tattoo magic?" Audrey's eyes lit up. "We need to hang out. I am dying to learn how that works. I can see the spells, but without a proper teacher—"

"Audrey, *focus*." I pointed at my head.

"Right, sorry." Audrey tapped her lower lip.

"Maybe it thinks you're trying to get rid of it?" offered Gavin.

"I *am* trying to get rid of it," I pointed out.

"Right, but maybe it thinks you're trying to get rid of it permanently."

"Oh." I touched the icicles. "You're worried that I've changed my mind." I felt a faint pulse of magic from the crown. "I think you're right, Gavin. Faerie loves a good vow, but I only agreed to be queen while talking to Kylian. If I'm more clear with my intentions, maybe the crown will feel more secure about this arrangement." I closed my eyes, trying to focus on the magic of Faerie, but it was like listening to someone talking from far away. "This might be easier outside."

I stood. Gavin and Kylian both stood as well, the two obviously worried as I wobbled slightly.

"I'm fine." I rested my hand on the table for balance and turned to Kylian. "Maybe you should come along, anyhow."

"Of course."

As soon as we exited the cottage, Fluffy flew down and landed on my outstretched arm.

"I hear you had a rough day." I scratched the owl's head. "I'm glad Estrid could fix you up."

Fluffy bumped his head against my cheek. *It seems that your day was not much better.* He peered up at my head. *But you came out of it with an excellent roost!* With a hop and a flutter, he settled on my antlers. *Perfect.*

I gave Kylian a look. He shrugged with a smirk.

"It was heavy enough without you," I complained to the owl.

Yes, but think of how imposing you are with me up here, said the owl. *I'm doing you a favor.*

"Are we imposing?" I asked Kylian.

He nodded. "Extremely."

Fluffy ruffled his feathers smugly. *I don't understand his babbling, but I could tell he admired me.*

"All right," I conceded. "But watch out. I'm actually trying to make it disappear. For now," I added hastily to the crown, which hummed nervously. "Okay, this is a good spot." I sat down in the grass amongst the clover. A beautiful yellow toadstool grew nearby, which seemed like a good omen. The chickens wandered around the meadow surrounding the cottage, uninterested in my magical drama.

"And you sit here." I pointed to a spot behind me, and Kylian sat down back-to-back with me.

"Will this help?" he asked as I used him for a backrest.

"Who knows? I'm just tired. I needed someone to lean on." I reached for his hand and closed my eyes. "Time to talk to a crown."

Chapter 41

Niamh

"OKAY, MAGIC." I DUG THE FINGERS OF my free hand into the grass and clover of the meadow. "I know you're worried. I've been fighting this, but I'm ready to be queen. I promise—"

I paused, remembering how the magic had reacted to my promise to the unicorns. Kylian squeezed my hand in support.

"I *vow* to do everything in my power to protect the Unseelie Kingdom and all the creatures who live here."

The magic swelled up hopefully.

"I will be your weapon against Moriath," I promised, "and your shield against any who try to follow in her footsteps. I will be your queen. I *am* your queen."

The magic rose up, almost overwhelming me with its intensity. Fluffy ruffled his feathers, and Kylian inhaled sharply.

"You feel that, too?" I asked him.

"Yes," he answered softly.

"Good." I turned my attention back to the magic. "I vow to be your queen for as long as I live. But I'd like to take a nap without a dozen spikes and two large antlers poking holes in my pillow. So, can we make a deal?"

The magic settled a bit. I could tell it was listening.

"Whenever we need to inspire awe, strike fear into our enemies, or just look super queenly, you make this crown for me."

The magic hummed happily.

"And the rest of the time, you let me fit through doorways."

I could feel the magic begrudgingly agree.

"Like now," I added.

If a tingling sensation of elemental magic from the Faerie realm could sigh, it sighed. The weight on my head vanished, and Fluffy fell on my head, wings flapping before he tumbled onto my lap.

"I did warn you." I righted the owl, and he hopped onto my knee.

Waste of a perfectly good roost, he grumbled. *If you weren't so fixated on going inside buildings, it would work fine.*

"I'm sorry." I gave the owl a little nuzzle. "Want a cookie?"

"Can I have a cookie?"

I jerked my head up to see Amber a few feet away. Liadan and my aunt Chloe followed behind.

"And was I seeing things . . ." Amber stopped beside me. "Or did you just have massive antlers?"

"She's received the Unseelie crown." Liadan smiled with her sharp canines. "And an owl familiar. You have been busy, child."

Kylian and I got to our feet, while Fluffy huffed and took off for the trees.

Amber sighed. "You looked totally epic in that crown. Some people really have all the luck."

"How did you get here?" Kylian looked unsettled.

"Oh, you know Miss Chloe. She always has a backup key stashed away." Amber flicked her mentor a sidelong glance.

"Well, I do need to be able to check on my godchildren." Aunt Chloe caught up to us, arms outstretched. "My dear girl."

I bent down to give her a big hug, sighing at the comfort only felt in arms that helped raise you.

"I'm so proud of you." Aunt Chloe patted my cheek. "What a queen you will be! And with this one at your side . . ." She grinned at Kylian. "Moriath had better run, that's all I can say." My godmother looked at me seriously through her gold-rimmed glasses. "I *am* sorry for keeping all this from you. I promised to keep you safe until you were ready, and this seemed like the best way."

I sighed. "I can't lie. I was pretty hurt. I spent my whole life wishing I knew more about my birth family, and everyone but me knew all along."

Aunt Chloe nodded.

"But now that I've met Moriath, I can see why you did everything you could to keep her away from me while I grew up." I gave the older woman another hug. "I forgive you."

"Thank you." She squeezed me back. "Well, let's go inside. We've got a usurper to overthrow."

"Finally," Liadan grumbled. "That woman needs to be taken down a peg. Do you have any peppermint tea, child?"

All the chickens decided to go back inside with us. Was it for the cookies or had they developed an interest in strategy?

Treats? Treats? Treats? Treats? Treats? Treats? Daddy?

Essie clucked last as she ducked under Audrey's feet, searching for her favorite person. Kylian scooped Essie up as he walked in. The hen sighed contentedly.

Audrey looked up, startled, when we re-entered the cottage

with our latest guests. "Miss Chloe! I thought you couldn't visit Neve until Moriath was overthrown?"

Aunt Chloe nodded. "Ordinarily, yes. But this cottage has strong anti-scrying wards. I crafted them myself when the dwarves built it." She winked at me. "This was your parents' romantic getaway cabin, after all."

"Too much informaaaaation," sang Amber, poking through the plate of cookies to find the best one. Good thing I had made a double batch. "Um, do the chickens eat cookies?"

Clementine sat on the table, watching her hopefully.

"Not chocolate ones, they don't." I gave the pale orange hen a look, which she pointedly ignored. "So, Aunt Chloe and Amber, did you ever find any clues about where Maeve is?"

"Nothing." Amber filled the kettle and set it on the stove. "From what you told us about the tower, it sounds like she's in Tír na nÓg, but no one has seen a tower like you described."

"Oh." I failed to keep the disappointment out of my voice.

I sat on the sofa, and Kylian sat next to me with Essie. Meringue immediately jumped onto my lap. The fluffy hen fell asleep within seconds. How did she do that?

"At least Maeve looked safe and healthy from what you said, my dear. Try not to worry. We'll find her." Aunt Chloe settled into the big armchair, causing Pip—who'd roosted on the back—to ruffle her spotted feathers grumpily.

Snickerdoodle flew up to sit beside the hen, fell off, and scrambled back up before sitting proudly as if nothing had happened. Pip gave the rooster a baleful look.

"You aren't still hoping she'll want to be queen?" Liadan moved Latte off the counter and started poking through cupboards.

"There's peppermint on the top shelf," I told her. "And, no. I'm queen now. I vowed to protect the Unseelie Kingdom, and that's what I'm going to do. I'd just like to meet my sister."

"I bet being an only child is peaceful though. Who wants tea, and who wants hot chocolate?" Amber set out a row of teacups.

"Ah, here it is." Liadan sniffed a jar she had grabbed from the top shelf, scooped the dried leaves into a teapot, then filled it from the steaming kettle.

Everyone gave their drink order, and Gavin added more milk and chocolate to the pot on the stove.

"So, Moriath can't see us here?" Gavin looked down as Latte sneezed by his feet. "How did she find Neve, then?"

"It must have been the tracking spell I saw on Neve's owl." Audrey sat at the table beside Estrid, and Gavin poured her a cup of hot chocolate. "If she could figure out where you were, Neve, then she probably used an amulet like the one Dylan had to come to the location. No scrying or gates needed."

I stiffened. "Fluffy has a tracking spell?"

"It's gone. I made sure of it." Audrey sipped her hot chocolate. "Don't worry. That amulet, though . . . Will she just come back?"

Kylian shook his head. "Not without the element of surprise. She's patient. She'll wait for a better moment."

"If I had a transportation amulet like that . . ." Audrey trailed off, then sat up straighter. "Wait a minute." She jumped off the chair. "Estrid! Grab that ink and come with me for a minute."

Gavin watched his girlfriend run out the door, Estrid following. "She'll explain later." He poured himself a mug from his pot and turned the stove off.

Liadan poured the tea. "The important thing is that Moriath can't spy on us here." She sat on a kitchen chair with her cup, and Waffles hopped up on the chair beside her, the black and white rooster looking for all the world like a wise royal adviser.

"Correct," Aunt Chloe said with a nod. "Which is very helpful in our current situation, as Moriath doesn't know that Niamh is alive and well."

"But Moriath didn't get the crown." Kylian stroked Essie's back. "Trust me, she will have noticed."

"The crown would never go to her," I scoffed. Everyone looked at me. "During my stay in Nidavellir, I met some Unseelie refugees. One of them told me that the small folk have always believed that the crown doesn't just automatically go to the most powerful Unseelie fae like the rulers believed. It chooses the person who will best protect and care for the people and the land. Power is part of it, but as I can tell you from recent experience," I said as I ran a hand through my hair, checking for icicles, "Faerie has opinions on the matter. But I guess Moriath hasn't figured that out. I don't think Faerie likes to talk to her."

"I didn't mean that Moriath thinks she *succeeded* in poisoning Niamh. Oh, thank you, my dear," Aunt Chloe added as Amber brought her a cup of tea. "Moriath knows that her plan failed, but she doesn't know that *we* know her plan failed."

"Huh?" I tried to follow her logic.

Amber rolled her eyes. "She's always like this."

"If we wish to launch an assault on Moriath . . ." Aunt Chloe paused to take a sip. "Oh, this is excellent tea!"

"Please, just keep explaining," sighed Amber.

"It is unlikely that we'll be able to lure her away from Skyretaine," continued Aunt Chloe. "Not after you nearly caught her this morning. She is wily and has always preferred trickery and disguises to direct confrontations."

"But we can't go to the castle," said Gavin. "The Ice Gate is only open to her minions. We only made it through last time because she didn't know Audrey had Bronach's key. At least, I assume that's what happened." He looked over at Kylian. "You really *weren't* trying very hard to catch us, were you?"

Kylian tilted his head. "Dylan reported it to me. But sometimes there were delays in my reporting things to Moriath."

"Thank you," said Gavin. "Anyway, she *has* noticed by now, and Kylian will be locked out, too. We can't get through the gate."

"You don't have a magical workaround?" Amber asked her mentor. "No extra key like you kept for the Frost Gate? No magic shoes or fancy bracelets?"

"Not this time," said Aunt Chloe. "I didn't have anything to do with the creation of the Ice Gate. Moriath and Oonagh's mother crafted it centuries ago under contract for Niamh's grandfather, the Unseelie king at that time. If she left any loopholes, she didn't confide in me about them. We weren't close."

"So, Moriath won't come out," I clarified, "and thanks to how my grandmother crafted the gate, we can't get in."

"Correct." Aunt Chloe took another sip of tea. "Until Moriath invites us."

"So *never* then," said Gavin.

"*Audrey*," bellowed Aunt Chloe. The chickens on the back of her chair jumped.

Audrey stuck her head in the door. "Yes, Miss Chloe?"

"Did you remove the sleeping death spell she put on Niamh or just neutralize it?"

"It's just dormant," said Audrey. "For now."

"*What?*" I yelped, making Meringue open one sleepy eye as Kylian turned a sharp look at Audrey.

"I tried to tell you that before we got distracted by the whole antler-crown situation." Audrey leaned against the doorframe. "Moriath's spells are amazing. She's had centuries to work on her craft. Even with Liadan's help, I've never been able to fully remove Gavin's spell." She glanced at her boyfriend. "It's the same with yours," she said apologetically to me. "It's already trying to grow back."

Alarmed, I looked down at the apple on my arm.

"With a few more decades of training, I should be able to remove it." Audrey grimaced. "Otherwise, it will unravel if Moriath—you know—dies."

"Let's go with that option," said Amber. She took another cookie, and Clem gave her a pitiful look.

"But, yes." Audrey turned back to Aunt Chloe. "The spell is still there." She ducked back outside.

"Perfect." Aunt Chloe smiled as she set her empty teacup on the saucer. "The other day, I tried to scry for Niamh's future. And do you know what I saw?"

"A glass coffin in the Unseelie castle and a gloating evil queen?" I guessed. "That seems to be the popular vision."

"Why, yes, my dear." My aunt gave me a proud look. "You've been scrying the future? Well done!"

I preened, while Kylian sighed and pinched the bridge of his nose.

"So, you have a plan for avoiding that?" he asked.

"Oh, no." Aunt Chloe smiled. "That *is* the plan."

"*What?*" Kylian surged to his feet, causing Essie to fly away in alarm.

Shocked faces ringed the room, but I wasn't worried. I trusted Aunt Chloe.

"Sit down, sit down." Aunt Chloe waved a hand at Kylian. "Niamh will be fine. Moriath knows that her poisoned tattoo put Niamh in a deep sleep, so deep that her heartbeat slowed and she appeared dead. But Moriath had to run before the spell finished its work, and she still doesn't have the crown. So either *Maeve* has the crown, or something went wrong with the spell on Niamh and it didn't kill her. Moriath will be desperate to see if Niamh is truly dead."

"But Moriath won't dare come here to check," Liadan added. "So Niamh needs to go to her."

"If she can be convinced that *we* think Niamh is dead, Moriath won't suspect anything. Especially if she already saw a vision of her victory over Niamh. All we need is a glass coffin. Not very easy to come by." Aunt Chloe tapped her chin.

"I have a glass coffin."

Everyone spun to face Estrid, who was still nursing her hot chocolate at the table.

"Well, I mean, it's not mine. It's Niamh's. Technically."

"Why do I have a coffin?" I squeaked.

We all stared at the dwarf. She wiped the chocolate from her mouth self-consciously.

"After that vision, the kings commissioned artisans to build the coffin. They didn't believe anything would happen to you," she added hurriedly, looking at me, "but they said that visions of the future were hard to decipher and that it was better to be safe. So they ordered it crafted in case you needed it for something."

"Perfect!" Aunt Chloe clapped her hands. "Ulrik and Ulf were right. We do need it for something. I always liked those boys. Now." She leaned forward, and we all avidly watched her. Even the chickens gave her their full attention. "Here's what we're going to do."

Chapter 42

Kylian

"You're *sure* she's all right?" I asked Audrey, not for the first time, as we stood with Gavin in a meadow not far from the cottage.

The spellcrafter rolled her eyes—although she also seemed a little tense as we looked down on Niamh under the glass, wearing the blue dress from the vision, which had been brought along by the ever-prepared Clíodhna and her apprentice. Niamh's skin was pale, her dark curls spread like black flames against the red velvet of the coffin as she slept. Well, more than slept. Audrey had fiddled with Moriath's death spell. Niamh lived, but no breath fogged the clear lid of the coffin. Her eyelids didn't twitch, and her chest didn't rise and fall.

Audrey pressed her fingers to the glass. "You should know better than me. Can't you feel her?"

I closed my eyes. The connection felt faint, but Niamh was there, like a tiny glimmer of sunshine in the back of my mind.

Audrey sighed when I nodded. "It *is* a bit creepy," she admitted.

Gavin slung an arm around his girlfriend. "She'll be fine."

"I'm just going to check the spells one more time before we do this." Audrey crouched down and ran her fingertips across the coffin's ornate gold base.

Estrid had fetched the coffin with Gavin's help, and then Liadan and Audrey had worked through the night enchanting the coffin to ensure that no one, not even Moriath, would be able to open it. Niamh's connection to Faerie powered the spell through a simple golden band on her little finger.

Only Niamh could break the spell and open the coffin, and only I could reach her in her deep slumber and tell her when it was safe to do so.

I adjusted the harness of my axe, even though it was already fine. So much could go wrong. I felt cold, despite the golden sunlight slanting through the mossy trees.

"It's perfect." Audrey straightened. "All right." She took a deep breath. "You boys ready?"

I nodded curtly, clenching and unclenching my fists.

"Let's do this." Gavin unbuttoned his shirt to reveal the inked tracking spell over his heart that had once bound him to me.

Audrey placed her hand over the tattoo, and Gavin looked down at her with such intensity that I paced a few steps away to give the couple their privacy. I wasn't the only one taking a risk here. A lot rode on the ego and impulsiveness of one mangy little wolf.

"Okay, that should do it. I'll unravel the spell again after this." Audrey stepped back. "He'll be able to feel it?" She glanced at me for confirmation.

I nodded. "I could sense your location right away whenever the spell started to grow back. Even Dylan should be able to feel it being fixed all at once like that."

"It's warm." Gavin touched the tattoo gingerly before buttoning his shirt back up.

"I gave it a little extra nudge. To make sure he noticed." Audrey pushed up her glasses.

I grunted and unstrapped my axe.

"The plan isn't to kill him, lover boy," Audrey reminded me.

"He might not come alone," I muttered.

"He will," said Gavin. "You know how eager he is. He won't want to share his glory with anyone else."

Sure enough, before a full minute had passed, Dylan appeared alone in a cloud of writhing black smoke, his sword already at Gavin's neck. As he made an awful retching noise, I ducked behind a tree.

"Are you okay?" Audrey's voice dripped with concern. "You know, I can have a look at that amulet for you. Maybe tweak it so you don't throw up all over your enemies whenever you arrive somewhere."

"Stupid girl," Dylan wheezed. "Don't you ever shut up?"

Audrey tapped her chin. "I don't think so."

Dylan pressed his blade against Gavin's throat. "Well, you can be as loud as you want when we torture you later," he sneered. "Now, get over here, or your dear boyfriend will be an ex one more time. Ex-alive!" Dylan laughed at his own joke.

"Wow, that's bad," said Audrey. "But no, we actually brought you here to talk. You aren't very observant, are you?"

"What?" Dylan snapped.

This was taking forever. I emerged from behind my tree, axe twirling.

Dylan startled but quickly recovered, the sneer back on his face. "Back off! Even someone as cold as you can't want your ally to die."

"I'm not talking about him, you idiot," Audrey groaned. "We're here to ask a favor."

"Huh?" Dylan struggled to keep up.

Belatedly, Audrey remembered that she was supposed to be heartbroken. She sniffled, even managing to squeeze a tear out. "Your stupid queen killed my friend!" she wailed, pointing to the glass coffin.

"Whoa, is that the princess?" Dylan's grip on his blade loosened as he peered down for the first time. His hostage put his hands in his pockets, unbothered by the sword wobbling in front of him. "That's a weird coffin."

"Would you rather she be buried in a box?" Audrey put her hands on her hips. "She's the crown *princess*."

"I suppose." Dylan scratched his head.

Gavin ducked away from Dylan's sword and quietly stepped to the side.

"Huh." Dylan stared down at Niamh. "She really does look dead."

"Are you trying to rub it in?" Audrey cried.

I sighed. This was going to take a while if no one explained it to him. "The princess deserves to be laid to rest with her family in the royal crypt," I said.

"At Skyretaine?" Dylan tapped the glass, peering in to look for any signs of life.

"So why don't you run along, little pup?" I narrowed my eyes. "Deliver the message to the queen. It's the least she can do after defeating us."

"Right . . ." Dylan glanced at Gavin, clearly still wanting to capture him.

I snapped my fingers in front of his face to get his attention again, axe resting casually on my shoulder. "*Now*, pup."

Dylan scowled. "Fine. Next time." He pointed a finger at Gavin.

"Sure, sure," said Gavin agreeably as Dylan disappeared in another cloud of black smoke.

"Do you think he'll puke on Moriath when he gets there?" asked Audrey wistfully.

"Hopefully not." I set my axe on the ground. "We need him to stay alive to deliver our message."

Clíodhna had been sure that Moriath would want to see the vision come true, to see Niamh's body with her own eyes. I had to agree. The queen didn't like to leave anything to chance.

"You're sure she won't just come back herself?" Audrey sat on the mossy ground.

I shook my head.

"Why risk a possible trap when you have someone so willing and disposable to do it for you?" Gavin settled down beside her.

I paced, my gaze fixed on Niamh, still as death in her blue silk dress. "What will you do if Moriath is defeated?" I asked the pair, desperate for distraction. "If you no longer have to run?"

"*When* Moriath is defeated." Gavin laced his fingers through Audrey's. "We can settle down. Build a home?" he suggested, a soft question in his voice.

Audrey leaned her head on his arm. "It will be nice not having to look over our shoulders everywhere we go," she admitted. "But I already have a home." She smiled up at the faoladh. He raised an eyebrow. "Anywhere you are, wolf boy." She kissed Gavin, and he smiled.

"I could get you a proper coffee maker, though," he said. "The big kind that Liadan won't let you put in her kitchen."

She perked up. "One that makes espresso? So I can have americanos?"

He kissed her forehead. "I'll bring you one every morning."

While Audrey gushed over her plans to run a coffee maker on Faerie magic, I looked back to Niamh.

Home.

For just a moment, I let myself dream about what a lifetime together would look like. At a Skyretaine without the layer of ice. The sun shining once more through the castle windows. Niamh baking pie for the courtiers. Me using my axe to build instead of destroy. Chickens flying through the ballroom.

"I'll take care of you," I whispered to her. "I promise."

I could have sworn I felt an answering glimmer in that spot in my mind where the bond connected us.

"*Blech.*" Dylan reappeared, retching once again. He braced himself on the coffin and coughed as the dark smoke dissipated, then turned to spit bile on the ground.

Audrey leaned across the coffin and examined the amulet hanging from Dylan's neck.

"Stop that!" Dylan snatched the black iron pendant away.

"No wonder that makes you feel gross." Audrey looked green. "You boys do *not* want to know how she made that thing. I take back what I said about wanting to study it."

"Queen Moriath," Dylan said pompously, lifting his chin, "has decided, in her great benevolence, to grant you this boon." He put his hand on the coffin. "I will take her to the royal crypt."

"I go with her," I told Dylan.

He narrowed his eyes at me, suddenly suspicious. "You want to walk into Skyretaine? I know you *liked* the wench." He tapped the glass again, and I gritted my teeth. "But, seriously, have you got a death wish now?"

"I need to see her resting with her family," I ground out. "It's my duty. Besides, you're going to vow not to hurt me or let anyone else hurt me."

"Dylan's worried that he doesn't have the power to take you both." Audrey crossed her arms.

"I'm the *Huntsman* now, little girl. I can manage just fine," Dylan huffed, but he still didn't agree.

I could see the wheels turning in his head. Most people would be suspicious that a fae known for strategy, like myself, would propose such a weak bargain with so many loopholes available. They could imprison me without hurting me. Someone could hurt me when Dylan wasn't around. They could even kill me without hurting me.

But Dylan was predisposed to believe himself smarter than everyone else, so he smiled gleefully.

"Of course, of course, Kylian. I vow not to hurt you or let anyone else hurt you. Did you two want to come along as well?" He turned greedily to Gavin and Audrey. "See your friend resting in peace?"

"It's all too much for me." Audrey blew her nose into the sleeve of her hoodie. "I can't bear it. I'll say goodbye to her here." She pressed her fingers against the glass. "See you on the other side," she whispered.

"Yes, yes, I'm sure you'll have lots of fun together in the afterlife. Time to go. Unless you also need to say a tearful goodbye?" Dylan glanced sidelong in Gavin's direction.

"I'm sure you already know how much I'll miss you, Dylan." Gavin winked.

Dylan curled his lips and reached for his amulet, his free hand on the glass coffin. I gripped his arm just a little tighter than was comfortable, causing Dylan to muffle a squeak, but of course his ego wouldn't let him admit that it hurt. A moment later, blackness and a wrenching sense of nausea rolled over me. Audrey was right: the amulet had to be a powerful blood-magic spell.

When the smoke cleared, we stood in Moriath's throne room. She was taking no chances this time. Her fingers and crown dripped with gems, doubtless brimming with power stolen from the unicorns. Her favorite sapphires encircled her neck.

"Dylan, come." The queen snapped her fingers, and Dylan transformed into a wolf again. The gray wolf whined as he trotted to sit at her side. She still kept him on a tight leash, even after all his scheming.

A quick glance around the room revealed more wolves than I remembered. At least a hundred surrounded us, their teeth bared. The queen must have been busy recruiting. It was almost as if she were afraid of something. More beautiful young men lured to her side with promises of love and power, only to find themselves the latest in a long, long list of furry familiars.

"My dear Kylian." Moriath grinned widely, all white teeth and cold eyes. "No matter which side you're on, you just can't seem to win. After all your struggling, here we are, just as the mirror revealed."

I bowed my head, trying to look humble and defeated, when really I wished to throw my axe at her head. Not the right moment. "As you say," I murmured. "Please allow me to escort the princess to rest with her ancestors."

"Oh, we can do it. Don't trouble yourself." Moriath waved her hand, gems flashing, and six faoladh surged up into their fae forms. "That lovely coffin must be heavy."

I fingered my axe. "It is my duty." I allowed my voice to break, to sound heartbroken.

Moriath must have been itching to kill me on the spot, to break the glass and use her dagger to ensure that Niamh was truly dead, but she hadn't become queen without learning a great deal about patience. She knew how strong I was. I had already escaped this room once. Moriath would wait until I was somewhere more secure. And the queen would ensure Niamh's death when I couldn't protect her.

The queen inclined her head. "Of course. But we will help you by carrying it," she insisted.

"Of course," I echoed her. "Thank you, Your Majesty."

She settled back into her throne, stroking Dylan's head as the six faoladh picked up the coffin.

"I'll ask you one more time, Kylian. You can still come back to my side. Be my Huntsman again."

Dylan whined, and Moriath smacked his snout lightly in warning.

"Your precious princess doesn't need you anymore, after all." The queen smiled.

She had truly never understood love or the connections between people beyond using each other for power.

"If you ever had a heart to break, you wouldn't ask me that." I turned to go, and the six faoladh followed me out of the castle with the coffin, toward the icy stairs of the crypt.

So far, so good.

Chapter 43

Kylian

In addition to the coffin bearers, I counted at least twenty more faoladh trailing us by the time we reached the doors of the crypt. Moriath and Dylan remained behind in the throne room, which only made it more likely that she was planning an ambush while staying safely out of the way. It would seem that Moriath planned for me to join the previous Unseelie rulers in their final resting place. I pretended not to notice, my gaze fixed on Niamh's still form as they carried her into the ancient mausoleum.

They slid the glass coffin onto a stone slab between two marble pillars, a statue of a winged fae with a sword in each hand guarding the spot.

The sound of the thick doors shutting behind us echoed in the room of cold stone, punctuated by the thud of a heavy plank barring the doors from the outside. That would have taken two wolves, which left twenty-four for me. Moriath had watched me fight for years. She knew that ten, maybe twelve, trained warriors should be able to subdue even me.

I chose to view the extra minions as a sign of respect. I closed my eyes, the picture of a bereaved bodyguard, and focused on that tiny glimmer in the back of my mind.

Keep sleeping, Princess, I told her, the nickname coming automatically as the term of endearment it had always been. My thumb activated the little gold ball in my pocket that Liadan had promised would prevent all sound from leaving the room. *But, if you could lend me your strength, it would speed things up.*

With a soft, sleepy brush of Niamh's mind against mine, I felt the bonding rune warm on my arm. I glanced down. All my rune tattoos shimmered faintly as the power of Faerie filled me. Even the runes on my axe glowed one by one.

Thank you, Niamh. See you soon.

I spun and blocked the sword arcing toward my head with the shaft of my axe, then quickly activated my runes for speed and strength. With so many enemies in the room, I was tempted to keep a shield around my vital areas, but it would be too hard while focusing on the battle around me.

It was difficult to take on twenty-four faoladh at once—some fae, some wolves, each given the form they fought best in—but it was even more difficult to do it without killing any of them.

I fought in a blur of speed, far out-pacing even their magically enhanced forms, but if any of their hearts stopped beating, Dylan would feel it through their tracking spells and alert the queen. That would complicate things. We needed time and a safe space in the castle to put our plan into motion, so I reduced my deadly axe to a blunt weapon as I spun, kicked, and cracked heads against stone pillars.

Wit hin minutes, I stood panting in the center of the crypt, the unconscious bodies of the faoladh strewn between the pillars and statues. The gold device seemed to be working, because I didn't hear anything from the two faoladh outside.

I dropped to my knees beside Niamh's sleeping form. Now came the moment everything hinged upon. She had to wake up or all of this would have been for nothing.

Niamh, sweetheart. I pressed into the place in my mind where I felt that glimmer.

Just a minute, came the faint reply.

What? I grasped onto the bond and tugged. *Niamh! Time to wake up.*

But instead of pulling her to me, I found myself back in her dreamscape. This time, I didn't recognize where I stood. Mist surrounded me, with swirling thorny vines all around covered in pale pink roses.

"Niamh?" I peered through the mist.

"More visitors?" asked a strange female voice. "It's turning into a party in here."

The vines surged past me until I found Niamh, standing in the same blue silk dress she wore in the coffin, talking with a brown-skinned girl with long straight black hair.

"This is Kylian." Niamh threaded her fingers into mine. "He's—"

"Your true love," finished the girl wistfully. "I could really use one of those about now."

I blinked, confused by this turn of events. Who had Niamh found in this strange sleeping realm? I didn't have time to figure it out.

"We have to go." I squeezed Niamh's hand. "They won't stay unconscious for long."

Niamh nodded and turned back to the girl, reaching out to grasp her hand. "I'm sorry. I'll see what I can do to help. I won't forget you this time, I promise."

"Does anyone ever remember the things they dream?" The girl sighed. "Thank you for visiting me, at least. It's been a long time since I've had anyone to talk to. But it sounds like you have something important to do."

The dream world faded to mist around us, and in a burst of pink rose petals, I fell back to the waking world.

I scrambled to my feet, the strange dream fading from memory as I stared at the glass coffin. Niamh didn't stir. Why wasn't she waking? Panic gripped my chest, and then I saw it. The movement was faint, but her chest rose and fell. Dark eyelashes fluttered.

She suddenly inhaled a deep breath, and I felt a surge of power burst from her. The glass shattered into millions of pieces. I flinched, throwing up my shield, only to find one already there, protecting me from the sharp fragments until they vaporized into sparkling dust, falling down like snowflakes.

"Kylian." Niamh blinked her eyes sleepily.

I had never been more relieved to hear someone's voice.

"I'm here." I bent down and kissed her gently on the lips.

Her mouth curved into a smile against mine. "This is how I always want to wake up from now on."

I chuckled, helping her sit up.

"That's a *lot* of faoladh." She blinked, looking around. "But not too much for you, it seems."

"Not too much for *us*," I corrected her.

Niamh grinned up at me, but her smile was short-lived. "I sent you all the power I could, but it didn't feel the same as when we fought the ice construct."

"Maybe it's because you were asleep?" I suggested. "You seemed far away. Maybe the magic took longer to reach me."

"Maybe." She didn't sound convinced as she pulled her phone from the pocket of her dress. "One hundred percent power. Audrey's magic charger seems to have done its job. That girl is crazy smart."

"You're lucky to have her," I agreed.

"I'll just send her the text . . ." Niamh tapped at her phone, then set it down, folding her hands on her lap. "And now we wait." Her eyes roamed around the carved marble of the room. "Is this really where my parents are?"

"Over here." I helped Niamh down and led her over to a pair of marble sarcophagi.

She ran her fingers over their names carved into the marble lids. "I wish I had more memories of them." She looked up at me. "I want to make them proud of me."

I smiled, wiping a tear from her cheek. "How could they not be?"

She sniffed. "Do you think . . ." She trailed off, her eyes widening. "Well, that feels strange."

"Are you all right?" I swept her hair aside and examined Audrey and Estrid's new design, the *eihwaz* rune inked on the base of Niamh's neck. I understood the necessity, but still, untested runes were not without risk. Especially this one. Before she could answer, sparkling gold smoke filled the room. I gripped my axe.

"That was a *crazy* feeling."

I relaxed as the sound of Audrey's voice broke through the shimmering cloud.

"Anyone feel like puking?" the spellcrafter continued. "No?"

"We're good," called Amber's voice.

"No one warned us that *puking* was a possible side effect," came a young male voice.

"Well, it's technically blood magic, so you never know,"

Audrey continued. "But powering the iron dust with the blood of the person wearing the rune instead of—well, you don't want to know—seems to have made it less *icky*. But no puking. Yay us!"

"Would knowing that have changed anything, Jac?" came a sharp female reply.

"Well, I would have eaten less breakfast," grumbled Jac.

"Lies." Another male voice.

"So only ten of Calder's pancakes instead of twenty?" teased another female as the smoke started to clear.

"Declan? Is Treasa allowed to tease me?" groused Jac. "Aren't there rules about rookies and respect? *Ow!* The dragons are here."

The air cleared, and in front of us stood Audrey, Gavin—with a black cat on his shoulder—Amber, Clíodhna, and nine fae warriors armed to the teeth with four small dragons leaping around them. Or *on* them, in Jac's case. The four women and five men were bickering as they disentangled their arms from one another and tried to capture the small dragons.

There was no sign of Niamh's owl. Had Fluffy refused to travel with anyone else?

"Liadan?" Niamh squinted at the cat as it leapt down from Gavin's shoulder.

"Do you know any other cait sìth?" asked the cat.

"I guess not." Niamh crouched down by Liadan. "You're using one of your nine transformations for today? You're very cute."

"Of course I am." The cait sìth groomed her ears.

I scanned the rest of the group and then froze, all my attention fixed on the tall woman staring back at me with the same wide eyes. Not just the same expression of shock, but the same eye color, the same *shape*. Her nose was a more delicate version of my own, her skin a shade darker from living in sunnier lands. She stood nearly as tall as me, with her black hair in twists.

"Kyauta," she whispered. "You're really here?"

I couldn't say anything. I hadn't seen my sister since she had been sent to the Seelie court. I had heard tales from the faoladh of the fearsome warrior who called the new Seelie king "brother," but I'd taken great pains to ensure that we never crossed paths. For I had known I wouldn't be able to pretend. Known that if I'd come across her in battle, everything would be lost, for there was no way I could have crossed blades with my own twin.

"Safiya," I finally managed.

"Saoirse now," she said quietly.

I nodded in understanding. I too had chosen a new name when I'd arrived in Tír na nÓg. Why keep the name given to me by parents who were willing to trade their children away for power and influence? Better to have a fresh start. To pick something a little princess could easily pronounce.

"Kylian," I told her as I crossed the distance between us and held out my hand.

She clasped it gingerly, and we stared at each other for another beat before she pulled me in for a hug. I felt tears slip down my cheek. When had I last cried? Niamh had truly melted my heart. I'd barely begun to believe that I could have love, never mind feel the embrace of family.

I swallowed and we stepped back, realizing that everyone was watching us.

Niamh's hand covered her mouth, her eyes shining. Clíodhna practically beamed. Of course she had known my sister would come. I couldn't fault her for this secret.

"Queen Niamh, Kylian." A warrior with pale skin and shaggy dark hair approached. "The Seelie king's personal fianna is at your service." The man bowed. "I'm Declan, and you already know my co-captain, Saoirse. What are your orders? Shall we go teach those Unseelie dogs a lesson?"

Gavin cleared his throat.

Declan winked at him. "Present company excepted."

"One question," called Amber from near the doors. "How do we get out of here?"

Chapter 44

Niamh

"JAC'S OUR SPELLCRAFTER. HE CAN TAKE CARE of the doors. Right, Jac?" Declan nodded to a lanky, blond fae boy.

"Let me take a look." Jac examined the doors and their hinges.

While we waited, the fianna tied up the unconscious faoladh, and I found Amber, who pulled my sword—sheathed and on its belt—out of her purse and handed it to me.

"I need a bag like that!" I admired the little purse. The gold-embroidered pattern of leaves and dragons was bumpy in places, and the dragon looked a bit cross eyed, but the bag hummed with magic.

"My first spellcrafting project," said Amber proudly. "I mean, I don't have the Sight, but Miss Chloe helped me. A faerie godmother always needs to be prepared. Speaking of . . ." She pulled out a set of leather straps and set to work hiking my skirt up to my sword belt.

Kylian glanced over as Amber fussed with the dress. "Wouldn't it be more practical to cut the skirt off? She has pants under it."

"We are going for *drama* here!" Amber put her hand to her chest in indignation. "The Seelie queen herself designed this dress for Neve. It's constructed for maximum queenly vibes while still offering ease of movement and range of motion." Amber fluffed the back of the skirt out. "How is she supposed to stand out in a crowd in leather pants?" She gestured around the room. Indeed, everyone but her, Audrey, and Aunt Chloe was in full leather fighting gear. "A queen needs to *inspire* her troops and make her enemies *cower* before her. Cut off the skirt . . ." she grumbled under her breath.

"Would this help?" I summoned my crown. It didn't feel as heavy as it had back at the cottage.

Amber nodded. "Definitely completes the look. And it makes sense to keep it small until we're outside."

Worried, I looked at Kylian. He smiled back, but I could feel his concern through the bond. Why wasn't the magic reaching me here like it had everywhere else in the Unseelie Kingdom?

"All right, I can do it, but these are pretty thick," called Jac from the doors. "It's going to take a lot of force to blow them open."

"There are two more of *these* outside." Kylian nudged one of the unconscious bodies with his foot. "So if we could direct that force outward, it'd be preferable."

Jac frowned, considering. "I'll do my best, but everyone should probably hide behind a pillar or something."

"I've got this." I channeled power and erected a barrier across the crypt.

The spellcrafter's eyes widened appreciatively. "That's a wicked shield, Your Majesty."

I smiled back, but inwardly, I worried. The shield would hold—it wasn't too big an area—but it wasn't as thick as I wanted. Why couldn't I channel more magic?

"Should we wait on the dwarves and the piskies?" asked Gavin. "We're hidden here, but once we blow those doors, the battle will start."

I shook my head. "Estrid will use her new *eihwaz* rune to get here as soon as she can with whoever she can convince to help. But we can't count on them. Most of them are crafters, after all, not warriors. And the piskies are flying here."

Estrid had been insistent that Prince Darach be informed. I had to admit that his tiny knights had been more helpful than I had expected against the ellén trechend, but I still worried about involving them in this battle. I knew Estrid was right, though. This was their kingdom, too. They deserved the chance to fight for it.

Kylian and his sister took up positions on either side of the door, just inside my shield. I couldn't get over how similarly they moved, with the same deadly grace. Not a family I'd like to be on the wrong side of.

"All set." Jac unrolled a fuse until he was inside the shielded area. "You're gonna need to replace the doors," he called over to me apologetically.

"Put it down on the maintenance list," I teased.

"Everyone cover your ears!" Jac lit the fuse, and we watched it burn through the shield toward the pile of explosives against the doors.

The doors blew outward with a deafening crash, bits of wood and stone glancing off my shield. There was no way that blast had been dampened by Liadan's artifact. The whole castle must have shaken.

"Think you used enough explosives, Jac?" a white-blonde fianna member asked the younger fae, her eyebrows raised.

Jac shrugged. "It's always better to be safe."

We all looked at the rubble where the doors used to be.

"*Very* safe," he added.

I dropped my shield, and Kylian and his sister rushed out, dispatching the two stunned faoladh outside.

"Clear!" called Kylian.

I followed the fianna out into the stairwell and then froze when I saw the two lifeless bodies.

Kylian glanced back and turned to grip my shoulders. Concern flashed across his face. I must be as pale as I felt. "I'm afraid you won't regain your throne without bloodshed."

"I know. I just . . . Surely we don't need to kill them all. Aren't they my subjects now, too? Moriath has caused enough pain. I hate to add to it."

He bent down to look me in the eye. "These were not good people, Niamh. I fought beside them, remember?" He jerked his thumb to the left. "This one abducted children from the human world for Moriath's sister, Bronach, to sell. And this one . . ." He looked at the other faoladh and paused. "You don't want to know."

"We need to get going," called Saoirse. "They will have noticed we're here, and I'd rather not be fighting at the bottom of the stairs."

The fianna were already creeping their way up, Audrey and Gavin at the forefront, but I stood rooted to the spot.

"The faoladh can't *all* be that bad," I insisted. "Do they even have a choice to fight for her?"

"Each one chose to join Moriath, knowing what she is," said Kylian. "And they've eagerly served her ever since. I don't enjoy this either, but they don't deserve your pity."

"But what about Gavin? He's different!"

"And that's why he's on our side. Come on." Kylian guided me up the stairs, his hand on my lower back.

I looked at the bodies one more time and gripped my sword. I understood what Kylian meant, but it still didn't sit right with me.

"Niamh." Saoirse, who had been listening, turned to face me. "I don't know if my brother's right or not about the wolves, but in the end, it comes down to this. Are you willing to let Moriath continue to bleed your kingdom dry? To twist its magic and enslave its inhabitants?"

"No," I answered immediately.

"Then we must defeat anyone who comes against us."

"We can't just knock them out like those guys back in the crypt?"

She shook her head. "That's harder than it looks. I'm honestly not sure how Kylian managed it against so many."

"Niamh lent me her magic through our bond," Kylian said.

Saoirse nodded. "Not an option for the rest of us, then. This battle is going to be messy, Niamh, and we need to keep you alive, okay?"

What she didn't say out loud was that it was also more dangerous for everyone else. Her friends and mine.

"Okay." I took a deep breath. "Let's go."

I heard a *pop*, and a small silver-blue dragon appeared in front of the male warrior with long black hair.

"They're coming," he called back. "At least seventy."

"Thanks, Haru!" called Saoirse.

"Now take your siblings and go back to Auntie Ella at the castle," Haru told the little dragon, who made a grumbling noise but chirped to the other dragons before they all disappeared together.

I couldn't see Liadan anywhere. She was probably smart enough to keep out of the fighting. The same couldn't be said for Audrey, who ran at the front of the pack, her red hoodie bright against all the leather fighting gear. What was she thinking?

"We need to beat them to the courtyard." Kylian grabbed my hand, and we bolted up the stairs after the fianna, Aunt Chloe in her red cloak with Amber at the rear.

It felt strange seeing the castle—where I must have lived as a child—for the first time while waging war against it. Had they carried my unconscious body along this walkway lined with trees of ice? Had I played here as a little kid? I shook my head and focused. Moriath's faoladh were pouring into the courtyard. Audrey dashed out in front of the fianna, Gavin behind her, shifting into his wolf form as he ran.

"Audrey!" I lunged for my friend, but Kylian grabbed my arm. "She's gonna get herself *killed*!" I tried to pull away from his iron grip.

"So shield her," said Kylian. "Do not run into danger after her."

"But—"

"Trust your friend," he said in my ear. "She's the genius, remember?"

"It's time!" Audrey reached the center of the courtyard and threw a tiny golden object into the air.

In a burst of shimmering light, my beautiful owl appeared. Fluffy trailed golden dust as he circled the momentarily stunned faoladh. Most of them just sneezed the dust away, but more than a third of them stood a little straighter as an emblem of a flying owl shimmered gold against their chests, over the place where their faoladh tattoos were inked.

Audrey spun and dashed toward the fianna, Gavin at her back, protecting her from the oncoming enemies with his teeth and claws. "Owls are on our side!" she hollered as our warriors clashed with the faoladh.

Sure enough, all of the men marked with an owl turned and fought alongside the fianna, making the numbers a lot closer to even. Close enough. With the way the fianna fought, they put my training to shame.

Saoirse smacked Kylian on the arm. "There was never a better time to be wrong!" she yelled, then ran to fight with her fianna.

Kylian looked ashen as the fighting swelled around us. "I would have killed them all," he whispered.

"But you didn't." I brought up my sword as an enemy faoladh lunged for me. I blocked his blade and kicked him back.

"But that was my counsel to you." Kylian still looked stricken, even as he spun me behind him and struck the fae rushing at me. "You can't still think—"

"I would have let them *all* live," I interrupted, slashing at the arm of a fae following Audrey as she reached us. "When two-thirds of them must have been given a chance to switch sides and didn't. Am I right?" I asked Audrey.

My blonde friend nodded, gasping for breath as she leaned on her black wolf of a boyfriend.

"Yeah," she said. "Gavin and I have been recruiting for months. I'm sorry," she added, giving me a quick hug. "We couldn't tell you. Vowing to keep it a secret was the only way the faoladh would trust us. But we were careful. We did background checks on all of them, and we made sure to ask each one that joined our side who else he thought might be fed up with Moriath." She ducked and Gavin leapt, taking the enemy who had swung his blade at her to the ground. "I wouldn't exactly call them, like, *best friend* material. But they'll be loyal."

"So, we were both wrong," I told Kylian as we took down an enemy together. "That's why we need each other."

"And me," added Audrey. She dug through her bag and pulled out a gold bell, then made a face and threw it back in.

"Obviously." I grinned at my friend.

Did you see how majestic I was? Fluffy soared near me.

"*Very* majestic," I called back. "How did you get him to help you?" I asked Audrey.

"Liadan can speak to animals when she's a cat. She appealed to your owl's epic nature."

The courtyard grew quieter as our allies finished off the last of the enemy faoladh. But before I could relax, we heard a sound like ice cracking and popping.

"We need to get out of the courtyard," called Kylian, "or we'll be trapped."

Saoirse nodded from across the courtyard and began moving, the fianna and our faoladh behind her.

"What do you mean?" I asked Kylian, sprinting alongside him.

"Moriath's renovated the exterior of the castle since you lived here," he explained unhelpfully, his hand on my back as he glanced upward.

"Well, it's not like I *remember*."

When we broke out of the courtyard into the wide space in front of Skyretaine Castle, I skidded to a stop. As I stared at the tall spires of ice, I suddenly realized that I *did* remember. My home had been one of graceful stone arches and vine-covered towers. The courtyard behind us used to be an apple orchard. I had a sudden memory of being right here, looking up at the castle, a mossy stone path underfoot. My parents had each been holding one of my hands, swinging me between them as we walked to the castle.

Now, everything was frozen and still, the castle so encased in ice that it looked like it had been crafted from it, cold and deadly like its mistress.

Another loud crack made me jump, and the memory broke. All my warriors stood around me with open mouths, staring upward as giant creatures of ice broke away from the castle walls.

Chapter 45

Niamh

The smaller creatures—gargoyle-like combinations of animals and beasts of various sizes—broke free first, scattering splinters of ice as they shook out their wings. But I hardly noticed them as I watched a giant serpentine dragon of ice flex its taloned feet and stretch away from the castle's immense main entrance it was curled over.

Kylian and Gavin had warned us about Moriath's guardian ice construct, but nothing had prepared me for the sheer size of it.

I threw up a shield over the group and winced at its flickering thinness as the smaller creatures tested it with their claws and fangs. All around me, our allies regrouped for battle. The fianna and our faoladh formed a protective circle around the rest of us. Audrey and Jac compared explosives in rapid speech, while Aunt Chloe and Amber held a large green gem—glowing brighter by the moment—between the two of them.

More monsters broke out of the ice as the dragon worked to wrench its long tail free of the wall.

I gulped.

"We can do this." Kylian squeezed my hand. "We took out the ellén trechend together, remember?"

"I remember." I hesitated. "There's something wrong, though. Look at my shield."

I lent Kylian my Sight through the bond, showing him what I saw as another gargoyle slammed against the barrier, making it flicker.

"I can barely feel the magic here," I whispered, not wanting to worry the others. "The power I'm channeling feels so faint, like it's coming from far away."

Kylian looked down at our feet. "Moriath is draining the land itself."

I nodded. "How tall are my antlers?"

He didn't say anything.

"That's what I thought."

Not tall enough to roost on, grumbled Fluffy, circling under the shield.

"Where are the dwarves?" I asked, wishing Estrid had one of Audrey's magically hacked phones. "And the piskies? Fluffy, can you look for the piskies and see if they're close?"

"Do you think they'd turn the tide of this battle?" asked Kylian, gripping his axe more tightly as the dragon launched itself at our group.

"No." I gritted my teeth, but the shield held as the giant construct smashed into it. "I think they should stay away," I whispered, staring up at the ice dragon.

"Behind you!" shouted one of our owl-marked faoladh.

I spun to see two Clydesdale-sized wolves made of ice creeping up behind us, hackles raised.

"Now!" yelled Aunt Chloe. She and Amber ran through the shield and threw the gem they'd been holding at the ice wolves. The gem exploded into sparkling dust, taking the ice wolves with it. They burst into splinters of shining crystal as Aunt Chloe calmly raised her hand. A gold ring sparkled while she threw up a shield protecting her and Amber.

"Do you have any more of those?" I asked hopefully as the dragon launched at us again, its icicle claws scraping along my shield.

"Two more." Aunt Chloe stared grimly at the fifteen or so beasts that now surrounded my shield. "And they aren't strong enough to take out that big one."

I grimaced. This was supposed to be my job, but when we had discussed all possible options, I hadn't considered that the magic wouldn't be able to reach me.

"Do we need to retreat?" I asked Kylian.

"How?" He glanced behind us at the cliffs surrounding the castle. "The gate is likely still sealed."

I nodded. I could feel its cold magic.

"And everybody with the *eihwaz* teleportation rune is here except . . ."

I looked at him. "Except Estrid. Do you think she's still under the mountain? We could go to her and regroup."

They're flying in! called my owl. *The dwarves!*

You mean the piskies, I sent back to him.

I think I can tell the difference between a piskie and a dwarf. Fluffy flew down.

I held my breath as he plunged between the icy monsters and through my shield, opening his wings to bank down onto my wrist.

They're flying fast. Almost here. He jumped up to settle on my shoulder.

"But dwarves don't—"

"Look!" Kylian pointed up.

My jaw dropped as five giant dragons—*real* dragons with glittering scales of purple, white, and green—dropped from the sky. Each dragon had one or two tiny figures on their backs. If I squinted, I could see the magic holding them in place without straps or saddles. Crazy dwarves.

"Watch out! This is going to get messy," hollered Estrid from the back of the purple dragon.

The dwarves all activated their rune-powered shields before crashing into the ice constructs surrounding us.

"Everyone who can shield, *shield!*" I poured all my strength into my shield as Audrey and Jac threw barriers up above mine, powered by devices pulled hastily from the depths of their backpacks.

Aunt Chloe and Amber added their ring-powered shields above them.

I gritted my teeth and held mine with everything I had as the dragons broke apart the ice constructs. They attacked the smaller ones first, crunching the ice and swallowing the golden power sources with relish as two dragons held the giant serpent at bay.

The ice beast thrashed against the shields, breaking what remained of my friends' outer protections and leaving only mine. It flickered under the weight.

"I don't have enough power," I gasped.

"Take some of mine." Kylian threaded his fingers between mine.

"Are you sure?" I had always been the one giving *him* magic. I had never considered the reverse.

He nodded. "Stronger together, right?"

"Right." I nodded firmly and our combined magic flowed through our bond, strengthening the shield as the dragons tore into the serpent with teeth and claws.

The dwarven warriors screamed in triumph as the snarling ice construct finally went down in a shower of icicles—some shards taller than I was—each of which glanced harmlessly off the shield Kylian and I kept over our group.

Kylian's magic faltered as the last piece of ice slid down the side of the glittering gold dome. When he wobbled unsteadily on his feet, I threw my arms around him.

"Was that too much? Are you okay?" I pressed myself against him as he regained his balance.

"I'm fine," he said weakly.

"You'd better be. No more self-sacrifices," I reminded him. "We've talked about this."

"Don't worry, Princess." He took a deep breath and leaned his forehead against mine. "I'm not leaving you. I promised. But I could use some of your cookies."

"Oh yeah?" I pulled back to look at him.

"At least two for—what did you call it? Plus twenty stamina?"

I laughed shakily.

"Don't tell me you didn't bring any," he teased. "I thought you always kept some in your pockets."

"They were too full of plots and secrets for cookies today."

I turned as someone sighed behind us. Amber handed one of my chocolate cookies to Kylian.

"Luckily for you, a faerie godmother is always well prepared." She winked. "I don't think I can take credit for *this*, however," she added, looking in awe at the giant dragons perched on the castle.

The shiny purple dragon landed in front of me, still munching on the golden artifact that had powered the ice dragon. Fluffy took off hastily.

"I'm sure she won't eat you," I called after my owl.

I'd rather not find out, thanks. Fluffy soared off to watch from overhead.

Estrid slid off the dragon's back. "Thank you, Sofie." My friend turned to us and grinned. "So, pretty sweet, right?"

"How did you get them to help us?" I asked. "Can you talk to them?"

"Not exactly, but they understand us." Estrid smiled up at the purple dragon.

Dwarves don't live long enough to properly learn our language, sniffed Sofie. *But you have your father's talent, I hear, little queen.* She peered down at me.

"I do." I bowed my head. "Thank you for saving us. How can I repay you?"

The small ones say that the usurper queen has amassed more than her share of gemstones?

"That's probably true. She stores her stolen magic in them."

Delicious. The dragon licked her snout, showing her long sharp teeth. She nudged Estrid, almost making the dwarf topple over with the force. *This one suggested that you might be willing to part with a few in exchange for our assistance.*

I smiled at Sofie. "You are welcome to the entire treasury."

Excellent. The cold one has been queen too long not to have an excellent hoard, but don't worry, little queen, we won't leave your cave empty. After all, a queen must have her snacks around.

I laughed.

"It's early in the day to be smiling, little niece."

I froze.

Black smoke cleared from the top of the castle stairs, revealing Moriath, her falcon on her shoulder. Twenty more of her faoladh were at her back, all looking rather ill. Dylan swayed on his feet. It was probably too much to hope that he would pass out from too many teleportations.

"Should we attack?" Saoirse looked to her brother, who held up a hand to wait.

I sidled over to Audrey. "I don't suppose any of those guys are going to join us?"

She shook her head grimly.

"Those wolves are the most loyal to Moriath. Every one of them would die ten times over before allowing anything to happen to her." Kylian followed close behind me, reaching out to hold my hand again.

I sighed, all traces of humor gone.

"Dylan doesn't strike me as the self-sacrificial type." Audrey tapped her lip.

"No," agreed Kylian. "But he knows he's dead anyway if anything happens to her."

"Pay attention!" the queen snapped.

A wave of power washed over us, dropping all the faoladh and most of the fianna to their knees. Saoirse and Declan managed to stay upright, teeth gritted, and Kylian and I pulled enough strength from each other through the bond to appear unaffected.

"Nice crown," I shot back.

Moriath narrowed her eyes, touching her false crown self-consciously. "But what about yours?" she crooned. "I haven't seen it for decades, but I seem to remember it being much . . ." She waved a hand. "Bigger."

"Not jealous, are you?" I didn't have to touch my own antlers to know how small they were. How little magic I could pull from the barren wasteland Moriath had created around her castle.

"A temporary problem." The queen descended the stairs. With a snap of her fingers, the faoladh behind her collapsed into their wolf forms and prowled down the stairs around her. "You're out of allies." She smirked up at the dragons on the roof, who were straining to move against the force of her power.

She was right. I looked at all my friends. Even Audrey was on the ground. I couldn't battle Moriath here. It was all I could do to stand.

"Should I bargain?" I whispered to Kylian.

I saw my fear reflected in his dark eyes, but I knew his worry was for me.

"We're not done yet, my dear." Aunt Chloe came up beside me, flipping the hood of her red cloak back. "Moriath," she called. "You look, well, as *evil* as ever. Isn't it exhausting?"

"Clíodhna," Moriath snarled. Then she brightened. "All my problems solved in one day. How lovely."

"Behind you," my godmother whispered in my ear, squeezing my hand before stepping up to meet the queen, Amber close behind her.

"Your years in the mortal realm have taken their toll, I see." Moriath smirked.

"It *has* been a while." Aunt Chloe laughed. "Hold these, Amber dear." She pulled her gold-framed glasses off and handed them to her apprentice.

In a blaze of light, my elderly aunt transformed into the most majestic fae I had ever laid eyes on.

Chapter 46

Niamh

SHE STOOD AT LEAST SEVEN FEET TALL, with pale blue hair that tumbled down her back between golden butterfly wings so tall that they reached high above her head and trailed down to the ground. Like her hair, her long dress of floating gold silk drifted around her, moved by some unseen breeze.

A crown of golden leaves and fluttering, translucent butterfly wings sparkled on her head.

"Clíodhna," whispered Kylian in awe. "Ancient Banshee queen, patron *sídhe* of love and beauty."

She turned, caught me gaping, and winked one blue eye—still the color I remembered, with the twinkle I had always known—in a face of unearthly beauty. Then she turned back to Moriath, who, like her wolves, stood stunned as Clíodhna lifted her arms above her head and, with a blast of magic, sent them all stumbling back.

"Hurry, back here! While she's distracted." Amber grabbed my hand.

Kylian squeezed my fingers before releasing me. "I'll keep an eye on them."

"Did you know she could do that?" I asked Amber as she led me away.

She shook her head, clearly impressed by her mentor's transformation. "But I do know that she can't match Moriath for power. She's only distracting her."

"I can't *leave* her," I protested, slowing down.

"We're not running," insisted Amber. "We're going to get you your magic. Look."

I turned. Coming through the courtyard behind her on hooves of gold were . . .

"Unicorns," I breathed.

The herd of unicorns surrounded me. Liadan, still in her cat form, sat on the back of the silver unicorn in front, and fluttering in the air above them flew a cloud of little winged piskie knights, tiny swords at the ready.

"Liadan! This is where you disappeared to?"

The black cat blinked smugly. "I knew she had them around here somewhere. It did take some poking around, but luckily, nobody bothers to notice a cat. I can communicate more easily with other animals in this form, so I explained the situation to the herd."

The piskie prince landed beside the cait sìth and cleared his throat.

"But I never would have gotten them free of their chains without the help of the piskies," Liadan admitted with unusual humbleness. "Their spelled swords make much better lock picks than my claws." She examined her paw, claws out. "I'll have to put these to use in other ways." She leapt off the unicorn's back and trotted toward the battle.

"We're just happy that our path here took us past those cursed stables." The small prince bowed. "Enchanted iron chains. *Nasty* things." He shuddered.

I smiled at the piskie. "You have my gratitude for helping me keep my vow to a young unicorn."

You've seen the rest of the herd then? The silver unicorn perked up. *My daughter?*

"Safe," I promised her. "They're all safe with friends. They miss you very much."

"You'd better hurry," said Amber. "Moriath's not going to be distracted for long."

"We can help with that." The piskie prince twirled his sword.

I glanced back. Most of our warriors were still pinned to the ground as Moriath and Clíodhna's power clashed in a shower of sparks. Her wolves were held at bay by Kylian and his sister for now, but they were outnumbered. They needed help, but the piskies were so small.

"She's very powerful. Are you sure?" I winced.

"Moriath won't see us coming until we're upon her," scoffed the piskie.

"Be careful."

The prince nodded and lifted his sword. "For Queen Niamh!" he yelled.

The tiny knights all echoed his cry and flew off to support Clíodhna and Kylian.

"You'd better power up fast, Neve," Amber called before running after them, another glowing gem in her hand.

Now it's our turn to help. The silver unicorn nudged me.

"Are you sure you're strong enough?" I glanced at the unicorns. They all looked gaunt and underfed. Their horns and hooves didn't have the luster of the herd I had met in the forest.

The unicorn nodded. *Moriath has been using us to channel magic into her gems.* She snorted. *She can't reach the magic herself like a true ruler.* She inclined her head to me. *She forced us to drain the power around the castle.*

"But if the magic here is gone, what can we do?" I asked.

We may have misled Moriath about our ability to reach the land's magic. The unicorn tossed her head. *We let her believe we had pulled from as far as we could. Selfish as Moriath is, she never guessed that we would let ourselves become weak just to protect the kingdom. The magic we draw is what gives us strength, my queen. Not hay or oats.*

"So this will help you, not hurt you," I clarified.

The unicorns all nodded in agreement, butting up around me.

"Stronger together," I whispered, closing my eyes.

Distantly, I could hear Moriath's sneers turn into cries of annoyance as the piskies joined the battle. I hoped their talent for distraction would be enough to loosen the magic she was using to hold down my allies.

I exhaled, blocking all of that out to focus on the unicorns around me and my connection to my kingdom through them. It felt faint at first, little more than the trickle I had been feeling all along. But, like water running downhill, the magic picked up speed and strength as it grew closer. The distant hum became a rush as Faerie eagerly filled in the magical void Moriath had left. I inhaled as the power filled me like never before. It felt eager to wash away the blight on the land.

Slowly, I opened my eyes. Silence had fallen over the battlefield as everyone stared at us. Then the dragons launched into the air as Skyretaine Castle shimmered, then exploded. The thick layer of ice covering everything shattered into sparkling dust before melting into tiny raindrops that fell down all around us, revealing the stone castle beneath.

I wanted to take it all in, the graceful arches, sunlit windows, and balconies crawling with growing vines and flowers. To watch as the magic continued to pour outward, grass and flowers bursting through the snow around my feet. But I wasn't finished yet.

I strode forward, sword drawn.

That's more like it! Fluffy swooped down and perched on my antlers as I walked toward Moriath. *I'll help you look imposing.*

I didn't need to touch the crown to know that the icicles were taller, the antlers growing more prongs than ever before as I stood before the false queen.

Moriath snarled, her gems flashing with stolen magic as she pushed back against my power. Her wolves seemed to grow even larger around her. Kylian, Saoirse, and even the piskies around her fell to the ground this time, and Clíodhna stumbled back a step.

The ground crackled as a circle of frost emanated from her.

"*No*," she snarled. "You can't have it. Not after everything I've done. Some little human-raised *baker* is not going to steal this kingdom from me."

I couldn't help it. I laughed at hearing my own argument from months ago thrown back in my face.

Moriath's brows furrowed in annoyance.

"You're right." I sheathed my sword. "That's exactly what I am. A baker raised by humans."

I thought of my mom and dad in our snug farmhouse as I stepped up to where Kylian knelt in front of the evil queen.

"Humans who taught me through baking pies," I continued, with a smile at Estrid, who winked back at me, "and love, everything I needed to be a queen." I pulled Kylian up beside me, lacing my fingers through his while he gripped his axe in his other hand.

Still smiling, I shoved back with my magic. Moriath's eyes widened as all my allies rose to their feet, weapons in hand, both bladed and magical.

"Get them!" she snarled.

Ránach launched toward me with a battle cry, but Fluffy met the falcon midair. My owl seemed to grow bigger as he swooped down on the peregrine, driving her back to cower on her mistress's shoulder. Moriath's wolves lunged forward, and I pushed my magic out again, throwing all her minions back.

Moriath screamed in rage, lifting her rings. That was enough of *that*. I felt out with my magic and found her stolen power, squeezing until all the gems on her fingers and false crown cracked. They dulled one by one until only the blue stones around her neck sparkled, unaffected by my magic.

She paled, fingers raking over her jewels, fumbling for the iron amulet around her neck. Her icy eyes widened when she found it missing. Baring her teeth, Moriath raised her arms one more time, and I tensed. Was she hiding one last trick up her sleeve?

But nothing came. Instead, she spun, picking up her skirts as she ran for the stairs behind her. Toward the only exit.

The Ice Gate.

Chapter 47

Niamh

Moriath's wolves scampered after her, except for one who had the poor luck to run past Saoirse.

The former queen raced up the stairs, her crown crashing to the ground behind her.

"You can't let her escape." Kylian took a step forward, but I put my hand on his arm.

"She won't. I promise."

I waited for Moriath to notice as she rushed forward up the steps, expecting her to hesitate, to check. But, even now, her pride won out. She couldn't believe that the gate her mother had created, that she had controlled with her own ice magic for hundreds of years, could be turned against her. And so it wasn't until her feet hit the ice surrounding the gate and her jeweled shoes slipped that she realized the gate was melting.

Faerie had pulled the magic from the gate, leaving nothing more than regular ice dripping in the warm sun.

Moriath's pale eyes widened.

I lunged forward. "No!"

I hadn't meant for this to happen, but there was no way to reach her as she slid, wolves surging around her, through the collapsing gate and over the cliff.

Ránach dove after her mistress with a cry. There was a scramble as the wolves in the back tried in vain to stop the momentum. Dylan yelped as he skidded on the melting ice before following his mistress to their doom.

In a matter of seconds, they were gone.

Kylian and I climbed the wet stone stairs—the carved ice that had covered them now gone with the gate—and carefully stared down, down, down into the distant forest below. Fluffy flew past us and drifted lower and lower in circles below the cliff.

"She's really *gone*?" I swallowed. I knew in my head that Moriath would never have stopped fighting for the crown. Everyone would tell me that she had only gotten what she'd deserved, but I was never going to be comfortable with death. This was something I'd have to learn to live with.

"They built the gate in a spot that would ensure no one would survive when it closed against them." Kylian tugged me back from the melting pile of ice at the cliff's edge. "As she made sure of more than once."

"I didn't mean for . . ."

"I know." He squeezed my hand. "But it's for the best."

"Well, you're a better person than I am." Audrey stepped up beside us and shielded her eyes from the sun as she squinted at the last icy chunks tumbling off the cliff. "I wish I could be as conflicted as you about my nemesis falling off a cliff. Sadly, Dylan really was the worst."

Kylian barked out a surprised laugh.

"Seriously, if I had been closer, I might have given him a bit of a push. Am I right, Gavin?" Audrey glanced back, but Gavin wasn't looking at her. He was too busy unbuttoning his shirt.

"Hold on, hot stuff." Audrey threw up her hands. "It's not *that* warm out."

Gavin pulled his shirt aside, and we all watched as the tattoo over his heart smoked and then faded to a dull black, only a small Celtic knot design in the center glinting with gold.

"She's really gone." He looked up, eyes wide.

"Let me have a look." Closing her eyes, Audrey placed her hand over Gavin's heart.

"You're right." She reopened her eyes. "The tracking spell is gone. There's not even a hint of it trying to regrow like before."

"Then why is there still an enchanted tattoo there?" I asked.

Audrey frowned. "That's from my tampering with the spell, I think." She peeked under her hand. "When I hacked it so that Gavin could shift at will instead of being bound to wolf form at night and fae by day, that part of the spell must have broken free of the rest. I couldn't remove it before," she murmured, "but I can see now that it's not tethered to anything else . . ."

"That's okay." Gavin put his hand over Audrey's. "Maybe I like having a little part of you over my heart."

Audrey's expression melted. "You just like to be furry," she teased.

"I mean . . ." he hedged.

"So floofy!" she said.

"Aw, come on."

I looked away as they kissed.

The other faoladh were checking their tattoos as well. Cries of happiness rose all around when they found the spell gone.

I started down the stairs and paused halfway to take a deep breath and glance at the rubble mixed in with fresh greenery and flowers. The castle windows were broken from centuries of ice. There was a lot of work to do.

"Okay, so who knows where I can find—"

"Long live the queen!" the piskies interrupted, flying overhead with their swords raised.

Fluffy soared up to fly with them, joining in with the piskie chorus as the faoladh all fell to their knees

"Um." I froze as the unicorns bowed their heads.

Even Liadan—once more on a unicorn's back—did something between a bow and a cat stretch, then pretended she hadn't.

The fianna weren't my subjects, but they still beamed at me beside a loudly cheering Amber and Aunt Chloe, still in her majestic fae form.

But even Audrey and Gavin passed me on the stairs to drop to their knees. Kylian stepped around me and tried to lower himself in front of me as well.

"Don't you dare!" I pulled him back up beside me.

"Surely, after all the work I've done to put you on the throne, you can't deny me this moment," he insisted.

"If you *ever* bow to me . . ." I poked him in the chest and then paused, trying to think of an appropriate threat.

"You'll never bake cookies for me again?" he teased.

"Well, no, that would just be mean."

I hauled him toward me. His axe and my sword clattered to the ground as we kissed, my hands against his chest, his mouth warm against mine.

We broke away when the cheering grew even louder. Kylian's eyes widened as I smirked at him.

"What did you—?" He reached up and found a circlet of icicles and antlers sprouting from his own head.

I shrugged with a smirk. "You promised."

"Long live the Unseelie queen and king!" Amber tossed a handful of golden acorns into the sky. They immediately burst into sparkling fireworks overhead.

"You think you can just get away with this?" Kylian narrowed his eyes at me.

I smiled innocently, waving to the cheering crowd.

"I'll get you back in training," he threatened, brushing his lips against my ear, careful not to tangle his crown with mine. "Make you do laps around the castle. In armor."

"Whatever you want," I answered. "As long as you're beside me."

And the cheers rose again as I kissed my Unseelie king.

CHAPTER 48

KYLIAN

WITH SOME EFFORT, I MANAGED TO DISMISS my new crown. Saoirse strode across the courtyard, looking uninjured save for a thin line of red on her cheek where a wolf had gotten in a lucky graze before meeting its doom on the end of her blade. The way my sister handled herself in battle would have made our childhood weapons master proud.

She pulled me aside. "Tiernan asked me to find out what happened to his father. I expected to come against Fiachra in the battle, but I didn't catch a hint of him anywhere."

I raised an eyebrow. "From the stories I've heard, I'm surprised your king has any wish to see his father. Didn't Fiachra try to have Tiernan's new bride killed before they even made it to the wedding ceremony?"

"*Wish* might be too strong of a word," Saoirse said with a

sigh. "Tiernan doesn't trust his father, and he certainly doesn't hold any lingering affection for him. But he does want to know what happened to the old bastard. When he ran off with Moriath after the whole wedding fiasco, they appeared to be allies. Do you know how to find him?"

"Come with me."

I kissed Niamh—she was having a rapid-fire conversation with her godmother—and told her where I was going before leading Saoirse into the castle. Already, Skyretaine felt brighter and more hopeful as the sun shone through the cracked windows.

"You're close with your king." I glanced over at Saoirse.

"He's my brother," she said simply. "He and the fianna are my family."

I knew it was true. I'd heard stories through the years, of course, of the Seelie crown prince and his warrior foster sister. I wasn't jealous. It had comforted me to know that my sister had found a family when I couldn't be there for her.

"I think Tiernan hopes that if he can talk to his father one last time, it will give him some sort of closure." Saoirse shook her head as we walked through the corridor. "I told him that I hadn't found conversations with estranged parents all that helpful, but he's forever optimistic."

"You've been to see them, then?" I asked. "Our parents?"

Saoirse nodded. "With Tiernan. He wanted to visit his younger brother. The one they traded for me," she added bitterly. "It seems that the brother had a happy childhood and is now married to one of our cousins. I'd say our parents treated him like their own child, but clearly not, as he's the one they let stay in the forest with them."

I opened the door to the back tower, and we started up the long, curving stairs.

"Apparently, they lost Niamh's sister before she even arrived," Saoirse continued, a couple of steps behind me. "And then hid it from Moriath so she wouldn't kill you. I suppose that shows at least a bit of affection. I was surprised. You were always their favorite. I didn't think they'd be so eager to get rid of you. Moriath must have scared them even more than Fiachra."

I shook my head. "She didn't threaten them at all. The exchange with the Seelie Kingdom for you brought them more influence, a new trading partner, and powerful allies as long as they kept the Seelie prince safe. They wanted more. After all, you only need an heir and a spare, and there were five of us kids."

"What are you saying?"

"*They* set up the engagement with Niamh, not Moriath. Though she jumped at the chance to send off Maeve. But you're right, they wanted to exchange Lekan. I convinced them to trade me instead."

"Why?" whispered Saoirse.

"Because of you." I shook my head at the naive princeling I'd been. "All I understood was that I could go to a kingdom in Tír na nÓg. I had no concept of the size of this land. I thought I could run away and find you when I got here." I rubbed the back of my neck as I climbed. "But everything became complicated rather quickly."

"You had to save your princess."

"Yes." I clenched and unclenched the fist at my side. "Still, I should have tried to come for you." Although I didn't know what choices I could have made differently.

"Kylian." My sister grasped my wrist, and I turned to look back at her. "I was fine," she said. "Truly. If anyone needed help, it was you. You were just a kid, too. I'm ashamed to say that I believed the rumors. I thought you had become a monster."

"I did," I said softly.

"No." She squeezed my hand. "You didn't. I can see that now. I thought my favorite brother was gone. It was as if you were dead."

I closed my eyes. The boy I used to be, Safiya's beloved twin brother, might as well have died. He felt so different from what I had become.

"I'm sorry." She stepped up beside me and wrapped me in a tight hug. "And I'm so glad to have you back."

I could feel the tears on Saoirse's cheeks as I hugged her back, and it felt like she somehow squeezed back together all the parts of myself. The young prince, full of hope for his future and love for his twin sister. The battle-hardened Huntsman, willing to do whatever it took to protect the princess and the kingdom. The good king I was determined to be at my queen's side.

Saoirse pulled back, rubbing at her eyes. "Hugging and crying, twice in one day? Don't tell my fianna. They'll never let me live it down."

"It'll be our secret." I grinned at my sister, and we climbed the final steps together.

The tower door swung open with a touch, its locking spell unraveled with the rest of Moriath's legacy. The door opened to a simple but comfortable room. A frail old man looked up at us in bewilderment from where he sat on the narrow bed.

"Fiachra?" Saoirse stared at the white-haired man, his once-sharp eyes cloudy with age. "What happened to him?"

"He lost the blessing of Faerie," I said. "Along with the long life it provides. He's as mortal as he would be in the human realm."

Saoirse gaped. "I didn't know that could even happen."

I nodded. "I've never seen anything like it either. When Moriath vowed to give him safe haven after he fled the Seelie Kingdom with her, I'm sure she expected a more useful ally."

"Who are you? Is it time for lunch?" asked the old man in a quavering voice.

"Well, I'll take him back with me, I guess." Saoirse shook her head. "Tiernan will want to see him. I'd better go. Declan's waiting with the dragons."

I nodded, not wanting her to go but knowing that her home, her family, was not with me.

"I'll see you tomorrow? Or will it take a couple of days to get a new gate set up?"

I looked up at her in surprise.

Saoirse grinned. "Tiernan and Ella will want to meet you guys immediately. It was all we could do to keep them out of the battle."

Hesitantly, I smiled back. "I'd like that."

"Don't worry, Brother." She gave me another tight hug. "Now that I've found you again, you won't get rid of me that easily."

Chapter 49

Niamh

THERE WAS A LOT OF WORK TO be done to set the Unseelie Kingdom to rights. Starting with the castle, we gave each captive enemy and castle servant the choice between swearing fealty or being exiled. But the challenges stretched far beyond Skyretaine. When powerful evil rules a land, smaller evil is emboldened to grow unchecked. Audrey, Gavin, and Liadan were working on a list, the top of which was Moriath's sister, my other evil aunt, Bronach. My friends had narrowly escaped the child-stealing witch when Audrey first came to Faerie.

But the first order of business was a happy one. I had a vow to fulfill.

The day after the battle, we stood surrounded by unicorns in the courtyard where Amber and Aunt Chloe—back in her unassuming librarian form—had been working on turning the stone archway into a temporary gate. I watched them finish while Fluffy attempted to find a comfortable roost in my antlers.

"Stop wiggling, or I'll make them disappear," I threatened the owl.

No! Fluffy froze. *I want my sisters to see how impressive we are.*

"This is just for now." Amber screwed the last enchanted gold plate into the stone. "We are going to make you a much safer and, let's be real, more stylish gate than Moriath's icy death trap."

"This is perfect," I assured her. "As long as we have something."

Because, without the Ice Gate, teleportation runes were the only way in and out of Skyretaine for those of us who weren't blessed with wings. Estrid and I had convinced Sofie and her fellow dragons to fly the fianna to the nearest Seelie gate, but unicorns weren't built to be dragon riders.

"Okay, my dear. It's all set." Aunt Chloe straightened and dusted her hands on her slacks.

"I'll meet you in the meadow with the rest of the herd," I promised Kylian with a kiss.

He nodded. "*Stop that,*" he added to his crown as it attempted to send little icicles up through his black locs, encouraged by the magic of the unicorns milling around him.

The herd had been told by the piskies what Kylian had done to save the kingdom, and I knew the unicorns' trust in him was helping to heal one of the raw spots in his heart.

Amber pulled out a gold pocket watch. "We need to get going."

"What's the hurry?" I sputtered as Amber yanked Aunt Chloe and me through the makeshift gate.

"There's one more thing I have to do before I can become a fully fledged faerie godmother," Amber explained as we stepped into Kilinaire's sunlit garden of blooming roses.

"Oh? *Ack!*" I struggled to keep my balance as Fluffy launched off my antlers to find his mother and her flock of birds. His excitement to see his family must have won out over his plan to make an epic entrance with me. "What do you have to do?"

"Get my first faerie godchild!" squealed Amber, clapping her hands.

"Technically, she's your niece," Aunt Chloe reminded her apprentice.

"She can be both. Come on!" Amber pulled on Aunt Chloe's arm as she dashed up the gravel path, leaving me with the roses. "I'm going to give her the *best* christening present."

"A musical voice?" asked her mentor.

"Better."

"Grace and beauty?"

"Are you kidding? She's related to me, so those will come naturally."

The doors to the castle opened, and the sound of new lungs wailing drifted out.

Amber squealed again and dashed inside, Aunt Chloe following at a more sedate pace.

"You don't want to see the baby?"

I looked down to see a brown otter at my feet.

"Seems like a family moment," I told him. "Besides, I'm not really a baby person."

The otter nodded. "They *are* awfully smelly. I'm Tait. Come on. I'll take you to the unicorns."

Tait leapt up, turning into a shaggy, black bunny-like creature with a long tufted tail as he ran. Phouka, I remembered from the illustration from my book.

"I'm Niamh," I called as I ran after him. "And I think I already know—"

I didn't bother finishing as Tait transformed again into a sparkling purple baby unicorn, leaping the fence and running around with the little foals in a game of tag.

The elderly black unicorn met me as I crossed the flower-filled field toward the herd.

So, you've done it. He looked up at my crown, proudly tall in the presence of the magical creatures.

I nodded, a lump in my throat as the little silver unicorn jumped happily around my feet. *You found Mama?* she squealed.

I grinned, catching the little foal up into my arms where she nuzzled my cheek.

"I found them all," I said. "It's time to go home."

I led the young and elderly unicorns through the Rose Gate. Their backs were covered with even more birds than before, thanks to a good spring for hatching chicks.

We stepped into an enchanted forest, nothing like the barren, eerie woods we had left behind months ago. I counted horns to make sure that every little foal had made it through—and no extra purple babies—before stopping to stare at the lush green forest.

The tiny magical meadow had been just a hint of what a full herd of magic-channeling unicorns could do to transform their home. As far as I could see, moss, ferns, and wildflowers covered the forest floor. Above us, the giant hawthorn trees were in full bloom with gold-dusted white and deep pink flowers.

All the birds but Fluffy and his mother took off in every direction through the treetops, sparkling dust trailing behind wherever they brushed a gold-veined green leaf in the shimmering canopy overhead.

Mama! I'm coming! hollered the little silver unicorn.

Whinnying and giggling, the rest of the young unicorns took off after her through the ferns that stood waist high on me. Soon, I could only see little pearlescent horns, shimmering brighter and brighter as they ran off through the flower-dotted ferns.

The grandpa unicorn sighed. *Well, we'd best catch up with them and make sure everyone's all right,* he muttered, but his shining eyes gave away the same excitement about seeing the rest of the herd.

Was it my imagination, or were the elderly unicorns moving less stiffly than before as they trotted after the foals?

That left me and the two large white owls sitting on a leafy branch beside me.

Your Majesty. The mother owl observed me solemnly. *I hope Frederick here has acquitted himself well as your familiar?*

Fluffy straightened, chest feathers puffed. *I've been very—*

Hush, Fluffy, said my owl's mother. *Let the queen speak.*

"He's been the perfect companion," I assured her.

And has he been properly dignified in your presence? pressed the mother.

I grinned at Fluffy, remembering all the times he had tumbled off my vanishing antlers or begged me for more cookies.

"He's been exactly the right amount of dignified." I held out my arm, and Fluffy hopped over to me.

His mother nodded, satisfied. *I'm very proud of him,* she added more gently.

Fluffy puffed up his feathers and stood a little straighter on my arm.

He's always been a good boy. She looked us over, satisfied, before launching off the branch.

Fluffy wistfully watched her go.

"Do you want to stay here with her?" I asked the owl.

He looked at me, eyes wide. *Are you trying to get rid of me?*

"No! I just want you to be happy."

By suggesting I stay with my pesky sisters? In the forest? His voice pitched up a little. *With* no *cookies?*

"Shhh." I stroked the owl's head, and he calmed down a little. "You just looked sad to see her go."

I most certainly was not, he huffed. *I was simply thinking that they were all going to find a nice place to sleep, as proper owls should. Do you know how high the sun is in the sky right now?*

"You wanted to come," I pointed out.

If only I had a nice roost, mused the owl.

I quirked an eyebrow.

Where I could take just a little nap . . .

I pointed at the branch his mother had just vacated.

Without worrying that my queen might try to leave me behind for my sisters to torture . . .

I sighed and stopped fighting the magic around me. The crown hummed happily, making my antlers immediately grow taller with wide prongs.

Why, thank you! Fluffy pretended to be surprised. *That will do nicely.*

I rolled my eyes as he hopped up to find a comfortable spot to nap.

Maybe I'll miss her a little bit, grumbled the owl sleepily. *Don't tell my sisters.*

"Never," I promised. "And I'll keep this gate open so you can visit anytime you like."

That would be . . . nice . . . His sleepy voice trailed off as I made my own way through the ferns.

I ran my hands along the tree trunks, just to watch the moss and tiny mushrooms sprout beneath my fingertips. Even without a trail of green—now that everything was green—the magic led me right to the middle of the joyful equine family reunion. I smiled when I saw the little silver foal nuzzle up to her mama.

One thing was missing.

I reached out through the bond. *You're hiding.*

Never from you, Princess.

I smiled at the nickname. It had made me so annoyed when we met, but now, it was full of affection. I never wanted him to change it.

I followed the thread connecting us until I found Kylian leaning behind a tree at the edge of the meadow, *ansuz* rune activated to help him hide.

I don't want to ruin their moment. He looked to me like he needed a hug—which was to say, he had *zero* expression. But, between the size our crowns had grown to—thanks to the unicorns—and the sleeping owl in mine, I wasn't sure I could manage it. So, I reached for his hand instead.

You know they've forgiven you. I squeezed his hand.

The ones who were at Skyretaine, maybe. But I'll only scare the little ones. He leaned his free hand against the tree trunk and then pulled it away as sparkling green moss grew under his fingertips.

It looks like Faerie has forgiven you, too. I felt the magic hum happily. *Actually, I take that back.*

Kylian looked at me with distress.

Faerie was never mad at you, I clarified. *So there's nothing to forgive.*

He looked unconvinced.

Do you think the magic just hands out crowns to anybody I kiss?

Kylian raised an eyebrow before brushing his lips against my knuckles. *Let's not test that.*

Obviously not. But my point remains. The magic knows you've been protecting the kingdom. As do I. I tugged his hand, and he reluctantly stepped out from behind the tree. "So drop your armor," I said out loud, waving at the glowing runes on his arm. "And come with me while I tell the little ones a story."

Are there cookies in the story? whispered a little voice at my feet.

I glanced down to see the little silver unicorn looking up at both of us, no fear in her wide eyes.

I knelt and smoothed her mane with my hand. "Luckily for you, a very well-prepared faerie godmother gave me a bag of them."

Is she my *faerie godmother?* asked the unicorn.

"You know what?" I straightened. "I bet she'd love to be."

And with my fingers again twined through Kylian's, I found a spot in the middle of the meadow where I could tell a tale of the big, scary Huntsman who believed he had a heart of ice, and how his love for the kingdom of the Unseelie fae led him to become their king.

Chapter 50

Kylian

"Come on, come on!" Niamh bounced impatiently in front of the newly crafted Ice Gate. The full skirt of her knee-length blue dress swished around her like bubbling water.

When the asrai had returned home to take down Moriath's dams and rebuild their villages, they had sent a gift of ice from their enchanted waters. Liadan, Audrey, Clíodhna, and Amber had all worked together to craft a new gate from the ice. It stood in the courtyard, between blooming apple trees, at the end of a path of stepping stones etched with the emblem of owls in flight. had carved an elegant arch of antlers traced with gold. The whole structure sparkled with feathers of frost, and sparkling floating crystals drifted around it like the Frost Gate by the cottage.

"Frost for my mother," Niamh had requested, along with a variety of small iced animals perched on the antlers. "For my father," she had said.

Niamh had cried when she had seen the finished gate, still mourning the parents that were only a child's memories. But now, she was bursting with excitement.

"How's the crown?" She bent her head down for my inspection.

"Still gone," I told her. Only a satin ribbon a shade darker than her dress broke up her dark curls.

Fluffy flew down from a tree branch and landed on Niamh's arm. He inquired something with a hoot, and Niamh shook her head.

"Why do you even want to come? It's morning. Aren't you tired?"

The seven chickens—happier than ever with a whole courtyard to run around in and a palace cook with clear instructions to spoil them—clustered around our ankles, squawking for Niamh's attention.

"No, I mean it. No birds." She attempted to give them a stern look, and the chickens clucked mournfully. "There's no way my dad will let eight birds into the house."

Fluffy hooted again.

"Okay, only Fluffy because he won't come inside anyway. No one else!"

The bird fluffed his white feathers proudly and hopped up onto Niamh's shoulder. Essie bumped her little black head against my leg and looked up at me with her sad chicken eyes.

I picked up the hen. "But your parents will want to see how big they are. Right?"

"Fine. *Two* chickens." Niamh scooped up Pip, while Fluffy flapped to keep his balance on her shoulder. "Only two!"

The remaining chickens continued to cluck sadly.

"I'll bring two of you next time," she promised, exasperated.

"And *you*," she snapped, turning to me as I quickly hid the gingersnap I had been feeding Essie, "are not helping."

"Calm down, Niamh," I said patiently.

She narrowed her eyes.

"Because your antlers are growing." I tried not to trip over the chickens milling underfoot.

"Ugh!" She closed her eyes and took deep breaths until the tiny icicles and antler nubs disappeared under her hair again.

"Who wants apples?" Niamh's best friend hollered from across the courtyard.

The chickens at our feet perked up and disappeared in a flash, running across the courtyard with wings flapping to where Audrey and Gavin stood with a bowl of apple chunks.

"Thank you!" called Niamh before she turned to me. "Quick, before they notice!"

She dashed through the gate with her two birds. I fed Essie the last crumb of gingersnap and then followed at a more leisurely pace. We had, after all, spelled the new gate to keep unwanted guests from arriving at Skyretaine and to keep rogue chickens from leaving.

A step later, I caught up to Niamh in the forest outside Pilot Bay.

"I know everyone kept telling me about faerie time and human time," she said, spinning slowly with Pip clutched in her arms, "but it can't have been more than a week or two since we left."

Niamh was right. The evening forest had become greener while we were gone, the grass taller and ferns slightly unfurled, but the air still had the smell of spring.

"That's good though," I reminded her, knowing how disorienting it could be to travel between realms. "It means your parents won't have missed you for as long."

"Right! Let's go." She started walking and then stopped. "Um, is it this way?"

I laughed and pointed her in the right direction.

"You'd be a terrible Huntsman," I teased, adjusting Essie in my arms.

"Good thing I have you, then." Niamh grinned at me.

Fluffy soon took off into the trees overhead.

"He says he heard something delicious. I think he only came along because he keeps asking me how mice taste in the human realm and has been very disappointed in my lack of personal research. Oh!" She broke into a run as the old white farmhouse came into view, Pip squawking protests in her arms. "Mom! Dad!"

Niamh's adopted parents burst through the door while I continued at a slower pace, enjoying the sight of their happiness as her parents caught her up in a big hug. Pip flew out in distress as they embraced her.

"Lord Kylian." Niamh's mom waved me over. "Neve's dad just made pie. Come on in, and I'll put the coffee on."

"That sounds perfect." I set my chicken down on the porch.

Look at you, accepting pie like a normal person! Niamh grinned at me.

I have to see if yours is really the best. I winked at her.

Niamh laughed and then followed her mom. Her father watched them go with a smile that turned into a frown when the two chickens followed them in.

"Neve!"

"Don't worry, Dad," she called back. "They promised not to poop in the house."

"They what?" He shook his head. "Never mind." He turned and put his hand on my shoulder. "Thank you for everything you've done to keep our little girl safe."

I nodded, not knowing what to say under the weight of his fatherly affection.

"When Clíodhna visited to update us on all that happened, she mentioned that you two are co-ruling together?" He raised his eyebrows. "Is that just a political thing or . . . ?"

"I love your daughter very much," I told him, willing myself to relax. I had defeated more opponents than I could count, but I had never been as nervous as that confession to Niamh's father made me. When they had envisioned her future as a queen, they couldn't have thought—

"Wonderful!" he interrupted my spinning thoughts, his face breaking into a wide smile. "I'll worry less, knowing that she has you to take care of her."

"She's the one who takes care of me," I answered honestly before the man shocked me by pulling me into a bear hug.

"Good, good." He squeezed me once more before letting go. "That's how it should be, son."

Son. I blinked back tears. Was I going to cry at everything now?

"Come on inside." Niamh's father clapped me on the arm. "Tell me about your plans. How many kids do you think you want?"

"I . . . uh . . ."

"Dad!" Niamh yelled from inside. "We are *not* discussing children. No one's even *engaged* yet."

"Sorry, sweetie." Her dad walked through the door. "I'm just excited to bake cookies for my grandchildren."

"Excellent," she called back. "The chickens love cookies. You should make them your honey snap recipe!"

Her dad glanced back to give me a pained look. "Please tell me I don't have grandchickens."

"Look how they've *grown*," called Niamh's mother from the living room.

"I'm sorry, sir." I followed him into the inviting glow of the farmhouse, and it didn't take long for me to see just how Niamh had gotten her steadfast joy and hopefulness as her family surrounded us both in warmth and love.

Chapter 51

Niamh

"SHOULD I BE CONCERNED, FLUFFY, THAT THE Unseelie queen is leading me off to some unknown destination up a cliff?" Kylian called from behind me as I scrambled up a grassy, rock-strewn mountainside.

I would be, Fluffy said from just overhead. *Who knows what she's got in that giant basket she's lugging up the hill?*

"That's enough out of both of you," I panted.

It was enough to make me miss the days before my bond with Kylian had intensified to the point where my familiar and my co-ruler could understand each other and gang up on me. I supposed I should be happy that my king hadn't found his own bird familiar yet.

On the other hand, the look on Kylian's face the first time he had realized that all the chickens called him *Daddy* had been priceless.

"You!" I pointed up at the owl. I set down the heavy basket and pretended I needed to adjust the full skirt of my pink floral sundress, when all I really needed was a moment to breathe. "You were only allowed to tag along because you said we would need you to keep a lookout. So, go keep a lookout!"

Fine. Fluffy soared on ahead.

"And *you.*" I pointed back at my one true love, who wore a navy blue tunic today. We were working on branching out from black-on-black, but it was a slow process. Baby steps. "You have been here before. Well, down there." I waved back toward the plain forest gate at the bottom of the hill. "Last month, remember? When we cleared out that nest of beithirs? And you don't forget anywhere you've been, so don't pretend you're lost and helpless here."

Kylian smirked at me, not bothered by my outburst. I'd never get tired of seeing him smile. In our first spring and summer as king and queen of the Unseelie fae, we had spent the majority of our time cleaning up the messes Moriath had made, which included relocating the creatures she had allowed to get a little too comfortable rampaging the countryside. All the Unseelie fae were our subjects, not just the cute ones. However, a giant venomous lizard in its natural cave habitat was quite a different matter from a giant venomous lizard rampaging through a glaistig village's apricot orchard.

It was hard work, even with the magic of Faerie eager to help restore balance to the kingdom and with Audrey's inventions and Estrid's new runes to support us. Still, with every situation we resolved, I could feel Kylian's heart growing a little lighter. He still wasn't exactly what you would call perky, but he smiled more. At least for me.

"Just let me carry that basket." Kylian swiped for the handle, and I heaved it out of his reach with a grunt.

"*My* basket," I panted, lugging it over a particularly large rock. "I planned this special outing for you, so I'm carrying the basket."

"What if the thing that would make me happy on my *special outing* is carrying your basket?" teased Kylian, reaching for it again.

"Back off!" I stumbled to the side. "Anyway, we're almost there. See?"

We reached the top at last, and I set down the basket with a wheeze. Admittedly, the hike had been farther from the crossroad gate than I had bargained for. But I hadn't trained daily for months and battled monsters on the regular without gaining some muscle. I was never going to manage *graceful and ethereal* no matter how much I trained, but I was rather proud of my biceps.

I wiped my brow and put my hands on my hips proudly. "I knew it, this spot is perfect."

We stood in a hanging valley, high enough in the mountains to be covered with heather, blooming pink and purple in the late summer sun. To one side, streams cascaded down in sparkling waterfalls, turning into mist at the bottom of the mossy cliffs. When we turned, the view opened into the majestic peaks of the *Bhanmhor Sliabhraon* range.

I only knew the names of a third of the peaks, but I had nearly a thousand years to learn the rest, and I would do it. I would get to know every inch of my kingdom.

"So." Kylian admired the view beside me. "When we were over *there,*" he said, pointing at the forest below, "fighting a rogue beithir, you glanced up here and thought, 'what a good spot for a picnic'?"

"Yes." I nodded my head firmly.

"While it spat venom at us, and we tested that new antitoxin rune Estrid developed, and you nearly got eaten, you were planning a *special outing?*"

"I am excellent at multitasking, which is a valuable quality in a queen."

Kylian gave me a sidelong look. "*Multitasking*," he said. "*That's* what we're calling it? Not 'being easily distracted by every little thing in a situation that could get you killed'?"

"But I wasn't." I smiled sweetly. "And look at that view!"

He sighed. "I worry about your priorities."

"I don't." I gave him a kiss. "Because I know that you've always got my back, right?"

I ignored the dark look he gave me and pulled out the quilt I had tucked into the basket.

"We couldn't sit on rocks?" Kylian helped me spread out the brightly patterned blanket. "This must have doubled the weight."

"Stop being so *practical* on your special outing. This is a picnic. Thus, we needed a picnic blanket." I pointed at a corner of the quilt. "Sit!"

"Yes, Your Majesty." Kylian gave me a mock bow and unstrapped his axe before sitting. I unslung my own sword—also on my back for ease while hiking and possibly the only practical choice I had made—and set the basket on the blanket.

"What have you got in there?" Kylian peered into the basket. "Did you bring any of those spiced molasses apple cakes?"

I smacked his hand away. "For someone so adamantly against baked goods for so many years, you certainly have a sweet tooth."

"I'm just making up for lost time." Kylian watched as I pulled out flatbreads stuffed with arugula, soft crumbling cheese, slices of tart apples, and little toasted hazelnuts.

Next came a bottle of sparkling peach and ginger juice, mini mushroom and thyme quiches—the eggs a gift from my chickens, of course—and, yes, two small spiced molasses apple cakes wrapped in waxed cotton.

As we munched, we chatted about light topics like the treaty talks with Álfheimr and what to do about the Cù Sìth terrorizing cats near the southern border.

"Well, at least we won't be swapping foster children as hostages." I licked my fingers clean of sticky molasses. "No children here."

"What if they asked to swap hostage chickens instead?" Kylian's eyes danced as he wiped his fingers with a napkin like a civilized person.

"Not the chickens!" I gasped. "We'd just have to go to war instead." I sobered, watching his face. "Is that something you want?"

"To go to war over chickens?" He paused, considering. "Do you think we could teach them to battle? Daggers in their beaks? Back-mounted crossbows, maybe?"

"No. Children."

Kylian stilled. He looked out over the distant mountain peaks, and I couldn't even guess his feelings through the bond.

"I'm not sure," he said finally. "It's not something I've ever really considered. Do you?"

I relaxed a little. "I don't want to say *never*. My life is looking a lot longer than I once thought it would be, but I'm so content right now. I don't feel like there's anything else I need."

"Neither do I," he agreed. "But are you sure? Not even more chickens?"

"Well, there is this one breed I saw in Nidavellir—Stop distracting me! I have something I need to talk to you about."

"I knew you didn't drag me up here just for peach juice," Kylian teased, reaching for my hand.

I pulled back, turning my wrist to examine the black design on the underside of my arm.

"These betrothal runes. I don't even remember getting mine." I traced the intersecting lines. "And I know it wasn't something I had any choice in."

"Did you want to get them removed?" asked Kylian carefully.

"Yeah, I do," I admitted, and felt his heart squeeze through our bond. "No, no, you don't understand." I grabbed his hand. "I've been talking to Estrid. She says that even if our bond started with these runes when we were children, it's far beyond anything enchanted ink can do. She and Audrey examined mine, and they say that apart from the occasional power sharing, it's not even doing anything anymore. Our bond isn't *here*." I tapped Kylian's matching tattoo. "It's *here.*" I pressed my hand over his heart.

"That sounds right to me." He relaxed, curling his hand over mine on his chest. "But did that require a *special outing*? You could have told me that back at the castle."

"I was thinking we should get new engagement tattoos," I whispered. "Something that we choose ourselves."

"Princess . . ." He nudged me with his shoulder. "Are you proposing?"

"Yes." I stared down at our hands. "You promised you'd never leave me, but we never officially—"

"Yes," Kylian cut me off. He ran his hand up my arm before threading his fingers into the curls at the back of my head, tipping me up to look at him.

"Are you sure? Because I hear that *'til death do us part* is a long time here."

Kylian brushed his lips against mine. "I'd spend a hundred lifetimes with you," he whispered. "I'll never let you go. We're stronger together, remember?"

He kissed me again, long and deep. When we broke apart, he gave me a look.

"There's something more, isn't there?"

"Yes." I drummed my fingers against his arm. "I hope you don't think it's silly." I turned to rummage through the wrappings of food at the bottom of the basket. "Liadan says that rings are just a human custom, and even with humans, the guy doesn't usually get a ring until the wedding ceremony." My hand finally closed around the little silk bag containing the gold band with intricate runes that I'd had commissioned. "But Estrid's brother is such an amazing craftsman that I couldn't resist . . ."

I looked up and fell silent as Kylian lifted his outstretched hand to show me the little velvet box he held.

"I hope it's not just a silly human custom to you," he said, "because both Audrey and your mother insisted that even if I could tell you were scheming something on your own . . ." He opened up the velvet box, and I gasped. Inside lay a delicate circle of gold blossoms with a round ruby framed by little apple leaves on the top. "Something like this would be the best way to reassure you that I want to spend all my days with you."

He slid it onto my finger and then paused. "We're still into apples, yes? Even after the cursed tattoo incident?"

I beamed at him through happy tears. "Moriath can't ruin apples for me. My whole life, I've held on to that scrap of a memory that told me I was loved. It's perfect."

"Then it's just right for you." Kylian kissed me again.

I showed him the ring I'd gotten him, with runes for *love, happiness,* and *forever* etched into the band. Then we sat in the meadow until the setting sun turned the waterfalls into streams of gold, dreaming about our life together.

Finally, Kylian gathered up the basket, firmly forbidding

me from carrying it back down, and I called Fluffy over. The owl had kept his distance, unimpressed by our strange habit of *face pressing,* as he called it.

We hiked back down the mountainside hand in hand and emerged through the Ice Gate to find our friends, family, and all the castle staff waiting for us in the courtyard.

"Yes!" Amber squealed. "Took you two long enough. Am I right?" She turned to Aunt Chloe, who nodded in agreement.

"Let me see the ring!" Audrey ran up, tackling me and a surprised Kylian in a hug before examining my finger.

"Didn't you help design it?" I asked.

"Yeah, but I need to see how it looks *on* you." My best friend sighed. "So perfect. It must be so nice to be *engaged,*" she said wistfully. "And to be getting *married.*"

I glanced over her shoulder at Gavin.

Audrey's boyfriend winked at me. *Don't worry,* he mouthed behind her back.

I stifled a laugh. Clearly, her wolf boy had plans. I'd have to track him down later for details. It was about time that I got to be the one with a secret.

Aunt Chloe had brought my teary-eyed parents to the castle, and even Kylian's Seelie sister and her co-captain Declan were there, giving us both back-thumping hugs.

Estrid was there with the dwarven kings, who had brought along snacks for the wait.

"Don't worry," Ulf whispered to Latte. "They're just fried mushrooms. We didn't want to make things awkward," he added to me.

All the castle staff we had gained in the past months cheered from the edges of the courtyard, and Liadan—still small and furry—watched smugly from a tree branch while the chickens did their best to trip unsuspecting visitors.

My heart was full, but there was still one person I wished could be with us. "You won't stop looking for Maeve, will you?" I asked Aunt Chloe.

"Never." My godmother gave me a hug. "Although, I will admit I'm a bit frustrated. I've been all across Tír na nÓg, and there's been no hint of a red-headed fae girl in a tower in the woods like your vision showed."

"What did you say?" Declan, who had been deep in conversation with Saoirse and Kylian, turned sharply towards us.

"Which part?" I squinted at the fianna captain. "Maeve? Red-headed girl?"

He stepped over to me. "Describe your vision."

"Um, well, I saw my sister. She had long red hair under a scarf, and she was picking mushrooms by a tower in the woods. That's all the mirror could show me, and no one can figure out where she is." I saw Kylian and Saoirse exchange a look. "Why?"

Declan examined my face. "She has blue eyes, just like you."

"How did you—?"

"Of *course* she's your sister." Declan ran a hand through his messy dark hair. "The girl in the tower. I met her in the forest, and then she vanished. I've been looking for her for eight years now."

"You never said anything." Saoirse nudged her friend, but he didn't even register it, lost in his thoughts.

"I have to go. I need to talk to Tiernan about this." Declan looked up again, as if remembering that we were there. "Congratulations. I'll see you at the wedding. I'm sure we'll all be there." He stalked off toward the new Ice Gate. Saoirse hurried after him, pestering him with questions.

I watched Declan go, stunned. "Do you really think he'll be able to find her?"

"I do." Kylian smiled at me. "You've got me feeling hopeful these days."

"Not just me. Look at all these people who believe we can make a better future together." I wound my arm around his waist.

"This wedding is going to be an *event*, isn't it?" Kylian surveyed the crowd with a pained expression.

"Yes," I confirmed.

"With a lot of people."

"We're Faerie monarchs." I patted his arm. "Eloping isn't really an option."

"I'll have to wear something . . ." He paused. "Formal."

"Yes!" I squealed.

He sighed and went quiet for a moment. I hoped he wasn't regretting our mutual proposal.

Then he looked over at me again. "Do you think we can train Meringue and Essie to scatter flower petals down the aisle?"

I gaped at him, my mind racing as I considered the possibilities. "We could put Snickerdoodle and Waffles in little bow ties," I whispered. "This will be the best wedding *ever*," I said in awe, and then pulled Kylian in for a kiss amidst the crowd of cheering loved ones.

Epilogue

Amber

"WHAT DO YOU MEAN *SHE'S NOT DEAD?*" I hissed at my mentor from my hiding place behind a shrub. "Did you see the height of that cliff? Did she sprout wings and fly? Speaking of wings, I still haven't forgiven you for not telling me about yours."

"Sorry, my dear. Keeping secrets is second nature when you're a faerie godmother. I'm sure you'll understand in a century or two." Miss Chloe hid beside me, rummaging through her purse.

The bag was adorned with her favorite Thor chibi keychain and stuffed with regular items (keys, wallet, paperback romances) and not-so-regular items (sleeping potions, enchanted gemstones, a ring that she forbade me to touch but I was pretty sure made the wearer turn into a snail).

"Aha!" She whispered, pulling out a vial of small gold pebbles.

"So how did she not hit the bottom and die?" I pressed, peering at the Wolf Gate through the branches of my shrub. Nothing yet.

"Oh, she hit the bottom all right." Miss Chloe tossed a pebble in front of the gate. "Nasty business."

"For the love of all that is sacred, will you *please* explain, you maddening fae!" I ducked down as Moriath appeared in the arch of branches, then I looked up in case her falcon spotted us.

"Don't worry about Ránach. She won't be coming," whispered Miss Chloe, beckoning me to follow as she crept away from the former Unseelie queen. "You remember back when Moriath kidnapped you and your sister, Lily?"

"Kidnapping is a rather memorable event."

"Isobel traded a very powerful artifact to get you back." Miss Chloe rolled another pebble onto the path.

We both held our breath as Moriath bent down to pick up the first gold stone. Now that I was over my shock, I could see that she looked like a shadow of the fearsome Unseelie queen I remembered. Her white hair was snarled in a tangled braid, her cotton dress too loose. No antlered crown or enchanted gems. Nothing but a necklace of dull blue gems, the surface of the biggest stone cracked through the middle.

"The necklace?" I followed Miss Chloe while she kept just close enough to watch Moriath, who found the second pebble and peered through the trees in the direction of Pilot Bay, the town just visible in the distance. Her eyes flashed with hatred. Yikes.

"The Sapphires of Airmid were relics from the days of the Fomóirian Wars, long ago. They can heal any injury short of death itself. I didn't think even that necklace would be enough for her to survive the plunge she took, but she must have boosted them with all her personal power, as well as the life forces of Ránach and her doomed wolves, as she fell. The woman is tenacious. You have to give her that." Miss Chloe considered a third pebble but put it back in the vial. "Don't want to be too obvious. I just want her to know she's in the right spot."

"So her power is gone? Forever?" I'd feel bad for the woman if she weren't a raging sociopath. "That's why all her spells unraveled?"

Miss Chloe nodded. "I've never seen anything like it. She doesn't have even a drop of magic left to tether them."

"Why isn't she old like Fiachra?" We had all been shocked when Saoirse had walked out of the castle with the old king.

"That must have taken time. But it's hard to say what the magic will choose to do." Miss Chloe tilted her head. "In Faerie, given enough time, it's possible her power might trickle back. The natural magic hates a vacuum, and Moriath's insides are one big black hole. That's why we need to keep her here in the human realm. I've been trying to track her down ever since the battle. I found the bodies of the wolves and the falcon in the forest, drained of their power before they fell—not a pretty picture, might I add—but no Moriath."

"Couldn't you just scry for her?" Miss Chloe had been teaching me to use her enchanted mirror of water, and I knew she had more skill than I ever would.

The faerie godmother shook her head. "Nothing came up. I had almost decided that my theory was wrong when Liadan discovered her at her sister's cabin. Bronach's wards had muddied my search."

Audrey had told me about their run-in with the child-stealing witch. Neve and Kylian wouldn't be happy to know that she still lurked in their kingdom.

"And she's here now because . . . ?" I blanched as Moriath pulled a dagger of black iron from her leather belt. "She's feeling murdery?"

"*Very* murdery," agreed Miss Chloe. "She's wanted me dead for centuries, and recent events have not improved our relationship. Liadan helped me by 'accidentally' showing her this gate to Pilot Bay, and Moriath is here to enact her revenge."

"And this is a good idea?" I stared at my mentor in disbelief.

Moriath strode toward town faster now, but without her magic or sneaky falcon, she still hadn't spotted us stalking her in the trees.

"How's your reception, my dear? Can you make a call?" Miss Chloe paused as we reached the edge of the forest.

I pulled out my phone and showed her the three bars.

"Perfect. Call 911 and tell them we spotted a wanted criminal at the end of . . ." She peered at the street below through her gold-rimmed glasses as if she needed them. Always the actress. "Elm Street."

I did so, watching Moriath pace as she tried to decide where to search for her librarian nemesis.

"What's she wanted for?" I asked when the police assured me they'd be at our location in three minutes. Benefits of living in a small town. "Is being an evil queen a felony in British Columbia?"

"Money laundering, child trafficking." She looked back at me. "Kidnapping. Only a handful of the crimes she's guilty of, but it was the best Audrey and I could find proof of when we planted the warrants in the police database."

I shook my head in admiration as the police arrived, sirens roaring as all three of Pilot Bay's patrol cars surrounded Moriath. The cornered ex-queen hissed when the police leveled their guns at her, and she attempted to slash one officer before being shot with a taser and falling to the ground.

"So that's it, then?" I sat on the grassy bank and watched them load her up into a cop car. "Should we tell Neve and Kylian?"

Miss Chloe shook her head. "Neve is too sweet. She'll want to try and rehabilitate Moriath, which is beyond the power of even her pies, and Kylian will attempt to solve the problem permanently with his axe. Better to keep him from ending up in prison as well. The humans have enough evidence—collected over years of patient observation on my part and gifted to them by Audrey and her computer skills—to keep Moriath locked up far from any power sources for the rest of her unhappy life. Which will be considerably shortened without the magic of Faerie to sustain her."

"Huh. That sounds terrible." I stood and brushed off my pants as the police cars drove off. "I really am learning from the best."

"I admit that my work does bring me a lot of satisfaction." Miss Chloe smiled and hiked down the bank toward home. "And speaking of your education . . ."

"Do we have a new project?" I scrambled after her down to the road. "Bears getting their porridge stolen? Rogue gingerbread men?"

"With Moriath safely tucked away, I think it's time for the next stage of your apprenticeship."

"What do you mean?"

"I have a situation that needs your special touch. Just you."

I almost tripped, staring at Clíodhna in shock. "*Alone?*"

"That's right, my dear. It's time to see if you've got what it takes to be a real faerie godmother."

Curious about Amber's first solo
adventure as a faerie godmother?

Her story will continue in:
The Gold Gate, a Retelling of Rumpelstiltskin.

THANK YOU!

THANKS FOR READING THIS SPECIAL EDITION OF The Frost Gate. Don't stop here, keep going to read a special epilogue novella featuring Niamh and Kylian's wedding!

I hope you enjoyed your time in Faerie with Niamh, Kylian, and their many feathered friends! If you have a minute, would you leave a review on Amazon, Goodreads, or tell a bookish friend about The Frost Gate? Reviews mean the world to small authors like me, and truly help others to find my books.

And I hope you'll love the gorgeous mini comic of one of my favorite scenes in the book by my dear friend Sonya Lindsay. You can find out more about her comic, Druin Saga, on Instagram at: @Sonya_Lindsay_Art

My version of Tír na nÓg is loosely based on Irish folklore. If you'd like to learn more about the world and the faeries that inhabit it, go to my website where you can find a map and a list of the various races with a little bit about each of them.

At my website you can also see the illustrations I drew for all the books and sign up for my newsletter. I use my newsletter to send you updates on my books, peeks at upcoming art, and fun printables.

www.HannaSandvig.com

I knew it, this spot is perfect!

So, when we were over there fighting a rogue beithir,

you glanced up here and thought 'what a good spot for a picnic'?

Yes.

I am excellent at multitasking,
which is a valuable quality in a queen.
Multitasking.
That's what we're calling it?
Not 'being easily distracted by every little thing in a situation that could get you killed'?
But I wasn't.
And look at that view?
I worry about your priorities.
I don't.
Because I know that I've always got you at my back, right?

A Frost Gate Epilogue

Of Frost and Feathers

Hanna Sandvig

CHAPTER 1

NIAMH

NO ONE HAD EVER WARNED ME THAT my happily-ever-after would include a daily scavenger hunt.

"Why did I even give you nest boxes?" I grumbled to Meringue before picking up the sleeping chicken.

The hen didn't even wake up, her fluffy white legs dangling as I checked for an egg in the soft, red-velvet-lined nest box.

There were five such boxes set into the wall of the royal chicken coop, one for each of my hens to lay her eggs in, marked with a golden nameplate attached to the front.

Meringue had laid her cream egg in Clem's nest box, but I supposed chickens couldn't read the golden nameplates affixed to the front of their boxes, which were spelled against mess and egg breakage and kept at a comfortable temperature year round.

Possibly too comfortable.

"You're supposed to sleep on your roost," I scolded the silkie, setting her on the fresh wood shavings of the coop floor beside Waffles. "Or not at all. As it is, you know, ten o'clock in the morning."

Treats? Meringue clucked sleepily, looking up at me through her fluffy mop of feathers.

"Yes, yes, the cook spoiled you again. Go look outside." The head chef at Skyretaine had a soft spot for my chickens and a rather broad definition of scraps, often sneaking muffins and pancakes into the chicken bowl along with the vegetable peelings.

Meringue sighed happily and ambled out through the little chicken door to the yard.

I put my hands on my hips and surveyed the remaining birds. "You lot have the best possible life a chicken could ask for." I waved my hand around the luxurious chicken coop, truly a palace for my feathered family members with roosts carved to mimic blossoming apple tree branches, an airy ceiling with skylights spelled to give them exactly the same hours of sunlight year round, and individual water bottles hanging on the wall with gold spouts. The wood shavings on the floor were changed every day and their bowls filled with the best mix of seeds and grains, thanks to the royal chicken keeper who loved my spoiled birds as much as I did.

Maybe more, at the moment. He didn't have to play chicken games for eggs.

"Latte," I said, pointing a finger at the fluffy silver hen who promptly sneezed, "is the only chicken in her own nest box today." I lifted Latte to find . . . nothing. I set the hen on the floor. "You," I continued, pointing a finger at Snickerdoodle, "are not even a hen. What are you doing in there? That's Pip's box!"

Eggs? The rooster tilted his head in confusion, the feathered crest flopping as I picked him up.

"No, you don't lay eggs." I sighed as I deposited him on the ground. "Where did you hide it, Pip?"

The speckled orange hen scowled at me from Meringue's nest box, her longer face feathers bristling. *Want chicks.* She nestled down further until she looked like a little orange chicken puddle.

"No chicks." I peeled her off the nest, and sure enough, there were two brown eggs, cozy and warm under the grumpy chicken. "Neither of these eggs is even yours."

Pip glared daggers at me as I deposited her on the ground before tucking the eggs into my apron.

Chicks.

"Nope. No one is going broody. I cannot deal with broody right now. My wedding is tomorrow. Do you understand me? You can be broody next week. Now where's Clem?"

Apples! The cheerful hen clucked faintly from outside. *Laid egg for Pip!*

"Okay, everyone outside before Clem eats all the food again."

The remaining chickens sped for the little door.

"Everyone but you, Paprika." I picked Pip back up and narrowed my eyes. "Tell me where you hid the egg, chicken. I know you're not actually broody."

The hen tilted her head. *Where Essie?*

"You're not distracting me that easily—Wait, where *is* Essie?"

Kylian, I called through our bond, *have you seen Espresso?*

"Looking for this?" rumbled Kylian's voice.

I jumped. He was *much* closer than I had expected.

My tall and deadly fiancé leaned against the coop's door,

dressed as usual in black leather pants and matching linen tunic with at least three visible daggers, although his large silver axe was absent this morning.

He had freshly clipped the sides of his hair and tied up his waist-length locs at the back of his head. Under one arm, he held the missing hen, and in the other . . . He raised an eyebrow and revealed two eggs. One chocolate brown and one a pale cream.

"Where were they?" I set down Pip and gave Kylian a kiss.

"This one was on the chicken coop roof for some reason." He glanced at Pip, who was making her escape out the chicken door.

"She's mad at me because I don't want her to go broody." I tucked the cream egg into my pocket. "This is not the way to prove your maternal instincts to me!" I called out to the chicken yard.

"And this one was in my sock drawer." Kylian raised an eyebrow at the little brown and black hen he held. "Again."

"Sweet, sweet Espresso." I gently extricated the chicken from her favorite person and held her up to eye level. "You need to start using your nest box. You can't keep leaving your eggs in Kylian's room."

Why? the hen chirped at me.

"Because the day after tomorrow, we'll be living in the same room, and I don't want to discover an egg in my slipper . . . with my foot."

Hmmm. The little hen didn't make any promises.

"Thanks for bringing her over. I know you're busy this morning," I added to Kylian.

"I came to tell you that our guests have arrived." He glanced over his shoulder at the other end of the courtyard where the Ice Gate stood.

"*What?*" I froze, clutching Essie to me. She clucked happily. "I thought they weren't coming until eleven!"

"It's eleven-thirty." Kylian's eyes danced with amusement. He was used to my rather loose grasp of time. "Come on, they're in the library."

"I can't greet guests like *this*." I gestured to my egg apron over a chunky old sweater and rumpled pants tucked into snow boots. "Can you stall them?" I pleaded frantically.

Kylian arched an eyebrow. "And how would you suggest I do that?"

"I don't know. Make small talk?"

He grimaced.

"I know, I know. I just need ten minutes to get these eggs to the kitchen and make sure my hands don't smell like chicken. No offense," I added to Essie as I set her down and gave her a gentle nudge toward the chicken door.

"Ten minutes?" Kylian asked. "You're not going to leave me with Tiernan for an hour again?"

"Well . . . maybe fifteen," I hedged. "I *do* need to change. Besides, I thought Tiernan was your bestie. I'm sure I heard him say so."

"He's very . . . chatty."

"I'll be fast. I promise." I went to squeeze past Kylian, but he caught me around the waist. I looked up at him. "What is it?"

"This." Kylian pressed me back against the doorframe and tilted my chin up to kiss me, soundly and unhurriedly.

"Oh," I managed breathlessly. "Hi."

"Hi." He leaned his forehead against mine and, for a breath, nothing else existed in the world. Just us.

Niamh! Kylian! There are faeries decorating my tree! Why are there faeries decorating my tree?!

And Fluffy.

I peered out past Kylian and found the large white owl looking disgruntled as a team of piskies draped his favorite apple tree with ribbons.

"They're decorating the whole courtyard," I called back to my owl familiar. "It's going to look lovely, I promise."

It's not very dignified to have so many bows on my roost, groused the owl.

I smothered a laugh, and Kylian smirked, overhearing the owl through our bond.

"Okay, I'll see you inside." I gave my fiancé another quick kiss.

"Fifteen minutes," he called after me as I dashed down the path cut through the deep snow.

"Yes," I promised with a wave. "Well . . . maybe twenty!"

CHAPTER 2

NIAMH

FORTY-FIVE MINUTES LATER, I SKIPPED DOWN THE plush carpeted stairs toward the library in my gray kitten heels. The full, knee-length skirts of my dark pink, almost-red dress flounced around me, belled out by a crinoline that was somehow neither stiff nor itchy, of course, as it was one of Ella's designs. The talented designer had occasionally helped me tailor vintage dresses to fit my curves back in Pilot Bay, and while I had missed her skills during the year she had spent in Faerie ahead of me, we were more than making up for lost time now.

This velvet, three-quarter sleeve dress was just one of the amazing designs Ella had come up with for me, combining my beloved fifties silhouettes with the magical textiles available to her in Faerie. More than just making me look amazing, the Seelie queen had patiently listened and given advice while I rambled at length about my worries and struggles as a new fae monarch during my fittings. In the process of turning me into a stylish queen, we had become fast friends.

I hesitated at the foot of the stairs as I felt the Unseelie crown growing excitedly through my dark hair. "Behave yourself," I whispered to the incarnation of Faerie's magic. "No icicles taller than two inches and only three prongs on the antlers."

The magic sighed, and I felt with my fingers until the crown subsided to a more manageable shape.

"Thank you." I patted my curls—freshly cropped to chin length—back into order. "You'll have plenty of time to go all out tomorrow. I promise."

The magic hummed happily.

"Why, yes, Kylian, I *do* have more marriage advice for you!" Tiernan's cheerful voice drifted through the open doorway. "Have you considered livening up your wardrobe a little? Seafoam green would look wonderful on you. Don't you agree, Saoirse?"

"It would certainly make Niamh see you in a whole new light," teased Kylian's sister.

"*Ansuz*," I whispered, activating my silence rune before peeking into the study.

Audrey lay sprawled on the rug in front of the fireplace, wearing the navy Sailor Moon t-shirt and jeans she had arrived in yesterday. Her eyes were closed, and Liadan—still in cat form—was perched on her chest, watching her. To be fair, I *had* kept my best friend up rather late last night. It was just so fun having her here for wedding preparations. Gavin—also in jeans and t-shirt—was pouring two mugs of coffee at the refreshments table set up under the window.

Isobel and Amber sat on either side of Ella on a velvet

settee as the Seelie queen flipped through her sketchbook, explaining her fashion designs in a low voice. All three wore pretty winter day dresses, but none of them could compete with the adorable baby in a yellow floral cotton dress who sat on Isobel's lap. Little Neala, almost a year old, did her best to chew on the corners of the ever-moving sketchbook pages.

I hadn't spent much time around babies before Neala was born, but Isobel and Leith had become great friends of ours over the past year, and I was loving being an honorary auntie to their little daughter.

On the matching settee across from the ladies sat my handsome, black-clad fiancé sandwiched between Tiernan and Saoirse. Kylian had also sprouted a modest crown. Faerie must think that we needed to look extra royal to meet our guests. The Seelie king patted Kylian's shoulder as he continued his advice while Saoirse bit her lip, eyes dancing with barely controlled mirth as she fed a little green Japanese dragon bits of a cookie.

Kylian's eyes met mine immediately from across the room. He could always find me, even with my silence rune activated. *Quit spying and come save me,* grumbled Kylian's voice through the bond. There was a pause, and then he added a pained, *Please.*

"Perhaps a little silver trim for accent?" Tiernan adjusted the sleeve of his stylishly embroidered, royal blue suit jacket. "What do you think, Leith?"

"Stay strong, Kylian." Leith didn't look up from the paperback he was flipping through. The Rose Prince also wore black with perfectly tailored trousers and a casual black linen shirt, the sleeves rolled partially up, as he perused one of Kylian's favorite cozy mysteries, *Doughnuts, Draoi, and Death-threats.*

I dispelled the silence rune and swept into the study, smiling at our guests. "Hi, everyone. Welcome to Skyretaine!"

Our friends all called out greetings—well, Audrey groaned hers—as Kylian extracted himself from Tiernan, causing Essie to squawk at the commotion from the back of the settee. I hadn't even seen the little brown-black hen perched by her favorite person. How did she keep getting out of the chicken yard? And how did she always know where Kylian was?

Kylian narrowed his eyes as he kissed my cheek. *You said twenty minutes.*

I widened my eyes innocently. *And you believed me?*

"Neef!" Neala lunged forward, and Isobel laughed as she caught her daughter and helped her to the floor. Yes, my name was one of the baby's first words. I may have won her over with cookies, but I was still very proud.

"Watch this." Isobel knelt down beside Neala, steadying her under her armpits.

From the corner of my eye, I saw Leith set down his book to watch with a grin. I crouched down, too, and squealed when my little honorary niece toddled one . . . two . . . three steps before pitching forward and wrapping her pudgy arms around my neck as she fell.

"You're amazing!" I exclaimed, sweeping her up into my arms and relishing in her giggles as I peppered her with kisses.

"Down," ordered Neala with another wiggle.

I kissed the silky brown hair on top of her head one more time before setting her down next to her father. She immediately began navigating the edges of the furniture, grabbing knees and boots for balance as she practiced. Neala shrieked with joy when she spotted the little dragon, who launched herself into the air off Saoirse's lap and disappeared with a pop. Obviously, Kiyohime had met toddlers before.

"So, what were you all looking at?" I asked, leaning over for a look as Ella and Amber rose to give me hugs.

"No peeking." Ella flipped her sketchbook firmly shut before giving me a tight hug. "It's bad luck to see the dress before the wedding."

"I don't think that applies to the bride," I grumbled.

"Well, before the designer wants you to, anyway," laughed Ella.

"Dress?" Audrey opened one eye.

"Yes, human child," grumbled Liadan as Audrey displaced the cat, sitting up to receive what I knew for a fact was not her first cup of coffee today from Gavin. "Even *you* wore one to your wedding, if you'll remember."

"Yes, yes, I'm aware." Audrey sipped her coffee and sighed happily. "I just want to see it, that's all."

"Me too!" I bounced on my toes.

"How are you so perky after keeping me awake all night long, gushing about how *handsome* and *romantic* he is?" Audrey asked me accusingly before closing her eyes for another sip.

Oh, really? Kylian smirked.

Stop fishing for compliments, I teased back. *Maybe I was talking about Snickerdoodle.*

"As if you weren't just as bad." I grinned at my sleepy best friend. "On and on with every single detail about the joys of married life."

"How many details?" Gavin raised an eyebrow at his new wife, who blushed fiercely.

"I . . . that's beside the point." Audrey took a gulp of hot coffee and coughed. "Anyway, why all the secrecy? Don't you need Niamh for a dress fitting?" she asked Ella. "*Someone* woke me up two hours ago saying I was needed for maid of honor tasks." Audrey glared at Liadan.

"You had been sleeping for *hours*." The cat examined her paw. "You should just take more naps."

"I want Niamh to get the full experience of seeing the dress for the first time when she's wearing it," Ella explained. "But, yes, it *is* time for the fitting."

"Ooh, yes." Amber clapped her hands. "Dress, dress, dress!"

I squealed as Audrey struggled to her feet.

"Cara was just helping me set up everything in the queen's parlor for you," Ella continued. "She's got all your things moved over to your new rooms."

Kylian and I had each chosen quarters in the family wing of Skyretaine. Neither of us had wanted to move into the monarch's suite before the wedding, choosing to wait until we could start our lives there together.

Ella waved her finger when Kylian stood as well. "No boys."

"Are you sure that you don't need any help?" Kylian eyed the other men.

"You just keep hanging out with your besties." I gave him a kiss on the cheek.

Traitor, he muttered into my mind.

Kylian, you can't come to the dress fitting. Secrets.

No, but Tiernan has lots *of ideas about fashion.*

"Nope. It's a hard rule," said Ella, heading for the door.

"I'll stay back with the boys," added Saoirse. "Keep Tiernan out of trouble."

Kylian relaxed a little bit.

"I've got Neala," added Leith from where he was attempting to keep his daughter from pulling out an infinite number of books from the Royal Seelie Library shelf.

I really needed to move that higher before their next visit.

You're fine? I asked Kylian.

I could feel his rumbling laugh in my mind. *Of course. Don't worry about me.* "I've got something I need to do today, anyway," he added out loud.

"Ooh, secrets! I love it." I pulled him down for a kiss.

"Break it up. Break it up." Amber hooked her arm through mine, and I pouted as she dragged me away from my love. "Lots of time for that tomorrow. Let's check out this *dress*."

Chapter 3

Kylian

I WATCHED THE GIRLS GO WITH A pang in my chest. I loved seeing Niamh so happy. The way she lit up with her friends here and her excitement in planning our wedding was infectious. But we had both been so busy with preparations all week, and there was nothing I wanted more than a quiet evening watching Niamh experiment with a new recipe, talking my ear off while I attempted to read my mysteries.

Two more days, Niamh said through the bond. I felt it like a whisper in my ear. *And then you can kidnap me. Drag me off somewhere like you love to do, Huntsman.*

I smiled. *Thirty-five hours, Princess,* I corrected her, *and then you're all mine.*

I already am. I felt the ghost of a kiss on my cheek.

"Are you just gonna stare into space with a dopey smile on

your face?" Saoirse poked me in the ribs, snapping me back to my surroundings. "Or are you going to tell us what this secret project of yours is?"

"Give me five minutes." I plucked Essie from her perch on the back of the sofa. "I'll return this one to the coop and meet you all in the kitchen. Gavin knows the way," I added.

"The kitchen!" Tiernan clapped his hands together gleefully. "I would love to help—"

"No!" exclaimed Leith and Saoirse firmly.

"I was *going* to say," Tiernan sniffed, offended, "that I would be happy to help by holding Neala." He leaned over and tickled his goddaughter, who giggled in Leith's arms. "Because we all know that your daddy will be more help in the kitchen than me," he cooed at Neala.

"You can bake?" I asked Leith. Tiernan would make any excuse he could come up with to hold the baby. I'd even seen him offer to change her diaper once when it was clear there was no other way he could pry her away from all her doting aunties.

The prince shrugged.

"Oh, trust me," Saoirse said. "You'd rather have Leith. Tiernan will be about as helpful as Neala. Maybe they'll at least keep each other out of trouble."

"See you in five minutes," I told them, smiling at their teasing banter as I left with Essie under my arm.

Nice friends, Essie commented contentedly as I carried her outside, and I almost missed a step when I realized she was right.

Friends. Over the past year, we had certainly become that. How had it happened?

After dropping a very disappointed Essie back into the chicken yard—a lush, green, climate-controlled patch of the courtyard magically protected from the deep midwinter snow surrounding it—I entered the kitchen. Precisely when I said I would.

Nobody likes a smug Huntsman, drifted Niamh's voice down the bond.

Stop spying, or I'll send Essie to tell me what your dress looks like, I teased her and then felt her mental shields come up with a snap and a huff.

Gavin was chatting with Niamh's adoptive parents as they worked on treats for the reception. Sam piped spice-flecked icing in precise lines onto tiny apple turnovers before Roberta plated the flaky golden pastries neatly onto a three-tiered dessert tray.

Tiernan was making faces in an effort to distract the squirming baby in his arms while Leith and Saoirse quickly blocked lower cabinets with chairs and jammed drawers shut with wooden spoons before the curious Neala could dig through them. An easier task here in Niamh's small, personal kitchen than it would be in the large, main castle kitchen.

This bright and airy kitchen with its mint green cabinets, marble counters, striped yellow curtains, and pink wallpaper featuring apples and blossoms had been my birthday gift to Niamh last summer. Estrid had helped outfit it with dwarven, crystal-powered appliances, and it was furnished with the various implements her parents had brought when they sold their farmhouse and café in Pilot Bay to move here to Skyretaine Castle not long after our official engagement.

"I don't want my grandchickens to grow up without knowing my face," Roberta had teased, making Sam roll his eyes good naturedly.

"We'll just get out of your hair and head back over to the main kitchen to see how preparations for tonight's dinner are coming along," Roberta said now, smiling at me as she plated the last pastry.

"You're sure you don't need any help, son?" Sam asked as he neatly stacked the baking sheets and piping bag in the deep farmhouse sink.

"No, sir," I lied.

He raised an eyebrow.

"Dad," I corrected myself, still having trouble naturally using the title despite months of Sam working on me. "And we can clean up those dishes for you." That part at least was true.

"Well, looks like you've got lots of help." Sam gave my shoulder a squeeze. "You just let us know if you need anything."

I nodded, spinning the gold ring from Niamh on my finger, then making myself stop before they noticed the nervous gesture.

"You'll do great," Roberta added with a warm smile. "I can't wait to try a slice."

The couple left the kitchen then, Roberta grumbling that she did *not* need assistance as Sam tried to take the pastry-laden serving dish from her.

"So, brother." Saoirse leaned against the pantry door while Neala grasped her boot and pulled herself upright to pry at the beveled wooden doors. "What's the project? What are we working on?"

I sighed. I really did need all the help I could get.

"I offered . . ." I winced. "To make the wedding cake."

"*The* wedding cake?" Leith raised an eyebrow.

"Yes," I confirmed.

"I didn't know you could bake!" Tiernan said, surprised. "You've been holding out on me."

"No, I haven't." I opened a cupboard and pulled out Niamh's recipe box. "My skills lie firmly in the simple cooking and occasional snacks category. That's why I need your help." I paused, trying to put into words why I was attempting this insanity. "For Niamh, baking is how she shows her love to those around her. I just want to do that for her tomorrow. As a . . . surprise."

"Well, she'll certainly be surprised," muttered Saoirse unhelpfully.

"Gavin?" I looked pleadingly at the faoladh. "You can bake, right?"

He ran a hand through his tousled brown hair. "The only thing I know how to bake without a recipe is cheesecake." He looked thoughtful. "Which, I *suppose* you could make into a wedding cake. It might be difficult to bake one big enough," he pondered. "And it would take some engineering to make tiers . . ."

"It needs to be an apple cake," I said firmly. "I'm hoping Niamh has a recipe in here . . . somewhere."

I set the wooden recipe box on the island. Note cards, scrap pieces of paper, and at least two paper napkins were bursting out of the box with dividers that said things like: *Yes*, *Dad*, or *Soup*. Which sounded helpful until you realized that nothing in that section was a soup.

"*Anything* could be in there," Tiernan pointed out.

"All right." I took a deep breath. "First task: see if we can find a recipe for apple cake. I know she's made them before." I dumped the recipe box out onto the marble surface. "Everyone take a pile. Let's see if she happened to write it down."

Chapter 4

Niamh

I GUIDED MY FRIENDS DOWN THE HALL that led to the royal suite, then paused for a moment in the doorway, taking in the cozy space.

Audrey ran into me from behind. "Don't spill," she yelped.

"Why?" I turned to see a flare of magic sparkle over my friend's coffee mug, which kept the contents from sloshing on me. "Oh, you were talking to your coffee again."

"By which you mean to say: 'Sorry for causing a traffic jam in the doorway'?" Audrey stepped around me and collapsed on one of the two red velvet settees in the sitting room, her coffee sloshing up against its invisible barrier.

"Oh, sorry." I stepped aside and let everyone else in. "I just haven't seen it finished yet. They only moved everything in this week. The last time I was in here, it was just another echoing, empty room."

Like so much of Skyretaine, these rooms had sat empty during Moriath's time here. The servants informed me that my evil aunt had preferred a different wing of the castle. Maybe the memory of my parents living in these rooms had made even her icy heart feel a bit guilty.

For two hundred years, the castle had been mostly abandoned with no royal family members or nobles needing apartments. Moriath had kept only the minimum amount of staff necessary, and her wolves had slept in their kennel dormitory, so the rest of the castle had fallen into disuse.

Over the past year, the much-expanded castle staff had steadily worked through the rooms of Skyretaine, repairing broken windows and split wood from centuries covered in ice. The artisans and decorator had done an amazing job with the sitting room. The space was inviting and warm. You could almost imagine we had lived here for years.

Dark wooden wainscotting paneled the lower walls, perfectly complementing the pale green wallpaper above. I had commissioned the wallpaper myself. The pattern appeared to be just leafy branches, but if you looked closely, you might see a glimpse of a unicorn's horn or an owl's eyes peering through the trees.

Liadan gracefully leapt onto one of the wingback chairs flanking the carved marble fireplace lit with a crackling fire. My sword and Kylian's axe hung on the wall above the mantel. "Wake me when there's a dress," the cait sith murmured, closing her golden eyes.

I dashed across the room, my shoes sinking into the plush cream carpet, aiming for what appeared to be a dress stand covered with a sheet. Thick velvet curtains neatly pulled back with gold cords framed the draped mystery. The sun shone through the diamond-paned windows behind it, sparkling on the frost feathering the glass.

"Don't touch." Ella lightly smacked my hand as I reached for the cloth, then frowned. "I don't see the shoes. Miss Chloe promised she'd have them here."

"I'll go find her," Amber called from the doorway before whirling to run down the hall.

"I *still* can't look at it?" I gaped at Ella in disbelief.

"I want you to see it *on*." Ella waved at the large oval mirror standing near the dress.

I sighed. "Fine."

Through the bond, I suddenly felt Kylian feeling pleased with himself for being so punctual. We could only sense strong emotions, especially at this distance, but he was feeling *very* pleased, the insufferable man.

Nobody likes a smug Huntsman, I mentally called to him.

Stop spying, or I'll send Essie to tell me what your dress looks like. I could feel his smirk as I snapped up my mental shields. Surely, he wouldn't dare.

"Well, let's check out the rest of your rooms." Audrey sat up suddenly and took another sip of her coffee.

"You haven't seen them yet?" asked Isobel, who had been poking through the row of books on the mantel.

"Not since I walked through the rooms with the designer," I admitted. "And only that one time. It made me sad to see them so empty."

"Oh, well, they're not empty anymore." Audrey cracked open a door to the right of the sitting room. "Oh, nice bathtub!"

I poked my head in after her. It *was* a nice bathtub, huge with golden claw feet—or, rather . . .

"Are those *chicken* feet?" asked Isobel, peeking in.

I laughed. "I couldn't resist." The chicken-footed tub was just as cute as I had imagined, resting on the floor of green marble tiles. "It feels like it still needs *something,* though," I muttered, taking in the golden shower head on its stand above the tub, the cozy white towels neatly stacked on shelves, and two plush robes on hooks by the tub.

"You need some plants," said Ella. "A nice moss bath mat, and maybe something viney with white flowers, I think."

"You're so Seelie," I teased her. "You and your plants everywhere."

"You know I'm right." She grinned back. "I'll bring some over next time I visit."

The bathing room connected to a small room with a large double-sink vanity and an alcove with a toilet tucked in it.

"I was afraid you wouldn't have plumbing up here," said Isobel.

"The dwarves helped," I admitted. "The original pipes were all broken from ice."

Next came a dressing room filled to the brim with Ella's creations in a rainbow of colors and patterns on one side, the other half containing our fighting gear. Racks of weapons, beautiful but deadly, gleamed on the wall, and a *very* small selection of black pants and tunics hung at the end.

"I don't know if Kylian's ever going to wear seafoam green," commented Ella, "but Tiernan might have a point about him branching out a little."

"I don't suppose you know what he's wearing to the wedding?" I eyed Ella speculatively.

She gave me a grin and a wink before leaving the room.

"She's just as bad as Aunt Chloe," I muttered to Audrey, who nodded.

The door on the left side of the sitting room opened to the bedroom, and my breath caught at the sight of the giant four-poster bed with its rich red curtains, heaped high with feather pillows and a plump duvet.

"What is it?" Audrey linked her arm through mine and leaned her head on my shoulder.

I shook my head mutely as a hint of a memory flashed through my mind. I had climbed up into this giant bed—even bigger as I had been so small—to snuggle between my parents, my little sister on the other side of my mother, asleep in her arms.

"I thought I didn't have any memories of this suite," I said quietly. "But I seem to have set up this room just the way my parents had it. Even the balcony." I waved my hand at the glass double doors that led to a magically climate-controlled balcony with a table and chairs for private meals.

My friends all clustered in to hug me, Liadan twining around my ankles. Surely, it was supposed to be comforting and not an effort to trip us all.

"They would be so proud of you, Neve," Audrey whispered, and I nodded, wiping my eyes.

"The shoes are here," called Amber. "Let's hop to it. Time's a-wasting!"

"I still can't believe you made her an official wedding planner," sighed Isobel. "It has definitely gone to her head."

I huffed a laugh and wiped my eyes again. "Okay." I took a deep breath. "No tears on the wedding dress."

"I should hope not," Ella teased with another squeeze. "Do you know how hard it is to source good quality *Tsuchigumo* silk?"

CHAPTER 5

KYLIAN

AFTER HALF AN HOUR OF SEARCHING, WE had discovered five apple cake recipes, three of which were the same recipe with various things crossed out, and *No* scrawled across one of the note cards in block letters.

"Then why did she put it back in here?" Tiernan asked, squinting at the offending recipe.

"I've learned not to ask." I started stacking all the soup recipes back into the box. In the Soup section.

"Is she going to be mad at you for reorganizing that?" asked Leith, looking over as he walked hunched circles around the island, Neala grasping his fingers for balance as she practiced taking weaving steps. "Was there a system?"

"She'll say there was a system." I made a neat stack of the pie recipes. "But there is not a system, and she won't mind,"

I added with a smile. Niamh loved to create with a chaotic disregard for process, organization, or cleanup. She had told me more than once how grateful she was for someone willing to do the dishes and reorganize the drawers so that they would close again.

"*Better together!*" she would say with a wink and a laugh.

"You've got a problem," said Gavin as he scanned the recipe cards.

"Make that two problems," called Saoirse from the pantry.

I winced. "Gavin first," I said.

"There isn't a recipe in here that we can use, not if you want it to look like a traditional wedding cake."

"What about the molasses one?" I pressed.

"That one's not sturdy enough for tiers." Gavin shook his head. "And it's so moist and crumbly, you won't be able to decorate it at all. You could aim for something rustic?"

Tiernan winced, and I couldn't help but agree. I was marrying the queen of the Unseelie fae. I didn't want the cake to look like a mess.

"What's the other problem?" I asked my sister.

"How many apples would you say we need, Gavin?" she asked, hauling out a large basket.

Gavin looked at a couple of recipes, and I could see him multiplying the number of guests in his head. "I'm not exactly sure," he said. "Thirty to fifty? Depending on the size."

"Well, I hope these are on the larger size, then." Saoirse tipped the basket to show four lonely apples rolling around the bottom.

"That was full yesterday," I said in alarm. Then I remembered Niamh's parents. "The apple pastries," I groaned.

"Surely, you have other apples in the castle somewhere," said Saoirse.

"These are the last ones from our trees last summer," I sighed. "Niamh has been hoarding them for baking. Apparently, the other apples in cold storage are for eating."

"That makes sense," said Gavin. "Baking apples are firmer and more tart. We could use the other apples in a pinch, but we still need a recipe."

I closed my eyes and laid my head on the cool, marble counter. I didn't want to call Niamh's parents back in. I knew they were very busy today. Besides, if I asked them for help, Sam would happily make the cake. But then, not only would I have to admit that I really didn't have this under control, he'd also gently but firmly take over, and I would be reduced to cracking eggs, if I was lucky. It wouldn't be a cake from *me* anymore.

Tiernan suddenly straightened from his slouching over the island. "What you need is an expert baker!"

"Yes, Tiernan, obviously." Saoirse rolled her eyes. "And yet, here we are with *you*."

"I know, I know." Tiernan waved his hand at his foster sister, then glanced over at Leith. "Are you thinking what I'm thinking?"

Leith nodded. "We need Tuala's recipe."

"Who?" I asked.

"Princess Tuala from the Lily Court," Tiernan said. "She's a truly exceptional baker, and you should have seen the cake she made for last year's Lughnasadh party."

"Oh, yeah, that *was* an apple cake." Saoirse nodded. "And it was tiered like a wedding cake. It was huge."

"And delicious," added Leith. "I had three pieces."

"We still don't have enough apples," Gavin pointed out, stacking up the cake recipes.

"We have some good baking apples in storage at Kilinaire."

Leith scooped his squirming daughter up to perch on his hip. "I can go fetch a basketful."

"I'll send a note to Tuala to let her know we're coming to get the recipe," said Tiernan with a nod. "And I'll help you carry the apples. Why is there never a ryu around when you need one?"

Leith laughed. "No amount of cookies will persuade Falkor to come anywhere near Neala."

The knot in my chest started to release as they made their plans. Maybe we could really do this.

"Take Saoirse," I told them as Tiernan rooted around in drawers to find a pen and paper. "The Ice Gate is set up to let her through any time."

"Good idea," agreed Saoirse. "Someone's got to keep them from chatting the day away."

Leith snorted. "Can you hold her for a second, Kylian?" He passed me Neala.

I held the baby awkwardly. She looked at me. I looked at her. Then she grabbed one of my locs and started shoving it into her mouth. "I don't know if that's—" I began, but Leith took his daughter back before I could finish, and she reluctantly released my hair.

"Thanks." Leith settled Neala into the fabric baby carrier he had strapped on.

Tiernan cracked open the window above the sink. The striped curtains danced in the frosty breeze as a little black-headed jay flew in. The dark blue bird perched on Tiernan's hand and tilted her head, one sassy white eyebrow aimed at the king.

Tiernan lifted the jay to eye level. "Morna, I'm sending you to Tuala of the Lily Court. Remember Tuala?" He dug in his jacket pocket and pulled out a handful of birdseed.

Morna happily pecked at the seed on the counter while Tiernan tied the note around her ankle.

I watched wistfully as the bird flew out again and tapped into my connection with Faerie's magic to make sure that she exited through the Ice Gate safely. Tiernan caught my expression and quirked a thoughtful smile at me.

"Still nothing?" he asked quietly.

I shook my head. Months ago, late one night as Ella and Niamh gushed over dress designs, I had confided to the Seelie king about my worries. Yes, I had the Unseelie crown, one proof of the blessings of the land, but no bird familiar. Every fae monarch in history, even Moriath, bonded with a bird that they had a special connection with. Owls in the case of Niamh and her parents.

But in all our travels, no owl or any other bird had chosen me the way Fluffy had chosen Niamh. Had Faerie not *truly* forgiven me for everything I had done?

Tiernan clapped his hand on my shoulder. "Don't worry," he said softly. "It'll happen."

We turned back to the others.

"Okay, ready to go." Leith adjusted the last strap on the baby carrier.

"I'll see you soon, baby brother," Saoirse teased. "Don't get into any trouble while we're gone."

"You're five minutes older than me," I grumbled.

She winked. "And yet, so much wiser."

As they left Gavin and me in the kitchen, I realized that I had never told anyone else about my worry over my lack of a bird familiar, and I suddenly wondered about all Niamh's teasing that Tiernan was my bestie. Was it actually true?

CHAPTER 6

NIAMH

ELLA STOOD IN THE CENTER OF THE sitting room and clapped her hands to get everyone's attention. I straightened in my seat between Amber and Audrey on the settee. It was hard to believe that my friend struggled so much with anxiety. All of it disappeared when it came to her absolute confidence as a designer.

"Okay, shoes." Ella pointed at Aunt Chloe.

Aunt Chloe leaned over from her seat on a wingback chair and presented me with a carved wooden box secured with a red satin ribbon. "For you, my dear." Her blue eyes sparkled, the only hint of her true form.

My godmother had glamoured herself back to her comforting, curly-gray-haired form, thanks to her enchanted gold-rimmed glasses. "*It's easier to get things done when people aren't staring at you in awe all the time,*" she had remarked when I asked why she rarely took them off.

I tugged the ribbon free and opened the box to reveal beautiful, classic closed-toe heels of golden fabric.

"They're beautiful, Aunt Chloe." I picked one up and traced my finger along the embroidery of apple blossoms in a pale pink thread with little sparkling pink crystals at their centers.

"Are those actual gold?" Amber peered over my shoulder. "Do you ever craft shoes out of anything practical?" she asked Aunt Chloe.

I turned the shoe over. The sole and heel did appear to be solid gold, but it wasn't heavy, and the sole flexed gently when I bent it.

"Well, it would have been tricky to enchant them the way I wanted with just gold thread and tiny crystals," said Miss Chloe airily.

Sure enough, once I looked harder with my Sight, I could see the drifting patterns of the spell floating around them.

Audrey snagged the other shoe to examine it. "Enchanted against blisters and sore feet . . . Handy for dancing," she added to Liadan who was on her lap with one paw on the shoe. "As well as speed, agility . . . and protection against death and dismemberment?" Audrey looked at Aunt Chloe with wide eyes. "What kind of wedding do you think this is going to be? Moriath and Bronach are both gone. Are we expecting a fomóire attack?"

Aunt Chloe shrugged. "With the life these two lead, one never knows what might happen."

I imagined what Kylian would say if I wore these on our next adventure in keeping the peace and laughed.

"Okay, next. Underthings?" Ella gave me a questioning look.

I nodded. "I'm already wearing the ones you had made up for me."

"Then we're ready to get you dressed." She extracted a satin scarf from her pocket. "Stand here," she ordered, waving me to the center of the room.

"This isn't some bachelorette nonsense, is it?" I laughed nervously as I obeyed.

"Do you trust me?" asked Ella.

"I do." I sighed and turned so she could blindfold me with the scarf.

"All right, ladies," the designer called out. "If you please."

I was quickly stripped of my dark pink dress and helped into a giant skirt of some sort. Fitted sleeves were tugged up my arms, and I yelped as icy fingers did up a row of buttons against my back.

"Sorry," came Amber's voice. "It was cold outside."

"Okay, here are the shoes." Ella's voice came from down low as she guided my feet out of my gray heels and into the golden shoes. They did, of course, fit perfectly.

Then I was turned, and I could hear a swish of satin as the dress settled around me.

"May I present . . ." Ella's voice was behind me as she untied the scarf. "The bride!"

I opened my eyes and gasped at my reflection in the mirror.

The sheer white sleeves covering my arms somehow enhanced rather than obscured my tattooed sleeve of pink blossoms, red apple, and dark knotwork before they finished in a thin gold cuff at the wrist. Matching embroidery edged the sheer vee against my collarbones, framing the outstretched wing of my tattooed white owl above a sweetheart neckline of white satin. A satin bodice skimmed my curves before belling out below a pale pink satin sash into a huge white skirt sparkling with intricate golden snowflakes—clearly sewn by tiny piskie crafters—and interspersed with scattered crystals. The embroidery grew thicker near the bottom of the skirt where it transformed into graceful swirls that, at one glance, looked like frost on a windowpane and, at another, swirling feathers with just a hint of rose gold. Pink crystals sparkled along the hem. The *giant* hem.

"It's so beautiful, Ella," I said, "but how am I going to fit through doors?"

"Well, it is an outdoor wedding," Isobel pointed out, and they all laughed.

I turned and looked over my shoulder. Audrey and Isobel adjusted the train as I took in the way the sheer fabric showed off my top four runes, the rest hidden by white satin as I had requested. I still didn't think everyone needed to know how many runes I had gathered over the past couple of years. The skirt swept into a short train, glittering with more of the pink crystals.

"I've never worn anything so beautiful in my entire life," I whispered, tears shining again in my eyes.

"That's not all." Ella held up a finger. She murmured a word of enchantment and tapped the back of the bow. "For dancing," she announced.

All the ladies in the room gasped as the heavy satin skirts dropped to the floor, revealing a full knee-length skirt underneath, embroidered with dramatic pink sparkling apple blossoms.

"Oh!" I spun and bits of sparkling gold tulle peeked out from the bottom, sending little motes of golden light into the air as the dress twirled. "It's perfect," I breathed. I could feel my magic hum in agreement. I didn't stop the antlers as they stretched up into three, then four prongs, the icicles growing higher through my hair.

"I don't know," mused Amber. "I think it's missing a little something."

"What could it possibly be missing? Oh!" I exclaimed as I felt my transportation rune warm on the base of my neck. "*Eihwaz*," I said, activating the rune.

"Estrid!" I cried, bending down to hug my small friend, who had appeared in the room beside me.

"I'm not late, am I?" asked the dwarf when I released her. "I was just finishing it up." Estrid's hands were clean, but there was still a streak of ink across her freckled face, and her red hair was escaping its crown of braids on her head.

"Late for what?" I asked.

Estrid smirked. "Presents, of course!"

"I thought presents were for after the wedding." I looked around at my friends, who were all grinning. "Other than the shoes and the dress, obviously."

"Well, there were a few things we thought you could use beforehand," said Isobel. "You go first, Estrid."

Estrid cleared her throat and flipped through her notebook. "I've been thinking about the marriage rune design we were talking about to replace the *ingwaz* runes," she said, "and after some experimentation, I found a way to replicate that shimmery gold ink Moriath used on your apple." She jerked her head up and looked at my friends. "Um, without the blood magic sleeping spell, obviously. What do you think?"

I pulled up a footstool to sit at Estrid's height and took the notebook. On the open page, she had painted two matching lines of runes, one in a delicate swirling script and one with elegant but simple strokes.

"They're so beautiful." I examined the drawing more closely. "I don't recognize the runes."

"They aren't runes we use in spells," explained Estrid with a smile. "It's a line from an old mansöngr, a love poem. It says:

I will forever dream of the one who makes my heart smile. Kylian found it in a book last time you visited Nidavellir."

Tears pricked my eyes again. It was a good thing I wasn't wearing eye makeup today. It wouldn't stand a chance.

"I know humans exchange rings when they marry, so I designed it to fit around your fingers," she went on. "I hope that's okay. I know you have engagement rings already. If you like it, we can do it tonight after dinner."

A sparkling gold poem chosen by my love for a wedding ring. "I can't think of anything more perfect." I hugged my friend, hoping I wasn't soaking her tunic with my happy tears. "We'll swap our rings to our right hands, so don't worry about that."

"My turn!" Audrey set down her mug. How much coffee had been in it? She reached into the pocket of her jeans.

"You're carrying that around in your pocket?" hissed Liadan. "After all the time we spent crafting it?"

Audrey shrugged. "Well, you don't have any pockets." She pulled out a delicate strand of gold blossoms with pink gems sparkling between the flowers on a thin gold chain.

"Thank you," I whispered, touching it gingerly as Audrey fastened the clasp. I stood and checked the mirror. The necklace floated above the neckline of the dress perfectly. Clearly, they had been working with Ella on this.

"Ooooh!" I noticed the threads of a spell dancing around the necklace. "What's the enchantment?"

Audrey laughed. "It will always reappear in your jewelry box, no matter where you set it down. I've seen how long it takes you to find those earrings I made you for your birthday."

"You know me so well." I pulled my oldest friend in for a hug.

"It matches the earrings, by the way, and we enchanted them last night when you were sleeping." She narrowed her eyes in a mock glare. "Liadan found one in your apron pocket. You're lucky she can track down her own spellcrafting."

"Oops." I smiled winningly. "Thank you, Liadan!"

"It was good for Audrey to practice some actual spellcrafting," the cait sith responded with a sniff. "She spends too much time playing with her human technology."

"And I made you this," Amber pronounced, thrusting a small golden bag at me. The golden fabric matched my shoes perfectly, as did the pink embroidered owl looking cross-eyed at me below the gold clasp.

"You're improving," I said, turning it over in my hands.

"I know, right?" Amber plucked it out of my fingers, clicked it open, and then stuck her entire arm inside. "See, it's enchanted, like my bag. You said you needed one, remember? Now you can bring anything you want to the wedding and still look stylish. Extra lipstick, emergency cookies, your sword, the essentials."

"That's amazing, Amber. Thank you." I gave the young fairy godmother a hug.

"One last gift." Isobel opened a white hat box to reveal a wreath of pale pink apple blossoms and dark pink roses, tied at the back with a ribbon that matched the sash on my dress. "We know you already have a crown." She nodded to the excitable icicles and antlers on my head. "We didn't want to offend it by giving you a wedding tiara . . ."

The magical crown sniffed in agreement.

"So, I thought this would be perfect."

"It's so beautiful," I whispered as she nestled the flower crown on my head before securing the ends with the ribbon. "But it's winter. How did you get the blossoms?" I touched the beautiful fresh flowers, and little golden motes floated around my head.

"I stored them in the library at Kilinaire." Isobel gave the bow a final tug and stepped back to admire her handiwork. "The preservation spell for the books kept the flowers fresh. Then Miss Chloe helped me enchant them once I finished the crown."

I gave my friend's hand a squeeze, touched that she had been thinking of me last summer.

"All right, let's get this skirt back on." Ella held up the long swath of satin.

"Do we have to?" I swished the short skirt one more time.

"Just for a minute," she promised.

"Your mom's on her way up to see it," added Aunt Chloe.

"Oh!" I helped them tie the dress up just as my mom burst in with tears in her eyes and a bundle of something white in her arms.

"Oh, sweetheart, look at you!" She gave me a tight hug, and I sank into her embrace.

"I knew you would never fit into my wedding dress," she began, and we both laughed. Mom was at least a foot shorter than me, and I had seen how petite she had been in my parents' wedding photos. "But I did save one thing for you." She shook out a long veil that I recognized from their pictures. "Your aunt Chloe helped me adjust the trim," she went on, "and we added these hooks."

With Ella's help, my mom carefully attached the veil to the flower crown so that the sheer fabric floated around me and down my back, its newly embroidered gold trim nearly touching the ground.

"Now it's perfect," pronounced Ella, and all the ladies in the room nodded in agreement.

A growl emanating from my stomach broke the awed silence. I clapped my hands over my mouth and laughed.

"I think," I said with one last swish of my skirts, "that it's time for lunch." I wrinkled my nose as I looked in the mirror. "Also, I might need some help." I stretched up my arms. "I'm not sure how to get all this off."

CHAPTER 7

KYLIAN

"HAVE YOU EVER TALKED TO HIM ABOUT your brother?" I asked Gavin, passing him a mixing bowl to dry. We were taking the opportunity to tidy up the stack of dishes Sam and Roberta had left while everyone else was away on their missions.

"Tiernan, you mean?" Gavin kept his eyes focused on his work as he dried the bowl off with a floral tea towel.

I nodded, washing another bowl. "I've noticed you don't speak to him directly unless you need to. But you don't seem . . ." I tilted my head.

"Bitter? Murderous? Vengeful?"

"I saw how you were after that battle."

The newly turned wolf had been inconsolable. Gavin hadn't cried—one didn't cry in the kennel—but losing the older brother he had devoted everything to try saving had broken something inside him. Gavin had pledged his life to Moriath just so that his brother wouldn't be alone. After Ruarc's death in a skirmish with Tiernan's fianna, a quiet rage had burned under Gavin's casually cheerful exterior until the day when he finally ran away.

"No, I haven't." Gavin let out a sigh. "Tiernan is easy to hate from a distance. You can convince yourself that all that charm is just a mask to hide another uncaring Seelie king." Gavin continued drying the dishes as I handed them to him. "But it turns out he truly *is* a good man, and I think he's haunted enough by the lives he was forced to take while in the fianna without me adding more pain to it. Who knows how many brothers' lives *I* was responsible for taking? I think," he added after a pause, "we've all paid enough penance for our past. And perhaps I want peace more than I want vengeance or painful apologies." He let out a huff. "After all, if I can become friends with the Huntsman who kept me on the run for years . . ."

I chuckled quietly. "It *is* a strange thing," I acknowledged, "when those you held as your greatest enemies become your truest friends."

I was happy for my young friend and proud of the peace he had managed to find. Of all the faoladh, Gavin had joined with the purest heart. He'd never truly been taken in by Moriath's lies or had a personal lust for power, and it had been hard to maintain my persona as an uncaring Huntsman when I saw that innocence slowly eroded over the time he had spent with the wolves.

Once again, those old doubts crept in. Had I done the right thing? Was the result worth the cost? Could Faerie truly forgive me? I just wished I could know for sure. Where was my bird?

I shook my head. Gavin was looking at me with concern, and today was not a day for dark thoughts.

"So I don't have to worry about being down a groomsman?" I teased, trying to lighten the mood. "No wedding murders?"

"Have a little faith in me," Gavin said with a laugh. "Audrey would have my head if I didn't wait until *after* her best friend's wedding."

"The truly frightening one is Amber," I pointed out as I pulled the plug and rinsed out the sink. "She actually threatened me with violence if I didn't have the same number of groomsmen as bridesmaids. Do you realize how many friends Niamh has?"

Gavin dried the last pan and slid it into the cupboard before clapping me on the shoulder. "It's starting to look like you might have some too."

"Well—" I paused, tilting my head. "They're back." I felt my sister, the two men, and little Neala as they came through the gate, and then one more. I frowned. "And they brought someone along."

"We have arrived!" announced Tiernan, striding through the door. "Eeep!" the king yelped, tripping into the room as a small, dark shape darted between his legs.

Don't worry, I'm here! Essie leaned against my leg.

"Tiernan, keep it down," Leith hissed as he entered behind his friend, pointing to his back where little Neala slept in the carrier. Her light brown eyelashes were fanned against her pudgy cheeks, two fingers in her rosebud mouth.

"Did you find enough apples?" I asked, scooping Essie up. Something relaxed in my chest, my worries melting away as I stroked her soft feathers.

"Right here." Saoirse hefted a bulging sack as she stood in the doorway.

"And the recipe, I hope?" asked Gavin.

"Even better." Tiernan rubbed his hands together. "May I introduce you to the finest baker in the Seelie Kingdom!"

"I think that's actually my father," came a soft voice from behind Saoirse.

"Beauty, wit, spreadsheets—the Princess Tuala!" Tiernan dramatically gestured to the door.

"Hi!" A strange woman stepped out from behind Saoirse, tucking a dark brown ringlet behind an ear with a rounded point that marked her as half human. "I hope I'm not intruding." Tuala wrinkled her nose, scrunching the freckles that dotted her golden-brown skin.

"Thank you for coming." I gave a slight bow. "I'm Kylian."

"*King* Kylian." Tiernan rolled his eyes. "And his pet chicken, Esso."

Essie glared at the king.

"*Essie*," I corrected him. "It's short for Espresso. And this is Gavin." I introduced my friend, who shook the girl's slim hand.

"You're the Lily Princess?" Gavin asked.

"Oh, that's my mother's title for a few decades yet, I hope," the princess laughed. "Until our little ones are grown."

"Hopefully Tiernan didn't drag you away from anything important." I gave the king a look. "I know he's a hard person to say no to."

Tiernan put his hands in his pockets and looked around innocently, but Tuala just laughed.

"I insisted," she assured me. "Baking for *romance*." She put a hand on her heart, pressing against the linen apron she wore over her simple pink dress. "How could I resist? But don't worry. Saoirse and Tiernan told me that *you* want to be the one to make the cake, and I agree, that's very sweet. I'm just here to answer any questions and give advice."

"And because she's nosy," said Tiernan. "Apparently, she's a big fan of your wife."

"You've met Niamh?" I asked, surprised.

Tuala shook her head, and a little blush bloomed across her golden cheeks. "No, but I used to follow her recipe blog, *Pie in the Sky*. She posted really . . . sporadically, but her flavor combinations were always amazing. Did she ever get that apple pie recipe figured out?"

Apple? Essie clucked, looking at me hopefully.

"In a minute," I told the chicken, then smiled at Tuala. "She did, but she's upstairs for a dress fitting now, so you'll have to ask her all about it tomorrow at the wedding."

"Oh!" she exclaimed. "I wasn't fishing for an invitation."

"I insist," I said firmly.

"The more, the merrier," Tiernan put in. "You should see how much food they've got over in the kitchen."

"Everything but a cake," Gavin pointed out.

Tuala grinned and pulled a notebook from her apron pocket. "Tiernan said you needed a recipe for apple cake?"

I nodded, setting Essie down on a stool to take the notebook.

"It's a bit of a thing for them." Saoirse pulled the four remaining apples out of the pantry and set them on the counter. "Do you need somewhere to lay Neala down?" she asked Leith, holding up the empty basket, which was indeed about the size of a one-year-old.

"I can get a blanket," I added.

Leith shook his head. "If I move her, she'll wake up. This is the only way she naps right now, and she was up half the night. We will *not* disturb her." He looked pointedly at Tiernan, who was reaching out a hand toward the baby's curled-up fingers.

"Sorry, sorry!"

I ignored them and flipped open the notebook, Gavin reading over my shoulder. The recipe was written in precise, neat handwriting and perfect detail with one page for ingredients, two for detailed step-by-step directions, a third containing decoration ideas, and a fourth with a chart multiplying the ingredients out for the number of guests, noting the changes in bake times and pan sizes as it increased.

"I hope you didn't do all this work just for me." I looked up at Tuala, worried.

The princess laughed. "Oh, no, this is my regular system. Once I get a recipe the way I like it, I transfer it to one of my notebooks and spell the pages against stains and smears. That way, it's easy for me to make again later."

Sure enough, the rest of the notebook proved to be filled with more tidy recipes. I couldn't help but glance over at Niamh's pile of mismatched notes.

Tuala's eyes brightened, no trace of judgment in them. "Do you think her final apple pie recipe is in there?" she breathed.

"I *think* I saw it somewhere?" Saoirse looked askance at the heap.

"May I?" Tuala edged closer to the recipes. When I nodded, she sighed happily and pulled up a stool to begin sorting through the notes.

"Do you need this?" I held up her notebook, but Tuala waved me off.

"I always have an extra." She pulled a second notebook and a pencil out of another apron pocket.

"All right then, let's get started." I scanned the recipe once more. "I'll find the equipment we need. Gavin, you can start on the dry ingredients."

Gavin nodded and snagged an apron off the hooks on the pantry door.

"Saoirse, you can start peeling apples."

Now apples? Essie perched on the stool and flapped her wings excitedly.

"Saoirse will peel into a bowl for you." I patted the little hen on the head, and Saoirse laughed.

"I'll set up right here, you little vulture," she teased my chicken as she set a bowl next to Essie's stool.

Am a chicken, Essie grumbled, watching intently as Saoirse peeled a long spiral from the first apple.

"Leith, can you peel too while Neala sleeps?" I asked.

Leith nodded. "I can do anything," he said, "except sit down."

"Tiernan . . . You can help them peel?"

Saoirse violently shook her head behind Tiernan's back.

"Really?" I tilted my head. "He's been training with blades for over a century. Shouldn't he have knife skills?"

"You would think that," my sister sighed. "Hey!" she exclaimed when Essie snagged the apple peel out of her hand. "Okay, okay, hold on." She went back to peeling.

"Okay, could you separate the egg whites?"

Saoirse wobbled her knife hand in a maybe gesture, and Tiernan grimaced.

"He can mix," said Tuala, not looking up from the notes she was making, and Tiernan brightened. "Just make sure he has two spoons," she added. "One for dry ingredients and one for wet ingredients."

"Oh, yeah, I wouldn't have thought of that." Tiernan removed his velvet jacket and considered the apron collection for a long moment.

We all looked at Tuala, and she laughed. "That's how I let my two-year-old help in the kitchen."

"I would like to be offended," said Tiernan, tying on a green-checked apron. "But I *am* very good at mixing."

Four hours later, I surveyed the perfectly golden cake rounds of various sizes cooling around the kitchen with satisfaction. The air was filled with the smell of apples, cloves, and cinnamon. Thanks to Tuala's detailed notes, everything had turned out perfectly. Although, it had been a near thing when Tiernan almost dumped pepper into the batter instead of allspice.

"Now, you won't be able to decorate until everything is fully cooled," said Tuala, inspecting one of the largest cake layers.

I froze, my eyes widening.

"You forgot we had to decorate, didn't you?" Saoirse raised an eyebrow at me.

"Possibly," I allowed.

"The most common way to decorate a wedding cake is with fondant," said Tuala. "I don't have any with me, though, and it's not the most delicious." She tapped her bottom lip, thinking. "How are your piping skills?"

"Piping?" I asked. What did pipes have to do with cake?

"I mean, I'd be happy to help you, but I need to get back. Maybe if I brought the children over . . ." she trailed off thoughtfully.

"No, we've imposed on you enough." I shook my head. "We'll figure something out."

We thanked the princess again, and Saoirse walked her out.

"Any ideas?" I looked around the kitchen as if cake-decorating inspiration might be hiding on a shelf.

"I could maybe find some roses?" suggested Leith by the sink where he was cleaning raspberry jam out of Neala's hair.

The toddler had enjoyed her post-nap snack of bread and jam *very* much and had giggled while feeding her crusts to Essie.

"Are roses edible?" asked Gavin.

"I think so? Ena makes rose hip jam every year, but that's not exactly the same thing." Leith scrubbed Neala's face before she grabbed the cloth and started chewing on it. "But why would people eat the decorations?"

I looked over at Gavin.

"I usually just put some sort of fruit sauce on top of things," he admitted.

"I don't think applesauce is fancy enough." Saoirse walked back into the kitchen. "What about if we found some *really* pretty daggers and—"

"You're all hopeless," interrupted Tiernan, not looking up from the piece of paper he was scribbling on. "It's a good thing *someone* around here has a sense of style."

He slid his paper across the island toward me, and I studied the sketch with its arrows and notes.

"That's a pretty good drawing." Saoirse smacked Tiernan's shoulder. "I'm impressed. I didn't know you had it in you."

"Ella's been teaching me." Tiernan grinned proudly.

"You know . . ." I tapped the drawing. "I think this will work."

"It's actually a really good plan," agreed Gavin.

"Thank you, Tiernan." I set the sketch down on the island. "You've saved—"

"That's enough!" Saoirse cut me off. "I won't be able to live with him if his ego gets any bigger."

"It's true though." I looked around the room at my unlikely group of friends. "Thank you all for helping me. I could never have managed this on my own."

"It's just like your wife-to-be is always saying." Tiernan

shrugged. "Stronger together, right? That counts for friends too, you know."

I smiled in spite of myself. "That's true," I said. "Stronger together."

CHAPTER 8

NIAMH

IF YOU HAD TOLD ME TWO YEARS ago that I would be the queen of the Unseelie fae, preparing to walk down the aisle to marry my king, I would have laughed in your face and then checked your temperature, because clearly you would have been delirious.

Two years ago—before a certain grumpy Huntsman burst into my life—I had thought that I had everything I needed in the small town I had grown up in, working in the bakery with my parents. My only future plans had been of the chicken variety.

I had been happy, but it had been a small happiness. I hadn't known how much more my heart could hold.

"Okay, the chickens go first," announced Amber, clipboard in hand.

She muttered under her breath, trying to count the chickens as they milled around my bridesmaids and parents, cleverly avoiding the grasping fingertips of Neala, who crawled after them, giggling. You had to watch your step in the small side entryway, that was for sure.

"...four, five, six..." Amber said. "Niamh, you seem to be down a chicken."

I bent down and straightened Snickerdoodle's golden bow tie. "I think Essie is with the groom's party."

Amber peeked out the door. "Oh, she is. All right, chickens, line up!"

Everybody listen to Amber, I told the chickens. *She has your favorite cookies in her pocket.*

The chickens scampered toward the door, looking up at Amber with adoring eyes.

"Okay," she told the chickens. "Go find Kylian."

The chickens all clucked in agreement, and Amber opened the door, allowing Waffles strutting in his bow tie to lead his little flock out into the courtyard. Each of the little hens wore a golden apple blossom magically affixed to her head. Aunt Chloe had crafted the blooms to scatter a trail of golden petals behind them. She said she had missed the weddings of too many godchildren and had gone all in with the decorations for this one.

"Okay, bridesmaids next in order of height, just like we practiced. Estrid first."

Indeed, Amber had been a bit of a drill sergeant the night before.

My dwarven friend flashed me a grin. Her red hair was braided into an elaborate crown adorned with apple blossoms that matched her bouquet. The sparkling gold of the knee-length gown she had complained about during the fitting suited her complexion beautifully.

"Saoirse gets to wear pants," she had grumbled to Amber.

"She's on the groom's side. Bridesmaids wear the dresses Ella designed." Amber had been firm.

"I mean, I'm friends with Kylian too," Estrid had commented thoughtfully.

"No. The sides must be *balanced.* It's a royal wedding. Think of the *aesthetic.* You're. Wearing. The. Dress." Amber's eyes had narrowed, her voice heavy with implied threat.

Estrid had huffed in reluctant agreement.

Today, the dwarf seemed to be rather enjoying the swish of the full skirts as she went out the door, but I knew better than to comment on it. I had seen her strap a dagger to her leg.

"Isobel and Neala next," Amber called, tapping her clipboard.

"Coming!" Isobel hoisted her daughter up on her hip. Neala's dress had a bodice of golden satin to match her mother's bridesmaid dress and a short skirt—so as not to interfere with crawling—in sparkling, pale gold tulle. The baby reached eagerly for the flowers in her mother's hair, but Amber quickly distracted her by tying a posy of enchanted gold flowers on her wrist with a little pink ribbon. Neala tried to shake it off and then squealed with delight as sparkling golden petals flew around her, scattering all over the floor. Luckily, they would disappear in an hour.

Amber handed Isobel her bouquet and opened the door while the Rose Princess muttered something about heavy babies and slippery dresses as she exited after Estrid.

Ella went next, elegant as always and glowing with well-deserved satisfaction as she took in my dress and Audrey's one more time before following the others out the door.

Audrey flung herself at me in a tight hug. "I'm so happy for you, I could burst," she whispered to me. "Whoever would've thought we'd end up here?"

I squeezed her back. "I suspect my godmother had an inkling about it," I murmured, and Audrey laughed before dashing out the door.

"I'm gonna slip out now so I'm not a distraction," said Amber. "Wait for the music to change and don't forget to cue your owl."

I nodded and held out my arms. Mom linked hers on my left, and Dad on my right. They were both dressed up far more elegantly than I would have believed them capable of, although my father tugged his cravat irritably when he thought no one was looking.

I pulled them both closer. "Thank you for giving me away today. So much has changed in my life, but I've never been able to picture my wedding without you here with me."

"It's a little funny," admitted my mom, "to give you away to the man who gave you to us in the first place."

I laughed. "I never thought of it that way."

"Besides," added my dad, "you're not getting rid of us this easily."

I leaned my head against his for a moment. "Thank goodness," I teased. "I never have been able to figure out what the secret ingredient is in your chocolate cake."

"It's mayonnaise," said Mom.

Dad gasped. "How *dare* you? I'll have you know, it's actually love," he told me.

I heard the music shift outside.

Are you ready, Fluffy? I asked my owl. I could sense him perched on the roof just outside the door.

It's a formal occasion, grumbled the owl. *Please don't use my baby name.*

I apologize. Are you ready, Frederick Otus Sharpbeak the Third?

Thank you, he said, *I am.*

Then get your fluffy *butt going!*

My parents opened the door, and we stepped out into a corridor of spring. Our unicorn friends had arrived the night before, and while swirling snow still blanketed most of the Unseelie kingdom, the courtyard was an explosion of green grass carpeted with tiny white fairy bells. I could have sworn those hadn't been there when it was actually spring. Mom and Dad escorted me between rows of blossoming apple trees as Fluffy flew overhead, sprinkling shimmering golden dust from the wreath of leaves Aunt Chloe had given him.

Everyone we loved waited in the audience, most sitting on the rows of chairs amongst the trees. I spotted Kings Ulf and Ulrik munching on a bag of crunchy fried mushrooms, sitting in a row with some of the other dwarven friends we had made during the past year. Ahead of them sat all the freed faoladh and Tiernan's fianna, our allies from the battle against Moriath. Cara sat with a delegation of asrai, including her mother, and there were representatives from the glaistigs, dearg due, draoi, grogachs, and even a handful of sheerie—who had *promised* to behave—along with any Unseelie nobles who weren't too much trouble. Politics or not, I was not breaking up fights on my wedding day.

Darach and his piskie knights sat near the birds in the overhanging branches. Below them was a pretty girl with dark bouncing ringlets and a gold tiara with lily designs. She grinned at me from her seat beside a handsome blond man and three small children. I smiled back, wondering who she was, and saw Kylian and Saoirse's two brothers and younger sister with their families.

The unicorns stood at the edges so they wouldn't block anyone's view, with Liadan lounging on a black one. Perched on the castle roof were three giant dragons, including Queen Sofie.

As we got closer to the front, I was dimly aware of a very stressed-looking Amber trying to lure chickens back into place with cookies while Neala shrieked and crawled around chasing them. Both the baby's parents were trying to capture their daughter, but the task was further complicated by the youngest of the baby unicorns and a ryu or two bounding around amidst the chaos. The laughing bridesmaids and groomsmen dressed in black weren't enough to bring the air of royal formality Amber had hoped for.

But, honestly, I barely noticed any of it. I only had eyes for my Huntsman. My king. My Kylian. He watched me with wide eyes and a dumbstruck expression on his face. I grinned and gave him a cheeky wink.

I didn't think you could possibly look more beautiful, Princess. His voice brushed against my mind as he slipped back into his old nickname for me.

I searched for a witty response, but all I could come up with was, *Wow*, as I took in his navy velvet suit, the jacket trimmed with swirling gold embroidery that matched the frost designs on my dress. A gold cravat was tied at his neck and flowers matching my headdress and bouquet were pinned on his chest. His locs fell to his waist unbound, the golden antlers and sparkling icicles of his crown growing taller in a majestic display above his head as I watched.

My parents each kissed me on the cheek and hugged Kylian before sitting down.

Kylian took my hand in his and drew me to stand with him in front of our new Ice Gate where Aunt Chloe waited, a twinkle in her eyes for us.

Everyone, go sit down, I firmly told the chickens, ryu, and little unicorns.

You should perch up on his crown like this, I heard Fluffy instruct Essie as he landed on my antlers, his favorite perch in the whole world. *It's part of our job as familiars to help them look as majestic as possible.*

Essie perked up, and with a flop of her chicken wings, landed a bit awkwardly on Kylian's antlers. The golden prongs rearranged themselves before my eyes to make room for the little hen. I smothered a giggle with my hand, but then looked up to see a tear running down Kylian's cheek.

What is it? I asked him.

I'll tell you later, he whispered, but I felt a sense of peace radiating from him that hadn't been there a moment ago.

The ceremony was short but beautiful. Saoirse stepped up with a golden cord in her hand, looking elegant in her wide-legged black satin pants and tailored vest, her kinky curls piled up high on her head and tumbling to the side. Audrey helped Saoirse wrap Kylian's left hand together with mine, and then they stepped back for the vows.

Aunt Chloe knew Kylian didn't love to be the center of attention for long, and that I couldn't be trusted to get through vows we had written ourselves without bawling. So we repeated after Aunt Chloe, promising to love, support, and protect each other for all of our long fae lives. The rings Estrid had inked onto our fingers the night before flared with golden light before fading into a soft shimmer. When our vows were complete, Kylian looked at me with the most intense expression I had ever seen on his face, and before Aunt Chloe had a chance to say anything, he wrapped his free arm around my waist, pulling me tightly against him and kissing me deeply. I heard our familiars take flight with a squawk as I placed my unbound hand on the back of his neck to pull him even closer.

As the cheers of the crowd reminded us of where we were, my eyes flew open. From the corner of my eye, I could see the whole crowd on their feet, the animals resuming their rioting, and birds and piskies tossing glittering flower petals from overhead.

"You guys can stop kissing now," whispered Saoirse from beside us.

"I'm not so sure about that," I told her, giving Kylian another quick kiss before looking up at our combined crowns. The icicles were taller than ever, the antlers twining together. "I think we're stuck."

Chapter 9

Kylian

I WANTED NOTHING MORE THAN TO DRAG my new wife away through the Ice Gate the moment we convinced the magic of Faerie to allow us to separate, but I still had to share her for a little while longer. First, we had to greet all our guests, including my younger siblings, who had come to represent my side of the family. After much debate, we had decided to invite my mother and father to the wedding. They had sent their regrets, and I couldn't say I was sorry about it.

Maybe one day, Saoirse and I would learn how to have some sort of relationship with our parents, but for now, it was enough to get to know the sort of adults my little brothers and sister had become. After awkward introductions and my sincere invitation to come for a longer visit another time, Saoirse took our siblings and their families under her wing and showed them around while Niamh and I continued greeting our guests.

"May I introduce Princess Tuala from the Lily Court," I said, presenting the princess to my wife.

"I'm *so* excited to meet you." Tuala grinned, stars in her eyes. "This is my husband, Naven." She patted the arm of the blond man I had seen earlier. "Evie and Remy." She touched the blonde curls of a girl who looked around seven, then the short dark wavy hair of a younger boy. "And our youngest, Étienne." She hoisted the toddler on her hip. "I just have to tell you what a huge fan I am of your blog! Some of the flavor combinations you come up with? Amazing."

"Thank you! You like baking?" Niamh smiled. *I almost forgot I ever had a blog*, she admitted to me. *I wonder if I should update it sometime?*

I think you have enough to do right now with ruling a kingdom, I reminded her.

"I hope you don't mind," continued Tuala, "but I copied down your completed apple pie recipe when I was here yesterday helping with the cake."

"The cake?" asked Niamh.

"Oh, no." Tuala's hand flew to cover her mouth. "Was that a surprise? I'm so sorry."

"It's fine," I assured her. "I have something to show you," I said, turning to Niamh.

"It was nice to meet you," said Tuala.

"We'll catch up later," Niamh promised. "Maybe you can come over for tea and chat recipes with me after the honeymoon?"

"Oh, I would love that!" Tuala gushed, then gave a little squeak when Niamh hugged her tightly. Little did she know how quickly you could go from being a stranger to a friend on hugging terms with my sunny wife.

"Did the princess help my dad with the wedding cake?" asked Niamh as I took her hand and led her through the castle.

"Something like that." I opened the tall wooden doors to the ballroom.

"Oh, wow. Clíodhna and Amber went all out decorating for our first event in here!" Niamh held out a hand to catch one of the tiny shimmering snowflakes drifting down from the vaulted ceiling of the ballroom. It disappeared in a puff of golden sparkles on her hand. "It's amazing!"

"Amazing," I agreed, watching her eyes light up as she took in the frosty wonderland, the inverse of the spring orchard outside. Golden trees with sparkling bare limbs grew out of mossy patches on the ballroom floor and reached up toward the vaulted ceiling strung with icicles of crystal. "Wait, *first*? How many are you planning?"

"Well, I've been thinking that the Unseelie Kingdom could use more parties." She turned to take in the magical space, her wide skirts gliding across the polished wood of the floor. "What do you think about a Beltane ball?"

"Whatever you want," I promised, watching a snowflake land in a shimmer of gold on her rosy cheek.

"Oh, good, because I've already found the *cutest* bunnies for the party."

"What?" Surely, I had misheard her.

"Weren't you going to show me something?" she asked, batting her eyelashes.

"Hmm, yes." We'd discuss the wisdom of live rabbits at a ball another time. "The cake is this way."

"The cake, right! Dad's been so secretive about it," she said.

"I asked him to keep it a secret. You know how you're always baking," I said, leading her past tables draped in white linen, "and you give nearly all of it away."

"Well, yeah, I want people to know how much I love them. That's why I was cranky when you wouldn't let me feed you for so long."

"I know." I glanced back at her. "That's why, for once, I wanted to do the same for you." We stopped in front of the table where the six-tiered cake stood, framed by an arch of golden branches.

"Kylian," Niamh whispered. I could feel the joy building inside her and reflecting in my heart as she turned her wide eyes on me. "You *made* this for me?"

"Well . . ." I scratched the back of my neck. "I mean, not by myself. Saoirse and the guys helped me."

"*That's* what you were so secretive about yesterday." Niamh grinned as she inspected the abstract, swirling texture of the spiced cream cheese frosting.

"The decorating was mostly Tiernan," I told her. "He said he didn't trust us to not screw it up."

Niamh laughed. "That sounds like Tiernan."

"Saoirse and I collected the blossoms this morning," I continued, still feeling nervous as Niamh examined the tiers sprinkled with apple blossoms. "Once the unicorns had been in the orchard long enough for it to bloom. And the apples on top are from Leith's trees at Kilinaire."

"They have good apples." Niamh admired the two pink-and-red apples on the top of the cake and then reached out and touched one of the seven feathers fanned out behind the fruit, each one unique.

"The chickens wanted to give you something too," I told her. "Tiernan thought it would add drama, but Gavin insisted that feathers weren't hygienic and had Audrey magically clean them before he covered the ends in gold wax."

"And it's an apple cake?" Niamh sniffed thoughtfully. "With cinnamon . . . cloves . . . and . . ."

"Cardamom," I finished. "Princess Tuala's recipe. Apparently, she made it for a party that the Seelie folk went to last year."

Niamh's dramatic crown shrank into nothing, and for a moment, I worried that she might not be happy after all. But then she flung herself at me and tucked her head under my chin.

"This is the sweetest thing anyone's ever done for me," she whispered as I brought my arms around her waist. "There's only one problem." Sorrow tinged her voice.

"What?" My heart dropped. What had I missed?

"We won't get to eat it for like . . . an hour or two," she moaned. "There are more people we have to greet, and we have to eat all the rest of this incredible food." She waved at the covered serving dishes on the surrounding tables, each dome topped with an enchanted gem to keep it at the perfect temperature.

With a chuckle, I extricated myself from her arms. "I thought you would say that." I reached around to the back of the cake. "So, I made you this." I presented her with a single spiced apple cupcake, topped with a swirl of buttercream and one pink apple blossom.

Niamh shrieked with delight, nearly making me drop the cupcake as she tackled me for another kiss on the cheek. She sighed happily when I set it onto her outstretched hands.

"Have you tried it yet?" she asked, then frowned when I shook my head. "Kylian, testing is an important part of baking."

"Old habits," I said with chagrin, holding out my hand as she broke the cupcake and handed me half.

"We'll eat together, then." Niamh held up her half and waited for me to do the same. "On three. One . . . two . . ."

We both bit into the cupcake, which tasted just as good as it smelled. Apples and spices combined in a comforting flavor, the spiced buttercream not too sweet or overpowering with a hint of cream cheese. But after that first bite, I was distracted by the look of pure bliss on Niamh's face as she chewed. I watched her take another bite, transfixed by the way she licked the icing off her red lips, and wondered how much longer I would have to wait before I could get her somewhere more private.

"Kylian," she groaned, drawing me down for a kiss, and I had to admit that the cake did taste pretty good.

"I hope we're not interrupting anything," Tiernan's voice called across the ballroom.

"Actually . . ." I gave him my best Huntsman glare, but he just grinned as he urged his wife forward, yet another person completely immune to the persona I had spent centuries cultivating. I must be losing my touch.

"We have news!" he continued as they drew closer to us.

"We don't want to make a fuss on your big day." Ella gave her husband a mock frown.

"Which is why we're telling them *in private*." Tiernan squeezed Ella's hand as they stopped in front of us.

"I'm—" she began.

"We're having a *baby!*" Tiernan crushed Ella against him, making her laugh.

Niamh squealed and rushed forward to hug her friend. "How far along are you?" she asked.

"Not very." Ella looked down at her still flat tummy. "I only just found out this morning."

"*I* just found out ten minutes ago," Tiernan groused. "She avoided me all day."

"Because I knew you'd be able to tell through our bond if I was close by! I can't ever keep secrets from you." Ella patted his arm with a laugh. "I didn't want to disrupt the ceremony. You've already *privately* told Leith and Isobel, Saoirse, Declan, and the whole fianna. How you managed to keep secrets from your father all that time is a mystery to me."

"It's very easy to not tell my father things." Tiernan kissed his wife's temple.

"I'm so happy for you," I told my friend before pulling him in for a hug. "You'll be an excellent father."

"He's hugging me, Ella!" whispered Tiernan. "It's a wedding miracle."

I rolled my eyes and then thumped him firmly on the back before releasing him. It was just a hug. No need to make a fuss about it.

"We'll let you get back to . . . whatever that was before we interrupted you," teased Ella. "I'm sure Tiernan has someone else that he has to *very quietly* announce our news to."

"Well, we *do* have to tell Tuala and Naven." Tiernan tugged his wife back across the ballroom. "They've been harassing us about having kids for years now."

"Speaking of babies." Niamh turned to me when our friends were out the door. "I've been meaning to talk to you about something."

My mind raced. The topic of children had not been discussed recently. Niamh had always been firm that while she would never say never, she was content to enjoy being an honorary auntie. Had that changed? I wasn't sure parenthood was something I'd ever be comfortable with, but if it was what Niamh wanted . . .

"Would that make you happy?" I asked hesitantly.

"It would make me *very* happy . . ." began Niamh sweetly, ". . . to let Paprika hatch some eggs when we get back from our stay at the cottage. Wouldn't chicks be adorable?" She looked up at me with a wicked gleam in her eyes, one that told me she knew exactly what she was putting me through.

"Troublemaking princesses don't get seconds of wedding cake." I tapped her nose in reprimand.

"I've already eaten some," she announced as we walked

across the ballroom to greet more of our guests. "It was incredible. I can die happy now."

"Well, I hope not," I said, opening the door for my sassy wife. "That would definitely put a damper on the reception."

Chapter 10

Niamh

THE REST OF OUR WEDDING DAY WAS a blur of visiting with friends and family, eating delicious food, and dancing. Having everyone here and happy in this castle after everything the kingdom had been through made me content in a way that I didn't know how to express. Once I shed my heavy overskirt, I even convinced my new husband to dance with me, and despite his protests, Kylian had a pretty good sense of rhythm.

Tiernan and Ella must have *quietly* told twenty more people, if my guess was right. I even saw Gavin clasping Tiernan's hand and saying, "I'm happy for you, man." It was very sweet. I didn't know they were friends.

And, well-behaved princess or not, I *did* enjoy two slices of the incredible apple wedding cake. I still couldn't believe Kylian had gone to all that trouble for me.

I was dancing with Audrey when I noticed that the top tier of the cake was missing.

I stopped in my tracks. "What happened to the cake?"

"I packed it up for later," Kylian said from behind me, making me jump. My husband snagged his arm around my waist and pulled me back against him. "It's time to go, wife," he murmured low into my ear, and I shivered.

"I'll catch up with you later," said Audrey with a laugh, hugging me goodnight. "I need to find Gavin before he gets all partied out, turns into a wolf, and escapes into the night like he threatened earlier."

"Shouldn't we tell people?" I protested as Kylian tugged me toward a side door.

"I'm sure they'll figure it out." Kylian kissed my temple as he reached around me to open the door.

"Do I need to grab anything?"

"I've got the cake and some of those mushroom turnovers you were devouring earlier." He gestured to the bag slung over his shoulder. "And everything else is at the cottage already," he assured me as we stepped outside to be accosted by the chickens.

Cottage? Cottage? Cottage? clucked the chickens milling around our feet.

"Not tonight," Kylian told them firmly.

Essie looked at him with extra pitiful eyes, so he picked her up and gave her a pat.

"We'll bring you next time," he promised her, then turned to me. "Did you know?"

"Know what?" I asked, distracted by how the moonlight glimmered on the planes of his face.

"That Essie was my familiar?"

"I hadn't really thought about it," I admitted, "but it makes sense. There's a little more magic around her than the other chickens, and when Fluffy said something, I realized it was the same as my connection with him and with Faerie. But *you* didn't know?" I asked slowly.

"I had worried," Kylian admitted softly, "about what it meant if I didn't have a familiar. If Faerie hadn't decided to make that connection with me."

"Oh, Kylian." I leaned against his arm. "I didn't know that you were still struggling with that."

He looked down at the little chicken. "I can't believe I missed it. She's just not what I expected," he said as Essie snuggled deeper into his arms and closed her little chicken eyes.

"It's true that Faerie monarchs usually have a familiar that's more imposing. *Dramatic*, as Fluffy would say." I glanced up at my owl, who roosted in a tree nearby. "But you're imposing enough on your own. You don't need the help like I do. Maybe Faerie knew that what you needed was comfort." I stroked the little black and brown chicken's soft back feathers.

Kylian nodded in agreement. "Not what I expected." He looked up at me. "But better."

I could tell by the shine in his eyes and the contentment that radiated out from him through our bond that he didn't just mean the little chicken—or even me—but this life we'd been given to share with each other. Then, with a lazy smile, he set the protesting hen down, pulled a cozy blanket out of his bag, and wrapped me in it before swooping me up into his arms.

I laughed as he carried me past frolicking unicorns and sleeping dragons toward the new Ice Gate. "Are you going to carry me all the way to the cottage?"

"I shoveled a path yesterday," he said, "but you're still not walking through the snow in those shoes."

"And what about you? You don't even need a coat?"

He glanced down at me with that inscrutable look of his, and I laughed again, tilting my head for a kiss as we stepped through the Ice Gate and into our happily ever after.

“Don’t worry,” I promised him. “I’ll keep you warm.”

Futhark Runes

These are the runes used in the tattoo-based magic system by the Dvergr (Dwarves). Two would be spoilers, so you'll just have to read on and find out what they mean for yourself!

Ansuz	(AHN-sooz)	**Silence**
Daegaz	(DAH-gahz)	**Sight**
Eihwaz	(AY-wahz)	
Ingwaz	(ING-wahz)	
Perthro	(PER-thro)	**Truth**
Raidho	(Rah-EED-ho)	**Speed**
Sowulo	(So-WEE-lo)	**Healing**
Teiwaz	(TEE-wahz)	**Stamina**
Thurisaz	(THUR-ee-sahz)	**Shield**
Uruz	(OO-rooz)	**Strength**

Pronunciation Guide

A Note on Pronunciations

My version of the Faerie realm contains countries inspired by fairy folktales from around the world. While I love and respect the lore and languages represented in these myths and folktales, I am not a native speaker of any language but English. Neither my Irish nor my husband's Scandinavian ancestries have given us any abilities to pronounce the names of people or places perfectly, but I have tried my best to research the proper pronunciations for you here.

I hope this guide will help give you an idea of how the names in The Frost Gate would be spoken. If you are a native speaker of one of these languages and notice something I got wrong, I'd love to learn from you.

Characters

Aelfred *(ay-el-fred)*
Dwarf - Doctor at Nidavellir

Amber *(am-burr)*
Human - Apprentice fairy godmother, Isobel's younger sister

Audrey *(auh-dree)*
Human - Apprentice spellcrafter

Bronach *(bro-nahk)*
Tuatha - Moriath and Oonagh's sister

Brynjar *(brin-yahr)*
Dwarf - Former runecrafting master at Nidavellir

Cara *(cah-rah)*
Asrai - serving staff at Nidavellir

Chloe/Clíodhna *(klee-uh-nah)*
Fairy Godmother

Calder *(call-dur)*
Tuatha/Dearg Due - Cook for the Fianna

Darach *(dah-ruh with a hint of ck)*
Piskie - Prince

Danu *(dah-new)*
Mother goddess of the Tuatha Dé Danann

Declan *(deck-lan)*
Tuatha - Co-captain of the Fianna

Dylan *(dill-in)*
Faoladh

Ella *(ell-ah)*
Human - Seelie queen, married to Tiernan

Ena *(eh-nah)*
Brownie - Housekeeper at Kilinaire

Eimear *(ay-mur)*
Asrai - Cara's mother

Estrid *(east-rid)*
Dwarf - warrior and runecrafter, Ulf's daughter

Falcor *(fal-core)*
Ryū - Isobel's pet

Fiachra *(fee-ah-chra)*
Tuatha - former Seelie king, Tiernan's father

Fionnbharr *(fyun-var)*
Tuatha - former Unseelie king, Niamh's father

Frederick Otus Sharpbeak the Third aka Fluffy *(fred-rick)*
White Eagle Owl - Niamh's familiar

Gavin *(gav-in)*
Faoladh - Audrey's boyfriend

Gustav *(goos-tahv)*
Dwarf - head chef at Nidavellir

Haru *(hah-roo)*
Kami - Fianna member and ryū daddy

Hedda *(head-ah)*
Dragon

Hreidmar *(hreed-mar)*
Dwarf - Former dwarven king

Isobel *(is-o-bell)*
Human - The Rose Princess, Amber's older sister, married to Leith.

Jac *(jack)*
Tuatha - Fianna member and spellcrafter

Kylian *(kill-ee-an)*
Aziza - Moriath's Huntsman, Saoirse's older brother

Leith *(like leaf, but a th instead of an f)*
Tuatha - The Rose Prince, married to Isobel

Liadan *(lee-a-dan)*
Cait Sìth - Audrey's spellcrafting master

Maeve *(mave)*
Tuatha - Niamh's younger sister

Moriath *(mor-ee-ath)*
Tuatha - Unseele queen, Oonagh and Bronach's sister

Neve *(nev)*
Human - baker in Pilot Bay

Niamh *(neevf just a hint of the f)*
Tuatha - Unseelie crown princess

Nora *(nor-ah)*
Glaistig - Kitchen staff at Nidavellir

Oonagh *(oo-nah)*
Tuatha - Former Unseelie queen, Niamh's mother

Ránach *(ra-nack)*
Peregrin falcon - Moriath's familiar

Saoirse *(sur-sha)*
Aziza - Fianna co-captain, Kylian's younger sister

Sofie *(so-phi)*
Dragon

Solveig *(soul-vay)*
Dwarf - Former dwarven queen

Tait *(tate)*
Poukha - Staff at Killinaire

Tiernan *(tear-nin)*
Tuatha - Seelie king, married to Ella

Treasa *(tra-sa)*
Tuatha - Newest Fianna member

Ulf *(oolf)*
Dwarf - King of Nidavellir, Estrid's father, Ulrik's brother

Ulrik *(ool-rik)*
Dwarf - King of Nidavellir, Estrid's uncle, Ulf's brother

**Tuatha is short for Tuatha Dé Danann*

Locations

Álfheimr *(alf-hey-mer)*
The Norse faerie country

The Forests of the Aziza *(uh-zee-za)*
The West African faerie country

Huath Forest *(hoo-ahr)*
The hawthorn forest where the unicorns live

Kilinaire *(kill-ih-nair)*
The castle of the Rose Court

Nidavellir *(need-ah-ve-klihr)*
The Dwarven home in Tír na nÓg

Skyretaine *(skyr-tain, rhymes with rain)*
Home of the Unseelie monarchs

Tír na nÓg *(tear-na-nog)*
The Celtic faerie country

Faerie Glossary

Here are the faerie types that have been mentioned so far in the Faerie Tale Romance series, and their pronunciations.

Aonbheannach *(in-va-noc)*
Unicorns.

Aos Sí *(ees-she)*
Any faerie smaller than a high fae. Also called the small fae or the small folk.

Asrai *(ash-ray)*
Fresh water faeries who live in ponds, creeks, and rivers.

Aziza *(uh-zee-za)*
West African high fae. Human-like in appearance but tall and with pointed ears.

Brownies *(brown-eeze)*
Household keepers.

Beithir (*bah-hee-ear)*
Venomous wyverns dwelling in mountainous caves.

Cait Sìth *(kate shee)*
A powerful race of fae who can shift into the form of a black cat nine times.

Cirein-cròin *(kir-in kron)*
Giant sea serpents, rumoured to eat whales or even large ships.

Cù Sìth *(koo shee)*
Giant green hounds with glowing red eyes. Their bark is an omen of death.

Dearg Due *(dah-ruhg du-ah)*
Vampires. Drinkers of blood.

Draoi *(dree)*
Woodland fae with bark-like skin and hair that resembles leaves.

Dvergr *(dv-ur-gur)*
Dwarves, originally from Álfheimr.

Ellén Trechend *(eh-lane treck-end)*
A giant three-headed bird.

Faoladh *(fay-lah)*
Fae who are cursed to shift into a wolf when the sun is down.

Fomóire *(fov-or-uh)*
Ancient Giants.

Leipreachán *(leh-pre-kan)*
Shoe makers and leather workers.

Glaistig *(glass-tick)*
Horned fae whose bottom half is like a goats. Similar to a faun.

Grogach *(grow-gahck)*
A small hairy faerie with a messy appearance.

Kami *(kah-mee)*
Japanese high fae. Human-like in appearance but tall and with pointed ears.

Merrow *(mare-ow)*
An ocean faerie, also known as a mermaid.

Peiste *(peesh-tah)*
Giant serpents that lurk in lakes, bogs, and moats.

Phouka *(poo-kah)*
Shape shifters. Natural form is like a shaggy black cat crossed with a rabbit.

Piskie *(pih-skee)*
Tiny, winged faeries.

Ryū *(ree-yoo)*
Small Japanese dragons.

Sheerie *(shear-ree)*
A tiny, glowing swamp faerie. Also called will-o'-the-wisp.

Tuatha Dé Danann (*too-ha day dan-on)*
Celtic high fae. Human-like in appearance but tall and with pointed ears.

Acknowledgments

Dear readers, my early drafts of this book were messier than a grogach's den after a beithir rampage. Which is to say, *very*. Every draft increased my word count by at least ten thousand, and it needed it. I couldn't have written this book by myself.

Sonya, thank you for reading my early drafts and listening to me talk at length about this book on our walks for the past year and a half. I'm not exaggerating when I say that I owe you my sanity. Oh, and thanks for that bag of apples you gave me for my birthday, they made an excellent spiced molasses apple cake!

Thank you to my beta readers, Valia, Tess, Mar, Lissa, Justene, Belinda, Jocelyn, Risa, Becky, Jacque, Laura, Marissa, Cacy, and Victoria. You ladies helped me sort out the tangles in the most complicated plot I've ever written.

Thanks to my mom, the amazing Christian Contemporary Romance author, Valerie Comer, for believing in my ability to tell stories, if not my ability to use commas.

Thanks to Becky for editing this book. I sent her a hilarious amount of messages that went something like "It'll be ready in June, it's about 70k words long." Friends, it was December, and it was 98k words long. And thanks to Becky it also conforms (mostly) to the rules of grammar.

I bet you'd think that after fifteen beta readers and two editors the book would be ready for readers. You would be wrong. I blame dictation, dyslexia, my newly diagnosed ADHD, and the failings of my high school English teachers for the fact that my manuscripts are absolutely riddled with grammatical errors and typos.

A big shout out to my typo hunters: Bethany, Kay, Cwang, Tirzah, Shannel, Jennifer, Precious, Sarah H, Katie, Genevieve, Rachel, Marilyn, Ami, Cedonia, Karen, Claire, Rebecca, Lisa, Mara, Sarah D, Jacquelin, Jillian, Emelia, Kali, Bree, Alana, Emily, Isabelle, Sheila, Christine, Delene, Lavay, Susan, Jani, Carrie, and Tamara. I put that colon in for you guys because I refused to use them in the book, no matter how many times you begged me to. Did I use it right??

A special thank you to the lovely members of my Patreon community for reading the rough chapters of Of Frost And Feathers as I wrote it, and giving me your feedback. I've never let anyone see my first drafts before, but I had so much fun sharing them with you.

Thanks to my daughters for discussing chicken antics and glowing mushrooms with me. I love seeing your creativity and storytelling grow every year as you do.

Thanks to my husband, Craig, for supporting me in all my artistic endeavors. We've always been better together!

And to God for filling this world with more magic and wonder than any Faerie realm could contain.

Thank you.

Connect with Hanna

Instagram:
@HannaSandvig

Facebook:
www.Facebook.com/Groups/HannaSandvig

Patreon:
Patreon.com/HannaSandvig

About The Author

HANNA SANDVIG IS TURNING YOUR FAVORITE FAIRY tales into faerie tales with some sweet romance and enough sass to keep things interesting.

Hanna is living out her personal happily-ever-after in the mountains of BC, Canada with her husband, three daughters, and giant cat. When she's not writing, drawing, or reading, she can be found sewing, taking photos, baking, and desperately trying to not pick up any more creative pursuits.

If you drop in to visit, please bring plenty of chocolate and strong black tea.

www.ingramcontent.com/pod-product-compliance
Lightning Source LLC
Chambersburg PA
CBHW020242030826
48979CB00030B/2486/J